CRITICS ACCLAIM
WILLIAM DEVERELL'S

MECCA

"Packs a saucy wallop... Here is another world-class thriller, fresh, bright and topical."
—*The Globe and Mail*

"A readable thriller that matches the newscasts. Action. Action. Action. Literature in the fast lane. Sit back in your easy chair, dear reader, pour yourself a drink, and read about the end of the world."
—*The Toronto Star*

"William Deverell has confirmed his place in the front rank of thriller writers with his new novel *Mecca*. This up-to-date thriller includes all the classical ingredients of the genre: violence, intrigue, chases, escapes and captures, sex, vivid descriptions, and a series of breathtaking double-crosses and hidden agendas which it would be unfair to discuss further. Great escapist fiction in the bestseller class."
—*Quill & Quire*

Now, turn the page for more raves for William Deverell's bestselling thrillers...

HIGH PRAISE FOR THE BESTSELLING THRILLERS BY WILLIAM DEVERELL

NEEDLES

"Seamy and steamy, sexy and sassy, a winner all around."
—*The Globe and Mail*

"Spellbinding, first-rate...a brilliant craftsman of suspense."
—*The Buffalo News*

"A find, a find; it must be shouted from the housetops."
—*The London Daily Telegraph*

"He makes the evil of his plot breathtaking and his surprises like shattering glass."
—*The Philadelphia Bulletin*

"Swift, exciting and vivid, its natty plot-twists prove compulsive."
—*Saturday Night*

HIGH CRIMES

NOW, PLUNGE INTO THE TERRIFYING WORLD OF...
MECCA

Bantam-Seal Books by William Deverell

HIGH CRIMES
MECCA
NEEDLES

MECCA

William Deverell

SEAL BOOKS
McClelland and Stewart-Bantam Limited
Toronto

This low-priced Seal Book
has been completely reset in a type face
designed for easy reading, and was printed
from new plates. It contains the complete
text of the original hard-cover edition.
NOT ONE WORD HAS BEEN OMITTED.

MECCA

A Seal Book / published by arrangement with the author

PRINTING HISTORY

McClelland and Stewart Limited edition published October 1983.
An Alternate Selection of Literary Guild
Seal edition / February 1985

ISBN 0-7704-2012-5

Seal Books are published by McClelland and Stewart-Bantam Limited. Its trademark, consisting of the words "Seal Books" and the portrayal of a seal, is the property of McClelland and Stewart-Bantam Limited, 60 St. Clair Avenue East, Suite 601, Toronto, Ontario M4T 1N5, Canada. This trademark has been duly registered in the Trademarks Office of Canada. The trademark, consisting of the words "Bantam" and the portrayal of a rooster, is the property of and is used with the consent of Bantam Books, Inc., 666 Fifth Avenue, New York, New York 10103. This trademark has been duly registered in the Trademarks Office of Canada and elsewhere.

PRINTED IN CANADA

COVER PRINTED IN U.S.A.

U   0 9 8 7 6 5 4 3 2 1

For my mother, Amy Grace,
who possesses the gift of caring

MECCA

I

The Confessional

A wide variety of names have been coined for the art of obliterating one's enemy. In one country they put him to death "legally" by an executioner and call it the death penalty; in another, they lie in wait with stiletto blades behind hedges and call it assassination; in another they organize obliteration on a grand scale and call it war. Let us, then, be practical, let us call ourselves murderers as our enemies do, let us take the moral horror out of this great historical tool. If to kill is always a crime, then it is forbidden equally to all; if it is not a crime, then it is permitted equally to all. Murder, both of individuals and masses, is an unavoidable instrument in the achievement of historical ends.

Karl Heinzen, *Der Mord*, 1849

1
Monday, September 26, Gran Paradiso, Italy

Giuseppe Nero's body was floating free, and he feared his mind was floating free from his body. Sanity was diffuse, uncertain. His hands were encased in thick foam mittens (a precaution, because yesterday Nero had ripped the oxygen mask from his face and had nearly drowned). The mask, the mittens, the electrode patches on his skin: otherwise he was naked in the nothingness of this dense saline solution, hearing the voice.

"Giuseppe Nero, where is Carlotta Calza?"

The voice of the old German general, calm, quiet, compelling. A terrible taste of nausea came to Nero's throat each time he failed to answer, or answered with lies, but he could not vomit. He kept trying to will his brain back to his body.

Concentrate, or you will hear the voice. "The armed struggle of the urban guerrilla points toward two essential objectives," Nero intoned.

The general's voice cut through: "Giuseppe Nero, where are Carlotta Calza and her daughter?"

The words came to Nero from a microphone, through the cord that was taped to the air hose, into the zero-buoyancy isolation tank, known locally as The Confessional. The tube carried Dioxygone as well, the truth drug, addicting, pleasure-giving. But when the subject did not tell the truth, nausea.

"The first objective is the physical liquidation of the chiefs of the armed forces and police." Concentrate, or you will hear the voice.

"Nero!"

"No . . . no." Metallic green, the colour of sickness, swirled about his eyes, and sickness engorged his throat, and he felt as if someone were moving through the rooms of his body, clicking off switches. Nero's central nervous system was being torn by conflicting forces, the need for Dioxygone and its pleasure, and the need to fight it. "The accusation of terrorism no longer has the pejorative meaning it used to have." His voice was flat, drained. "It has acquired new clothing. . . ."

"Giuseppe Nero, who is holding Signorina Calza and Giulietta? Is it The Shrike? Is it the Rotkommando?"

He tried to rotate his body in this black nothingness, biting his lip savagely and drawing blood. Yes, I feel pain; therefore I exist. "In order to function, urban guerrillas must be organized in small groups. The firing group—"

"He's just spouting communist shit. This is a waste."

General Hesselmann turned off the microphone after Hamilton Bakerfield's outburst. "The communist shit, as you elegantly put it, are passages from his Bible. Marighella's *Mini-manual*."

Hesselmann knew he must curb the tendency to speak sneeringly to the American, who must have thought he was an overbearing prig. But Hesselmann couldn't help it—he was not a warm person, was as stiff in his manner as in his bearing, which bore the stamp of old Prussian pride. He was the son and grandson of generals, ascetic, thin, bespectacled, immaculate except for a short thatch of white hair that obeyed no comb or brush.

Hamilton Bakerfield was Hesselmann's second in command, a veteran of the CIA who had achieved a reputation as a terrorist expert. He had quit the agency a few years ago, completed his Master's at the University of Chicago, developing his thesis into the standard text for handling hostage situations. He was a son of the south Chicago slums, a working-class Buckleyite, free enterprise all the way, down with the welfare cheats. At fifty-three, he was large, bony, bald, pink-complected. His face was an angry russet colour now.

"It isn't working," he said. "It's hare-brained." He glowered at Dr. Laurent Pétras as if the psychiatrist were to blame for their frustration.

"We must give it time," said Pétras, looking coldly back at

Bakerfield. "You had him for five days. You did nothing but harden the man's will to resist."

Pétras was a spare man of middle years with furry mutton-chop whiskers as bookends for a plain, flat face. The confession gas, Dioxygone, had been developed at his clinic in Brussels. The chemical was humane, he claimed, while Bakerfield's old-fashioned methods were clearly not: there had been bruises on Giuseppe Nero's body when the young astrophysics instructor had been placed in the isolation tank. Pétras had achieved some successes with volunteers on Dioxygone, but those volunteers had held no dark secrets.

"He will survive this, Dr. Pétras?" Hesselmann said. "You are sure?"

"Of course." Any mental aberration will disappear." Pétras spoke with confidence. "The matter yesterday, it will not be repeated. We did not have a chance to reduce the Dioxygone in his system." Late yesterday, after Nero had torn the oxygen mask from his face, and before he had been pulled from the tank, he had passed into a state of frenzied paranoia that lasted for five hours.

Our methods are humane, thought Hesselmann. We represent a civilization of law, we are better than the enemy, we are just, and we call this business humane. One rationalizes: this is not torture, for the prisoner brings on his own pain with his own lies. He is his own torturer.

The whole thing was getting Hesselmann in the gut, and his gut was where his various forms of unhappiness gathered, bunching up his soft tissue, creating sores that cut like sharp stones.

"Perhaps you would take over, Mr. Bakerfield. I propose to take some air." He spoke English with the accent of an Oxford don.

Hesselmann put on his greatcoat, took his cane from a coat rack, and walked from the laboratory, straight and stiff, with a gamey-leg limp. He closed the heavy pine door with a flood of relief. The laboratory was a place that Hesselmann despised. There were old memories—human experiments, human guinea pigs.

Outside, he braced himself against the cold fall wind sweeping up from the Orco River valley. The camp of Group Seven International was located atop a palisade in the Italian Alps, high above the valley which twisted its way toward the plains of the Po River and the factories of Turin. It was an abandoned forestry camp. Access was by a tortuous trail, and only a four-wheel drive would dare the assault up the eastern flanks of the Gran Paradiso range to these secret cliff-top headquarters. A helicopter was better.

The laboratory building, once a sawmill, had been built of thick, rough-hewn timbers, and its builders, thought Hesselmann, had been mountain men of curious bravery—they had put it at the edge of an escarpment that dropped sheer, almost seven hundred metres of rockface, before it levelled and clothed itself with pine and fir. To the west, only ten kilometres away, was France, the valley was to the south and east, and to the north were the shining permanent snowfields of the Gran Paradiso range. Soon there would be snow at this lower level, too, for September was dying.

Up the slope from the cliff edge were other log buildings, one of which housed Group Seven headquarters, Hesselmann's office, and the intelligence centre. A trail led to a barracks and combination canteen and mess hall, then to several cabins that housed senior staff. Beyond was a subalpine meadow, rising by steps to the snows. Hesselmann could see men and women high up on the playing field, chasing a soccer ball. Others were in track suits working their way around an oval. Members of the assault teams, always running, always exercising. Everyone seemed to be waiting for something to do, waiting for Giuseppe Nero to break, to give them his list of houses, to open the doors, perhaps, to all of the Rotkommando. We wait, he thought. There is nothing else.

Hesselmann limped up the stone stairs to his cabin, unlocked the door, and went to his medicine cabinet for his drug, the dreadful syrup which coated the lining of his stomach. He took two spoonfuls of the liquid chalk and bore himself stoically.

Then, as he had done almost every day for the last three weeks, he took from the drawer of his desk a file and, from the file, a photograph. He searched the cool blue eyes of Karl Wurger, The Shrike, seeking purpose in them, seeking some hint of grace, some insight into the soul of this killer. The eyes of a man just before a kill. Those two pale sapphires were focussed on a lunchpail, upon the lens of a miniature camera hidden inside it. Not hidden well, it had turned out.

The photograph had been taken by a Group Seven agent, one of the best, recruited by Hesselmann from his old staff at military intelligence in Bonn. One second after the shutter had softly clicked, Wurger had taken from his jacket pocket what witnesses described as a small pistol—a Landmann-Preetz, doubtless, Wurger's favourite assassination tool—and had shot the agent in the face and heart, killing him instantly. Wurger and his three companions had then run from the restaurant, a workingman's place in Zurich, and they had separated, disappearing into the old city. The agent had had no back-up. That had been a mistake.

Hesselmann studied the profiles of the men sitting at The Shrike's left and right. Giuseppe Nero was one: until then known only as an associate professor, Turin University, an astrophysicist. The other was Ferrante of Rome, also a captain of the Red Brigades. Of the fourth, his back to the camera, Hesselmann wasn't sure. Perhaps one of the Palestinians. Perhaps their new man, Cuyfer, the Dutch-American. But the meaning was clear. This meeting in Zurich was proof that the Red Brigades had joined Wurger's growing army, the Rotkommando, the Red Commando.

And just as surely the kidnapping of Carlotta Calza and her daughter was the inspiration of Wurger, master of the large gesture. Signorina Calza, the grand lady of the Italian cinema, a Jew, was a friend of the rich and influential, had been outspoken about terrorism, and had become a target.

I will destroy you, Herr Wurger. I will find you. Because Giuseppe Nero will lead us to Carlotta Calza and to you. I have the means now.

Now, five months from its inception, Group Seven International had its first lead into the inner workings of the Red Commando. Haupt General Heinrich Hesselmann's new supranational police organization would now begin to pay for itself, to return the investments of the seven allied powers which had given him the men and the women and the money.

Group Seven was the general's own invention. He had stepped down as chief of NATO intelligence to run it, selecting as personnel the best from the anti-terrorist police and commando units from West Germany, Britain, France, Italy, Japan, the United States, and Canada.

As a young lieutenant in the Abwehr, before Hitler dismantled it, Hesselmann had been the wunderkind of German intelligence during the Second World War, adjutant to Colonel Count von Stauffenberg, the leading figure of the plot against the Führer of July 1944. Von Stauffenberg's bomb had failed to destroy the German dictator in the Gästebaracke at Rastenburg, and he along with two hundred other officers had been strangled with piano wire while the cameras rolled. Hitler had watched those movies with glee, and had sworn to the world he would execute Hesselmann, too, but the young officer escaped to Switzerland, and was taken from there to London, where he worked with Allied command.

After the war, during the Adenauer years, Hesselmann became head of military intelligence for the Federal Republic and later served as officer commanding his country's anti-terrorist kommando, the Grenzschutzgruppe-9 of the Federal Border Guard which, under him, was West Germany's equivalent of Britain's Special Air Services Regiment. After that came the NATO posting.

But Hesselmann, impelled by forces he did not clearly understand—having to do with a sense of duty, a sense of debt, a sense of shame—and bored with NATO's cold war, returned to the real war of the closing decades of this century, a stylized, guesswork war with invisible fronts, fading targets; a war with an infinite subtlety.

He turned his mind to Giuseppe Nero. He prayed that the capture would be worth the cost. Already Nero had become an expensive prisoner, because after an initial euphoria over his capture—while he was delivering a ransom message—the public had grown restive as Carlotta and Giulietta Calza remained at risk. The terrorists had sent a tape-recorded plea from the actress to a Rome television station and all of Italy had been aroused.

And now the Group had been condemned by the media for having interfered with the plans of an Italian industrialist—once Miss Calza's lover—to redeem the captives with a hundred million lira. The Italian government seemed about to bend under, offering to negotiate the terrorists' second demand, the release of the Milan Nine, arrested two months ago and soon to be tried. Libya was prepared to accept them. For humanitarian reasons, Ghaddafy had announced. Humanitarian reasons: Hesselmann smiled a bitter smile.

But how much more public anger would explode around

them if Hesselmann didn't break Nero by four o'clock this afternoon? At that time, three hours from now, the terrorists were going to cut off both thumbs from the hands of twelve-year-old Giulietta Calza—unless Giuseppe Nero were released. The kidnappers had made the threat in a letter to the *Osservatore*, with the child's inked thumbprints on the envelope. They claimed to have been betrayed: their emissary, Nero, had been on his way to pick up the hundred-million-lira ransom when grabbed by Group agents.

But we will break Nero today, Hesselmann thought. And not just for the hostages. Through him we will break every safe house of the Rotkommando, for if Nero was on the Central Committee with Wurger he was the possessor of its darkest secrets. Do this right, and the Rotkommando will perish in the blood of its well-born fanatics, the psychopathic refuse of the bourgeoisie.

He took more of his chalky goo.

"He shows extreme discipline," Pétras said. "He has obviously been trained for... exigencies such as this." As seen on the computer monitor Giuseppe Nero was floating upside down, his feet almost at the sealed tank-top. "For a man under stress—I've never seen anything like this before."

"You have never *done* anything like this before," Hamilton Bakerfield said. "Except maybe with rats and rabbits."

The microphone was open. "Execution is a secret action in which the least number of guerrillas is involved," Nero was saying in a flat voice. "One sniper, patiently, alone, unknown...."

Hesselmann pointed to the small cylinder tank containing compressed Dioxygone, and asked Pétras, "How much of this can he take?"

"How would *he* know?" said Bakerfield, bitchy with fatigue.

"I have told you, I am certain we can go to sixty pressure," said Pétras. "Triple his present intake."

"What would happen to him?" said Hesselmann.

"He will be more malleable. There could be, perhaps, a minor psychotic attack, but that would pass."

"Sixty?"

"Fifty, perhaps sixty." Hesselmann did not like the uncertain tone in Pétras's voice. "The computer will tell us immediately if a problem is forming."

"Raise it to thirty-five," Hesselmann said.

Pétras turned a valve. Bakerfield watched with narrowed, doubting eyes.

"Giuseppe Nero, you will have your freedom, the new identity, the money, everything we have promised," Hesselmann said into the mike.

"The first sin of the guerrilla is to . . . underestimate the enemy . . . to think him stupid. . . ." Nero was giving evidence of struggle.

Hesselmann's voice was controlled, commanding. "Wurger is with your friends from the Turin brigade, yes? They have Miss Calza?"

"The second sin . . . is cowardice."

Hesselmann winced, feeling the man's pain and nausea.

"Answer the questions and you will feel no pain. Does Wurger have Calza and her daughter?"

"Yes." Furious struggle. The needles of the readout gauges on the computer auxiliary panel were pulsing wildly. *"NO! NO! DIO!"*

"But we know this anyway. We ask you only to confirm." Calm, reassuring.

There was the sound of sobbing. Hesselmann glanced at Pétras, who smiled confidently, nodding, as if to say, "You see, it's starting to work." He pointed to the cylinder valve and arched his eyebrows at Hesselmann in a question.

Hesselmann took a deep breath then mouthed the word *"Cinquante,"* and Pétras turned the dial. The readout needles seemed to settle back.

"Giuseppe Nero, can you hear me?"

"Yes." The voice floated from the speakers as if from a great distance.

"You must answer my questions now, and you must answer them truthfully. Because if you do not you will be in an eternal hell of lunacy and pain. Do you understand?" Hesselmann glanced at Bakerfield, hoping to see some support from him. Bakerfield's face had clouded.

A long pause, then a soft laugh from Nero. "Yes, I understand. You will kill me." His voice was oriented, in control. He sighed. "Everyone dies anyway. What matters is how, and how you lived. Fighting the militarists and the pigs as a human being for the liberation of man, loving life, disdaining death, that is how I lived and that is how I shall die."

Hesselmann looked at the smiling Pétras. Dr. Mengele. I, the inquisitor. Auschwitz. "Where is Signorina Calza?"

A scream that strangled in the throat. "Parasite! My death will explode upon the conscience of the masses!"

"Is she with Karl Wurger?"

Another scream. *"DIO! SI!"*

"Who else is in the group?"

"Grazzoni!" The name exploded as if from between clenched teeth.

"Yes, who else?"

"Cuyfer! Zahre!" Wurger's girlfriend. "Pergo, Bellini. That is all. *Cristo!*"

"Where is Signorina Calza being held?" Do not let him rest.

"In Turin." The voice was suddenly calm. The readouts showed that Nero's resistance had ended. He had been broken.

"Address."

"Apartment 2-B, Caradoso Strada, 21."

Hesselmann nodded to Bakerfield, who went to the intercom unit by the front door. An assault group would leave by helicopter immediately, and radio would be in quick contact with Italy's Squadro Anti-Commando.

He decided to pump this man empty.

"The Turin house, your unit, where is it located?"

Nero gave an address in a working-class area.

"The main Paris house. Address please."

"I do not know." The voice sounded eerie, words from outer space.

He asked about the Berlin, Zurich, and Amsterdam houses, but Nero did not know where they were either.

"You are on the Central Committee?" Hesselmann believed at least eleven persons were on Rotkommando's controlling body, representatives of Italian, German, Japanese, Palestinian groups, loners like Cuyfer.

"Yes."

"What is planned, Giuseppe Nero? After Calza, what has been planned?"

No answer. Tremors among the indicator needles. Surely Nero knew the Central Committee's next target.

"Rotkommando is training soldiers for a major operation, yes, is that so?" Hesselmann persisted. There had been evidence of a recruiting campaign, of disenchanted youths disappearing from the streets of Europe.

Nero was struggling again, gasping. His arms were jerking. "God," he said, "I have stars in here."

Pétras made the okay sign with his fingers.

"What is the next operation?" A trap could be sprung.

"I . . . I . . . ."

The needles were pulsating.

"*Dio!* Stars!"

"What is next?" The question was barked.

"MECCA!"

Had he heard correctly? Mecca? Saudi Arabia?

"I am with stars! They are exploding!"

"What will happen in Mecca?."

"You promised!" Nero screamed. "You promised I would be sane! I have left my body! *Dio!* I have left my body!"

Nero's voice rose to a high pitch, then cracked. Dials were jumping and the screen was flashing red numbers among the green. Pétras's colour was white.

"Mecca—what is that?" said Hesselmann.

A cackling laugh. Then a shriek. "Stars, they are exploding! Hydrogen! Hydrogen! Oxygen! It explodes!"

"Jesus *Christ,*" Bakerfield said, looking at the flailing, spastic motions of Nero's image on the screen.

Pétras, seemingly frozen in position, was blinking his eyes, staring at the monitor. Then, without pausing to shut off the Dioxygone valve, he raced up a metal staircase to the top of the immersion tank and like a man possessed began spinning the wheel that broke the seal.

"I EXPLODE!" Nero's voice was inhuman, high-pitched, shattered. Now there came a peal of hoarse, gravel-throated laughter from the speakers.

Pétras sprung open the tank top. Bakerfield joined him and they reached deep into the water, hefting Nero from the tank by his flailing legs. Now came his arms, his hands in foam mittens as big as soccer balls, his torso, his head, his eyes, stark above the oxygen mask and sunk darkly into their sockets.

Hesselmann just stared at this fantasy, at the naked guerrilla suddenly freeing himself from Pétras and Bakerfield, dancing crazily on top of the tank and upon the steel-ribbed stairway platform, his voice triumphant. "I am of the stars! I am of the stars!"

Nero kicked, and swung his arms at Bakerfield, who was trying to grab him. He had cleared his mouth from the oxygen mask, and with his teeth was tearing the foam encasing his hands, freeing them. Hesselmann ran to the Dioxygone cylinder to turn it off, but as he reached it, it was jerked away from him, Nero pulling it up the wall of the isolation tank by its hose.

Grasping the end of the hose, he swung the cylinder in a great circle, forcing Bakerfield and Pétras to duck low, and the cylinder splintered the glass and wooden framework of a pair of windows looking down over the chasm of the Orco Valley.

"Achenar, Antares, Sirius! I am a star! Red star exploding!"

Nero took a perfect swan dive through the open window and passed into eternity.

2

Sunday, October 2, Gran Paradiso

Heinrich Hesselmann listened to the news from the portable radio in his office.

"...following a phone call from their kidnappers, they were found alive today in an abandoned farmhouse near Turin, where they had apparently been moved following the capture of Professor Nero. Both are said to be resting in hospital, Giulietta receiving treatment for her two maimed hands. In the meantime, the prosecutor's office in Rome has announced that criminal charges have been withdrawn against the Milan Nine and the prisoners flown to Libya. A spokesman for industrialist Eugenio Serri has refused to confirm whether ransom money has also been paid in the securing of—"

He flicked off the switch, donned his greatcoat, and went outside. He walked slowly, limping, to the escarpment, and looked over the vast panorama of the valley. He stood like a sentry, back straight, legs straight, his cane tucked between elbow and waist.

He stood there for nearly an hour.

He watched the sun set in the southwest, watched it die behind clouds that had turned orange in receiving it, then red and violet as the sun passed beyond the far mountains. Now the gloom of night was spreading across the sky from the east, and the last swallow was diving for its nest in the recesses of the cliffside below.

He wondered what they were saying, his old comrades-in-arms, in the officers' mess at German intelligence. Old Heini Hesselmann, growing senile, can't stop playing the game. Fell flat on his face over that business with the Jewish actress and her daughter. Thinks the people he's dealing with are gentlemen, like Russian spies. It's age, of course. Poor Hesselmann.

My damn gut.

I am an old soldier. But I cannot quit. I owe too much.

He swivelled smartly, winced as his lame leg gave slightly, then marched slowly to his quarters.

II

Le Grand Slaque

*Happy it is for mankind
that Heaven has laid on few
men the curse of being poets.*

Frank Frankfort Moore

3

Thursday, December 15, Cuba

His Muse, that formerly fecund goddess of his art, was
barren. Many times had Jacques Sawchuk lashed out at her:
"You sexless whore! Speak to me!" His Muse rewarded him
with a writer's block that sat on him, smothered him, crushed
him.

Never had he known this. In the sixteen years since he had
first been published (*Chansons d'Immoralité*, Aardvark Press,
$2.85. "The author of this salacious romp, only sixteen, is a
poet of the so-called 'Beat' generation...."), never had a
writer's block of such awesome dimension gripped Jacques
Sawchuk. It had been going on now for nearly seven months.
All he had been able to compose were book reviews and
some political commentary, including an excoriation of his
host government which had just appeared in the *New Left
Quarterly*.

Sawchuk had tried everything. Meditation. Alcohol. Ancient Ukrainian garlic cures. Mostly he had sat in front of a
Remington upright that had been beaten cruelly by the
writer over the years, and had waited and waited, staring at
the machine, memorizing its bolts and screws.

He had rapped out babblings, hoping they would somehow
transform into verse. He had stared out the window watching
the waves break on the white sand. Crunch, swish. Crunch,
swish. For a few weeks he had whipped himself mercilessly
through the pages of an intended short story, but with no
artistic impulse, no images from the mind's eye, just his brain
propelling the fingers over the keys, putting dead words and
dead people on the pages. He read it and shredded it.

Sawchuk had been on a long glissando. He had peaked at

twenty-five, had been world-famous then, at least in radical-lit. circles. The decline had set in a few years after he had come to Cuba. Now, at thirty-two, he saw himself being regarded as very much passé. Rotting in the tropics. In Cuban asylum.

The literary world derided him now. His last book of poetry and his last collected stories had been panned. His publisher had 5,000 copies of *Various Views* still in their cardboard boxes. Was it critical and commercial failure, he wondered, that had shocked his Muse into this ultimate infertility?

Failure. Failure of talent, failure of the benison of acclaim. And failure of gods. Those gods of the Left that had succoured him, filled him with their idealistic milk. Gods that had fed him with a fervour for justice among mankind, for Utopias. But cracks of doubt had developed and his edifice of belief was crumbling, and it had been doing so more and more rapidly as Sawchuk saw in increasing focus the People's Democratic Republic of Cuba: all the pap and the propaganda and the endless tape and the ugly monotony and lifelessness of it all. "It is all supposed to work," he found himself saying softly. Cuba had been the hope of the Western hemisphere. Now they had become like the Russians.

Since the beginning of December, Jacques Sawchuk had begun giving in to sprees of drunken rowdiness—at the Liberación Bar in Nuevitas, at the cantina near his cottage, at beach parties. He would be back the next day pecking at his Remington, his head clanging, nothing of worth displaying itself on the page.

The block had begun to express itself in a physical way. He felt constricted: his throat, his chest, his mind. He felt threatened by the walls squeezing in on him. "I need space about me!" he had roared one day, and had ordered carpenters from Nuevitas to tear down the partitions in his four-room villa. It became a one-room villa. His space.

Jacques Sawchuk needed this space in part because he took up a lot of it. He was six feet, four inches tall, 220 pounds. There had been a time when he had been much fitter, back when he was on the run, and before that, when he had been a good amateur athlete. But now, he was so out of condition, his limbs seemed loose and ill-fitting. He was what one would describe in his native Quebec as *un grand slaque*.

At the centre of his space was a snowdrift of crumpled paper, the failures that had flowed unceasingly from his heartless typewriter, atop an old mahogany table. Above that table was a three-foot-square mandala, suspended from the ceiling there so that Sawchuk might find inspiration under the eye of God. Its wooden frame served as a perch for Chamberlain, the trilingual macaw, a large, multicoloured bird of uncertain age who would occasionally drop small bombs on the typewriter, like bad reviews.

A somewhat deflated basketball sat on the floor in the area one would call kitchen. The counters there contained several dozen jars of various grains and herbs, brown rice, dried fruit. A garlic ring hung near the propane stove.

Windows on the north and east walls overlooked a beach of ground coral and palm-tufted cays beyond the bay. Between the windows, against the walls, books were stacked, hundreds of them, works by ancient and modern poets, dramatists, fiction writers, sources of former inspiration; and Marx, Marcuse, Huxley, Sartre, sources of former truth and present disenchantment.

A silver-alloyed alto flute sat in an open case near the little side door that led to the outhouse, where Bach arpeggios were often played.

On this day, Sawchuk was sprawled atop a mattress on the floor in the sleeping area. Beside him was a young woman, her head cradled against his chest, her eyes open. She had been awakened by the sound of a motor vehicle driving up the road to the villa.

It was noon now, and Chamberlain, his head cocked and his right eye beamed at the front door, was listening warily to the approaching footsteps.

A knock at the door. The girl, Rosalia, shook Sawchuk, who tried to bury his head under the single sheet that covered them. He became aware first of all that he was mightily hung over. His literary frustration had driven him *boracho* the previous night; he had drunk Russian vodka until the dawn, roaring obscenities at his Remington, roaring them upon the beach.

Outside the door, standing beneath a rusted basketball hoop and knocking insistently, was Paolo Regalado, undersecretary to the Minister for State and Cultural Affairs in Havana.

He was bespectacled, prim, his shoulders hunched together as if they had been permanently pressed in a crowded elevator. In his waiting car were the mayor of the Town of Nuevitas—Rosalia's father—and the district police chief, both unhappy-looking men.

Regalado knocked again.

"*Adelante!*" Sawchuk shouted. He swore softly, clambered from beneath the sheet.

Regalado opened the door and saw Sawchuk naked, his face clouded and dreadful with ill feeling.

"Shut the door, Reglamento. Let us keep the flies outside." It had been Sawchuk's habit not to remember Regalado's name and to call him Reglamento instead, which in Spanish means rules and regulations. Sawchuk took a bleary measure of Regalado at the doorway, and he thought: what is this more-Marxist-than-thou functionary doing here? What have I done now, forgotten to file one of his forms? *El Reglamento.*

Regalado left the door open a crack, said nothing, watched as the big, red-bearded gringo moved unsteadily toward the sink, scratching the underside of a dissolute belly. Sawchuk dumped some Vitamin B tablets from a jar into the palm of his hand and chased them down with a glass of water.

"To what do I owe the honour?" Sawchuk spoke almost accentless Spanish; a low voice, rumbling. "Have you come to tell me I have won the Lenin Prize?"

He found a wooden match on top of the stove, struck it, ignited the gas beneath one of the elements with a puff of blue flame. He put a pot of water on. "Yes, Reglamento, what do you want? I warn you, my writing has gone bad, and this has made me short-tempered. I am not my usual buoyant and lightsome self."

"Put some clothes on," Regalado said. "Have you no sense of shame?"

"Shame? What are you talking about, *compañero*? There is no God in Cuba. No *official* God, though God knows there are priests. Plus Fidel who is the biggest father of them all. Why should I feel shame? What is this Christian morality you imply? Very unsocialist for such a head honcho Party man, Paolo."

"How low you have descended," Regalado said softly. "A living embarrassment to the revolution."

"Even if I were in a Christian country I would not be

ashamed of my naked body." But he took his worn cut-offs from a chair and buckled them on. "And if I believed in God, as you do in your secret heart of hearts, I would still not be ashamed to be seen in the garment God gave us and intended that we wear in dignity."

Regalado sniffed, observed the flabby shape of Sawchuk's garment. "When you first came here, the President toasted you at a banquet," he said. "Now, if my reports are true, you mock him. Slanderous imitations of his television broadcasts to entertain the crowd of bourgeois drones that collect each weekend at the Liberación Bar in Nuevitas." It was true: Sawchuk in old army fatigues was a red-bearded send-up of Fidel Castro.

"The real drones in the bar," said Sawchuk, "are the spies of the DGI. This country has more spies than whores have bed sores."

Sawchuk sprinkled some camomile and liverwort into the warming water and stirred oatmeal into it. He turned to the girl, who was sitting up now, clutching the sheet to her chest.

"Rosalia, stay in bed. This man cannot abide the sight of the human body. He must not see yours—it will drive him mad. Do you want some porridge, Reglamento? It is good for what sickens you. Your hemorrhoids are the result of twisted bowels, which in turn is a result of your poor diet."

Regalado backed up a step. His stomach was making known to him its terror of Sawchuk's oatmeal porridge.

"When you came here, we believed you were a great man," he said. "A great revolutionary. But you are a corrupter. You are no example to the world." He sneaked a look at the Sanchez girl, her breasts standing out under the sheet, hard little lemons. "You were honoured by our people. We gave you sanctuary when your own country sought to imprison you for political acts. Look at how you repay us. For seven years we have given you an allowance so you can live here in comfort while my two sons spend eight months of the year locked to their desks at the university and the other four months driving themselves to exhaustion on a tractor assembly line."

"*I* work," Sawchuk shouted. "I *write*." He paused in stirring the porridge. "Don't just stand there squinting your fervently socialist eyes at me. Tell me what you want and get out." Then he saw fat little Mayor Sanchez peering through the louvers of the front window. Sawchuk walked over and shut them tight. "It is about Rosalia?" he said. "She is here of her own wish, a fugitive from this tyrannical fat *cerdo,* like you, a Party *apparatchik.* I gather Mayor Sanchez has complained to you. He wants Rosalia home again, to beat her."

"I should go with them, Jacques," Rosalia said softly. "As you told me, they are looking for excuses to do you harm."

Regalado made a show of averting his eyes as Rosalia arose from bed and began to dress. "I am here for that, among other reasons. Señor Sanchez contacted the police. He thinks you have hypnotized her, and he wants them to charge you."

Sawchuk dug his big toe under the basketball and lifted it to Regalado, neatly, soccer-style. Regalado caught it before it could bounce into the empty vodka and rum bottles behind him.

"Take that and dribble back to Havana, Reglamento. Rosalia is seventeen, mature, a free Cuban woman, and she will do as she wishes."

But what Rosalia Sanchez was doing was packing her few things into a bag. Sawchuk watched her with a lugubrious expression.

"I am going, Jacques." She came shyly up to him, went high on her toes, kissed him quickly on the mouth, then backed away, averting her eyes.

Sawchuk stood stubbornly by his porridge, stirring. "Don't let this bully scare you, Rosalia. Dress a man up with a little authority and he begins to have the idea he may tell you how to run your life. It's the Russian mentality around here. Bolshevism pervades everything."

Rosalia slipped around behind Regalado. "*Te quiero,* Jacques," she whispered, and slipped out the door.

Regalado, emboldened by success, repeated Sawchuk's words, his tone acerbic: "'Bolshevism pervades everything.' Yes, I have seen that same view expressed in print under your name. Which brings me to the second reason for this intrusion into your subsidized writer's retreat: your very sardonic attack upon our revolution."

He brought from his back pocket a folded copy of the *New Left Quarterly,* the December edition. From the front cover, he quoted the title of the lead article: "'The Fraudulent Face of Latin Communism. By Jacques Sawchuk.' That essay in this purportedly Marxist, decidedly revisionist publication has been reprinted with glee by the Hearst newspaper chain in America. Quoted by the Voice of America Spanish-language service."

Sawchuk stared at him without expression. "Yes? Do I assume from your pinched, unhappy face that I am accused of incorrect thinking? I believe I wrote that a model of East European socialism has been imposed upon this latin country, that that design has destroyed spontaneity, killed the yeast that makes art. Do you wish to argue the point? It kills *my* art. I am in a mood to argue, Reglamento. Defend this bastardized, Kremlinized island and its surfeit of informers, cops, and petty clerks?"

Regalado cleared his throat and wet his lips. "The minister had hoped you might consider composing a further article. A redefining of your views."

"A redef—" Sawchuk stopped in mid-word, looked at the government man with contempt, began doling oatmeal porridge into a bowl, pouring cream on it. "An apologia?" he said. "A recantation of heresy? Put me on the rack, that's the next step. Or do you try to brainwash now, the Andropov way? Yes, hand me over to the KGB so I may be treated in a little hospital near Moscow, flush out all that poisonous Yankee propaganda from my brain. Then come back to Cuba a zombie like Paolo Regalado. Get out of here, you bureaucratic wimpshit."

"Our Soviet *compañeros* have also sent dissidents into exile. There is that alternative, of course: sending you back to Canada to face your courts. In fact, the minister has entrusted me with the responsibility of selecting the appropriate option—"

Sawchuk slammed his bowl of porridge on the kitchen counter. "Send me back!" he roared. "That will finally put the lie to the pretensions of Cuba, its pretensions of being a great asylum for the revolutionary Left. Send me back! *Then* I'll write about Cuba." He took a step forward.

Regalado stood his ground, two feet from the not-quite-shut door. He was still holding the basketball, like a shield. "You have not been good advertising for Cuba while in it. You would serve the country no worse outside of it. If anything, your leaving would help the tourist business."

"'Cuba Expels Revolutionary Poet.' Won't the world press

love that, Paolo." Sawchuk's voice had grown deceptively calm. Yet everything was combining to deepen his rage: Regalado's mewing mannerisms, the desertion of Rosalia, the clamour of hangover bells in his head, and the collected detritus of frustration and guilt and self-pity that had smothered his creative spirit.

Regalado, brave in the face of Sawchuk's passivity, began to twist the knife. "I have, by the way, read some of the reviews of your latest books. The critics heaped abuse. 'How the mighty have fallen,' said one. Another said your short stories made him physically sick. I gather that only the crazy magazines will publish you now."

Sawchuk looked benignly at his tormentor and stretched out his hand. "Do you have a forty-centavo piece, Paolo?"

Regalado took a coin from his pocket, tendered it to Sawchuk, stepped back, smiling. "It is said your latest poems were *replete* with scatology. Full of disgusting imagery."

"It is Cuba which inspired me, Paolo." Still calm. "I am going to flip this coin, *compañero*. Heads I will be utterly patient and reasonable with you. Tails, I will propel you into the people's democratic compost in my people's democratic garden."

Regalado took an uncertain step back to the door. "You are a failed artist, Sawchuk," he hissed. "A dead fire whose coals no longer glow. You are to be pitied."

Sawchuk caught the coin expertly on the back of his wrist. "Tails," he said.

Before Regalado could squeeze through the front door, Sawchuk, with two giant bounds, his voice thundering many-syllabled obscenities, had one hand around bunched shirt at the nape of Regalado's neck, the other at his pants. Sawchuk violently kicked at the door, smacking it against the head of the mayor of Nuevitas, who had been crouched outside, peering in.

Sawchuk took a long stride over the sprawling person of the little mayor, past the wide-eyed Rosalia, raised high the screaming, squirming body of Paolo Regalado, and threw him into a mound of rotting orange, lemon, and grapefruit rinds.

"You're a sanctimonious socialist sycophant, Reglamento. You're going to keep on sucking the Bolshevik cock and one day it's going to choke you. Fuck you and fuck your revolution."

4

Friday, December 16, Cuba

Jacques Sawchuk, dishevelled and weary after long ordeals with the authorities, had been freed—in a nominal sense—and was now in the post office at Nuevitas on a wavering long-distance line to Montreal. Chamberlain was pacing up and down on his shoulders. Sawchuk's voice was forlorn.

"Louise, I have an *exigisé* on my hands. Let me speak to The Mouth."

Two agents from Dirección General de Intelligencia were standing near the front door, waiting to accompany Sawchuk to his villa, where he would remain under house arrest for seven days.

"What have you done now, Jacques?" Louise sounded resigned, as if she were used to bad news.

"I need legal advice. Illegal will do. Rocky has got to come up with a brilliancy, as uncharacteristic as that might seem."

But what hope was there? He had asked the government to be allowed to leave voluntarily—for Mexico, Spain, Costa Rica—avoiding for Havana the political embarrassment of deporting him. Regalado had said no. The vengeful Regalado had the minister's confidence.

Rocky Rubinstein could try to do a deal with the RCMP, perhaps get him low bail, a short sentence. Maybe they would drop the charges: it had been a long time ago.

"Rocky hasn't been in the office all day," Louise said. "*Je suis tanné.* I'm fed up. His clients are screaming at me. He hasn't been answering his calls, other lawyers' letters. He didn't show up in Sessions Court this morning for a trial, and the judge says he has to appear by four this afternoon and apologize, or he'll jail him."

"Oh, God," Sawchuk moaned. His friend had always run a haphazard practice. "Louise, send a search party into the brothels and the *barbottes* or wherever that balding little *morviat* is gambling away his clients' money—"

A frantic male voice came on the line, cutting Sawchuk off. "I heard that. I could hear your drunken screams all the way down the hall. What is this perfidy you are speaking about me, Sawchuk?"

"Rocky? It's three o'clock in the afternoon. You're just getting to the office?"

"I forgot it was Friday, thought it was Saturday, went to the gym. Someone told me it was Friday. I got depressed, went home, watched TV game shows." Rubinstein talked like a machine-gun with a Brooklyn accent. His voice faded and returned on the weak line. "I had a rotten day. Everyone's on my case, including a fascist judge. Now this I've got to return to—your calumnies to my secretary. You hitting the bottle, Jacques? Still not writing, are you?"

"Rocky, is this line safe?" Sawchuk lowered his voice, glanced at the Intelligencia men, who were chatting with a man in the phone lineup.

"I pay people to keep it safe. What did you do, man, rape the police chief's daughter?"

"They are deporting me. Listen carefully. They are not letting me go to a country of my choice. A local Iago has whispered lies into the culture minister's ear about my political, as it were, reliability."

"Jeez, you had it made down there. Where am I going to spend my holidays this winter?"

"For Christ's sake, this isn't a joke," Sawchuk said angrily. "Look, these are the facts: they've served a Minister's Order on me. They have me on a flight leaving Havana next Friday, *Friday*, Rocky, not Saturday. Friday, the twenty-third day of December, two days before Christmas. Flight 41, Cubana Airlines, to—what's the new airport north of Montreal?"

"Mirabel." There was silence from Montreal, as if Rubinstein were letting the information digest. "This is serious," he said.

"Listen, you have to try to arrange a deal for me with the prosecutors."

"Don't even know if I can go to court for you. There are

disturbed lawyers, trapped into the system, who are trying to get me disbarred. I'm about to be thrown into the slam by Judge Pierrefonds if I'm not in his court in half an hour. I'm into a negative justice situation myself, man."

Rubinstein's attitude seemed flip, which infuriated Sawchuk. "Goddamnit, you little *détoureux* shyster, I saved your life years ago."

"Saved my life?"

"Saved your gizzard from being cut out by a Viet Cong with the blood of Yankee dogs souring his nostrils because I sneaked you across the Canadian border when you were a snivelling New York draft-dodging Jewish coward. Now *you* save *my* life. Do what lawyers are supposed to do—make a deal. Buy the prosecutor dinner. Tell them I'll agree to come back to Canada if they are prepared to give me, say, a couple of months. I can do a few months in the joint without breaking. Just remember to tell them I had nothing to do with the kidnappings."

Rubinstein spoke slower now, and ominously. "Jacques, I'm in a hurry, but let me lay this on you. Advocating force to separate Quebec from Canada: that's sedition, Section 60 of the Criminal Code. I quote—it's here in front of me—'Anyone who publishes any writing that advocates the use of force as a means of accomplishing a governmental change within Canada,' et cetera, et cetera, 'is guilty of an indictable offence and is liable to imprisonment for fourteen years.'"

"Rocky, it was meant as a . . . kind of joke. Everyone was going for the impact, the shock. We were trying to jerk people awake. We were just coming out of the *sixties*, for God's sake." Was that a defence? And had it been just a joke? Was it possible to separate the serious from the not-so-serious in those upside-down years?

"A joke," said Rubinstein. "Not only advocating, but giving *advice*. On how to blow up Parliament and kidnap selected members of the Cabinet. I guess you were too subtle. Nobody got the joke. I'll call a joke expert to testify. A Ph.D. He will explain to the judge that this was a joke you wrote. Because without some expert assistance, the judge ain't going to laugh. Especially when the labour minister was kidnapped only one week after you published the article— and shot dead in the head days later. There's still a warrant out for you here, Jacques."

"I was only nineteen," Sawchuk said weakly. Chamberlain began to squawk. Sawchuk grabbed his beak, held it closed.

"You want you should be tried in juvenile court? Listen, you want my advice? You're best off going into this with a burst of glamour—lots of publicity. We can build up the image of a man who's changed his ways, found Jesus. Radical in his youth, he is aging and finding truth in the old-fashioned values. I'll explain to the press you're gonna become a walking billboard extolling the virtues of free enterprise—"

Sawchuk cut him off. "Can it, Rock. I'm not going to grovel to them, play the fawning Rigoletto. And don't go to the press, goddamnit. I don't want the airport loaded down with reporters. Just do a deal for me. I'm depending on you."

"Gotta go. Call me Tuesday. At this same time. I'll see what I can come up with, but I don't know."

Chamberlain, his beak released, uttered an "awk," a despondent note. Sawchuk hung up the phone, paid the fees, left the post office with the two Intelligencia men beside him. He coaxed Chamberlain onto his left hand, then flung that hand upwards, and the macaw fluttered uncertainly, squawked, settled onto the frond of a palm tree.

"*Adios*," called Sawchuk sadly.

"*Adios*," answered the parrot.

5

Friday, December 23, Cuba

Sawchuk sat in an aisle seat near the aft of the big Ilyushin-62, and he refused to glance out the window as the plane ascended, refused to look one last time at this country which had promised so much with Guevara's dream, which now was denying it. A bitter, black cloud of depression hung over the writer, on his way now to face the vagaries of Canadian justice, the likelihood of jail.

Rocky Rubinstein had not been in his office when Sawchuk had called on Tuesday. The secretary had not known where he was.

Sawchuk was resigned to letting fate carry him where it would. Could the imprisoning of his body be worse than the stultifying of his mind and his craft? He had allowed mind and body to grow fat in Cuba. Perhaps he needed a cold, northern tonic to reverse the arrest of his writing skills.

It seemed strange that Regalado had not put an escort on board with him. Or at least had not requested the Canadian Embassy to send their RCMP man Kessel, whom Sawchuk knew from casual, unfriendly encounters in Havana.

The plane was only two-thirds full. This was the beginning of the holiday season when more people were travelling south than north. Two seats over, by the window, was a florid-faced gringo in a cold-weather business suit, who had not smiled at Sawchuk, merely said hello, then returned to his Bible. His vibrations seemed fear-of-flying fundamentalist.

Sawchuk flagged down a flight attendant, ordered a bottle of Camus Napoleon from the duty-free stores and a double straight vodka—the only thing Russian he had learned to like. "*Por favor, señorita,* check on me every twenty minutes or so. To see that I have a full drink in my hands."

The man by the window gave him a nasty look. Sawchuk stretched his long legs down the aisle, affecting an easy, relaxed mood in counterpoint to the man's white-knuckled stiffness. He sipped. Fly high, the best way to travel. Especially when one might not enjoy strong drink for the next few years.

It was bitter and hurtful, this cancer of defeat which had visited him so early in life. Perhaps he had known success too soon, had gambled it away recklessly, had run out of high cards too quickly in the game. He had taunted success, and for that, karma was visiting him with punishments.

Jacques Sawchuk had thought he owned the streets of Montreal as a boy, a gangly, cheerful, wise-cracking preadolescent. Popular, surrounded by freckle-faced groupies, talented with words, he was a leader—captain of the Laurier Secondary basketball team, a track and swimming star. But there had been a bit of the flim-flam in him. In fact as a pubescent boy he worked the Main with his father, shilling. His father was a genius with a grade-five education and a 1930s mentality, a man whom Sawchuk loved and hated in equal instalments.

Sawchuk's mother had provided his genes with a suppressed store of seven generations of French resentment over English domination of Quebec, but it was the socialism of his Ukrainian-Canadian father that ignited those smouldering coals.

His rounder father had never been accepted into the conservative francophone world from which he had taken a wife. Marie Blais had been a strictly raised daughter of the Church, but had fallen uncontrollably in love with John Sawchuk, second-generation Canadian, escapee from a Prairie homestead farm, ex-carnival roustabout, bootlegger, pool player, an alcoholic Marxist who did nothing to change the system except shout his opinions in taverns. He finally got a union job, joined the telephone company as a lineman. He fried to death when he came in contact with a high-tension cable strung too close to the telephone line.

And his wife soon after broke a law of the Church. She committed suicide.

When Sawchuk recovered from the loss of his parents, the Age of Aquarius was in bud. Ferlinghetti. Ginsberg. Dylan. The Stones. An even more perfidious influence: Rocky Rubinstein, then eighteen, fleeing the U.S. draft.

A small press published Sawchuk's first collected poems when he was sixteen, and the book was seriously reviewed. He became a teenage literary lion in the Stanley Street coffee houses. Then, as the counter-culture revolution exploded, so did Sawchuk. He and Rubinstein, freaks and Yippies together, tripped on orange sunshine and purple passion dots, and egged each other on to crazier stunts.

In an age when the world seemed about to explode in a dynamite made of equal parts of violence and love, Sawchuk went to the University of Paris on a scholarship, already at seventeen committed to the passion of revolution. In May of 1968 he and thousands of other students battled with the police in the streets of Paris as ten million workers struck and a new republic seemed about to emerge. But de Gaulle bought the workers off, and Sawchuk had the first bittersweet taste of revolution's failure.

In his year in Paris he read Guevara, Marighella, Regis Débray, became Leninist, then Maoist, then anarchist in turn, sampling all the sweets from the tray of revolutionary ideology, feeling the fulfilling power of belief in each new dogma as he rejected the last one. He wrote workers' poetry and stories about the alienated, those who were being destroyed by a system which kept them fat and mindless. He became heralded as a brave voice of the Left counter-culture.

He held fierce thoughts: one writes history by shedding his blood for others. Revolutionary action generates revolutionary consciousness. The strategy of provocation educates the masses. *Qu'importe les victimes si le geste est beau.* Terrorism is theatre.

Back in Montreal, still filled with all of youth's naïveté and mutiny, he had been drawn to the Front de Libération du Québec as by a magnet. The French fact in Canada gripped him with all its wondrous potential for a free and just society, and he believed that only through struggle could the Anglo corporate juggernaut be smashed.

Reckless and passionate, he joined an F.L.Q. cell, went underground, wrote calls to revolution in stirring, rich language, immersing himself in the joy of rhetoric.

It was all a marvellous, electric, psychedelic circus—until Pierre Laporte, the Quebec labour minister, was kidnapped and killed by members of the Rose cell. Until James Cross, the British trade representative in Montreal, was taken hostage. Until the Trudeau government declared a form of martial law, when police swept across Quebec, arresting artists and intellectuals, holding them in secrecy, denying them bail.

Laporte's death had been traumatic for Sawchuk. The event planted a seed of terrible doubt.

It grew as he ran. Warrants were issued for him on the sedition charges, but Sawchuk slithered out of the police net. Aided by his buddy Rocky Rubinstein, by then a fellow university student, he escaped into the Weather network in the United States. There he travelled from safe house to safe house, still writing, still thinking, still wondering, becoming more despondent as he saw the turn the Weather movement was taking, toward violence for profit, a corruption of the system it sought to change, with men and women in it like Willy Cuyfer, who loved guns and bombs.

Cuba took him in, and he was treated like a hero there at first, given his villa on the beach, where he wrote furiously. He continued to search the writings of socialist thinkers for

answers but the answers seemed to become more muddled as
the nub of doubt grew within him.

As organized terrorist movements became more skilled and
as helpless victims were sacrificed upon the altar of the
strategy of provocation, Sawchuk became cynical, found it
impossible to rationalize. The allowance he received from the
Cuban government began to seem like blood money: he
knew his hosts ran camps to train international terrorists. The
fact that Western countries like the United States and its
Latin surrogates were doing so, too, did not appease him.

He began to sling stones at Cuba. Finally, he let go a
barrage: his article in the *New Left Quarterly*. His poetry and
fiction—that which survived increasingly exhausting and attritive
battles with his typewriter—became foolish and arid, and his
art withered. His work reeked of defeat and disillusionment.

The stewardess enjoyed Sawchuk's verbal attentions and was
generous with hers, topping his drink punctually every twenty minutes. The alcohol began to unleash some optimistic
thoughts. Perhaps after all Regalado, to save face for Cuba,
would deny that Sawchuk had been deported. Perhaps he
had not even informed the Canadian Embassy that Sawchuk
was on his way back, which would explain why there was no
police escort on board.

Canada was not like the U.S.: they did not keep lists of
wanted people at immigration desks. And they would probably not recognize his name. That F.L.Q. business had been
thirteen years ago.

He took two bottles of red wine with his meal. The food
itself he found too dreadful to touch—he could sense the
nitrites in it. But his neighbour ate piously, putting the Bible
aside only for the meal, mumbling a soft grace, returning to
the book afterwards.

Sawchuk opened his bottle of cognac and poured a rich
measure into his glass. The man gave a disgusted look but
returned squint-eyed to the scriptures as Sawchuk gave him a
sunny smile. The alcohol had begun to drown misery, substi-
tuting a frenetic, false happiness. "Wudd ye be afther havin' a
drap to celebrate the toime o' year?" he said.

"No, thank you," said the man. "I have not had to seek
refuge in drink since I discovered His path and understood
the power of His love."

"How grand. And when did the enlightenment occur?"

"Two years ago. It is when I had my last drink. I followed Satan before then, like you."

Sawchuk glowered at him, poured more cognac into his glass, and took an honest swallow. "This your first taste of godless communism, this trip to Cuba?"

"I felt His power here. He is everywhere. You will find Him in your heart if you search it."

"What were you doing in Cuba? You don't seem to be a sun and fun type, if you'll forgive me."

"I was only there a day."

"Yeah? What kind of business?"

"Government business."

"Civil servant?"

"Yes."

"What department?"

"Solicitor General. My name is Agent Walmsly, Canadian Security Intelligence Service. I'm escorting you to Montreal."

Sawchuk spilled cognac on his shirt as he withdrew the glass from his mouth.

"I feel I serve Him in the work I do today, Mr. Sawchuk. It fills me with joy to know this."

Sawchuk sank into an alcoholic depression.

Agent Walmsly returned to his Bible.

6

Friday, December 23, Mirabel Airport

Sawchuk continued stubbornly to drink and when the plane let down at the international airport at Mirabel he was *gazé, en boisson*. Agent Walmsly, speaking in a flat, toneless voice, had been describing his conversion to Jesus Christ, warming to the subject, while Sawchuk listened in misery, and when

the plane bounced onto the runway, Walmsly, without altering
that toneless voice, announced to Sawchuk that he was under
arrest. "It is my duty to warn you that you need not say
anything but that anything you do say may be used in
evidence at your trial."

I have made no friends in the world recently, Sawchuk
thought. Nobody likes me. Cuba throws me out. The critics
have turned against me. The Muse spurns me. A man so
vilified becomes an easy target for a bad-tempered judge who
wishes to make a statement about saving Canada. He saw in
his mind's eye the shocked expression on the judge's face as
the prosecutor read the scatological imagery from his last
book of poetry.

What if the judge decides to make an example of me?
Ten years, say. The remainder of my thirties, the important
years, putrefying in a cell.... Rocky probably hasn't got
me a deal.

He thought about escaping. He was not handcuffed. He
could outrun Walmsly. But drunk and wobbly-kneed, he
followed Walmsly out of the plane and aboard one of the
elevated transfer buses to the terminal building.

The agent showed identification and other papers to
immigration and ushered Sawchuk past the baggage car-
ousels. "Someone will get your belongings when they
come up. A few of us have some questions we want to ask
you."

Third degree. Sawchuk knew how the police got their
voluntary confessions.

They walked through the doors that led to the arrivals area,
jammed with Christmas travellers. Suddenly Sawchuk was
besieged by a media army: men and women gabbling questions at him, all talking at once, holding television cameras,
tape recorders, notepads.

He bolted.

Cameras and recorders flew as he plunged into the reporters, then into the middle of a tight ball of Japanese tourists
who fell like tenpins to a bowling ball. He aimed for the
automatic sliding doors, hoping for a taxi bank outside.

It had been a long time since Sawchuk had last run the
two-hundred-metre hurdles on the track at Laurier Secondary. Yet he would have made it had he not been drunk.
As he leaped over a large suitcase on little wheels that was

being pulled across his path by a startled old woman, the toe of his boot clipped the grip. He came down like a fallen fir tree.

Sprawled there, he looked up and saw in front of him a uniformed man levelling a gun at him with both hands.

"Arrest a bad poet," Sawchuk groaned. "Make the world a better place."

Sawchuk, handcuffed, was flanked by policemen on either side, and another was behind him with a gun. A fourth followed with Sawchuk's rucksack and duffle bag. They were marching along the covered walkway to the administration building and its airport RCMP detachment.

Agent Walmsly was waiting there. He motioned to the officers to take the prisoner around a counter, to an office about the size of a small boardroom. "Take the handcuffs off," Walmsly said.

Sawchuk was released, ushered inside. His bags were dropped inside the door. Walmsly shut it.

Sawchuk stood woozily—though sobered by time and the rush of events—before a table behind which two men sat. One was mean-looking, wore a fedora.

Here is where they go at me, Sawchuk thought. Here is where they take out on me all their sorrows, the nagging wife, the pot-smoking son, the mortgage rates.

"They told us you were smart," said the fedora. "But trying to escape—that was not smart."

"In this country," said Sawchuk hoarsely, "a man is treated fairly. He is forgiven his first mistake."

The fedora barked a laugh. "First mistake? Kidnapping the labour minister? That was a mistake which cost his life. The mistake is called murder, Sawchuk."

Sawchuk felt his jaw suddenly go unhinged. "That's a damned lie! You know I had nothing to do with that!" He tried to calm the anger in his voice. In his worst imaginings he had not suspected this, a frame. Had Rubinstein not talked to them at all?

"We know all about the F.L.Q. cell," Walmsly said. "We have statements saying you were present, attended at the murder, assisted."

Sawchuk ignored him and strode to the table and looked directly into the face of the third man, an older man who seemed to be in charge. "You know I wasn't there. You *know* that. You know who was—they were convicted."

"Not all of them," said Walmsly.

Sawchuk looked from face to face. "What are you trying to do?"

The older officer, white hair and glasses, sat motionless, recoiling slightly from Sawchuk's overrich breath. He studied Sawchuk for some moments, then said, "Thank you, Mr. Walmsly."

Walmsly nodded and left.

"We would like you to plead guilty to kidnapping the minister," said the hat, pulling two sheets of typewritten paper from a file in front of him. "We would like you to plead guilty to being a party to his murder. This is your confession. We would like you to sign it."

Sawchuk's stomach was bubbling, the alcohol mixing with the adrenalin and the acids in there.

"We have some gaps in your U.S. history, when you were with the Weather underground," the policeman said, holding out the papers for Sawchuk. "But we have arranged to locate a long list of charges for the offences you committed there. Bombings, kidnappings, probable homicides. We'll be going over them with you, one by one."

"I want to see a lawyer."

"Willy Cuyfer, he's one of the Weathermen you used to hang around with. A real cutie, that guy. Number two on the world's most-wanted list. Fifteen bank robberies, seven hired hits, two escapes. Last summer he blew up fifty million dollars' worth of oil tanker and fuel, the *Tegiko Maru.*

Now the white-haired man spoke. "The number-one man, ever since Carlos went on ice, is Karl Wurger. The Shrike. Doubtless you have heard of him and his group, the Rotkommando. The Red Commando. Remnants of Baader-Meinhof, the Red Brigades, the Sekiguu, loners like Cuyfer. They are recruiting. Hundreds, maybe thousands. Young people from the streets of Europe. Mostly victims of the recession, I suppose. We believe Wurger is creating an army."

"Who are you?" Sawchuk said. He knew now that this was something different. Something altogether different.

"My name is General Heinrich Hesselmann. This is Captain Hamilton Bakerfield." He barely paused before continuing. "Multinational terrorist organizations are not like rings of drug smugglers or jewel thieves. An agent may easily buy his way into such groups because they are oriented to money. Rotkommando is oriented to . . . an ideal, I suppose. A candidate must have a past of radical work and hold the correct views of history."

"A Commie background," said Bakerfield.

"We understand your own views have changed somewhat," said Hesselmann.

Sawchuk said nothing, stared red-eyed at them.

"We'd like to employ you as a spy, Mr. Sawchuk," Hesselmann said. "The hours are bad, the working conditions deplorable, but there is danger pay."

Sawchuk found a vinyl-covered chair and cautiously slid into it. For a fleeting moment he wondered if this was the world's most hilarious practical joke. Had Rocky Rubinstein, as he had sworn to, finally outdone him in the great continuing game of one-upsmanship they played?

"Hesselmann," he said slowly. "You're the guy—"

"Yes, I am the person responsible for that debacle in Turin three months ago. We are called Group Seven International. Canada is one of the seven sponsoring countries. We have never been able to get a man inside, Mr. Sawchuk. But we have come to believe that that is the only answer. We have been looking for a person with the right credentials. Credentials that will get him into the Central Committee of the Rotkommando."

"Somebody with a built-in cover," Bakerfield said. "We know you can talk their talk."

"Willy Cuyfer is your key to get in," Hesselmann said.

"Take a dive on the kidnapping and the murder, Sawchuk," Bakerfield said. He pulled another paper from the file, extended it to him. "That's a pardon. The Canadian solicitor general has agreed to sign it to clear your record. He'll do it if you agree to infiltrate the Rotkommando."

Careful here, Sawchuk. Stories of police chicanery are legion. Sign the confession, plead guilty—they've got you there for life.

"I would like to see my lawyer. That does not seem to be an unreasonable request." He slurred the word "unreasonable."

"You have the advantage of being multilingual,"
Hesselmann said. "A French-Canadian—"

"French-Ukrainian," Sawchuk interrupted. A point of
honour.

"Born and raised in an Italian section of Montreal. You
have Spanish, Ukrainian. Any German?"

"No. Some Russian. Tell me more."

Play along with these gentlemen, Jacques. If what seemed
to be happening was really happening, those prison walls
were starting to look far, far away. Not that he was going to
put his ideals on the line for these guys by becoming a
political informer, even against some fanatic like The
Shrike.

"We know that Wurger is searching for men and women of
commitment and talent," Hesselmann said. "Particularly those
who have shown they are capable of killing."

In that regard, they definitely have the wrong man, Sawchuk
thought. But he would hear them out.

Bakerfield said, "We've got information that says we can
trust you, Sawchuk. Although I'm not sure. I've met too
many fellow travellers in my time, and I never saw one
change for the better. You've got a history of being a troublemaker, an agitator, a comsymp, and we're going to want to
run you through some tests just to make sure we haven't got a
case of lunatic fringe on our hands. We'll find out if we have
the raw materials to put together some semblance of an
agent. We do know you're a bullshit artist, and I'm not saying
that won't come in handy."

A bullshit artist, Sawchuk thought. He felt injured. "I want
to think about this, gentlemen. A question: What happens
after I come in from the cold? Who saves me from the
assassins?"

"You will have new identification," said Hesselmann, "a
secure place to live, and money." He reached over to
Bakerfield's file and drew out another document. "Everything will be guaranteed in writing, with the appropriate
signatures."

"A contract? No, nothing happens without my lawyer."

Bakerfield made a face. "Samuel J. Rubinstein? Frankly, I
wouldn't hire that man to defend my dog."

Hesselmann clicked on an intercom and spoke into it.

"Agent Walmsly, send Mr. Rubinstein in now." He said to Bakerfield, "We'll leave and let them talk."

As they went through the door with their files, Rocky Rubinstein sauntered in, chirpy and beaming. He closed the door and turned on a small transistor radio that was strapped to his belt.

"Rock and roll fucks up their bugs," he said. "Okay, you Slavic schlang, so what do you think of the deal that your diabolically clever lawyer put together for you?"

7

Mirabel Airport

Rubinstein jabbed at Sawchuk with a flurry of soft lefts and rights. Such was his ritual whenever they met. He had often boasted to Sawchuk about his days fighting out of the Lower East Side Club in Manhattan, but Sawchuk had observed that his old friend was always vague about particulars of the alleged matches. There *was* evidence, however—in the form of a flattened nose.

"How's that for a little plea-bargaining, Jacques? I had them eating out of my hands." Rubinstein's words came rapid-fire from the side of his mouth. He was nearly a foot shorter than Sawchuk, who had not seen him for a year and noticed that the bald area was expanding at the centre of Rubinstein's curly fuzz-top. It looked like a fur nest.

"What have you got me into, Rocky?"

"I put together such a contract even Gary Carter don't have. A general amnesty for all your past sins, a hundred grand, and a lifetime pension. As your manager, I'll be by your side all the way—at least until we unleash you on the terrorists. I'm now a consultant to Group Seven."

In the absence of some form of blackmail, Sawchuk found that hard to believe. He lowered his voice to a level just audible over the rock music. His intoxication was yielding to early hangover. "Rocky, I will go along with this to a point if it will save me from the slammer, but I am *not* enlisting in the War on Crime."

"Sure you are." Rubinstein had a cagey grin. Sawchuk had never been able to figure out how much of Rubinstein was façade, and whether the lawyer had ever been committed to the progressive causes he espoused, or whether life and politics were to him technicolour movies. But there was always that glint of shrewd intelligence in his eyes—and sometimes those eyes were sad, betraying something sensitive behind the buffoon he pretended.

"I showed them your letters, about how you had begun to despise left-wing terrorists. That was a big item in the selling job. 'And he don't like Russians,' I said. To reactionaries like Hesselmann and Bakerfield those are the magic words, meaning you're one of the good guys. It's good guys and bad guys with these schleps. Bakerfield is a red-baiter and Hesselmann is an ex-Nazi. You bring any cigars? Jeez, you smell like a saloon."

Rubinstein did a little shuffle, a bob. His jerky speech and his quick bursts of movement had Sawchuk's head whirling.

"But Willy Cuyfer, that was the kicker, that's what finally put these boys in my clutches. 'Hesselmann,' I said, 'my man *knows* Willy Cuyfer. Big radicals in the Weather underground ten years ago. The Dutchman *loves* my client. They're like brothers."

"I hated the son of a bitch. Rocky, did you tell these guys that I killed people when I was hiding out in the Weather network? If you did, man—"

"No, that's for the public, part of the cover·story. All I think they want you to do is waste a few terrorists. You finally got your chance to save the world, like you always wanted."

"*Waste a few terrorists?*" Sawchuk felt as if he and Rubinstein were occupying alien worlds, trying to communicate through the ether of space. Did he actually think Sawchuk was going to work for political police? Kill terrorists?

"You'll be like James Bond, man. Licensed to kill. At least that's what I figure they want you to do. They didn't actually spell it out clause by clause, footnote by footnote, in the contract." Was Rubinstein kidding? Probably. His voice suddenly lost its levity. "You're looking at ten years on the sedition beef, Jacques. The crown won't make a deal. Okay, if that looks like a lever to convince you to go for this contract, that's probably what's intended. And they're talking about you being an accessory before the fact to the murder of the labour minister. If the Rose gang was encouraged by that article you wrote—the satire, ha-ha—to kidnap and murder Laporte, maybe they can prove a case. I don't know."

"Can the sales pitch, Rocky. I'm going to go for it—to a point. I may turn out to be the Clouseau of political spies, but that'll be their problem. But I am *not* going to be a leftwing stool pigeon. Where are they going to send me?"

"I asked: did you bring any cigars from Cuba? They're going to take you to Europe, some secret camp in the mountains for training."

Sawchuk decided he would play everything by ear until he could assess his chances of going AWOL or, better, getting fired for incompetency. He tugged open the cord of his duffle bag, reached deep inside, pulled out a cigar box, and handed it to Rubinstein.

"Romeo y Julietta double coronas." Rubinstein admired a long cigar as fat as a German sausage. He took the wrapper off, bit a chunk from the end, lit it, and puffed contentedly. "These suckers cost a bitch up here. I'm smoking my way into the poorhouse."

"How did you manage to get this together so fast, Rocky?"

Rubinstein leaned back against the table, blew a column of smoke. "Jacques, you've been away a long time. Things have changed in North America. The shit-disturbers of old are the power brokers of today. Jerry Rubin sells stock on Wall Street. Eldridge Cleaver makes speeches for Reagan and Reverend Moon. Timothy Leary is a stand-up comedian. And Henri Gagnon is deputy minister of justice in the Parti Québécois government. Ten years ago we were anarchists, you, me, him, about half the McGill social sciences."

"Henri Gagnon," Sawchuk said softly. They had been at F.L.Q. meetings together.

"He's the top civil servant in the justice department. I called him Friday after I spoke to you. We met Tuesday in Quebec City. That night I met with a few other people who came up from Ottawa, Canadian Intelligence Security Service. I had your letters, that anti-Soviet piece you wrote in the *New Left Quarterly*, and I spieled them hard. On Wednesday, Hesselmann and Bakerfield flew in from Paris. We drew up the contract yesterday."

"Well, you figure out how I can break that contract without risking my ass."

"Jacques, look at it this way: you're becoming part of the system. When you become part of the system, there ain't any escape." He patted Sawchuk on the shoulder.

Sawchuk glared at him. "Rocky, there were reporters out there. What did you do, issue a press release?"

"A little ink don't hurt."

"I'm not going to get tied in with these Rotkommando crazies. They blow up airplanes. They cut little girls' thumbs off. They're sick, over the edge."

"Then why not do something about them?"

"I *won't* be an informer." Sawchuk backed off from the belching cigar smoke. His head was now aching with alcohol's raw after-effect.

"I knew you'd want me on your side during the trying times to come, so I insisted on a consultant's job as a term of your contract. I'll be going to Italy with you, make sure they train you right." He winked a sly wink. "In a few weeks I'll be running half their agents."

That had got to Rocky, Sawchuk decided. A chance to practise a little spycraft—Rubinstein's great stoned pipe dream. Somehow, unbelievably, the lawyer had silver-tongued his way into General Hesselmann's confidence. "Jesus, Rocky, they want me to plead guilty to the Laporte murder."

Rubinstein gave a reassuring wave of the hand. "Naw, I'm changing all that. You ain't going to plead guilty to nothing. You are going to be *found* guilty. We're going to give them a show trial." The lawyer pulled a copy of the contract from his inside jacket pocket. "It's all signed, sealed, and delivered. Hesselmann, Bakerfield, Henri Gagnon, the deputy solicitor general, they've all signed it. We just need you to sign." He pulled a pen from his pocket and gave it to Sawchuk.

Sawchuk looked the document over. He saw the signatures were there, a government seal. The clauses were clear: a new identity, a pension, a lump sum hundred thousand dollars in addition. ". . . Will perform to the best of his ability services as requested by the Party of the Second Part . . . ."

He signed.

"I just hope you know what you're doing. And what *I'm* doing."

"*Hey*, Jacques." Rubinstein put a brotherly arm high over Sawchuk's shoulder. "This is Sammy Rubinstein you're talking to. What are you talking, you hope I know what I'm doing? Say 'Thanks, Rocky, you saved my buns.'"

"Yeah, well, thanks, Rocky."

8

January, Montreal

Hesselmann flew back early to Gran Paradiso to organize Sawchuk's training program. He was a realist, and harboured no inflated optimism about Operation Sawchuk. The Canadian, he thought, would probably run. And if he did not, if he stayed with the project, he would probably die. As for Mr. Rubinstein, well, Hesselmann had a strong hide. Rubinstein seemed inescapably a part of the team. He would be coming to Gran Paradiso later with Sawchuk, and would have to be endured.

Hamilton Bakerfield, left in charge of things in Montreal, was not sure that Rubinstein's scenario for the grand trial was going to work as advertised. He would have preferred to use another lawyer, but was reluctant to bring in one more outsider. He couldn't get a handle on Rubinstein and this bothered him, because he was a professional cop and an expert judge of men. He knew this about Rubinstein: he played the game a little differently from most.

"We'll shoot the works," the lawyer said to him. "We dress him up simple, nothing garish. Clean pants and white shirt, open at the neck. And we got this little star pinned to his pocket. A little *red* star. A subtle touch. You don't notice it right away, and then suddenly you pick up on it, and there it is, and your eyes are fixed on it for the rest of the trial."

Let's not screw around," Bakerfield said. "Let's just prove the confession and be done with it."

Sawchuk had signed the confession with a heavy foreboding, but Rubinstein had been beside him, nodding and chattering, emboldening him.

"Judge and jury, Superior Court, the works. We want to get every newspaper in the world into that courtroom. It'll be a losing case for me, won't help my reputation, but the public's gonna know he got a good defence."

"Every day Sawchuk sits in jail waiting for the trial is a wasted day, Rocky."

"Jacques don't mind," said Rubinstein.

To Bakerfield's relief, and much to his amazement, Rubinstein handled the trial in a finished, expert style. He was a superb actor in the courtroom, playing for the headlines certainly, but giving credence to the trial. Only a few in the Attorney General's Department knew a charade was being played out. The prosecutor did not know, nor the judge, an irascible man with thin slits for eyes, his body hunched forward like a badger defending home and territory.

The jurors, faceless shopkeepers and clerks, kept peering around the courtroom nervously as if they feared a unit of the French-Ukrainian Liberation Army might suddenly burst into the courtroom hurling hand grenades.

Rubinstein stretched the trial out. During the breaks, Sawchuk complained.

"A three-day trial only gets three days of headlines," Rubinstein insisted. "A ten-day trial gets ten days' worth. Man, we were on the national news on TV last night. Look, I'm the expert. The patient don't tell the doctor how to amputate the diseased organ."

"Rocky, when is the escape supposed to happen?"

"Relax. It don't happen until you're sentenced."

"After I'm sentenced?" Sawchuk was not happy with this.

"For maximum impact. Listen, they're reading about you in Europe. Karl Wurger will be wetting his pants to get ahold of such a revolutionary as I'm painting you, a man who inspires by the firmness of the convictions he holds." By the end of the trial the jury had smiles for the pugnacious Jewish freedom fighter, who was always near them, chatting them up during breaks, cracking jokes, talking hockey.

Bakerfield had unhappy thoughts that Rubinstein might actually *win* the case. But the confession had been put before the jury, a document in which Sawchuk had boastfully admitted to the revolutionary act of murder. And Sawchuk rendered the issue certain as he personally made the closing speech to the jury, an hour-long buffeting of Western imperialism that ended with a note of arm-flourishing ardour.

"The revolution is in this courtroom!" Sawchuk's rich baritone boomed at the jurors, who flinched. "It is in our homes, in our schools, on the streets. It is in your hearts, in the heart of every man and woman who is not blinded and can seek it there. I call upon you to set tinders under it, to take flint to it, to set it aflame."

Sawchuk sat, proud of his own rhetoric. A scattering of applause came from members of the local Trotskyist League in the back of the courtroom.

The jury deliberated for eight and one half minutes and returned with a unanimous verdict of guilty.

The judge, in sentencing, described Sawchuk as a national obscenity. "Perhaps I should amend that," he said. "To adopt the wider scope which the prisoner employed in his windy summation, I should call him an international obscenity. I have decided to grant him the martyrdom which he so desperately wishes to claim for himself. Life imprisonment, no parole for thirty years."

Sawchuk felt a whap, for the briefest second forgetting that this was all a play, the judge an unwitting part of it.

III

Glickums

Here am I, O God, at thy command
Thou art one and alone. Here am I.

The pilgrim's prayer
at Mecca's gate

9

Friday, January 20, New York City

"You look worried, General."

"Who are you?"

"Charles M. Rubinstein. Don't you remember me?"

"I can't say I do."

"I'm Charles Rubenstein the reporter. I did the defence beat for the *Washington Post* two years ago."

"Oh, yeah, I remember you now. You did that story on Hank Naiboldt and the kickbacks. That almost got him court martialed. That was a hard knock for old Hank. You still with the *Post*?"

"No, I'm with the *Times*. Here, in New York."

"Sit down. Bring your drink."

Thus they had met, a week ago. Charles M. Rubinstein had been sipping a beer, relaxing on his favourite stool in his favourite bar in New York's SoHo, trying to think of an angle, a way to expose City Hall, dig out corruption in an NYPD precinct, daydreaming of that story which would restore his good name, which would turn the tide of his disastrous career as a journalist.

Sitting at a table by himself, looking besotted and sad, was General Rufus McKay, five stars, old Pentagon, not in uniform here, knocking back Scotches desperately. Charles had felt a little pissed that McKay had not remembered him at first. Two years ago he had interviewed the man for three hours when Rubinstein was hot on the track of General Naiboldt and a fix-price scandal involving high-technology defence contracts.

McKay was Chief of Staff for Defence Procurements, Sophisticated Weaponry Division. At the Pentagon he was known as quartermaster of missiles. And he was involved with high-level strategy, war plans, the Pentagon think-tank team.

Now Charles Rubinstein was going to meet General Rufus McKay once again in SoHo, in an area of former sweat shops, converted now into artists' lofts, under siege by a rich-hip crowd which was beginning to move the artists out. Why is General McKay hanging around this artsy, boho part of town? Charles had wondered.

In the bar, he had said he had a story. He had warned Charles not to tell anyone that they had met, even his editor. Fat chance, Charles thought. If there's a big story here, I'll sell it to the *Stone*, or *Mother Jones*.

McKay had stared at him with alcohol-dazed eyes, eyes that were unsoldierly—moist and soft—and Charles had perceived that the man was troubled. Charles Rubinstein, from the general's point of view, had been an anonymous-looking young man, dressed in tweed, neatly groomed. Charles always tried to look anonymous. His business was worming stories out of people, infiltrating targets at the top. He was taller than his brother Rocky, more easy-going, less raucous in manner.

But he shared much with Rocky. This is not surprising, given the stamp of common family traits and their Brooklyn upbringing in the seven-member family zoo. They shared a love for grand concepts, a ludicrous vision of the world, a talent for muckraking, a scorn for the establishment, and a brazen pride in their Jewishness.

But while Rocky was a lover of theatre, spy thrillers, fantasy, Charles was a fact nut. All his boyhood he had wanted to be a reporter. He had worked summers at small neighbourhood presses. He had eschewed the school of journalism route, the easy route, and starting with the lowest of the low, the service club luncheon beat at the Begonia, Illinois *Triweekly Record*, had done the journeyman reporter's tour of America. Almost always he had been fired or had quit because of the heat.

The highest he had risen was Washington correspondent for a racy daily tabloid out of New York. But he had been cashiered there when the paper collapsed in court. They had had to fork over $350,000 to a senator and the chairman of the senator's re-election fund.

The *Washington Post* bravely took him on probation—for Charles had a reputation as a digger—letting him fill in during summer holidays on the Pentagon desk. Charles had written the kickback piece on General Naiboldt. That had gone over well. Then he had written an informed-source story about some of the chilling second-strike game plans being played out in one of the Pentagon theatre rooms by a team with a big nuclear contingent. That story had not held up when the defence department put the heat on. Its press relations people had demonstrated many small inaccuracies, and Charles, refusing to name his informant, had been sacked before the end of August.

Now Charles M. Rubinstein was back to where he had started in his journalism career. Working for a neighbourhood newspaper in New York City. The *South Greenwich Times*, radical voice of the bedraggled, beaten remnants of Manhattan's counter-culture.

But now he might be onto the scoop of a lifetime. The *Washington Post* would beg to have him back.

He stood in front of a five-storey, red-brick building, fat and square. Take the elevator to the third floor, the general had said. If the front door is locked, buzz Weltz. Third floor of *this* place?

The door was unlocked. He got into the elevator and pushed the button.

When the elevator door opened, he found himself standing before a good-looking redhead. She might have been a dancer, she had the legs. But she was an artist: Charles saw the oil canvases banked along the walls. She was pretty hip. He liked the flouncy miniskirt.

"Are *you* from the private secretary service?" she said. "I was expecting to see a woman. I'm relieved." She was into erotica—big, distorted bodies, acrylic breasts and penises.

"My firm is called Secretary Birds, Inc.," Charles said. "Maybe that's what got you on the wrong foot."

She called over her shoulder. "The private steno is here, Rufus. I'll be back in half an hour. I'll get something nice for dessert. Wine?"

"Chablis," came the general's voice.

As Charles stood aside to let her pass, he saw McKay sitting on a block of foam on the floor, his legs stretched out, his back against a low window frame. He was smoking a big Peterson bent. He looked happy.

The elevator door closed.

"Take off your coat. Barbara will be back in half an hour. I told her I needed a little time to get some letters out, although I hate lying to her." The voice was friendly but gruff. Spencer Tracy in a multicoloured kimono, with a satisfied smile. To Charles he looked like a man recently fucked. "Last Friday night you caught me getting loaded. I had just got in from Washington, figured she'd be up here, waiting for me. God, all sorts of things went through my head when I unlocked the door and found this place empty. That's why I was in that little bar. I figured, Lord, there will be nobody I know in that greasy little hippie dive." He waved Charles toward a worn rattan chair. "It turned out she was at a meeting of her W.A.C. regiment—Women Artists for Choice."

"Was she all you were worried about, sir?" Charles removed his overcoat, hung it on a spike, one of several driven into a beam for that purpose, and sat in the chair. "It looked like something else was heavy on your mind."

"Are you still doing defence stories?" McKay asked.

"It's my best beat," Charles lied. Play this mighty cool, Charlie. This guy looks as if he is going to spew it all. Maybe I have got the whole military-industrial conspiracy about to fall into my lap. He resisted the urge to go too quickly for pen and pad.

"I come to New York most weekends. I tell my wife it's secret business. I wonder if she suspects what kind of secret business. In Soph-Weapons, a lot of the guys probably do suspect. They just have to look at me. They know I'm not on drugs, so I must be in love. I can't get the smile off my face. Hell, I even *took* some drugs. She had me smoking a marijuana joint with her last month. Just one, and it's the *last* one, I'll tell you that." McKay levelled his love-numbed eyes at Charles. "You don't name your informants—that's what I remember about you. I have to tell somebody. You protect your sources, so I'm telling you."

What's this? Charles thought. He asks me up here to tell me he's in love? This is a story?

"We have time for me just to give you a flavour of this thing. I am never to be quoted; my name is never to be mentioned."

Maybe he is crazy. A maniac on the loose in the Pentagon,

in charge of ordering Cruise and Pershing missiles, planning war strategy.

"I'll give you the phone number here and you can call me on weekends. You'll have to do some research between meetings. I can't give you anything except hearsay, but it's from a hell of a strong source. There are films and tapes, but they're in Mecca."

Mecca?

"You're Jewish," McKay said.

"No, sir. I'm an Aztec Indian. My real name is Xanthzetepec."

The general smiled, fumbled in a matchbox for a wooden match, and ripped it across the exposed bricks of the wall, then applied it rigorously to his pipe. "I like Israel," he said, working the fire into the bowl. "Spunky country. They got too many socialists in there, but I like the gutsy way its soldiers fight. I'm old West Point. I know and admire good soldiering. And now I'm like a damn lawyer, not a soldier, negotiating contracts with the sharks in the defence industries. I don't enjoy it."

The pipe was blasting hot clouds now, and they swept over McKay's shoulder and out through the open window. "I've always believed Israel is our only reliable ally in the Middle East. First line of defence there. Obviously the people in State disagree: the future is with the Arabs, they feel. Oil buys the strongest friends."

Mecca. Israel. What did Charles have here?

"I don't like Democrats. I thought Carter was puerile. I'm an Eisenhower Republican. Taft. Dulles. The honest, strong people we used to have around. I tell you this so you don't think I'm some kind of malcontent, a maverick."

"The thought never crossed my mind, sir. Ever thought of joining the sharks yourself? A high-tech contractor pays a retired general a few hundred thousand plus bonuses every year."

"I've had offers. You're way off on the salary. I have a friend on the board of the Typhon Corporation. In the service he got sixty thousand. Now he gets a million a year. This friend is Henry Naiboldt, the man you wrote the story about, the man you forced into resigning his commission. He's a crook, Mr. Rubinstein. And he's my best friend. He tells me things."

The Typhon Corporation was one of the great California technology giants, Charles knew. His pen and pad were screaming at him. But he kept his hands in front of him, clasped.

"This bunch they've got at the White House now, this California crowd, they're a different kind of Republican," McKay continued. "I'm not comfortable with them. They like guns too much. Does that sound strange coming from an army man?" McKay blew a couple of perfect smoke rings which crumbled, went out the window.

Charles liked this guy. He was different, all right, different from most of them.

"It's an unhealthy democracy when the people we elect go to bed with the military. And with its contractors. It's unhealthy when the people we elect get paid for fucking us, like prostitutes."

"Prostitutes, sir?"

"Fifteen-million-dollar prostitutes. Mr. Rubinstein, I'm going to pass you some sticks of sweating dynamite. Handle them carefully. I respect the *Times*, it's an honest newspaper, and it's as good as its slogan. And you have the research facility to get the confirming facts. That's why I'm giving you this."

Charles felt guilty. His paper, the *South Greenwich Times*, circulation five thousand and a little, had no research facilities.

"And maybe I'm giving you this because you're Jewish."

"Your girlfriend. She's Jewish, too."

"She's nice, isn't she?"

"A looker."

"Her parents have retired to a kibbutz in the Negev."

"General, I'm ready. What's the story?"

"You've been following the Glickums thing—the sale to Saudi Arabia?"

"You bet."

Glickums, for want of an acronym, was the in-phrase to describe GLCMs, ground-launched Cruise missiles. The White House was negotiating a thirteen-billion-dollar sale of Cruise missiles and installation sites with Saudi Arabia, ostensibly to counter Soviet threats from South Yemen and Ethiopia. The U.S. public was in a furore over it, although the administration had insisted that only conventional warheads would be supplied.

"We're giving Saudi Arabia the means to destroy Israel," the general said.

"That seems to be the view of the Israeli lobby." Charles

tried to sound neutral, but he was revolted by the deal. First F-15s, then AWACS, now Glickums. Saudi Arabia was the new reliable ally. "But you and I both know, General, that there isn't a snowball's hope of the bill getting through Congress." The bill, when presented by the President, would require approval of either the House of Representatives or the Senate. The House would likely give a big negative vote. In the Senate, it would be closer, but an informal poll indicated the nays would have it by a small margin.

"Reagan has written off the House," said McKay. "But he's got the Senate."

"He's what?"

"Typhon has the Glickums contract. Hank Naiboldt is executive veep of Typhon. And Hank has bought off two senators and blackmailed a third. With Saudi money. They've got fifty-one votes now."

"Come again, sir?"

The general sighed, shook his head slowly. "I've been holding onto this so tight that I can't tell whether what I am feeling is pain or relief now. Hank and I were out duck-hunting in North Dakota last November. He got really tanked. He got loose-mouthed. He told me he's given out fifteen million dollars in bribes."

"To a couple of *senators*?" Charles was aghast. "Who?"

"That's for you to find out. He didn't tell me."

10

Monday, January 23, East Berlin

"Sixty man-portable rocket systems and PGMs. And enough submachine-guns and automatic rifles to equip a regiment. What are you hoping to accomplish, comrade, take over a country? Perhaps the United States?"

"We are going to take over the Kingdom of Saudi Arabia," said Wurger. He sipped his tea.

Colonel Zuhair looked for humour in Wurger's eyes, found none, and had to smile himself. "With hand-held missiles, the Rotkommando will invade one of the most heavily defended nations on earth with its AWACS, its Mirage fighters, its Centurions. The Rotkommando with its three hundred young guerrillas against the Sauds' sixty thousand troops, its four hundred thousand reservists. May God be with you, Karl Wurger."

"We are taking over from inside. We have access to the summer palace of Prince Aziz near Mecca. If our timing is right, we may have the defence minister and the King himself. And some important Americans. Outside our Central Committee, Comrade Colonel Zuhair, no one knows but you."

Zuhair was the paymaster for the Rotkommando. Officially he was first military adviser to Moammer el-Ghaddafy, chairman of the Revolutionary Command Council of the People's Libyan Arab Republic. He had worked with this young German for many years, and he had not known him to harbour impossible dreams. The two men were meeting this day in a sitting room of the Libyan Embassy in East Berlin, a safe house for the Rotkommando.

"I have the power to bring that fetid kingdom collapsing at our feet like a colossus." Wurger's words rang with a passion that startled Zuhair. "In five months we can be ready, after our people graduate from Misurate. But you charge us dearly for training our soldiers, comrade, and our London accounts have almost dried up. And we need the arms."

"And doubtless you will need sanctuary when it is all over. For even if your attack succeeds, it will not succeed for long. In Saudi Arabia, one does not take the kingdom by simply taking the King. The Saud dynasty is not as monolithic as that. There exist three thousand heirs to the Saudi throne—a large family, comrade."

"If the army stays loyal to the King, we will exact a price before we take refuge in Tripoli. The price will be in the billions." Wurger leaned toward Zuhair, his eyes like blue flames. "And that money will be invested in your country—for the training of thousands more of our recruits at Misurate."

"The army will stay loyal to the Sauds," Zuhair said,

"because serving the King are fifteen thousand members of the National Guard, drawn from the loyal tribes of the Najd—and their role is to watch the army. And watching *them* are seven thousand members of the Special Forces, who are American trained, more fiercely loyal yet."

"Who knows what will happen? The country is a smouldering volcano, and the lava only needs a prime." Wurger knew that Zuhair was astonished at the scope of the Mecca operation, although he betrayed nothing behind his soldier's mask. He continued his selling job. "We will have hostages from the Pentagon and the Typhon Corporation. Who knows, maybe the Americans will invade. Then there would be war. And war means upheaval in the feudal kingdoms of the Middle East. Revolution. We need the arms, comrade."

Zuhair poured more tea—sweetened, with milk, in the English style—and looked long and thoughtfully at Wurger. "Sometimes we worry about the Karl Wurger who leads an army. We worry that when the Rotkommando grows too large, it will no longer need us as friends. And we have enough enemies."

Wurger reached out and grasped both of Zuhair's hands. "That hurts me. I am a brother to you, as I am a brother to Libya, as I am a brother to all who wish to see the Arab world transformed into a united socialist power."

Zuhair pulled his hands away. "Yes, comrade, you may have the arms. For an almost insignificant price. We have another name to add to your list. Execute him and you will have the arms for Mecca."

Wurger didn't have to guess. He had read the *Time* magazine profile on the famous British concert pianist who had described Ghaddafy in richly insulting phrases. "Sir Isaac Solomon, I suppose."

"Comrade Ghaddafy reads all the American news magazines," said Zuhair, smiling, some irony in his voice. "It will be easy to execute this Zionist. He is regularly on concert tour. The Saudi princes are truly enemies in the class struggle. But the Zionist entity must always be the first enemy. Execute this pig and you can come to Tripoli and take your pick of the rockets and the guns."

Wurger sat back, relieved. Yes, the execution would be easy, although the planning might take some months.

"Now tell me about the summer palace of Aziz," said
Zuhair. "You have someone who is close to the prince?"

"So close she smells his stench. So close she may soon
share his bed."

Prince Aziz ibn Saud al Saud, nephew to King Fahd and son
of a former king, carried the blood of desert zealots, the
Wahabis, whose austere Islam faith was the Shari'ah, the
Holy Law of Saudi Arabia, as interpreted by His Majesty, the
sheik of sheiks, the supreme religious leader.

Prince Aziz and the other three thousand members of the
House of Saud constituted a family which owned a country.
The Wahabi warriors, who were Aziz's direct forbears, took
Arabia in 1919 from the Hashemites with gun and sword, and
the clans of the Saud had since maintained their rule with
better guns, bought with oil.

Aziz had once been deputy minister of finance, but several
years ago he had gone into business on his own as a commission agent. He was now the richest man in the world. He
counted as clients General Motors, Rolls-Royce, Sony, IGN-
Farber, AT&T, another fifty such multinationals including five
oil conglomerates and a dozen Western banks, and the defence ministries of the United States, France, Britain, and
Italy. Several hundred million dollars' worth of contracts
flowed each month through his offices, which occupied the
thirteenth floor of the tower of his summer palace. The
fourteenth floor, the penthouse, was his personal suite.

The palace had been designed by architects from Paris and
Stockholm, a hodgepodge of arabesque and modern design
but an impregnable fortress of concrete and silvered steel and
bullet-proof glass, built at a cost of a billion *riyals*, high in the
Hijaz Asir, on the slopes of the Jabal Kabkab north of Mount
Arafat. It overlooked the narrow, searing valley of Mecca.
From its telescopes one could see the fifty-foot-tall *Ka'aba* in
the courtyard of the Grand Mosque, its surfaces draped in
rich black and gold hangings. And one could see the neon
signs of Mecca: Sanyo, National Panasonic, Kentucky Fried
Chicken. On a windless day one could hear the wail of the
muezzin calling the people to prayer.

Beyond Mecca, the palace overlooked the paleness of the
Red Sea, behind whose hazy distances a sun the colour of
blood died suddenly each night. During day, under that

omnipotent Arabian sun, the palace sparkled like a garish diamond. The walls around it and the other buildings in the compound were five-foot thicknesses of stone ridged with dog-tooth triangles. The gate was of steel armour, and could never be opened unless by order of Aziz from the console in his office, the command centre for all palace functions. He was in contact from there with palace rangers who controlled anti-aircraft batteries on rooftops.

The prince's guests came to the palace by executive helicopter from the bustling airport at Jeddah, where pilgrims to Mecca poured by the thousands each day from chartered and scheduled aircraft. The helicopter would land on a pad on the penthouse terrace above the fourteenth floor. Aziz had a stable of such helicopters, ordered personally from Sikorsky. They were plated with gold, with buttons of sapphire studding the kid-leather upholstery. The personal monogram of Prince Aziz adorned them, as it adorned his yachts and limousines.

There was no way except by air to approach the palace, unless a guest were prepared to scramble over ancient volcanic debris from the dead-end road five miles down the mountain. That road, built by the U.S. Corps of Army Engineers at a cost of three million dollars, had once continued all the way to the compound gate but, after the palace was built, Aziz had had the road bulldozed to keep sightseers away.

The bulldozers had levelled thirty acres of rock surrounding the walls, and earth movers had dumped thousands of tons of soil there. The lawns of Aziz's personal par-three golf course which surrounded the palace walls were so green in this country of grey and dun that the sight of them took the breath away. They were watered from the Qat oasis on the eastern side of the Hijaz, the water carried in an eight-inch pipe which wiggled through the desolate hills to the palace. It was pumped to the rooftop gardens, then allowed to descend freely in a series of waterfalls and pools over the multi-levelled palace tower before being carried into the golf course's underground piping system.

The pools were for bathing and swimming. But they were not to be used by the staff and servants or by the members of Prince Aziz's elite palace guard. They were for royal guests. Those who came here in the summer to enjoy the fragrant mountain coolness included not only sheiks of the House of

Saud but those on pilgrimages to Mecca. Such people were
important clients of Prince Aziz and were treated lavishly. In
recent years there had been visitors from the West as well,
from New York and Dallas and Minneapolis, from Paris and
Tokyo and Frankfurt, the elite of the elite from the multinational
boardrooms.

This afternoon, a group of such Westerners had just departed Aziz's circular office, together with the Saudi minister
of defence, who was half-brother to Aziz. From his office,
Aziz could feel the rumbling and hear the clatter of the
helicopter taking off overhead. It would take his half-brother
to Riyadh and the Americans to Bahrain for their flight to
Washington. These Westerners were special guests. They
represented a thirteen-billion-dollar arms purchase—many
times the true value of the ground-based Cruise missile
systems, Aziz knew, but his commission was twelve per cent,
half to be paid by his own government, half to be paid by the
Typhon Corporation. But what was money? *Jihad*, holy war,
was the important thing.

The ground-launched Cruise missiles would be coming off
the assembly lines of the Typhon Corporation in a year. The
bases would be built, and the technicians who manned them
would be trained, by personnel of Typhon, the California
high-technology giant which during the last decade had casually shrugged off the economic demons of recession and
inflation and had ridden a skyrocket to the top of the list of
the big new corporate stars: the high-tech powerhouses spawned
by the revolution in computers and the largesse of the u.s.
defence budget, a horn of plenty of seemingly infinite
proportion.

For this meeting, Typhon had sent its executive vice-
president, Henry Naiboldt, and two other retired generals
who were on its board. The Pentagon had sent a three-man
team, and the State Department an observer. Aziz feared
American politics might create problems. He often wondered
how America's leaders governed with so many complex and
awkward restraints: a Congress which would apparently have
to approve this package and felt entitled to poke into matters
not of its concern; newspapers which seemed to have the
power to print anything they wanted. But their President had
said yes, and surely that was the main thing. The people from
the Pentagon had promised that certain opposition within the

ranks of the defence department would be stilled. And Henry Naiboldt, a man of many admirable skills, had assured Aziz that the United States Senate would ultimately line up behind the President.

That promise by Naiboldt had been made in the course of a private discussion yesterday between the two men. Three senators whose votes had early been thought to be doubtful were now committed. Those votes would ensure a majority when the President's bill was presented. Aziz had requested and received as proof—after all, he was paying fifteen million dollars into private accounts in the Bahamas—original tape recordings and film, which he had locked in his office strongroom, in an eight-foot-high, twenty-foot-deep vault, built into a wall.

A powerful Jewish lobby was fighting the bill, but Saudi Arabia had deflected the thrust of their attack by assuring the U.S. government publicly that Typhon would construct the bases along the ill-defined border with the People's Democratic Republic of Yemen. There they could strike at the huge Soviet naval station at Aden and then reach farther, to the Soviet and Cuban installations in Ethiopia. Still other Glickums bases would be built near the Persian Gulf. Those Cruise missiles, with their maximum range of four thousand kilometres, would be programmed for targets in Iran—a potential enemy—and beyond the Caucasus and the Caspian Sea.

With the training from Typhon, it would be simple for Saudi computer technicians to reprogram them, Aziz knew. All of Saudi Arabia was within Cruise range of the occupiers of the lands that had been stolen from Islam. Israel was not too small a target for a Cruise missile, which could pick a streetcorner in downtown Tel Aviv. The U.S., of course, was supplying conventional, not nuclear, warheads. But soon, within another year perhaps, they would have the nuclear warheads from Pakistan. That business was a costly one, too—Aziz had earned commission fees on the loans to Pakistan. But God had given oil to Saudi Arabia for a purpose. That purpose was to do God's work.

Aziz watched through his windows as the helicopter fluttered east toward Riyadh. "They will be returning for further talks in March," he said. "I will give you a list of the people we want from Riyadh, from the defence and trade ministries.

They will be back again later for the signing. His Majesty will be here to greet them personally. Nothing must go wrong."

Latifa scribbled a note and nodded. She heard the helicopter speed away. She looked with distaste at the museum pieces that lined the walls between the windows in glass cases. Muskets, breechloaders, guns from every war of the last three centuries: Aziz's multi-million-dollar collection.

"We will send the 747 from Jeddah to collect them," Aziz continued. He began to dictate a long memorandum to her, from his memory of the discussions with the Americans. He preferred to carry on his business in the Western way—which meant using English. He preferred all things English. He had graduated from St. John's College, Cambridge, had read law and economics, had won blues for tennis and soccer. He wore a lounge suit from Hollinger-Smythe of Oxford Street. Only in public did the royal sheik wear a *thaub* or a *kaffiyeh*, and never outside his own country.

His private secretary was also Western-educated. Latifa's British school had been a lesser one, of course, but she had obtained there her Master's degree in English literature. The school had been one where radical ideas were discussed, and one of her young instructors had been a Palestinian, from whom she received confidences, during their quiet walks about the college grounds, about his work with the Popular Front for the Liberation of Palestine.

She had fallen deeply in love with this gentle but passionate revolutionary, and a hunger for liberation began to grow within her.

She had learned from him that women had not been born to be slaves of men. But she was a slave now to Prince Aziz—as she had been a slave to her wealthy father who had had her abducted from England when she refused to come willingly. Her father had literally sold her into Prince Aziz's service.

Aziz pointed to a folder on his massive circular rosewood desk, a folder that contained the missile capability reports. "Put that in the strongroom with the other files. Then fetch me a Scotch with a dash of soda."

Latifa pressed a button and a section of the wall slid open. She dialled the combination of the vault, opened it, took the papers inside. Then she came out, closed it, touched a switch on the underside of Aziz's desk and a section of mahogany wainscotting opened on a hinge, revealing decanters atop a small refrigerator. The switch had also triggered a tape machine. Arab love songs wailed softly from speakers hidden in the walls behind enormous Persian carpets intricately woven in the geometric designs sanctioned by the Koran.

Women were usually attracted to Prince Aziz. He was not yet fifty, was thickly built and handsome, with streaks of grey in his goatee, with dark eyes that were confident and strong. But Latifa detested this man.

Her face was composed, her thoughts hidden, as she poured the Scotch and soda and removed a silver ice bucket from the refrigerator.

Alcohol was not forbidden in Prince Aziz's palace, but that fact was not advertised. The possession of alcohol was a crime punishable by God's law, as interpreted by his uncle the King. But the *muttawiun*, the religious police, understood they were not to seek to enter the grounds of the palace. Aziz had not gotten rich by offering his Western guests sweetened tea or cardamom coffee. He had learned to drink Scotch, even bourbon.

"Pour one for yourself," said Aziz, smiling. "I know you had alcohol when you were in England. I suppose all the girls who study in the West learn the joy of falling from grace."

"I have never had alcohol, Your Excellency." Latifa stood poised but slightly nervous and extended the drink to him. Aziz touched her fingers as he took the glass and she trembled.

"In the four years that you lived among the English in the City of Hull you did not taste a glass of English beer? No sherry, no wine? Come. My wives drink cocktails in London, or when they are in the villa at Monte Carlo. You are not the innocent you wish me to perceive."

Koran law allowed a man, should he have the means, at most four wives, and Aziz had his full quota. These were jealous, vicious women whom Latifa feared. They had regarded her with unbridled hostility after she had been given into the prince's entourage four months ago.

"I do not drink alcohol, Your Excellency."

"Then in what simple sin do you indulge, Latifa? You are very good to look at. I suppose you know that. There have been boys."

"No, Prince Aziz."

"An innocent child of God. Relax with me. Pour yourself a

Kaki-Cola. I know business bores you, Latifa, as it bores all women. So we shall end our business and relax. Are you frightened of me?"

"Should I not type the memoranda?" Latifa's name translated as "gentle" into English. She suited the name: quiet, timid, even fearful. Her prettiness was hidden by makeup, heavy lacquered layers in the style preferred by Arab women and insisted upon by their men. She was dressed in the Western way, a blouse, a fawn-coloured suit of light silk.

"Come. Around the desk. Come up to me."

She hesitated. She could smell, from across the desk, the heavy perfume. She felt her heart nervously skipping in her chest. This would happen. She had been told that by her contact in Popular Front for the Liberation of Palestine.

She walked around to Aziz, her hands hanging loosely at her sides.

He reached out his hand and set it on the inner part of her knee, through the slit of her dress. She felt the hand there, hot through her stocking. She felt dizzy.

"I rather care for you," Aziz said. "Does that not make you feel more relaxed? I would not make love to you if I did not care for you. You are different from the other women here. There is something fresh about you, a vitality that you try to hide, but not well."

His hand slid up her thigh, parting the skirt. She closed her eyes.

11

Friday, February 24, New York City

Shortly after his last meeting with General McKay, Charles Rubinstein had journeyed to Montreal to spend a weekend at

his brother's flat. He had expected to find Rocky in the
dumps following his loss in the well-publicized trial of Jacques
Sawchuk, expected to be able to commiserate with him.
Charles was also a friend of Sawchuk; he had been an
accessory to Sawchuk's escape over the border in 1970, and
had hid him in his Manhattan apartment.

Rocky, to his surprise, had been in a merry mood. "Just
another loss, got to take the losers with the winners. Anyway,
I'm appealing. In fact, some think I'm *very* appealing."

Charles had not found things quite as funny. The burden of
carrying General McKay's revelations had been difficult to
bear alone, and in a beery, smoke-filled session on a Saturday
night, he disclosed to Rocky what McKay had told him.

Rocky had seemed unmoved and cynical. "What's a senator
going for down in the States these days? More than a judge?"

"Eight million in one case, seven in another."

What ex-General Naiboldt had drunkenly boasted to McKay,
and what McKay had disclosed to Charles, the reporter now
repeated to his brother: two senators had been bought, and a
third blackmailed. The fifteen million dollars had apparently
been provided by an agent of the Saudi government. As a
guarantee for that investment, secret tapes and film had been
made of Naiboldt's bartering with the three senators, evidence
which was locked in the private vault of that agent, Prince
Aziz al Saud, in his summer palace near Mecca.

"Who's your source?" Rocky asked.

Charles was wounded. "I'm a journalist."

"Jeez, Charles, here's your chance to scuttle the Cruise
sale."

"I need verification. My source can't be quoted."

Rocky said he'd help. "I got an underground information
network," he said vaguely.

Charles did not draw much hope from that. He believed
his brother read too much spy fiction.

Charles knew the fruits of success in his business were
harvested only with sweat, and so this young I.F. Stone had
returned to New York and begun spending long hours in his
weedy garden, the library of the *New York Times*, digging
through mounds of clippings. He was smuggled in there by
friends on the editorial staff whom he persuaded to give him
a blank I.D., a pass to which he affixed his own picture, and
typed and signed his name.

"These are my *Times* credentials," he had said to General Rufus McKay, during their second meeting in the artist's loft. "You have a right to see them." Charles felt guilty as hell about that, but what was a little subterfuge when it came down to nailing the biggest story of the year? Such matters must be kept in perspective. Doubtless the *Times* would be happy to hire him on as a hard-nosed political analyst after he exploded the Typhon-Saudi bribe and blackmail seam. In the meantime, he continued to work for the little *South Greenwich Times* and hoped the general would never notice his byline in it. Charles had given him his home number. "Don't want my editor getting suspicious," he had said.

Charles was now meeting McKay for a third time at his mistress's SoHo loft. The general's girlfriend had wrought serious changes in the man.

"Art is more important than guns," McKay confided. "She has released hidden talents in me." It was true. The general, wearing a paint-splotched smock, proudly displayed to Charles the little oils he had begun to create, still lifes.

"Little touch of Cézanne there," Charles said.

"She says I have to master this stuff before I get into free expressionism."

There was a mix of happiness and paranoia about the man, Charles observed.

"Sometimes I think I'm being followed," McKay said. "I wonder if my wife has hired a detective? Maybe it all has to end anyway. The kids are grown up. There's nothing left at home for me."

McKay told him that he had lunched with Naiboldt recently in Washington. The Typhon vice-president had seemed nervous, not wishing to engage McKay in debate about the Cruise bill, not wishing, perhaps, to be reminded of the drunken confidences of last fall. Or not wishing to engage in conflict with his old friend because it was known that McKay was one of the Pentagon's firm opponents of the Saudi sale.

Charles narrowed his list of senators to those whose support for the sale seemed inconsistent with their voting records. He had several suspects and dug diligently into their backgrounds, their possible financial difficulties, any predilection for unusual tastes which might involve scandal. There had been those rumours about the Senate page-boys.

The President's campaign to mobilize public support for

the thirteen-billion-dollar Cruise sale was in high gear. A State Department White Paper had warned of intentions by the Soviet Union to arm its surrogate state of South Yemen with ss-20s, threatening the Saudi oilfields. *Pravda* had described the White Paper as a tissue of lies. But the Soviets denied everything, all the time. Who was to know who tells the truth in these matters?

The Saudis, of course, had declared that the missiles would be used only for defensive purposes and would never be nuclear-armed. The u.s. government had assured the world that the Glickums would be programmed not for Israeli targets but against Soviet targets, their bases in South Yemen and Ethiopia and southern USSR itself.

"The Soviets are scared shitless about America's Cruise strategy," McKay said. "The Cruise is the future, for another fifteen years at least." Advanced air-borne and ground-launched Cruises were still being tested by the United States in Canada, being installed in NATO countries at European bases manned by Americans.

"They can be land-based, submarine- or air-delivered," said McKay. "They ride like a bat fifty yards above the ground, under radar, computer-guided, sensor-equipped. There is no defence against them. They're airborne mechanical bloodhounds."

But the Saudis, unlike the NATO allies, would not permit American soldiers on their soil to man the missile sites to be built there by the Typhon Corporation. The Airborne Warning and Control System (AWACS) surveillance aircraft, recently sold to Saudi Arabia as part of an eight-and-a-half-billion-dollar package, had likewise been given to the Saudis without controls. Only Saudi crews were allowed to man those planes. Only Saudi crews would be allowed to man the Glickums bases. Typhon technicians would train their Saudi counterparts how to program the missiles.

For its part, the Saudi government had recently been, making deceptively earnest talk about co-existing with the alien Jewish entity to the north, but Charles believed—as did most who had studied Saudi Arabia—that this was just pap, a public relations handout doubtless proffered to make the Glickums sale more palatable to America. The policy of Saudi Arabia was still *jihad,* a holy war against the Israeli state. That was also McKay's view, and he had access to more sensitive sources than the reporter for the *South Greenwich Times*.

But the worst thing was that Cruise missiles could be armed with conventional or with nuclear warheads. And the Saudis were on their way to obtaining the bomb. It was a fact that their government was financing three nuclear projects in Pakistan, projects that many—including General McKay—believed were designed to provide the first Islamic nuclear bomb.

So far, the President had not presented the bill to Congress. To stop him, the payoff-blackmail scandal would have to hit the front pages quickly and hard.

But all Charles had so far was a Pentagon general who refused to be quoted. And his own reputation for libellous mis-statement.

12

Saturday, February 25, Montreal

Sawchuk felt the sharpness of a cruel Canadian wind that bit through his denim pants and jacket and pricked at his face like needles. He had been smuggled out of St. Vincent de Paul Penitentiary through the laundry chute, into the back of a panel truck, then dropped near a skating rink in east-end Laval, in an unlit park. A young man from Canada's new intelligence service, c.s.i.s.; Serge Ouellette, was standing beside him, anxiously checking his watch. His nervousness did not make Sawchuk feel easier.

"*Maudit!*" Ouellette cursed into a small cloud of vapour. They were waiting for a car, overdue by several minutes.

"*Lâchez pas*," said Sawchuk. Don't have a heart attack, goddamnit. From what part of the backwoods had the Security Intelligence Service enticed this raw recruit?

Sawchuk gritted his teeth against the cold. He had lost his comforting layer of warm fat in the month he had spent in the penitentiary after his sentencing. He had been told not to contact anyone, even Rocky. He had worried the pounds away, constructing plots in his writer's mind—what if he had become the victim of a subtle police conspiracy, tricked into signing a confession, into accepting a life sentence? Contracts written in disappearing ink. . . .

But late yesterday, Ouellette, posing as a parole officer, had come to him with the escape plans.

Now came the growl of an engine and an ugly beast of a machine, a 1971 Oldsmobile Toronado, emerged from the darkness with its park lights on. "Sorry I'm late," said the driver. "Had 'to have a boost. I'm André."

Ouellette got into the middle of the front seat, Sawchuk beside him.

André seemed the other side of the coin from Ouellette, a brash young man with a crazy grin. They took off, spitting slush, and as they turned from a side street onto Boulevard Lévesque, along the shore of the north river, they heard sirens wail from the towers of the penitentiary, a few blocks away.

"*Sacrement!*" said Ouellette. "They found the dummy. Get going."

"I know what I'm doing," said André. Sawchuk hoped so. Police cars would be everywhere around here soon. They were half a mile from the Pie IX Bridge leading to Montreal.

Suddenly a police cruiser came hard toward them and spun to a stop with a squeal of brakes, salted slush thudding against the Oldsmobile's doors. André pulled over.

"It's the cops," said André. "We always pull over for the cops. Like good citizens."

Sawchuk, slouched down, heard the sound of boots crunching toward them over the snow-packed street. "Then we wait until they are both out of the car," the driver said softly. "*Alors, on fait de l'air.*"

Sawchuk was thrown back, an astronaut into launch, as the Olds' wheels spun, caught, as André propelled the car to the right, just missing the back bumper of the cruiser. The car hopped onto the sidewalk, then back onto the street, hurtling westward toward the bridge.

"*Calvasse!*" Ouellette cried, gripping Sawchuk's arm with

fingers like steel. André whipped the car across the centre line to pass an ambling Volkswagen, sent it screaming through a red light, then past another speeding police cruiser coming in the other direction, which tried to brake in the slush and skidded sideways into the parking lane.

They churned around a cloverleaf at the north end of the bridge, sped over it to Montreal Island, then off Pie IX Boulevard suddenly, into the darkened, narrow streets of Montreal North. André took them into a back alley, and they abandoned the Toronado there and walked to a waiting Pontiac Astre.

"We make the escape look good, yes?" André said in English, slapping Sawchuk's shoulder. Ouellette was trembling. Sawchuk, however, was charged with electricity, high on the narcotic of excitement. This was a rich tonic. He was enjoying a surge of life, a feeling that had not been with him for years. Goddamn, he had been decaying in Cuba.

They drove into Montreal's East End, into the thick-packed rows of two-storey homes, red brick with curved wrought-iron stairways outside, latticed like butterfly wings. Old working-class Montreal. It was home to Sawchuk. He had grown up in a neighbourhood like this. Looking back on it, his life had seemed blissful here. He suddenly remembered that he loved this city, had missed it, had been lying to himself about that in Cuba.

He had left a fugitive, an anarchist, an angry young man. And now he had returned as a . . . cop? A member of a secret police? He felt a stab of pain. His father must be throwing up in his grave. He stared at the old buildings of his childhood world as they drifted past him in the darkness.

Sawchuk found a shower down the hallway from the basement room that had been assigned to him in the Group Seven safe house. For fifteen minutes he stood under a hot torrent, then turned the water on cold and let it sweep away all the grime of jail that had collected in his pores.

He was unable to sleep, still wired, at four a.m. He clicked on the light, found a pen and some lined paper, and began to write poetry. He felt his mind unlocking. Swirling images, erotic, free. *Now it is time to run with the sun dogs. Sky-powered, high, erect as gods. . . .*

God, what was this strength he was feeling? This surge?

He heard seductive whisperings of power in his ears, felt something of an ancient pride, a former arrogance. What if he were to play the game with these people for a while? This business of being an *agent provocateur* among the Left was unworthy... and doing so under blackmail less worthy still. But these Rotkommando terrorists, were they really of the Left—or had they moved so far that way they had fallen over the edge?.

Now he began to browse through the books and papers that Group Seven intelligence had assembled for him on the bedside table. Writings of revolutionists, radical reviews full of windy declamations, Group Seven and Interpol reports stamped confidential, stiffly written analyses of structures and goals.

Later. I'll get to this turgid stuff later.

But some photographs caught his eye. A mug shot of Willy Cuyfer, ex-Weatherman, sometime soldier of fortune for the Left. A destroyer, a sociopath, a foul man. Sawchuk shuddered as he remembered the man's hateful outpourings.

And who was this? My God, what a beautiful woman. A photograph from a German fashion magazine, circa 1975. Kathë Zahre, with a long and slender leg flashing forward through the hip-high slit of a designer gown, walking toward the camera with a defiant smile, her hand brushing a wild strand of jet-black hair from her eyes. No round-faced, pouty beauty queen this, but hard-featured with dark, wide, and passionate eyes. Kathë Zahre, Wurger's lover.

And The Shrike himself, shown here sitting in a restaurant with three other men. His eyes, like pale-blue stars, seemed to study the lens of the camera and on his face was an expression of... not shock, but a sudden alertness. Something of a craziness, and something on that handsome, wide-chinned face of an intolerance. A look that said the man was superior to other beings.

What kind of terrible gamble was Sawchuk chancing? He was not afraid, was in fact tempted by intimations of power, but the thought of being an informer, employed by the kind of men he had been counselled by his father to detest, sat heavily on his mind.

The next day Sawchuk was flown by Canadian Air Force reconnaissance plane to Turin, was briefed en route by Group

Seven aides as to the kind of training he would receive. From Turin he endured a gut-churning ascent by wind-blown helicopter into the Gran Paradiso mountains, to the camp, where the bitter winds of late February sent sweeping sprays of powder snow over the chasm and across the roofs of the log buildings.

A smiling, gregarious Rocky Rubinstein, bundled into a parka, greeted him at the helicopter pad. Sawchuk had been told that Rocky had been here for a week. Somehow the little lawyer seemed out of context here among the stiff and unsmiling agents, but Sawchuk was glad to see his friend.

"That's the canteen," Rocky said, leading Sawchuk to the cabin they would share. "They got Berliner Kindl on tap. We're in fat city."

"Fat city? Did they tell you what they've got lined up for me? Target practice with missile launchers, for Christ's sake. Five miles a day on the track. Five hundred faces to be memorized. They're going to teach me how to cut people's heads off with wire loops."

"They'll make a man outa you. Look, in Israel, Mossad guys work like this for eighteen months. You're doing three. In Mossad, the candidate don't pass the test unless he can survive being dropped fifty miles into PLO territory with only a handgun. They've lost about forty trainees that way. Stop whining."

He showed Sawchuk the cabin: cozy with a stone fireplace, a refrigerator loaded with German beer. "Fat city, like I say," Rocky chortled.

"How long are you going to be here, Rocky?"

"I'm your *manager*, man. You're my *property*—the great white hope of the French-Ukrainians, two hundred pounds of raw fighting material I got to help whip into shape. I'm here for the duration, the three months. It's in the contract."

"What about your practice?"

"On hold. I adjourned my trials. I told Louise I'm away on one of my big international cases." He beamed. "In reality, I'm a spy."

Sawchuk was not given a chance to pop a beer cap. Bakerfield arrived, shook hands brusquely, took him to Dr. Laurent Pétras's clinic in the laboratory building.

He was run through a battery of personality tests, then underwent a long interview with the psychiatrist while wired to a polygraph linked to the Typhon 2090 computer newly installed in the lab.

Pétras asked how Sawchuk had felt when his father died. ("How was I supposed to feel? I was outraged. They claimed he was drunk on the job. No compensation. What a bullshit system we live under.")

He was asked about his motivation. ("Mr. Sawchuk, why have you volunteered for this assignment?" "*Volunteered?*" "Are you doing it for the money?" "A hundred thousand dollars isn't much if you're going to spend the rest of your life on a terrorist hit list." "Are there any other factors which prompted your decision?" "Blackmail.")

Pétras didn't much like the new agent.

"I will tell you right now that this man is dangerous," he told Hesselmann and Bakerfield later. "He is headstrong, ego involved, totally incapable of submitting himself to any kind of discipline. The multiphasic tests tell us that. He lacks motivation. Politically, he is not trustworthy. We should cancel him."

"He may be difficult to run," Hesselmann admitted.

"I still think he's some kind of fellow traveller," said Bakerfield, "so I don't know if he's got the right attitude for this business. But he looks like he might be hard to knock down in a fight, and he's got some weird kind of charm going for him. And we don't want some gutless panting spaniel for this job." It was enough that Pétras distrusted Sawchuk for Bakerfield to warm to the Canadian. Bakerfield disliked Pétras, with his precise, mincing manners, disliked his fancy tools, his computer, his truth drugs. He preferred to go with his gut feeling. "He's honest, that's the thing. He hasn't lied."

"Yes," said Hesselmann, after a long silence. "We'll see if we can't do something about his motivation before we unleash him onto the world."

Day two lasted forever.

"Picture shows tonight, Jacques," said Bakerfield. "Then you can go to the canteen. Your limit is two beers, two wine or one hard per night. I hear you put away five or six vodkas last evening."

Sawchuk, a collection of sore and angry muscles, issued a pitiful groan as he sat on a chair.

"I told you to go easy at first," said Bakerfield, who began to assemble a projector and a box of slides. "You didn't have to go through that workout like you were trying to miss the final cut."

"I thought I was in better shape," Sawchuk gasped. "They're trying to kill me, Rocky. Read them the Geneva Convention."

Hesselmann was sitting beside Bakerfield. Their faces, outlined by the white light of the projector, looked harsh and menacing. Rubinstein was reclining on two chairs he had brought together.

Karl Wurger's eyes, from the screen, seemed to be drilling small holes into Sawchuk's head.

"We know nothing about him that will help you," Hesselmann said. "No weaknesses that might be breached. He drinks only moderately—as *you* must do when you're in the field—and does not indulge in drugs. His writings say nothing about the man. They are obscure, laced with rhetoric."

"Communist mumbo-jumbo," said Bakerfield.

"Perhaps his Achilles' heel is his vanity," Hesselmann continued. "He is vain about his intelligence and tactical skills, his leadership, his power. He is also vain about his masculinity. He likes to be thought of as handsome. Blue eyes, blond hair."

"An Aryan god," said Rubinstein.

"Like all terrorists," Hesselmann said, "he suffers from a martyrdom complex. He is a German, and he carries the burden of our tradition—a romantic idealism wedded to the death wish. He has gone beyond philosophy. There are those in every age who become infected with a political blood lust, and it makes no difference what label they wear. Fascism is no longer chic, so he claims to be a Marxist."

That would be comfortable to believe, Sawchuk thought, making tasteless aspects of his job easier. Was he going to carry it out? He shifted in his chair, feeling the raw edges of his muscles grind against one another.

"We can trace him only to the late sixties," Hesselmann said. "We can find no family links, but he claims to be a war orphan from Berlin. He did study at the Free University there, and even took a teaching post in sociology for two years. Then he started a newspaper which became the centrepiece of Berlin's radical chic community. He was the darling of the set—romantic, free-wheeling, audacious, but with a violent temper. He got closer to the edge: Baader-Meinhof contacts, alliances with the General Union of Palestine Students and Workers of West Germany. Then private assignments for Lebanon-based 'groups like the Popular Front. Then he formed the Rotkommando and went underground."

"I've read the material, General," Sawchuk said. "He built the Rotkommando on business with Palestine revolutionary groups."

"Mainly the Popular Front for the Liberation of Palestine, Habash's organization. The PLO, however, has him on its assassination list. Fatah, their terrorist wing, is looking for him as hard as we are."

Sawchuk was not happy with this added complication.

"Rotkommando's international clients include Libya, South Yemen, Syria, occasionally Algeria, the so-called Arab revolutionary states. The PLO receives its major funding from Saudi Arabia and the Persian Gulf sheikdoms. Wurger's clients, including the Popular Front, have sworn to destroy the Saudis. They claim it's a feudal kingdom tied to American imperialism."

"But that's exactly what it is," Sawchuk said. "Saudi Arabia is just a minor playing piece of the oil and automobile multinationals, part of the game of keeping us locked into an oil economy."

"That kind of negative talk worries me," Bakerfield said. "You don't always impress as a true believer in the cause of freedom."

"Freedom is everybody's favourite meaningless word, Hamilton," Sawchuk said. "If we can cut the brainwashing for a minute, I just want to clarify something. The PLO is at war with the Rotkommando. They represent different sides in an internecine Arab struggle. Fatah is trying to assassinate Wurger. Yes?"

"Yes," said Hesselmann.

"And anyone else in the Rotkommando they can get hold of."

"That's true."

Sawchuk groaned.

"Don't worry, Jacques," Rubinstein said. "You'll win everybody over with your rascally ways."

"The Israelis have asked that you trace the lines right up through to the paymasters in Tripoli and Aden," Hesselmann said. "They are briefed, of course. We didn't want some Mossad fellow taking a shot at you."

"He wouldn't miss," said Rubinstein.

"They are particularly anxious to get you into the field," said Hesselmann. Sawchuk knew why—Wurger was behind the recent wave of killings of prominent Jews in Europe. It was obvious he was working from a hit list.

Wurger's picture disappeared from the screen. Bakerfield flashed photos of other known Rotkommando soldiers: Germans, Italians, Japanese, Arabs. Willy Cuyfer, in army fatigues, dirty-blond hair, a goatee, a long, rat-like nose. Kathë Zahre, with magnificent legs.

"Don't be fooled," said Bakerfield. "She's a killer. She's got two lethal weapons: a Baretta submachine-gun and a hot box."

"Please, Mr. Bakerfield," said Hesselmann.

"He'd better know. She sent her first husband into the Rhine on a suicide. That's when she was seventeen, a bigtime model already. Her second man used to be lead guitar for Kraftwerk, took two hundred hits of lysergic acid, plays his riffs to a padded cell now. A Commie playwright in England was next—he turned her onto politics—and he got busted for manslaughter when he caught her in his bed blowing the late theatre critic for the *Evening Standard*. She's a nymphomaniac, is what I'm saying. A love witch. Wurger is just a way-station for her."

"I'll be wary." Sawchuk was not going to get his private parts caught in any meat grinder, no matter how beautiful she looked.

"Now that you've met the artists, I want to show you their work," Bakerfield said. "The victims are artists, too. Real artists."

"I'm kind of beat, Hamilton."

Click-whirr.

"This is what an apartment looks like after a bomb goes off in it. Home of the late Julius Irving, the choreographer."

Click-whirr.

"That's Irving, on the stretcher," said Bakerfield.

"It is known as propaganda by deed, of course," said Hesselmann. "Famous people make for bigger headlines. Ever since the Israeli invasion of Lebanon, the Rotkommando has been targeting well-known Jews; artists, intellectuals. Diplomatic personnel no longer make news for them. Besides, they're too well protected."

Click-whirr.

"This is Mrs. Irving and her three teenage kids," said Bakerfield.

"Hamilton—"

Click-whirr.

"Maurice Samuelsohn, French sculptor . . . ."

The session lasted for two hours. At the end, the picture of Karl Wurger was returned to the screen. Wurger in the Zurich restaurant, about to draw his gun.

"You ever see that expression on his face, Jacques," said Bakerfield, "it means he wants to kill."

Sawchuk looked at the blond young man with his ice-blue eyes.

"Do you see?" said Rubinstein. "The master race."

Too exhausted for the canteen, Sawchuk returned alone to the cabin he shared with Rubinstein. He played a few desolate tunes on his flute and went to bed and saw in his sleep those terrible eyes.

13

March-April, Gran Paradiso

A humourless gym instructor regularly kicked Sawchuk out of bed at half-past four in the morning, often upon threat of violence, with Sawchuk hurling back foul imprecations. Rubinstein, who occupied the upper bunk in their cabin, found the morning routine unnerving, so he had to resort to

earplugs to stay cradled in the arms of Morpheus, in whose
company he remained until last call for breakfast.

By that time, half-past seven, Sawchuk had been forced
into the gym shower by his captors, punished with weights
and exercises for an hour, pumped full of milk and fruit-juice
and oatmeal, and sent reeling from classroom to classroom.
The cryptography section would have him for a while, the
electronics team would work with him, and then would come
basic vehicle and arms recognition. Then a second breakfast,
more massive, usually with poached eggs—from country farms,
Sawchuk had insisted.

Later, as a bleak sun rose over the Piedmont hills, Sawchuk,
bundled in a heavy sweatsuit, a towel wrapped around his
neck, would be chuffing around the track like an old bear.
Five miles a day.

"You never know when you're going to have to run," said
the tireless man who paced him.

Later, there were courses on photography, forgery, radio,
navigation, accent recognition, voice identification, flaps and
seals (the art of opening and resealing letters). A powerhouse
lunch, heavy on protein. More classes in the afternoon. An
hour of karate in the gym. Then to the mess hall for dinner,
and to the canteen for his drink ration. Sometimes he would
fall asleep on a chair there, a half-drunk bottle of beer
clutched desperately to his breast.

"They're killing me," he moaned to Rubinstein one evening.

"Stop kvetching. Mossad Unit 101, they drop their trainees
in Tangiers with five dollars and tell them to make their way
back to Jerusalem, across North Africa. No credit cards."

While all this was going on, the men and women of the
Group information section, a team of skilled propagandists,
launched themselves into action. Their work was vital:
establishing a high profile for Sawchuk, enhancing his credibility, his value to an organization like the Rotkommando.
Reports were leaked to the press through European police
offices that Sawchuk had made his way from North America
to France, and that he was suspected of being responsible for
a series of bank robberies and terrorist attacks in and near
Paris. The plan was to paint Sawchuk in lurid colours, a
one-man terrorist gang. Articles ostensibly written by him
would appear in underground newspapers expressing solidar-
ity with the cause of the more militant pro-Palestine groups.

Some unsolved assassinations were being attributed to him. A myth would be developed around his name: Red Jacques, the killer poet.

By the end of his first ten days, Sawchuk's brain had become a hopeless mush of disconnected tradecraft, his body a tangle of abraded and grating muscles. "*J'ai mon voyage,*" he would mutter. "I've had it." He had endured it at first because it was a matter of proving his—he was not ashamed to admit it—manliness.

By the third week he had his wind together and his body and brain were purged by hard exercise and hard thinking.

As to how long he would stay with Group Seven after he was released from its camp he was unsure. He still detested the thought of being an informer, a spy. Equally, he was filled with revulsion at having to deal with Wurger and the others, maniacal fanatics with their love of blood sport. A time would come when he would have to decide whether to run or stay. He wondered how serious were Bakerfield's hints of retribution if he refused, in the end, to play the game.

Bakerfield's threats had seemed serious enough. "Soldiers who don't take orders, terrible things can happen to them," he had said. "I've got to assume you're the kind of guy who doesn't follow orders too well, Sawchuk. I have a Book. I go by it. It is God. I obey the Book even when I think it is wrong. You will obey Bakerfield's Book, too."

But Sawchuk could tell that Bakerfield was secretly pleased with his progress. The ex-CIA man spent at least an hour with him every day, briefing him on anti-terrorist tactics.

"Bait money buys time. Delay, delay, delay. Co-ordinated delay. Terrorists holding hostages are primed for action at the beginning, willing to sacrifice themselves. But time takes the edge off."

"I'm not going to be involved in any hostage-taking cases."

"Who knows? Learn the Book, Sawchuk. We negotiate, negotiate, keep offering that quick, easy way out. When everything else fails we bargain in bad faith. If that fails we storm them. If we can get away with an acceptable loss."

"Of life."

"Yeah, life. Learn the Book, Sawchuk."

There was a Book response to every dreamed-of contingency. "Rule: Eat what they give you. They offer you sheep's balls for dinner in Lebanon, you eat sheep's balls. Can the vegetarian crap. Rule: Meld with people. You don't attract attention by being some kind of neurotic health-food faddist. Don't stand out. You're not taking your flute; it attracts attention."

"I'm *taking* my flute."

"Rule: Talk less than is your habit. Rule: Entertain wisely but not too well. Booze, drugs, and sex, their use is only to maintain survival level."

"That's the level they're at right now, Ham."

"Don't start making it with a lady so hard she falls in love with you. And don't *you* get infatuated with some good-looking Commie terrorist. Agents have been turned that way. I've known some who had to be taken out." That was jargon, Sawchuk knew. Tradecraft language for a bullet in the back. "Not that I think you're capable of falling in love with more than one thing at a time, and you love your own ass so much there's no room for anyone else."

"I love *you*, Hamilton."

"Always obey orders. That's rule number one in Bakerfield's Book. Number one in every agent's handbook in every country of the world. Think when you are ordered to think."

"You can count on me, Ham."

"*Always* carry your gun. We'll start you off packing a .357 Magnum, enough power to do what you have to do. Rule: If anybody makes you, blows your cover, kill him."

Sawchuk just looked at him.

"You can kill, can't you?"

"I love to kill. I get horny thinking about it."

"Never make a drop when there is the slightest possibility that you might be seen by anyone but the agent assigned to the pick-up. The notes are always to be folded in a newspaper, left on an empty chair. Bar, restaurant, lobby, wherever, only on an empty chair."

Sawchuk and Bakerfield became friendly. Sometimes the American would just chat, about his days in the FBI and CIA, about his loneliness at having been a bachelor all his years, his sadness at the recent death of a father who had meant much to him. Sawchuk had been deeply involved with his own father. He decided Bakerfield was not a bad guy—for a cop.

In April, fierce storms battered the mountain retreat and warm breezes began to melt the snows. But rain or shine,

Sawchuk was now doing fifteen miles a day on the track. He learned high-speed and evasive auto handling along the hilly roads. He was taken to Turin and told to-tail a stranger on the streets, an expert agent who knew all the tricks. In turn, Sawchuk was followed, and later there were critiques. Afterwards, more driving practice in the city.

He began to spend extra time in cryptography, fine-tuning the code he would use: a jargon code based on poetry. The disguise section began to work with him, then the acting instructor. And always Bakerfield, for more of his Book.

Sawchuk learned about bombs—everything from shipyard confetti to pipe bombs and plastique letter bombs to sophisticated explosives with photoelectric and x-ray fuses, RDX, PETN, Flex-U. He learned about guns, stripped and assembled M-21s, AK-47s, machine-guns.

There were memory-training sessions. A film would be shown, then the screen would suddenly go white. He had exactly thirty seconds to describe everything in the last frame. Or he would have a few seconds to study a table on which various objects were arranged. Then a cloth would be placed on top; Sawchuk would list the objects.

He got to be very good at these games. He was blessed with good memory and eyes so quick they could predict a coin flip seven times out of ten.

His recreation was The Confessional. A few of the snipers had introduced Sawchuk to the secrets of the isolation tank, its capacity to bring a man's body and soul together at the end of a hard day. Sawchuk quickly became a tank freak, and persuaded Pétras that an hour of floating in the warm, zero-gravity solution was worth five of sleep. This was better than any form of yoga he had tried. The tank slowed everything down to a drift, taught his mind how to close in gently upon itself—like a bird coming to rest—or fly off in some beautiful directions. Alone with nothing but one's mind... clouds like frilly panties drifting by one's head...skies expanding. And through the headphones, Beethoven chamber music, or the sound of Rampal's flute.

There was, however, an uncomfortable presence in there, of Giuseppe Nero, who had gone insane with Pétras's truth drug Dioxygone. *Mecca!* he had cried. Sawchuk had heard the tapes of his voice and had been beset with unease. Mecca: the final goal, the end of journeys. What had Nero meant?

Sawchuk was unaware that while he was being transported

to idyllic climes in his tank Dr. Pétras piped words through the headphones, beneath the music, just below the threshold of conscious hearing. The message said: "I can kill." The happy trilling of Rampal's flute began to sound sour to Sawchuk's ears. He quit the tank.

As for Rubinstein, he declined all invitations to take part in the physical training at Gran Paradiso and volunteered for the intelligence section. But he found the tasks stultifying—feeding into the computer the phone numbers taken from arrested terrorists' address books, collating the results: a chimpanzee could do that. Assembling in chronological order the data that flowed unceasingly to the Group describing movements of suspects through Europe: that was a task for a mindless clerk.

"I ain't interested in the mundane aspects anyway," he told Sawchuk and Bakerfield. "My forte is the grander picture."

Bakerfield groaned. "You're going to be kept out of sight, Rocky. Things might get boring when Jacques is in the field, so you better stock up on lots of your favourite reading material. Comic books, or whatever it is."

Rubinstein continued to fill his inner tube, complained about racist bigots at the camp, about working under a man who had served Hitler (albeit as an Allied spy), and generally carried on in such a way as would convince a stranger that he was camp commander.

Sawchuk continued to wonder at Hesselmann's tolerance of Rubinstein. He concluded that Hesselmann, influenced by some kind of reverse prejudice, was determined to put up with him as best he could.

14

Saturday, May 26, Gran Paradiso

The snows had retreated high into the mountains, and the air had become sweet with alpine flowers and the sound of

summer warblers. Sawchuk's three months at Gran Paradiso
were winding up. On the final afternoon, Bakerfield ran him
through a long review of timings, safe locations, code routines, and asked at the end, as he had asked many times:

"Do you think you can kill? Time you started to face that
question."

Sawchuk suddenly felt a headache. Memories of the quea-
siness in the immersion tank.

"I can handle myself, Ham."

"It takes one kind of balls to stand up to a man and fight
him," said Bakerfield. "It takes a different kind of balls to kill
a man."

"Balls to kill a man. What kind of balls are those?"

All drink limits were ignored at Sawchuk's graduating party.
He held forth until late, but afterwards, alone with Rubinstein
in their cabin, slid into an alcoholic funk.

"They have trained me to be a fink. It kind of takes the
romance out of it."

"A rat, that's what you are, Jacques. We have just built the
world's most expensive rat." He chortled, enjoying his digs at
Sawchuk. "Skulking about the camps of the revolutionaries—
it don't earn a very high standing in the community, but
you've got to admit it's more fun than beating your meat for
ten years in the penitentiary."

"A police spy," Sawchuk groaned. "We used to believe
l'informateur was an object of justified disgust, Rocky. I feel
crawly with vermin. I am a turncoat. Un vire."

"I'll give you credit. I wouldn't be able to do it. But that's
the price you gotta pay, Jacques." Rubinstein bounced off
toward the bathroom in his jockey shorts and began to fill the
tub.

"For what?" Sawchuk gave a desultory tweet on his flute,
and began cleaning it with a felt rag.

"For saving the world. I got some sad news that will
dispirit you even more. I got a big arson trial coming up in
northern Quebec next month, a six-weeker, and I won't be
able to get out of it. I'm not going to be around to monitor
your progress in the field as I hoped."

Rocky slipped off his shorts, tried the water with a toe,
then climbed into the tub. "I wouldn't leave you in the lurch
except I think you're ready to fly on your own."

Sawchuk was relieved. Rocky would be out of everybody's hair if the going got heavy.

He thought: How heavy is the going going to get? And will I stay in long enough to find out?

About that, he had still not settled his mind.

But in twenty-four hours he would be able to make that decision. He would be in Paris, alone. He would have money, false I.D., and access to other false papers deposited for him here and there in Europe. And he would have the skills to forge his own—to stay hidden from Group Seven.

But to be on the run all his life from agents of the world's most skilled, most unscrupulous police force—could his life be worth much? Far easier to stay, to feel around a bit, try to make a little contact with the Rotkommando. He could get out of it with a lifetime pension. He could get out of it with honour.

Honour? God, do I want to spend the rest of my life knowing only one thing certain about myself? That I was a police informer?

In the hierarchy of humanity as observed by Sawchuk's father there were many levels of degradation, bankers, labour scabs, arms dealers, men from the liquor and gambling squads, but Sawchuk had always been taught that beneath everyone else, at the very stinking bottom of the human compost heap, crouched the rat: the man who informed to the political police.

He remembered his father's vituperative descriptions of the men he believed spied on him and sent anonymous notes to his various employers. His father had believed that informers had destroyed all true people's movements over the centuries.

John Sawchuk had loved his son, and had wanted him to carry the red banner into the next generation. Now his son was prepared to soil their family name.

The quisling of the Left.

Sawchuk listened to Rubinstein in the bathroom, gaily slopping himself with water.

"Rocky," he shouted, "I don't want to do this."

"You got to be joking. What are you, a craven coward?"

"It's wrong, Rocky."

Rubinstein pulled himself from the tub and walked toward

Sawchuk, briskly towelling himself. His eyes lacked their usual sardonic glint. They were penetrating.

"I'm not doing this," Sawchuk mumbled.

Rubinstein smiled. "Sure y'are." He patted Sawchuk's shoulder in a manner more proprietary than brotherly. "Sure y'are, champ. You're gonna do it because it's the right thing to do."

"You're so sure of that, aren't you, Rock?"

"And you're gonna do it because if you try to skip out, Hamilton Bakerfield is gonna issue new guitar strings to his ten best loop men."

"He likes me."

Rubinstein uttered a grumbling, low laugh. "You poor, innocent baby. You're gonna do it, Jacques, for another reason. You're gonna do it, because you *gotta* do it. You're gonna do it because your swollen, misshapen ego is gonna drive you to do it. Otherwise you won't be able to live with yourself, you arrogant bastard."

IV
The Butcherbird

Like many predators, shrikes often kill more than they can eat, and when opportunity presents itself seem to kill for the joy of killing. Their well-known habit of impaling their prey on thorns has earned them the common name 'butcherbird.'

Austin and Singer, *Birds of the World*

15

Tuesday, May 29, New York City

"The *South Greenwich Times* regrets any embarrassment that has been caused to the Comptroller of Waterworks as a result of an erroneous report in last week's edition alleging 'siphoning' of monies allotted for the Bleecker Street improvement project...."

Charles Rubinstein stared bleakly at the copy, marked for boldface, intended for the front page of the next edition.

"I feel I've been stabbed in the back," he said.

"How do you think the water comptroller feels?" screamed his editor, a spiteful feminist.

"A paper that doesn't back up its people is a disgrace to journalism. No balls, Brenda, that's what you got, no balls."

"One goddamn story all week is what you produce, and for that we get socked with a *writ*, goddamnit."

"I've been busy on a big scoop. I got bigger fish to fry than some corrupt two-bit political hack."

"What scoop?" she yelled. "Don't bullshit me, what scoop?."

"I have got a story that will tilt this gullible dumb country backwards on its ass. When I get it finished you can bid for it along with *Time*, *Newsweek*, and the Hearst chain. I'm starting at a million bucks and we'll see where it builds from there. I'm not going for *Rolling Stone* any more, Brenda baby, this is something to feed the circulation wars of the big news empires."

"I want you should know, Charles *baby*, you are fired. You haven't produced twenty inches of honest column space in the last three weeks."

"Hey, cool it, Brenda. Listen, I'm gonna give you full personal credit for helping to support me while I am gather-

ing facts and background on a story of international intrigue—
I can tell you that much—in which America is shamefully
involved. The *South Greenwich Times*, circulation fifty-five
hundred, and a third of that giveaway, so poor we have to run
pornos in the classifieds. I mean, let's get serious, Brenda, I'll
give the paper ten per cent, as a kind of commission. Just
bear with me a couple more weeks."

"Charles, you're fired."

"Okay, you can publish it simultaneous with whoever wins
the bidding war. I'm going for the Pulitzer, baby. Woodward
and Bernstein, watch out, Charles M. Rubinstein is coming
around the bend charging."

"It's termination city, Charles."

"Aw, listen, I'm broke. You can't do this."

"It's thirty, sweetheart. You work on your own time from
now on. Two weeks' severance pay."

"All right, look, I'll just give you this little teaser—I meet
regularly with someone inside the Pentagon. He's just discovered
he wants to make love not war. I'm on the *inside*. All I've got
to do to buttress it is get the background facts. I was reading
the Congressional Record all day today. That's why I couldn't
come in until now."

"It's a quarter to five. I've been waiting all day so I could
enjoy this moment. Find a nice job writing fairy stories,
Charles. Hit the road."

Despondent, Charles walked the long walk to the New York
Public Library and settled down into his dig into the strange
world of Saudi Arabia. It seemed an unsavoury country in
many respects, ruled with steel by a family network, without
freedom of speech or assembly, a country in which the foreign
newspapers looked like lace, scissored by the censors, a
country without political parties or labour unions. Those
Saudis who dared express reforming ideas usually found
themselves in jail, in dungeons where prisoners were known
to go blind. The country was riddled with informers, members of the National Guard who returned to their villages
after their terms of service, becoming the eyes and the ears of
the Saudi rulers.

Two-thirds of the native population were illiterate, and the
average life expectancy was thirty-five. Yet the nation's oil

revenues were three hundred million dollars a day. Its per capita military spending was second highest in the world, more than double that of the United States or the USSR. And its foreign policy toward Israel was *jihad*: holy war. Its annual pledge to the PLO was four hundred million dollars.

This was the country to which the United States government was about to supply Cruise missiles.

The White House had finally sent the bill to the Senate, and a vote was expected late in June—a month away.

Charles had also dug, although it was like going through solid rock, into the Typhon Corporation. He had run up a telephone bill of hundreds of dollars trying to reach people in the corporation and people who knew people in the corporation. But Typhon was like a closed little country.

It was family-owned by the Boschuff brothers, sons of an immigrant German who made his fortune during the Cold War of the late forties in the development of small, hand-held missiles. It grew, expanded into computers, became one of the first companies to ride the defence budget gravy train into California's Silicon Valley.

The Boschuff brothers were said to be not merely conservative in their politics but on the very fringes of the radical right. But no one had ever interviewed them. They were as shy as hermits but as ruthless as werewolves. Ex-General Hank Naiboldt did most of their talking now, as executive vice-president. The other members of the small Typhon board, two of whom were ex-Pentagon, one ex-State, one ex-CIA, were all mercenary men as far as Charles could find out, chosen for their conservatism and a pitiless view of the business world.

As far as the three purchased senators were concerned, Charles felt he had zeroed in on the men. He had only the most circumstantial of cases, but he had a journalist's gut feeling.

The key was the Senate division over the AWACS bill in 1981. The President had fought like a demon, charming, bullying, trading, to get the fifty-one votes he needed and finally secured. A number of senators had announced their opposition early on, had stuck hard to their position, couldn't be enticed by promises of federal works for their states or threats to sabotage their nominations. And three of those seemingly principled men had now quietly lined up for the Cruise sale.

Stoffer Johnson, a Dixie dove, a political anomaly, had consistently voted against Middle East arms sales of any kind, except to Israel, and to that nation he had been known as a friend.

Charles had discovered that Senator Johnson lost a bundle in the 1982 recession: he had gone into a land development scheme that had left him with a fat mortgage on a falling real estate market. Two months ago he had come off the fence on the Cruise sale, stating simply that he believed it was in the best interest of America. He refused to elaborate, even in interviews. But somehow he had managed to avoid personal bankruptcy. A vague case, sure, but a lot of people in the journalism fraternity smelled something from this one.

Case number two: Senator Jack Grodsky, who came from a Midwestern State with a big Jewish population. And he needed every vote he could squeeze from his State—his plurality last time out was less than twenty thousand. Grodsky was a flamboyant high-roller with some ties, gossip had it, to New York theatre people. Gossip also had it that he had helped bankroll a recent Broadway flop. It was said, too, that the senator had friends in the mob, had used a Mafia machine over the years to help get his votes out.

Grodsky had cried hell and damnation when the President proposed selling advanced radar planes to the Saudis. But since the AWACS sale he had altered his position, stating that the Israeli invasion of Lebanon had shifted the balance of power in the Middle East, that it was time to bring things there back to even keel. (That was a tune the President had played quietly but effectively.)

One of those two men, Charles had it from McKay, had been paid eight million dollars by Naiboldt, the other, seven million. Everyone had his price, Charles thought bitterly. Even Grodsky, Jewish himself.

The third senator—an educated guess would be Kennington Budd, scion of a wealthy New England family. He didn't need money, but it was not through money that Henry Naiboldt had got to him; it was through a certain weakness. The story was going around that Budd liked boys in their early teens. That Senate page-boy business: no one was naming names but everyone who knew Washington seemed to know it was

Senator Budd. It wouldn't have been hard to set him up in an unpretty, scandalous situation. A thirteen-year-old boy in his bedroom, secret camera, secret tape recorder.

Budd had been a down-the-line Democrat. The President proposes, he opposes. Budd had been almost livid about the AWACS sale. But he was the President's puppy on this one.

Charles had read the senator's statement, made following a recent tour of Saudi Arabia: "After an agonizing reappraisal of the situation in the Middle East, I have concluded that Saudi Arabia has proved itself to be a responsible and important ally of this country and that its hostile attitude toward Israel is one of rhetoric not deed." Worded like a statesman. The senator had presidential aspirations.

But none of this constituted the kind of proof Charles had to have to scuttle the Saudi deal and deliver a great defensive blow on behalf of a certain hard-nosed little country where he and his brother Rocky had done their turns on kibbutzim. But time was running out.

Charles Rubinstein faded early in the library, broken as he was in spirit as a result of the latest calamity in his downward-spiralling career as a journalist. It was a bleak future that he faced. Where could he go now? What was lower than the *South Greenwich Times*? Public relations? Writing handouts? That would be worse. How about writing advertising copy for Bloomingdale's? That would be far worse. Or Toyota TV commercials? He performed this mental masochism as he got off the subway at Broadway and Seventy-Ninth and trudged up the stairs to his West Eightieth Street bachelor apartment.

Charles needed to make it with this story. But what did he have? A general who refused to be named and quoted and beans all else except rumour and circumstance. He imagined the reaction of the editor of the mass circulation newspaper as Charles was being hurled out of his office: "Informed source? Informed source? You're a menace to journalism, Rubinstein." No one was going to risk even a speculative piece about the Saudi-Typhon-Senate connection. Typhon would bankrupt any newspaper with the resulting libel suit. Unless corroborative proof could be found, such as the tapes and film in Aziz's palace. Or unless General McKay would agree to go on record. That seemed unlikely.

In near desperation, recalling his brother's claims of having access to a secret intelligence organization, Charles had tried early in May to contact his brother in Montreal and was told by an answering service that Rocky was out of the country conducting interviews. Charles had again called Montreal yesterday. This time his brother was somewhere in northern Quebec preparing for an arson trial.

Charles wondered what was going on with Jacques Sawchuk. He read he had escaped jail and was apparently in Europe, a one-man terrorist army, according to the newspapers. Charles found that hard to accept. He remembered Sawchuk as a personable kind of guy, not a killer, not a bank robber. Now he was looting and shooting. Wouldn't believe it if I hadn't seen it in the newspapers, he thought to himself.

He decided to hit the sack early, to try to sleep away his depression.

But that wasn't to be. In his apartment he found his kid sister Paula—he had lent her a key—and someone who looked like a college football player.

"This is Hugo," she said brightly, then came up to him and mumbled in his ear. "Do you mind? Like, maybe see a movie for a couple of hours?"

He wandered down to a bar instead, and got drunk.

16

Wednesday, May 30, Paris

Sawchuk awoke at eight p.m. He had not fallen back on old habits, but his work in Paris these last three days had kept him up late at night in the left-wing bistros, and he slept all day.

He rolled from the bed onto the floor, did thirty fast pushups, thirty situps, then stood to his full height and did some stretching exercises. The body that he saw in his wardrobe mirror was that of a professional athlete. The muscles were long and fluid and his stomach was ribbed and flat like a washboard. He was thirty-five pounds under his retirement weight in Cuba. His hair was short, his face clean-shaven. He put on a pair of rimless spectacles and peered again at himself. Jerome Miles, Yankee in Paris.

Paris had been chosen as Sawchuk's starting point because the city was the main switching station for world terrorism. Paris, with its magnetic appeal for the young, was the hub of international travel routes, a haven for political refugees who included half a million Arabs, mostly near Boulevard de Belleville or in the *bidonvilles*, the Arab shantytowns on the outskirts.

Sawchuk's hotel was on the Left Bank, and looked over the river to Notre Dame. His window was open and he could taste and smell the hot breath of the great city on this second to last evening of May.

He had spent his first three days of freedom moving about, enjoying Paris's bracing tonic. He had not been here since 1968 when the director of admissions at the Sorbonne had barred the red-bearded troublemaker.

Now he put on jeans—ordinary-looking but specially designed with secret pockets—and fastened them with a belt buckle engineered so that it might be disassembled into a number of lock picks. He pulled on boots that had two sections of a miniature camera built into the respective heels. He strapped on a watch in which the Japanese high-tech team had installed a recording device, a miracle of silicon engineering.

Across his naked chest he buckled a shoulder holster with the .357 Magnum, separate pockets for a silencer and extra clips of bullets. Every second bullet was live, every other one a blank, in case he had to fake a kill.

He put on a white, short-sleeved shirt, a light sportsjacket over that, and went to the window and looked out at Ile St. Louis, the vines of its cathedral trailing like God's tentacles over the walls and into the Seine, which lapped muddily below. He heard the noise and felt the energy of the street. He felt alive—full of ginger and hot sap. Paris seemed as far from his Cuban villa as the stars.

Sawchuk still did not know how far he would go with the Group Seven project. For now, he would enjoy himself while testing the waters in the revolutionary watering holes. The Group had recently planted a news item about a Paris robbery in which Sawchuk was said to have escaped with a two-hundred-thousand-franc government payroll. He could therefore enjoy playing the part of a man with money to spend, and the owners of certain brasseries in Les Halles and the Left Bank now counted as a friend the genial playboy known as Jerome Miles, from Schenectady, New York, a graduate student at the Sorbonne, apparently rich.

If the Paris Sureté were ever to check him, they would find, on the Interpol teletype, that there did exist such a Jerome Miles, six foot four. The Interpol records would show that Jerome Miles's only previous conviction was for criminally negligent driving in upstate New York. A Group agent inside Interpol—Hesselmann distrusted that organization with its Arab and East Bloc members—had slipped false cards into the files and computer banks: Jerome Miles, with Sawchuk's prints and pictures.

So Sawchuk, his wallet jammed with thousand-franc notes, left his hotel, and set off for Barney's American Bar on rue St. Jacques, off Boul Mich. Here, students played at being anarchists. There were no Americans in Barney's American Bar, for the tourists had been crowded from it. To hang out in such a place—a Hollywood joint with pictures of movie kings and queens decorating its mirrored walls—had become a fashionable political statement among radical youth, an in-joke. Arab students comprised about a quarter of the clientele, punks with dyed, close-cropped hair another quarter, and eco-freaks and various kinds of fringe people, the balance.

Sawchuk went in, picked up a glass of wine from the bar, and withdrew to a table in the corner. A young woman—he remembered seeing her the previous night—glanced at him a few times: little looks with questioning eyes. When he smiled at her, she approached his table.

"May I join you?"

Sawchuk nodded. She seemed what the doctor ordered: brash, baby-faced, *bien plantée*, as they say in Quebec. Sawchuk had led a spartan life for five months.

She placed her glass of wine beside his. "Where are you from?" she said, sitting. She didn't look at him, stared straight ahead.

"I am from America." He let a haunted quality inflect his words.

"I saw you here last night. But I have not seen you here

before." She was beside him, but talked as if to someone in front of them, as if to their reflections in the mirror across the room.

Sawchuk studied her in close profile. A spring bud, about nineteen, twenty. Tight jeans. A Save the Whales button on the breast pocket of her denim shirt. Save the whales. Sawchuk was all for it.

"I hope you are not waiting for someone." She talked softly, hardly moving her lips.

"No, I am alone." He stared off into innermost space, hoping she might observe the loneliness in his eyes.

Two flics in pillbox hats entered, looked about, then left. "*Les hommes de police*," Sawchuk said. He used the Quebec expression purposely.

She glanced quickly at him. "They make me tense, too." She looked ahead again, and continued to talk to the space in front of her. "I believe I know who you are."

Maybe, he thought, that is why she is acting a role from some 1940s spy movie: a secret meeting, two agents on a park bench, pretending not to know each other as they talked.

"I think your name is Jacques," she said.

He offered the merest hint of a wanted man's smile. "My name may be Jacques," he said softly, allowing a touch of Québécois accent. He picked up his half-empty wine glass and stared into it as if looking for answers. His face revealed he was a man beating back the pain of fighting for causes. Then he signalled the waiter and asked for a bottle of good Bordeaux.

The waiter returned. "Do you want to try it?" he said, showing Sawchuk the label, tugging the cork out.

"Of course."

The waiter poured a taster into a fresh glass—fancy service in Barney's American Bar—and handed it to Sawchuk, who swirled it to get the aroma up, sniffed it, took it in his mouth and rolled it around his tongue. Then he swallowed— unfortunately, the wrong way. He found himself choking helplessly.

"Good wine," he said in a strangled voice. The waiter put the bottle on the table and left.

"*Mon Dieu*," said the young woman. "Are you not well?" Recovering, Sawchuk frowned into his glass as if there had been something in it, perhaps poison. "It's my lungs" he said. "I'll be all right."

"You are Jacques, and you are from Canada."

"How do you know this?" Sawchuk worked to reassemble his cool. How *did* she know this?

She dug into her purse and pulled a folded clipping from it, an article from *L'Express* entitled "Le Nouveau Gauche." Sawchuk's photo—with beard—was in the middle of the page.

"You are this man," she said.

Sawchuk gave her a smile to let her know she was shrewd as well as attractive. He said nothing. A revolutionary groupie, he thought. He told himself it was wrong to feel guilty about this little seduction scene. Infiltrating the student movement—it seemed part of his job.

"It is okay," she said. "My name is Jeanne. I am a socialist." She added: "Not the Mitterand kind."

Sawchuk glanced at her well-filled denim shirt. He sighed. "Perhaps it would be wise for you not to be seen with me."

"Your secret is safe with me." She darted a quick look at him, then her eyes went straight ahead again. "Do you have a place?"

"There are different places. I move."

"I mean a place where you can be secure."

"There are no secure places."

"Do you have friends in Paris?" She leaned a little closer to him. He could smell the freshness in her hair. She was healthy-looking, milk-fed.

"I have no one."

"If you have no place tonight, I . . . please don't misunderstand. I have an apartment." Her words came charging out. "I am a student at the Ecole Polytechnique. At noon some of us meet with a few professors. We study Kropotkin, Emma Goldman, I have read your poems."

"There are police everywhere. I cannot ask you to share my danger, so I will have to move on tomorrow. It is always necessary to move."

"Yes, I understand."

"Do you have any wine?"

"I have wine. Hashish. You may have anything you want."

Sawchuk, hiding his happiness, stared impassively at the mirrors on the opposite wall. He caught the reflected image of two young Arab men, one in a frizzy Afro, the other with straight long hair. Tiny bells rang in his mind.

Then his attention went to another direction, to the front door. Willy Cuyfer had just walked in. He was looking at people's faces. Sawchuk knew, with an intuitive certainty, that Cuyfer had come to the bar looking for him. He felt his energy field start to pulse.

His eyes flicked back to the Arabs. One, then the other, quietly sidled out of the bar, past Cuyfer.

Cuyfer now spotted Sawchuk and strode up to his table, his head craning forward—a long rat's head with a rat's nose. The other features of his face were compacted: small eyes, small mouth, small goatee—tasteless decorations around the all-conquering nose. He seemed shorter than Sawchuk remembered, but broader in the shoulders. A mat of coarse hair showed through his unbuttoned shirt.

"Maybe your friend will want to visit the ladies' room for a few minutes," Cuyfer said, leaning toward them, his hands flat on the table.

Jeanne looked flustered, offered a weak smile.

"Hello, Willy," said Sawchuk. "Long time."

"Long time."

"So here we are. The debris of the American New Left. Cast up on Europe's shore."

"I'm not interested in that any more," Cuyfer said. "I don't use words. I don't think about it. I just do it. Get rid of her, okay? I've got two minutes, and this place is a heat can. It's a fucking PLO bar, and I'm a target."

Sawchuk turned to Jeanne. "Go to the w.c. Give me a few minutes."

Jeanne walked off quickly. Sawchuk was filled with tension. The two Arab youths—he tried to remember. Had he seen them in the Group Seven catalogues? But there had been hundreds of photographs.

"Nice-looking lunch," Cuyfer said, assessing Jeanne's bottom as she weaved among the tables toward the washroom. "I won't blame you if you don't want to come, but you can't pack her along." He talked fast, nasally, a hint of Dutch twang under an American accent. "We'd like to talk to you. We heard you've been dropping in here. I'm the search party. Like I say, this is a dangerous place. I offed a Fatah a few nights ago, and they're looking for me. Fucking Arabs, wherever you go, fighting each other, going crazy."

"Give me a phone number or some meeting place."

"First tell me if you're interested. If you're not interested now, you won't be interested in three or four days. We have something you might want to be a part of. There's big bucks in it."

Even in the heady, idealistic days of the early seventies, Willy Cuyfer had been devoid of values. Big bucks, it was obvious, still dominated his revolutionary ethic. But Sawchuk had also seen other members of the Weather underground evolve into a standard criminal pattern, lose their social motivation.

"I might be interested. Not tonight. I have other plans."

His plans now came out of the washroom door, still looking nervous.

The young Arab with the frizzy hair came back inside the bar, and now the bell that had been ringing in Sawchuk's head struck the right note. Mohammed Admal was the name. Picture number three, page twenty-four of the Palestine catalogue. A button man for Fatah. The second Arab now re-entered, and Sawchuk remembered his face from the book as well. All systems went on full alert within him.

Cuyfer was gabbling on: if Sawchuk wanted to come now, Kathë Zahre was outside in the car, waiting for them. If he wanted to meet later, they could decide on a safe place. But Karl Wurger wanted Sawchuk brought to their house, if possible.

Mohammed Admal moved cautiously toward them, and seemed to be studying Cuyfer from behind, then at Cuyfer's face reflected in a mirror. Admal's companion began moving off carefully to a corner, his eyes on Cuyfer, too. Sawchuk was trying to keep all his training together. He felt the weight of his gun in its holster and remembered: only every second bullet is live.

Jeanne reached their table.

"Get back," he said to her as he saw Mohammed Admal's hand coming out of his jacket pocket with a machine pistol.

Drowning the noise in the bar, and all the thoughts in his head, were the soft and incessant words: *I can kill, I can kill.* He moved, acting as if something outside his conscious will was working upon him. His shirt snaps flew open as his hand dove to the holster and plucked the .357 automatic from it, and he swept an arm hard against Cuyfer's chest, throwing him onto the floor.

I can kill.

Sawchuk clicked the trigger once, firing the blank, as he moved the gun around a short arc, but before he could take a shot with the live bullet, the Fatah guerrilla was pouring fire past his table, a fusillade that turned Barney's American Bar into a bedlam of screaming people.

Sawchuk lurched from his seat and dived to his right as Admal tried to centre his fire on him. The bullets exploded into the mirror behind Sawchuk, and shards of glass spun into the air as Sawchuk scrambled among the fallen chairs. The terrorist's fire swept a long arc just above his head, and the bullets slammed into the chest of Jeanne, cutting her dead, her scream choking dry in her throat.

For the slightest wink of an instant, Sawchuk saw himself from outside, saw a tall, hard man raising himself on one knee, coolly bracing his firing arm on his left wrist, his right elbow on his right knee, his eyes picking a point two centimetres above the bridge of Admal's nose, saw the gun kick as it fired once, twice, three times.

An incredibly sharp pain pierced Sawchuk from inside. Then it was over.

But his pain was nothing compared to Mohammed Admal's, whose skull shattered open just above the bridge of his nose. His head whiplashed back but, amazingly, despite the force of the bullets and the destruction they caused him, he stayed on his feet, staggering back two steps, three steps, four steps, his trigger finger working reflexively, the machine pistol firing rounds into the floor.

Now suddenly the man stopped in his backward tracks and his body was propelled forward, as if launched, and now Barney's Bar was echoing with the clamour of a submachine gun whose bullets were tearing into Mohammed Admal from the back.

Through the wash of blood, Sawchuk caught a vision at the door. Kathë Zahre: black leather pants tight to the hips and thighs, long, booted legs splayed wide apart, black hair streaming behind her, bouncing with the recoil of her gun, her teeth gritted, her Baretta submachine gun gut-high and level.

The second Arab terrorist had a pistol out now, seemingly unnoticed by anyone in the room except Sawchuk, who fired a blank as the man levelled his gun at Zahre. Then Sawchuk fired a live bullet into his chest.

There was no inner pain this time, no voice in his head reciting the mantra, *I can kill*. Sawchuk knew he could kill now. It had been easy.

Zahre turned and looked at the terrorist who had been about to shoot her, saw the life leave him, and she lowered her gun.

Her eyes met Sawchuk's. They were beautiful and dark. They spoke to him. Sawchuk felt the room whirling around him. Cries and moans were in his ears.

Willy Cuyfer had a snub-nosed .38 in his hand, but he hadn't got to fire it. He scrambled to his feet. "Let's go," he said. "Sorry about your plans."

He looked at Sawchuk with some respect.

But Sawchuk was still locked into Kathë Zahre's eyes. There was hot challenge in them.

17

Paris

I can kill. It no longer came as a voice in his mind. It came to him as a truth.

This was something to fear, the rush that came with the kill. Jesus, there is something terrible inside me.

A cold drizzle fell upon him like a slime.

Cuyfer jumped into the driver's seat of the vw-1300. "Get in the back, Kathë. We need Jacques' good gun up here.

"Damn," said Cuyfer. "Did you see those fuckers go to their maker? In their case, Allah."

Sawchuk and Zahre got in. The car lurched, almost stalled,

then sped forward. Cuyfer almost creased a Citroën as he wiggled the vw into a free lane.

"For God's sake, Willy, turn on your headlights," Zahre said, in English, a husky voice with a slight German accent.

They screamed through an amber light at St. Germain, continued moving south, through the university district. Cuyfer flicked on the parking lights. '

The thought of pretty Jeanne was making Sawchuk's stomach turn and knot. Her blood was in his hair, her dying cry in his brain. He willed himself to a state of near calmness.

"Did you see that guy blow apart in there?" Cuyfer exulted, sprinting for openings in the traffic.

"For the sake of God, slow down," Zahre said. "There will be police all over."

Cuyfer slowed and gave Sawchuk a rat grin. "Back-seat driver."

Sawchuk observed that Cuyfer *was* a bad driver, one who seemed destined to attract police attention. Maybe he wanted it.

"You opened that guy up like a pumpkin, Kathë," Cuyfer shouted. "But it was Jacques! It was Jacques!" He took his right hand off the steering wheel and slapped Sawchuk lustily on the shoulder, grabbing him by the muscles there, shaking him. "What a fucking good shot you are. You saved my life. Willy Cuyfer doesn't forget a thing like that." He called over his shoulder to Zahre. "Now we have Sawchuk. No one will stop us."

"You saved my life, too," Zahre said.

Sawchuk had not yet found the strength to turn around and look at her. But now he did so. She was breaking down the submachine gun, arranging the parts in a large satchel with a shoulder strap. Loose strands of her limp, black hair hung across her face, and she swept them back as she brought her head up. Her skin was stretched taut across the sharp planes of her face; her eyes were like pools of oil. She looked like a beautiful witch.

"Thank you," she said. "Welcome to the Rotkommando."

"What's that you're using, a Magnum?" Cuyfer said, glancing down at the gun that was still in Sawchuk's lap. "Good gun, but we've got more advanced stuff than that around these days. Vzor 7.65, Czech, most efficient automatics around.

We just got a bunch of Skorpion machine pistols in—same thing as that Arab that you drilled in the forehead used—chambered for 7.75 Browning cartridges. Eight hundred and fifty rounds a minute. And those Baretta subs, man, I'll stack them up against Uzis any time. Mind you, the Jews can make guns."

Sawchuk looked sideways at Cuyfer. The Dutchman, they called him. He had come to America as a child with his immigrant parents, Sawchuk remembered. He had been nothing more than a left-wing mercenary with the Weathermen, then had gone out on his own, hitting banks, doing contracts for Arab organizations as a button man until Wurger bought his rights, according to Hesselmann, ten months ago. Sawchuk's memories were that the man was foul in every way.

"Two bullets right on top of his nose," Cuyfer chuckled. He shouted back at Zahre: "You were shooting at a corpse, Kathë!" He dug a hand into his right jacket pocket, steering casually with the other, and brought out a dozen yellow and purple capsules. "Why did you go for the head, Jacques? Kind of a small target on that guy."

It had been easy, Sawchuk thought. It had been easy: that was the terrible thing. "I shot high, so no one would catch a bullet if I missed."

"You like this stuff?" Cuyfer asked, jiggling the caps at him. Bennies or Dexadrine, Sawchuk wasn't sure.

"No," he said.

"Please don't start doing speed," Zahre said.

Cuyfer popped four of the capsules into his mouth and swallowed them dry. "Never thought you could use a fucking gun," he said to Sawchuk. "Just your mouth, from what I could remember. To be honest, I was never turned on to you when we first met—what was that, about ten years ago? Philadelphia? Kathë, this guy is a pro, not like some of those great socialist fighters we've got at the house. If we had more pros and less true believers, we'd turn the capitalist system on its ass."

The windshield wipers slapped from side to side and the lights of the southern suburbs of Paris swam by, l'Hay-les Roses, Freshes, Orly airport on the left as they moved down the A-6.

"Too bad about the little lunch," Cuyfer said. "She'd be a pretty useless fuck right now."

Zahre exploded at him. "Willy, you are a pig! An utter pig!" To Sawchuk: "I'm sorry, was she a friend?"

"I had just met her. She was a . . . friend of the revolution."

"A friend of the revolution!" Cuyfer snorted. "Hey, you sound just like Karl. You can stow that stuff with me, Jacques, I don't talk the language any more. All that matters now is that the system is rotten from the top to the bottom, and it's all shit, and I'm going to do what I can to bring the whole fucking thing down. That's what I'm in it for now, as far as philosophy goes. My politics is I say we should jam the guns up the capitalists' asses and shoot them all. It doesn't matter what you replace it with, so long as it ain't cops and jails and rich snobs and private schools. Karl calls me a nihilist. He's got labels for everything."

"You will have to get used to Comrade Cuyfer," Zahre said. "Some aspects of the revolution seem bizarre to him. His ideal is quite deformed."

"Listen to her, so sweet and high-idealed. I don't go in for the bullshit any more, Jacques. To be honest, I'm mostly in it for the bread now. Three hundred grand—that's what I got paid for the last hit, the one on the Fatah guy. You work with us for a while, Jacques, and you'll get fat." He patted Sawchuk on the belly.

"I am sure Jacques admires your pure communist ethic," Zahre said icily.

Sawchuk glanced back at her again. Her look seemed sad yet brittle.

Cuyfer popped three more caps. "I've got to keep the batteries charged," he said. "Karl won't be able to meet you tonight. He's in Geneva doing a job; you'll have to wait until the morning to meet him. He's greasing a Libyan—"

"Willy!" Zahre interrupted sharply.

"What difference does it make? So he knows Karl is doing a hit tonight? We've got no secrets from Jacques. He's the *third* most wanted guy in the world." He smiled at Sawchuk. "After me and Karl. He's part of the *movement.* Karl says we're to bring you to the house, but we're not supposed to talk until him and you talk. Shit, I know you can be trusted. You and me, Jacques, we'll be like brothers, real professional brothers."

They went off the freeway, onto the N-7 through Pothierry and toward the Fontainebleau forests.

"Those Arab gunners back there, they were Fatah, the

competition. Guerrilla arm of the PLO. The PLO, they get their backing from Saudi Arabia. The Sauds don't support us, but we've got all the kick-ass countries, like Libya and Syria."

Now they drove off the highway, down a hill on a departmental road. Sawchuk caught flashes of light on moving water from between trees. They were near the Seine, in a deep wood.

"We're almost there," Cuyfer said. "You're going to like this place. Used to be owned by a French count. Ten hectares and a piece of the river. You'll dig our operation. I used to be on my own, just like you, but it doesn't pay."

The Volkswagen rolled to a stop in front of a large gate—wooden timbers and steel plate—a high stone wall on either side of it. A young man came from the shadows, grabbed Cuyfer's hand, then reached in and took Sawchuk's.

"We heard it on the radio," he said. "Welcome, comrade, it is a great pleasure. I am André."

He was about nineteen or twenty, his face a sea of blackheads. "You have been identified by witnesses," he told Sawchuk. "Now everybody knows you are one of us." There was much pride in his voice. His hand remained in Sawchuk's for a long time. It seemed limp and weak.

"Stay at the gate, André," Zahre ordered. "We were not followed, but stay at the gate and watch."

André unlocked a padlock, unhitched a chain, and swung the gate open. The road inside curled through unkempt orchards and vineyards. Old oaks like frumpy women lined the driveway, which came out onto open grounds, an area uncared for, with tall grass and spreading bramble. In front of the ugly baroque chateau was a fountain, whose cherubim spurted streams from mouths and penises, above lights of many colours under the water.

"We keep that fucker going day and night," Cuyfer said. "Psychedelic show for the kids. But it's just extra work, the way I see it, because we have to sweep the sludge from the pool ourselves. We don't hire caretakers around here." They parked in a garage behind the chateau and Sawchuk studied the building as they walked back to the front entrance.

The style was heavy rococo, and Sawchuk guessed it was probably no more than two centuries old. It was three storeys and involved much stone, plaster, many shutters, chimney pots, and grillwork balconies. On the steep-sloped roof were tar shingles, and at the peak was a copper-plated figure of a winged angel who, at some earlier time, must have been holding a weathervane. Also at the peak were a television aerial and a directional quod antenna, perched there like pop art. Small dormer windows peeked through the roof. Along the front wall were friezes of bearded god-faces. The main door was plated with brass fancily worked: cupids climbing vines, winged serpents above a greco-nosed woman, tits bold, a jug on her head.

Cuyfer led them inside. "Told you you'd like this place. Beautiful, huh?"

Inside the foyer, bright light from a chandelier caused Sawchuk to blink. On the hallway carpet he observed a blackened banana peel, a multiflavoured Lifesavers wrapper, and one tennis shoe. Two cats came snuffling up to him, and about six young people gathered around.

"Here they are," said Cuyfer, "the hope of the revolution. Toy soldiers who can't hit a barn with a bazooka."

"They'll learn," said Zahre.

There was a gabble of many voices as introductions were made. Two young Arabs, in military fatigues, a Japanese, a French boy in a red beret and two teenage girls—Yolanda, a Basque, who was chewing on a bar of Tobler chocolate, and Simone, equally lumpy and unattractive. Simone seemed shy, but Sawchuk thought it was possible she was very stoned. She gave him a crooked, glazed smile.

"Yeah, here it is, the Paris unit." Cuyfer was talking loudly as if still competing with the automobile engine. "We've got units in Berlin, Hamburg, Zurich, Milan, getting one under way in Turin with the deal we made with the Red Brigades—"

"Willy!" It was Zahre again.

"It's no secret," Cuyfer said. "The cops know we're all over. Come on, Kathë. Jacques is joining the team."

She sighed. "You know what Karl said. I have to lie down. If you will come up, Jacques, I'll show you your room."

"Naw, he's starving. You look like a guy who eats half a cow at a sitting, Jacques. Come on."

Sawchuk gave what passed for a smile to Zahre, then followed Cuyfer down a hall, past a huge library with empty bookshelves and a full-sized pool table at the centre and an

array of computer video games and pinball machines against
the shelves and walls.

The kitchen was grand, obviously once an important
workplace in this mansion. Sawchuk took the bench that
Cuyfer pointed to, and the Dutchman went to the refrigerator, took out salami and milk and blocks of various cheeses,
and placed them on the table.

Two of the young members of the Paris unit came to the
kitchen door but didn't enter, just lounged there, watching
Sawchuk with seeming awe. Another person was sitting at the
far end of the kitchen, a skinny young man who had not been
among the greeting party. He was on a chair, his legs propped
on a butcher's block, a book in his hands.

"This is Oskar Grubbler," said Cuyfer. "He ain't too friendly. Reads books, doesn't have time to enjoy life."

Sawchuk said hello. Grubbler merely nodded and returned
to his book.

"You're a real fucking bore, Oskar," said Cuyfer. "You
should spend more time down in the target room learning
how to shoot if you want to be any use to Karl when he takes
you out in two days. You can't win any wars reading books."

Grubbler looked up and glared at them. "We fight with
every weapon, including words," he said. "Ask Comrade
Sawchuk. He sees himself as a poet."

The boy was a little snot, Sawchuk thought. "Education of
the masses begins with the deed and with the gun," he said.
"Words are only symbols."

"You tell him," said Cuyfer, very cheery. "Jacques, you
sound just like Karl. That's just how he'd say it. Clear out,
you guys, I've got to talk to Comrade Sawchuk alone. This is
Central Committee business." He stared at Grubbler until
the young man, with great effort, rose from his chair and
shambled out. Cuyfer waved the others away from the kitch-
en door and closed it.

"I wanted these amateurs out of here while I tell you
what's going down. They're new, see? Green. We'll be sending them to Misurate, the training camp in Libya. It'll cost us
ten thousand Deutschmarks a head, but they know how to
make fighters there. Okay, the Central Committee is what
I'm on and what these jerks aren't on. Karl and Kathë, the
heads of the other houses, and a bunch of Arabs—that's the

Committee. We'll get you on it next meeting, this Sunday in Amman. We want you to come. Eat up."

Sawchuk had no stomach tonight, but he didn't want to reveal that, and he sliced a big round from the salami—eat what everyone else eats, Bakerfield had warned—and tore off an end of a loaf of stale white bread, and began to munch stolidly.

Cuyfer talked through a mouthful of crumbly blue cheese. "Karl is chairman—I've got to warn you, he's acting a little fucked-up lately." He tapped a finger to the side of his head. "I head up planning and strategy. I'm an expert, see. Karl needs people like me and you. I came to Rotkommando with this idea to take out a tanker full of oil, bound for Israel. Yeah, that was me that was behind the Jap tanker business last August." Cheese crumbs were spilling into his goatee. "We've been following you in the papers ever since your trial in Canada, and all the big jobs you've been doing here in Europe. Karl has been reading the stuff you've been writing. He wants you, Jacques. Another big name from North America—it'll help give us a stronger international image." Cuyfer lowered his voice and scraped his chair closer to Sawchuk. "Jacques, I want you in as lead gun in Operation Mecca. I'm not supposed to talk about it yet, but it's big. The sky's the limit."

Amman. Operation Mecca. Sawchuk had taken a rocket right into the centre of the Rotkommando with hardly a chance to catch his breath. Decisions were being made for him. He had not joined the Rotkommando; it had joined him. He wanted desperately to be alone, to think, to resolve his ambivalence about this terrible work. The worst thing was this: he was good at the work, and he felt an evil thrill of accomplishment.

Then he thought of young Jeanne, the anarchist.

The bread and salami, improperly chewed, had cornered a pocket of air in his stomach, and a belch was trapped there. He banged the side of his stomach with his fist, hoping for release, not finding it.

"Listen, Karl will have my nuts on a plate if he hears I've been filling you in on this." Cuyfer leaned even closer. "But you should know: in ten days, we're going to Saudi Arabia. We're talking about billions, Jacques. We can buy our own country when it's over."

This man was a talking fool, Sawchuk realized, a spy's good friend. Yes, this was almost too easy.

"I'm going to warn you about Karl. Now you've got to give him credit—he's the kind of guy that leads from the front, not from behind a desk. And he's the smartest son of a bitch I ever met. But lately he goes off on these tirades, see? It's got some of us worried. And the other thing I've got to tell you about is Kathë Zahre. She's a nympho."

"Uh-huh?" Sawchuk twisted his body, trying to provide a free channel for the recalcitrant burp. He remembered the hot look she had given him in the bar.

"Things are a little hair-trigger around here with Karl and her. She's got roaming eyes, and that gets the guy a little nervous. I'm just telling you, man to man, as a friend, don't try to get too close to her. Karl will mail your balls to the *Daily Express*."

"I wouldn't dream of it, Willy." Sawchuk was determined not to get himself tangled up with her. The job had too many inherent dangers as it was. The belch that had not been released was now a vicious gas pain in his stomach.

Cuyfer gave a little rat-face leer. "I don't think Kathë finds things very good with Karl—if you know what I mean. She's giving off these sexual vibes around here which are making Karl a real nervous guy just before the big Saudi job. Nobody wants a nervous hand at the helm, right?"

"Right, Willy."

"Enough said, friend to friend." He sat back and passed his hand over his beard, wiping away the cheese crumbs. Then taking another gulp of wine, and glancing at his watch, he said: "Okay, let's go down to the TV lounge and watch the news. Karl has probably got his man by now. Then we've got one more hit before Operation Mecca, one more people's sentence, as Karl calls them. A piano player." Cuyfer stood up and sprayed the room with imaginary machine-gun fire. "*Rat-tat-tat-tat.*" He was jumpy with the speed.

Sawchuk followed Cuyfer through a grand salon decorated with whorls and twirls of painted plaster and tapestries running twenty feet to the ceiling. The bookish terrorist known as Oskar Grubbler was lying on a sofa there, amid much clutter, reading. He didn't bother to look up as they passed through to the television lounge, a baronial anteroom crammed with ugly plastic appointments and chairs and sofas known in the trade as fat furniture. Sawchuk estimated that there was a small fortune in video and stereo equipment in here, a Betamax recorder, a giant screen, a library of hundreds of video and music cassettes and six-foot-high speakers.

Simone was lying on the floor with headphones on, eyes closed. One of the Arab boys was studiously cleaning and oiling a Skorpion submachine-gun. The others were watching the late news on the big screen.

An earthquake in Iran. Death toll in the hundreds.

"Come on, come on," said Cuyfer, "get to it."

Sawchuk found himself a place on a wobbly cushion filled with foam flakes, and as he sat he felt himself being swallowed up in it. His stomach was still knotted, still gaseous.

Now on the screen was an exterior shot of Barney's American Bar. Now the camera was panning through the interior, showing the wreckage. Someone in the room let out a cheer. Yolanda shouted, "Shut up, shut up, everybody."

The announcer described the carnage. Three dead, three bystanders cut by flying glass. The Sureté described it as a terrorist strike. A reporter began to do a backgrounder.

"Hey," said Cuyfer, annoyed. "He's got it all wrong. They've got *us* ganging up and doing a hit on the *Arabs*. They were gunning for *me*."

"I can't hear," Yolanda said.

Now Sawchuk was looking at a still photograph of himself, bearded. "Police have confirmed that the Canadian terrorist has joined the Rotkommando, the fanatic left-wing group headed by Karl Wurger. As had, only months earlier, one of Europe's most-wanted criminals, Willy Cuyfer...."

"That's me, he's talking about me."

"... whom witnesses identified as being the second man involved in the attack...."

"Where's my picture? They've got Jacques' picture, not mine."

"Shut up, Willy," someone yelled.

"It is okay," said the young Japanese. "We have it on tape."

As a police terrorist expert was being interviewed about the wave of assassinations that had recently struck Europe and the Middle East, the announcer cut back onto the screen with a bulletin from Geneva. He announced the murder of Ahmed Gebayesh, former Libyan ambassador to Italy, who had been shot while stepping outside his bullet-proof limousine. "No details are available, but it is known that no suspects have been arrested."

"He got away," someone shouted.

Sawchuk could feel the pain in his gut gnawing at him like a hungry rodent.

The announcer moved on to other news and Cuyfer flicked the screen off with a remote switch.

André, back from duty at the gate, was sitting in the middle of the room, a mirror in front of him, and he was chopping lines of cocaine from a pile of white powder at the centre of the mirror. He looked up at Sawchuk. "Peruvian flake," he said.

"Not for me. It always makes me want to rob and kill."

Cuyfer roared and slapped Sawchuk on the back. "Same guy that I remember, always got a funny line." No one else laughed. Cuyfer dispensed with the paper tube that André offered him, and Sawchuk watched with an expression of incredulity as the Dutchman brought his enormous inhaling machine to bear upon the pile in the middle of the mirror. Never mind the neat lines that André had cut. Never mind the tube. Just powerhouse it up that great fleshy vacuum cleaner. Cuyfer stuck an index finger up each nostril in turn and twirled it about, working the cocaine in.

Remember flower power? Sawchuk thought. Welcome to the 1980s.

For two hours Sawchuk talked airy rhetoric with the young members of the Paris house, befriending Grubbler with revolutionary cant that had seemed meaningful to him years ago, but was now barren and turgid. Were these to be the soldiers of Wurger's revolution? Hesselmann had said the Rotkommando were recruiting disaffected young people from European streets. What kind of war could these humourless chocolate-munchers fight? Oskar Grubbler with his cant— how could there be a revolution without the spark of humanity?

He tried to draw them out, but none seemed interested in talking about themselves. They enjoyed dropping names of the martyrs: Marighella, Guevara, Ulrike Meinhof, Gudrin Ensslin. They seemed haunted by visions of martyrdom. To be enshrined in the list of the honoured dead—maybe that would replace the afterlife as a reward for facing danger. But nothing about these children seemed worth remembering.

Yolanda wandered into the conversation with a distant,

strange voice. "I believe that when we die, we become like stars in the sky. Those we kill also become stars in the sky." Her mouth was brown and wet with chocolate.

Then Kathë Zahre came gliding into the lounge and came up to Sawchuk.

"Are you tired?" Her look drowned him.

"No, I'm not tired," Sawchuk said. "I'm enjoying myself. Did our loud talk wake you up?"

"I have been in bed, but I haven't been sleeping."

She made Sawchuk nervous. He felt there were unspoken words in her eyes. "When I do decide to crash," he said, "I'll grab a piece of foam, find a place underneath the stairs."

"You have your own room," she said. "In the south wing, overlooking the river and the eastern sky. It is just across the hall from the room that Karl and I share. Did everything go all right for him tonight?"

"He has performed his task," said Grubbler.

Zahre offered Sawchuk a strained smile. "I know he will be happy to meet you, Jacques. We are all happy that you will be joining us."

"We have some new movies in," André said "Want to take one in, Kathë? *Ordinary People*—it won an Oscar."

"I am going to bed." She turned slowly around. Sawchuk's eyes followed her as she walked in front of a light, the outlines of her body showing through the robe.

Just across the hall from the room that Karl and I share. Sawchuk breathed out slowly. "A movie sounds good," he said. He decided not to tiptoe down the south wing until Kathë Zahre was fast asleep. *He'll mail your balls to the Daily Express.* Yes, he would watch a movie, maybe practise a little more orotund gobbledygook with his fellow fervent revolutionaries.

18

Wednesday Night, the Chateau

Sawchuk outlasted everyone, including André, who had kept a cocaine tube up his nose most of the night; even Grubbler, who had talked and talked, full of confused dreams. Now only Simone remained, and she was stone-dead to the world, her thick buttocks splayed with gross invitation across a pair of foam cushions.

Sawchuk stared with gloom at the flickering grey images of an ancient Randolph Scott western on the television set. His watch said four a.m.

How had he allowed this to happen? He had been prepared to test the water with his toe. But it was as if some monstrous black power had grasped his feet, pulled him from the deck, plunged him into the roiling depths of terrorism.

He was responsible for that girl dying. And he himself had killed two others. And he feared he might be able to kill again. Because it wasn't that hard. And would get easier.

He felt little fear now, however. It was as if the gunfight had altered consciousness, like a powerful drug, a ten-day Indian peyote ceremony compressed into twelve seconds of carnage that had brought him a self-enlightenment that was cosmic, Zen-like.

He knew now that he could kill if he had to.

Randolph Scott was ambushed, his horse shot from under him, and he was heading for the mesquite.

I have their Paris house, he thought. I have Cuyfer, and tomorrow I'll have Wurger. Plus half a dozen zombies. Hesselmann might be satisfied with the booty. The Group could seize all of Wurger's records, too—Grubbler had mentioned to Sawchuk that Wurger kept an office in here.

114

He thought of his father. *My son, the informer.*

He could go over the wall and hike to Fontainebleau. A bus to Orly. And Jerome Miles, the professional student from Schenectady, could take what was left of his two hundred thousand francs and present himself to the Pan Am counter.

But shit, dad, these people are just maggots. Wurger with his thirst for the blood of great men. Grubbler, with his ugly cant. Outlandish Yolanda: *Those we kill become stars in the sky.* Cuyfer, that fun guy. Hesselmann had called them left-wing fascists—was it a bad description? Was there not a moral imperative to end the madness of the Rotkommando?

John Sawchuk, on the hospital bed, proudly speaking his last words: *I never sold out.*

He seemed unable to move, swallowed by his fat chair. Rubinstein had got him into this ugly dilemma. Tie the blighter to the mizzen, bosun, and twenty of the best if you would. What had Rocky said? *When you're a part of the system, there ain't any escape.*

His mind moved desperately away and on to thoughts of Kathë Zahre. Libidinous thoughts, immediately censored. Such thinking is deviationist and must be uprooted. Focus on Randolph Scott and his fine new horse. How straight in the saddle he rides.

Her hot look was something not to be misunderstood by men of ordinary experience. But getting too close to her would be like stepping on a nest of puff adders.

He returned to his quandary: Could there be honour in being an informer, a political spy? Where does the role of rat end and honest policeman begin? Surely he had blurred the considerable distinction between a skulking informer (as he saw himself through his father's eyes) and a noble protector of the peace (as he had begun to want to see himself through his own). These people were a cancer on the cause of the Left. They were justifying the end with means so corrupt that they themselves stank with corruption. And what kind of society could all their spilled blood bring except one that was suffused with the immorality of those means?

And he began to understand that he had been too much blinded by an angry and passionate father, too dominated by his father's scorn for those who sell themselves to the political police.

Such thoughts were fuelled by surges of excitement, by an

emboldened ego. Rocky's words: *Otherwise you won't be able to live with yourself, you arrogant bastard.*

He thought: Hesselmann will be stunned when he finds out how fast I got inside.

Sawchuk had always wanted to play some small role in history, in changing it. But had not Marx taught that men do not alter history, that history alters men? Perhaps he should test Marx on that.

He clambered out of his chair, wandered past the prostrate form of Simone, turned some lights out, then walked down the darkened hall.

Yes, he would continue to be a spy for a while. It tasted good.

He locked his father away in a small back room of his mind.

He felt strangely light-headed and alert as he slipped out of his boots and continued softly toward the door which, Grubbler had explained, led to Wurger's office. The Rotkommando's head office, he had learned, was in Amman, Jordan, moved there after the Israeli attack on Beirut. But there could be some interesting things in here.

He unhitched his broad leather belt and pressed the spring which disconnected its clasp from its loop. The parts of the clasp twisted apart like a Chinese puzzle, became a lock-pick set. Sawchuk tried several of them in turn, and finally the door clicked open. He went in and closed it behind him.

The room was dark except for a subdued light from the fountain outside. He would need a little more than that for photographs, even with his light-sensitive camera. But it would be dangerous to turn on a room switch.

Sawchuk—because of healthy diet, he liked to think—had good sight in dark places, and his eyes focussed on a wide metal desk, clean of papers; a single, four-drawer filing cabinet; chairs; a shelf behind the desk with an amateur radio set. He had seen no telephones in the chateau. Maybe Wurger believed, in these days of extensive phone tapping, that radio was safer.

He clicked on the transceiver and examined the rest of the equipment in the green glow of its panel lights. A whole single side band package here with a Priva-Com 3C. Sawchuk remembered them from the radio manuals. They were used for selective calling to specified units. There was a microphone and head set. A power amplifier.

Sawchuk touched pressure points on each of his boots, twisted the heels off. The two parts of the camera clicked together, and a soft glow was emitted near the lens. He had film in it that would take fifty micro-negatives.

The lock on the filing cabinet was easy. He held various files up to the light from the radio: research material, newspaper clippings, magazine articles, pages from books that had been run through copiers. Most of the files dealt with the Middle East, Saudi Arabia and Israel in particular.

The second drawer had more such files. The third drawer contained clippings, articles about terrorist ventures. Notes were scribbled in German on the margins of some. Sawchuk found a collection of stories about himself—his trial, his escape, all the planted stories prepared by Group Seven's propaganda section. There were also articles from left-wing and underground periodicals, under Sawchuk's name, full of vitriol about Israel, expressing common cause with those who believed only violence could unhinge the state.

Other files dealt with other terrorists. There was a list of imprisoned men and women, their countries, their jails. As the prisoners had been transferred from jail to jail, amondments were scribbled by their names. And here was Jacques Sawchuk on the list: St. Vincent de Paul Penitentiary, Montreal. A line had been drawn through that, and the word *"Frei!"* written beside it.

He found a file with a list of about fifty names, some crossed out: victims of Wurger's assassination campaign. He held the list to the light from the ham radio, turned the camera's light enhancement device on maximum, and took photographs.

He also found in that file copies of the London *Jewish Chronicle* with names of prominent Zionists circled in pencil.

Next to that was a thick file folder labelled "Solomon." It held charts and diagrams and what appeared to be a twelve-page timetable for the assassination of the British concert pianist, Sir Isaac Solomon. This was the "piano player" that Cuyfer had mentioned. Part was in German, which Sawchuk couldn't read, but it was clear the timetable was detailed to account for every contingency. The assassination was to take place this Friday night—forty hours from now—in the guest dressing room of West Berlin's Philharmonie, where Solomon was to play and von Karajan conduct Beethoven's Second Concerto.

Sawchuk's mouth had gone dry. Suddenly he felt an overwhelming sense of shame about his puerile concerns of earlier. No honour in being a spy? No honour in saving the life of Isaac Solomon? He knew he had to get to a phone quickly, or to one of the pick-up points. He began photographing the file.

The bottom drawer of the cabinet was empty except for a strange file of clippings from the personal column of the *Manchester Guardian,* most involving men of various ages offering their companionship to younger women. Sawchuk assembled some samples of these and took more pictures.

Then he turned to the desk. Its bottom drawers were unlocked and contained nothing but blank paper and stationery tools. The top drawer was double-locked, both by a built-in lock and a clasp welded between desk and drawer, fastened by a small combination lock. This, Sawchuk decided, must be where Wurger keeps the family jewels. He brought the microphone from the radio set against the combination lock, put on the headphones, switched the mike on, and listened to the tumblers drop as he played with the combinations. The lock eventually gave. The other one was easily picked. He slid the drawer open.

All that was in it was one black binder notebook, the kind a student might use in a lecture room. Pages and pages of penned lines, all in German, in what he supposed was Wurger's handwriting. Working quickly now against the coming of the dawn, using the growing light from the window, Sawchuk photographed as many pages as he could before his film ran out.

He left Wurger's office, locking the door behind him, and went upstairs to the south wing. His room was baronial, with a low built-in bed against one wall, a fireplace opposite. French doors led to a balcony that looked over the river, glowing softly grey now in the early gloom of an as yet sunless morning. He pulled the curtains shut, shrugged from his clothes, tucked the camera back into his boot-heels, laid his holster and gun on a chair in easy reach. Then he went to the bathroom and took a long, hot shower.

When he came back and sat on the bed, it swished and gurgled. A waterbed. He crawled beneath sheets that smelled as if bodies had been in them recently. He tried to calm himself to sleep with imagery and rhyme.

He dreamed he was on an inflatable raft, the kind he had floated around on as a kid in Lac Massawippi in the Eastern Townships of Quebec. Slop, slop, went the waterbed as he tossed on it. He had a fishing line out. Little rat-faced fish swam beside the boat, nibbling at his bait.

Then the dream turned bad. He saw his father on the shore, waving for him to come in. He looked into the purple water and saw his own reflection, a rat himself.

Suddenly he was wallowing crazily on a high sea, and he shot awake to find Kathë Zahre, in a black nightgown, sitting on the edge of the waterbed, on the sheet that covered Sawchuk, naked beneath it.

"I have to talk to you now, before the others get up," she said.

His eyes were nearly blinded by a stripe of focussed sunshine that knifed through a part in the curtains of the balcony window. What time was it? He looked at his watch. Six-thirty. He had slept only an hour.

"When Karl gets back, we may not have time to be alone, to talk."

What time is Karl getting back? he wanted to ask. But he said nothing, just blinked and moved his head so that Zahre's face blocked the sunray.

"Please do not join the Rotkommando, Jacques. It has all gone wrong. We are like the Corsicans, rebels who have succeeded at crime. We cannot stop now, for it is our profession. The ideals are dead. Karl is building a multinational corporation. Its commodity is death."

The sun streamed through her hair and made her face dark. She looked as sad as a folk song.

"Karl sees you—and your legend—as a source of more power for himself." Her voice quavered. "Your name, it is thought, will bring credibility to an organization that kills artists. Your name will bring hundreds more recruits. And more leverage at the bargaining table when contracts with that foul man from Libya are discussed. You will be used, Jacques."

"I want to find out what he offers." Sawchuk was sitting up now, against the headboard. She moved closer.

"Do not join the Rotkommando. I do not understand what we do. Karl's words confuse me now, and once they were so clear. I have lost the line between works for evil and works for good. We assassinate and we bomb in order to force the state to become oppressive and bring on the final battle for communism. We say we are doing works for good. Oh, God." She shuddered. "Don't join us."

"But you were searching for me. Why?"

"I do Karl's bidding. Most of the time." Her voice was hesitant. "Do you want my other excuses? Perhaps I, too, wanted to meet you. I've read your writings. I'm a fan."

Now she reached out and touched his forearm, and traced her fingertips along it, toward the wrist. Sawchuk didn't move.

"I am afraid," she said. "I am afraid of a man who teaches that to kill the enemy is liberating. The world lights up with the death of a fascist—that is what he puts in the heads of the new people. The Rotkommando army will be ghastly. Mecca will be ghastly. Friday night he kills Solomon, the pianist. He says the death will make a statement. I am afraid of him, Jacques. He is sick."

"Sick?"

"Delusional tirades. He suspects plots, accuses comrades not only of incorrect thinking, but of disloyalty. Paranoia eats at him like cancer. But there are so many sheep who think he is God. He is vain, addicted to the praise of sycophants. I am afraid of him, and I am afraid to run."

Sawchuk could see the outline of pointed breasts where the sun glowed through her robe. He was having trouble assimilating all this information, the libidinous energy coursing through him. Her fingers were still resting on his wrist. He could move it away. He didn't.

What time was Wurger due back?

"And he is jealous of everyone. He thinks I go to bed with others."

She drew one leg up onto the bed, a masterpiece of long bone and tawny skin bared thigh-high. Sawchuk felt the unwelcome urgings of an erection. Bakerfield's Book: don't get involved. This one was a love witch, a nymphomaniac. Agent Sawchuk did not wish to have his body vandalized with bullets from Wurger's famous Landmann-Preetz.

Her eyes were mercury pools, hypnotic in their mystery. He could not tear himself from them.

What if someone came down the hall, came to his door?

She kissed him on the mouth, so quickly he was defenceless. "I feel so desperately unfulfilled," she whispered, and she put her arms around him, pressed her body to his.

Sawchuk, caution vanquished, felt his loins exploding as she pressed against him, the bed rolling gently on a light sea. She raised up, pulled her gown over her head, revealed a body that was from a painting by Modigliani, pulled the sheet from Sawchuk's body. And went down on him.

At the pull of her lips, Sawchuk felt a galactic explosion building up, and he fought it, felt her hands upon his cock, and tried to fight it, failed, and like a volcano, erupted.

There were a few moments of silence. He heard her voice.

"It is all right. We have time."

Was there reproach in it? And how much time *did* they have? Ask her, Sawchuk. It is a simple thing.

"When does Karl get back?"

"The garage is below your window; we will hear his car." She got up from the bed, opened the French doors that led to the balcony, and Sawchuk could hear the sound of thrushes calling to each other. He watched Zahre walk into the bathroom, heard the tap. She returned, model-erect, naked, smiling. She crawled under the sheet with him.

"Did you know that I would come to your room?"

Sawchuk was unsure how to handle this question. He said nothing.

"I knew we would come together. I knew it when I looked into your eyes in the bar. You knew it, too. We both knew, Jacques. It was as if a current connected us."

He remembered the flash of her eyes across the bloodied ruin of Barney's American Bar. How to escape from this?

But he let her touch him until he became hard again, and she raised herself up, tossing back her hair with a sweeping brush of her hand, mounted him, and rode him with an expression that seemed a mix of agony and passion.

A waterbed does not co-operate with lovers, and Sawchuk's body kept falling into the trough instead of reaching up as she descended upon him. He put his hands to her waist and moved her gently onto her back. When they began to master the rhythms of the water moving beneath them, he felt himself being overcome again, broaching to in the turbulent sea. She stifled groans, dug her fingernails into his back, traced long welts across it.

He came like a cannon.

"Don't stop," she cried.

Zahre was shuddering, and twisting her head back and forth violently.

Sawchuk's ears caught the growing rumble of a car engine outside. He felt his own gears slipping.

"God, don't stop!" she shrieked. Her voice ricocheted like a bullet around the room. Sawchuk summoned hidden forces.

A car door slammed. Voices from below drifted through the window.

"*Du lieber!*" she cried. "I am coming!" She convulsed, uttered a wail of release.

The door swung open. Sawchuk had visions of a horrible death. Drowned in a bullet-ridden waterbed.

It was Cuyfer. "He's back, for Christ's sake." He disappeared, shut the door.

Sawchuk leaped from the bed in ungainly fashion, went first for his gun and holster, threw it over his shoulder, bounded into his blue jeans.

Zahre seemed to take an eternity to crawl from the bed, woozy from her release. Sawchuk grabbed her nightgown in one hand and lifted her with the other arm like a sack on his shoulder, and he raced outside, across the hall, into her room, where he deposited her on the canopy bed.

Back in the hallway, he heard someone talking in a high-pitched voice, in German. The voice seemed to be moving up the stairs. Sawchuk got as far as the doorknob to his room, but he froze there. Something told him: Don't open the door. Turn around very casually.

When he did, he saw Karl Wurger coming up the last stair, looking at him.

Sawchuk pulled away from the door as if he had just closed it behind him. Wurger: a blond man in a bland suit. He looked as if he had just returned from a sales conference. But the eyes were of ice, pale and terrible. Were these the eyes of a man before the kill? No, he decided. Not quite.

"I am Karl Wurger." He came toward Sawchuk and held out a hand.

"I'm Sawchuk." The grip was cold and the handshake sharp

and swift. Sawchuk saw Wurger's eyes move down the length of him, his naked chest, the holster strap slung over his shoulder with the butt of his pistol sticking from it, his belt undone, his feet bare.

Sawchuk saw the eyes move back up, as if taking the size of him for a coffin. Wurger's thin lips parted and he said softly: "I think I have heard a scream."

"It woke me up," Sawchuk said. "I was coming out to check."

"Kathë has nightmares." Wurger went to his bedroom door, entered, shut it behind him.

19

Thursday Morning, May 31, the Chateau

Willy Cuyfer looked at Sawchuk's bare back. He whistled. "Jeez, looks like a cat jumped on you. I hope Karl didn't see those scratches."

Sawchuk swore at himself for being a fool, an unmitigated disaster as a spy. He turned in front of the wardrobe mirror in his bedroom, saw the long, red welts that Kathë Zahre's fingernails had drawn across his back in evenly-spaced rows, *Had* Wurger noticed? He remembered those cold eyes ranging up and down his body.

"You son of a bitch, you've got more balls than the Ghengis Khan," Cuyfer said. He was sitting on the edge of Sawchuk's bed. Sawchuk was dressing again, after a hurried shower.

"Some nightmare." Cuyfer grinned, showing crooked teeth. "*'Du lieber,* I'm coming!' We all heard her from downstairs." Respect for Sawchuk showed in the Dutchman's eyes.

Sawchuk had none for himself. What had he let himself in for?

"Thanks for warning me, Willy. Now we're even."

"Naw, I still owe. You're going to need someone watching your back if Karl starts getting jealous. But maybe he's a chickenshit under it all, hey, Jacques? Maybe he ain't got the fire in the balls the way me and you do. Maybe we need someone running the Rotkommando that's got fire in the balls."

Sawchuk and Cuyfer went downstairs to the library. Grubbler was there, looking awkward, staring at Sawchuk with a curious expression. In a few minutes, Wurger came down and joined them. He had been transformed. He was jaunty, offered a warm smile to Sawchuk, strode forward and shook hands palms up, the revolutionary greeting.

"I welcome you. I welcome you as a brother." He stepped back. His expression was warm, without malice. "You will have to excuse me if I seemed under a strain earlier. It has been a long drive from Geneva, and I return to find that Kathë has been having her nightmares again. But she has told me everything—how you saved her life, how you have come into the fold of the Rotkommando so dramatically. Oskar, please prepare some coffee for Jacques and me, bring it to the office."

Grubbler jumped up and left.

"Comrade, last week Israeli bombs and planes killed twenty-two innocent men, women and children, people denied their Palestinian homeland. The imperialist world forgives, even applauds. It is not genocide, they say. It is a legitimate act of war. In response we will take a single life. Our executions are isolated, single, ringing messages of retaliation." Wurger's voice raised in pitch, and his face had suddenly become intense. "When the enemy kills, it is mass murder, a bloodbath. Twenty thousand Palestinians slaughtered in the last decade! They dare call *us* terrorists." He paused, breathing heavily, then spoke more softly. "Let them. To be a terrorist today ennobles an honourable man."

What was this leading up to? Sawchuk wondered. He could see how it would be easy for the uncynical to be caught up in Wurger's passion.

"You and I are revolutionaries, comrade. We both know that even revolutionaries have traditions. Ours, like most others', is blood initiation. Sir Isaac Solomon will be executed tomorrow night in West Berlin. He will be destroyed by two guns. One will be mine. The other was to be Willy's, but I am sure he will be pleased to give way to you. Will you do it?"

Sawchuk tried to settle this new unease that was working through him. *Go by the Book*, Bakerfield had warned. An assassination: the Book said agree to it. Learn the plan. Phone in fast. But he stalled.

Cuyfer grunted. "Go for it, Jacques. It's worth fifty grand to you."

"Why Isaac Solomon?" Sawchuk said. "He is an artist, a famous one."

"His politics poison his art," Wurger said. "Those who so loudly support Israel must know they cannot hide behind an artist's cloak."

Sawchuk understood that the recent Israeli bombing, as cruel as it was, would serve only to legitimize an act that must have been planned months ago.

"Will you do it?" said Wurger. "If your zeal for revolution is honed by the whetstone of profit, like Comrade Cuyfer's, there is the money, as he says. Or you may invest your share, as I will mine, in the training of soldiers in Libya. When the Central Committee meets in Jordan this Sunday, you will be elected to it."

"I'll do it," said Sawchuk.

Wurger was hearty again. "We will fly from Orly tomorrow to Tegel Airport in Berlin." He took Sawchuk's arm. "Come to the office. We will talk. There are things that need to be said."

Sawchuk followed him. Wurger opened the door with a key, one of several linked by a thin chain inside his briefcase.

"This is the operations centre for Western Europe," he said. "Our main offices are in Amman." He unlocked the filing cabinet and handed to Sawchuk the plans for Operation Solomon which Sawchuk had already photographed. "You must study these." He pointed to a chair, which Sawchuk took. "You will see how well-prepared we are. We have someone inside the Philharmonie." Wurger did not sit, but leaned against the desk and looked down at Sawchuk.

"It is an elusive shadow world in which we live, Jacques, and I am happy that our shadows have finally crossed."

The man had obviously not guessed that Sawchuk had made him a cuckold, so Sawchuk relaxed a little.

"One of the contradictions of capitalism," Wurger went on,

"is that its so-called free press—for the most deliberate of motives, to raise circulation and sell advertising—makes romantic heroes of its enemies. You have become the Che Guevara of the north."

"Contracts to kill, Karl—what kind of revolutionary program is that? Guevara would have been dismayed."

Wurger waved off Sawchuk's misgivings with an impatient flick of his hand. "Please understand that it is not cowboys and Indians any more on the revolutionary Left. We operate on the basis of sound business principles." He smiled wryly. "We apply capitalist methodology." He studied Sawchuk, as if seeking reaction to this heresy.

Sawchuk remained silent. Bakerfield's Book: Don't talk.

"Rotkommando is modelled after a profit-oriented corporation," Wurger said. "We steal the enemy's efficient ideas, but we do not steal his morals."

"Corrupted by the system we are intent on destroying."

Wurger shrugged. "We are children of capitalism. Perhaps we *are* corrupted by it. But the generations that will follow its destruction, they will be untainted, and the corrupted will be forgiven. I will be proposing to the Committee two hundred thousand dollars a month for your services. You can keep it. Or you can reinvest it in our operations. As I do." His eyes blazed at Sawchuk. "We have an Armageddon planned for ten days from now. We have many soldiers; we need more leaders. Join us in it. It will be the first battle of the final great war for mankind's liberation. You will know everything when you have sworn the oath before the Committee this Sunday."

Sawchuk felt dizzy. He had been hurled like a human cannonball into the tangled net of the Rotkommando, was still collecting his wits.

There was a soft rap on the door. "Come in," said Wurger.

An obsequious Oskar Grubbler carried in a tray with a pot of coffee and cups, cream, and sugar.

"Jacques will be joining us for the matter in Berlin," Wurger said.

"I have much to learn," said Grubbler. "I will do everything that I can to prove myself."

"Oskar will be the driver. Berlin is his home. *Danke,* Oskar."

Grubbler crept out. Sawchuk noticed that around Wurger he acted like a castrated slave.

"Comrade Grubbler learns quickly," said Wurger, pouring coffee. "Six months ago he was picking out the cobblestones from the sidewalks of Kurferstendamm, throwing them at the pigs, and in turn being beaten by them. He came to us after he had been ejected from his tenement by a speculator who emptied the building, and who still keeps it empty, waiting for the prices to rise. Our revolution will inherit the disinherited; comrades like Oskar. He will learn that there is more power in the barrel of a gun than in the cobbled boulevards of Berlin."

Sawchuk chose the cup nearest to Wurger. Just a little precaution.

Wurger spooned sugar into his cup, and stared into it, stirring thoughtfully, his eyes distant. He abruptly looked at Sawchuk. "You were deported from Cuba."

"I wouldn't have any truck with their corrupt revolution. If you have read what I have written, you will know that I believe it has failed, as the Russian revolution has failed."

"Yes," said Wurger. The light in his eyes seemed to fade again. "They all fail. They become soft and lose the ideal. We must not become soft. No, we must not become soft." The thought seemed an obsession.

Sawchuk's tone was easy and confiding. "Comrade, you and I understand one thing very well. The Soviets have failed. Cuba has failed. Even China is ruled by the new technocratic bourgeoisie. You and I share nothing with the self-perpetuating bureaucratic dictatorships of the East." He leaned toward Wurger. "We share a dream of a different world, you and I." He had read Wurger's published statements. He would go straight to what passed for his heart.

Wurger's eyes grew glazed again as the man sipped his coffee, then stared into the cup. Sawchuk remembered the photograph from Zurich—Wurger looking for his new world in a steaming bowl of soup.

When Wurger raised his eyes there was pain in them. "Sometimes it seems to retreat into the distance. It is as if we are walking across the desert toward a wonderful, shining city, and it retreats, retreats forever to the horizon."

"The world of brotherhood," Sawchuk said quietly. "Free of institution, free of the inequity of law." Now he spoke sharply. "They scorn Karl Wurger in Havana. I have read what the Soviets, too, have written about you: an elitist blood-thirsty adventurer who objectively serves the interests of the class enemy, masquerading as a communist. But they say worse of me. They fear us."

"They are rotting from inside." Wurger said this with a tight voice. "One day the walls will collapse upon them. When the war comes."

Sawchuk felt a chill. The war?

Wurger's eyes came clear, focussed on him. "But I have heard of other things that caused your expulsion from Cuba. I have heard of a degenerate life, sexual excesses." He hissed the last two words. "The struggle has no place for that."

Sawchuk showed injured innocence. "What do you talk about, a degenerate life? God, I have seen your people in this house popping benzedrine, snorting coke, smoking pot. Your soldiers are fat, pimpled with chocolate bars, wired into a million francs' worth of electronic gadgetry and software. A degenerate life, Karl?"

Wurger replied in heat, defensively. "These people have come from nothing. *Nothing*. And they themselves as yet are nothing. But they will become fighters. Living here, waiting for Misurate, they learn what they *can* have if we turn the world upside down."

His high voice began to rise, to crack like a whip. "They are ignorant savages, Simone, Yolanda, André, the others here and in our houses elsewhere. They are the malignant seeds that capitalism has shed, and we harvest them in our cities, and they will bloom into soldiers. There are millions more to draw upon in the jungles of the city—the innocent, the unemployed, the evicted, the disaffected, all yeasty dough for the struggle, hungry for war."

Now he began to speak slowly, looking closely at Sawchuk as if unsure whether to trust him with his thoughts. "You and I are the vanguard. The others are nothing. Jacques Sawchuk and Karl Wurger need not pretend that everybody is equally important to the revolution. It is time to speak of equality after we have won. But until then a small minority will be required to lead the way."

"Men like Willy Cuyfer?"

"There is a role for the Cuyfers. Was it not Bakunin who said that the bandit is the only true revolutionary: without fine phrases, without book-learned rhetoric, a fighter who springs angrily from the people?"

Wurger leaned toward him, as if impelled to share his thoughts, as if he had finally found someone, like himself, upon a plane above the others.

"You are shocked when I talk about money. I will explain. Ten thousand Deutschmarks buys a year's training under the veterans of the Popular Front for the Liberation of Palestine—their best men, their commando leaders. We have a hundred and fifty in Misurate camp in Libya now. And we have paid the tuition of another hundred and fifty who are recently graduated. Add the figures up. That is where our millions go. And that is where the billions will go that we will be given by the family of the Saud—in a matter of days." He kept his eyes on Sawchuk. "Soon we will have an army of a hundred thousand."

Sawchuk was stunned, and trying not to show it. Trained terrorist hordes under the command of this fanatic, wobbling on the edge of insanity, overcome with Napoleonic delusion. "Those who have been trained already—where are they now?"

"They are waiting for orders for our little Arabian Armageddon—and for the wars that are to come." He leaned close to Sawchuk. "One day our great army will give the Israelis a fight that the enemy could never have conceived as possible. And the day will come when we will have the strength to light the spark that will set the world at war! We will bring the revolution rushing across the West like a torrent of fire!" His voice cracked.

Now he moved away from the desk, to the window which looked upon the ugly fountain in the courtyard. He stood there, staring out, his feet wide apart, his hands clasped behind his back.

"But the years ahead are going to be very hard," he said. "We must be prepared to survive the fascist tyranny that will crush the life of every bourgeois institution. And *we* will be the authors of that tyranny, it is *we* who must attend at the birth of the monster that is hidden within capitalism. We have no choice. You understand that, Jacques. You do not deceive yourself. You and I know." He was trembling.

Sawchuk did understand, although he no longer believed. Followers of Marx had all had to face up to the great philosophical conundrum: is a brutal, right-wing regime the last stage before cataclysm, before the ultimate war for freedom? Or can a capitalist society transform itself into one of equality through a democratic political process? Those who chose to believe that the non-violent path was correct had joined the democratic socialists. The others remained true to a fundamental Marxist-Leninist prophecy: struggle will bring repression, repression will bring violence, violence will bring the final struggle. And capitalism, after reaching its final, most deformed condition, will succumb forever.

Wurger swung abruptly about to face Sawchuk. "Do you believe?"

"Of course."

Wurger's eyes softened. "Most of us will die in the struggle. The torturers will kill us." He took a deep breath and looked up and smiled. "I have monopolized you. Accept that as a compliment. But you understand. Even Kathë, whose mind and thoughts are wed to mine, even Kathë does not always understand."

A startling dampness in Wurger's eyes. Sawchuk looked away, embarrassed.

"Bakunin wrote that there is no place for love in the revolutionary's world," Wurger said. "Only the cold passion of the revolutionary cause—that is his pleasure and reward." His manner changed suddenly. There was a heartiness. "But I am being stupid. We have talked so closely that I have forgotten that you came here as a stranger. But you are a stranger no more. A comrade, and more than that, a friend."

He put his hand on Sawchuk's shoulder, gripped it, and looked squarely into his eyes.

"I have been a thoughtless host, Jacques. Perhaps you are tired still, from the events of last evening. Did you sleep well?"

"Hardly at all."

"But you were asleep when I arrived."

Sawchuk didn't drop his eyes. "Yes. Finally."

A long pause, while their eyes stayed locked. Then Wurger said, "I believe Kathë thinks most highly of you. And I hope you will think well of her." He punched Sawchuk playfully on the shoulder. "But not too well, yes? Not too well." His smile faded. "Some day the world will know another side of me," he said quietly. "Those who know me better—perhaps some see me as cold, the archetype of the emotionless, efficient Deutschlander. But those who are truly close to me—like Kathë, like Oskar, perhaps you, too, when you come to know me—have learned there is another, truer picture of Karl Wurger. The nightingale, not the shrike. Shall I share another secret with you, my comrade? I, too, am a poet."

20

Thursday, the Chateau

Sawchuk sat on a grassy ledge on the riverbank, composing. Swallows danced over the roiling, muddy river, danced around the river barges that toiled upstream and drifted down.

He had escaped the eerie Rotkommando house at midmorning after faking ebullient spirits over breakfast. The chateau with its dank odour of suppressed fear and misbegotten causes. He had gone outside and strode, frowning, about the grounds of the estate, as moody as Byron. All could see he needed to be alone, to pen the rhymes that would hail the revolution, with a mind free from the mundane.

He had found a spot, warm in the sun and out of view of the house by a grove of willows, and he was recording the Solomon plan in a notebook, in the form of coded poetry.

He felt changed, and good. He had replaced complex old causes with a simple, meaningful one: Save Isaac Solomon's life.

Ruin that ideal.
Bring Gods to earth,
Raise passion's flag . . .

Art joins the functional. Maybe I will publish some of this: addicts of cryptograms will become lovers of poetry. But it was bad stuff, composed according to laws not its own.

He was working with a combined polyalphabetic and open
null cipher. Common prepositions, articles, and conjunctions
would signal a plaintext letter in the following word pursuant
to a predetermined pattern. Only one letter in fifty was
significant, and eighty per cent of the words were nulls, filler.
So Sawchuk had to write great reams of verse just to describe
Operation Solomon. As to what he had learned of Operation
Mecca and the workings of the Rotkommando—these would
have to wait until he had more time. The murder of the
concert pianist was planned for the following night, while
Mecca was a week and a half away, and Sawchuk as yet had no
clear idea of its nature.

He was confident now that he would be able to make a
drop at Orly Sud or Tegel Airports. All he had to do was
phone in, let the Group know when he would be at the
airports. The Group cipher team would be able to break
down his code within seconds: the cipher was keyed into the
Gran Paradiso computer.

Sawchuk had been at work for two hours when he heard a
soft footfall, and he turned to see Kathë Zahre coming
through the trees in a silver-black shirt with billowed sleeves,
tight black leather pants—a Madonna from hell. In her hand
was a bouquet of wild daisies.

"You have found my place," she said softly, and sat on the
grass beside him. "It is a place for a poet to be." She faced
him in a tight yoga sitting position. "I told him I had been
dreaming. I will be in his bed tonight. It is not where I want
to be."

"He doesn't suspect?"

"About us?" She spoke softly.

"About our being in bed."

She gave him an intense look. "Jacques."

"What?"

"We were not merely in bed together. You can be mundane
for a poet."

"Okay, we were in a distant world."

She sighed. "Suspect? He suspects the whole of the universe."

"Kathë, tell me, because he may have seen some wounds I
suffered in that distant world."

Instead of answering, she told a story. "Two weeks ago he
came back from one of his people's sentences. I went to bed
but he refused to come and stayed in the office downstairs,

drinking coffee and brandy, working. He woke me up in the middle of the night. I saw tears in his eyes. He said, 'Do not let anyone know that I am weak.' God knows how much manhood he discharges with every bullet." She spoke with scorn. "To be thought weak, to have it known that he cannot physically fulfil his love, that would be the final horror for Karl. It would pierce his vain shell. Of course he suspects, Jacques. But he cannot let it be known; he cannot admit it to others."

That was small comfort. Still, Wurger seemed not so stalwart a foe as Sawchuk had thought likely. A man with fragile places, blind in his fanaticism. Dangerous from hell to breakfast, that was to be sure. Especially with Kathë Zahre stalking Sawchuk this way. But he would be damned if he was going to let Wurger run him off the ranch. Like a craving coward, as Rocky would say.

"Where is Karl now?" he said.

"In his office. Talking on the radio to Amman or some place." She touched Sawchuk's arm. "We will not be able to pretend for very long. It's so unnatural. Perhaps we should face up to him, confront him with this."

Sawchuk did not like that idea. Randolph Scott had nearly got killed in that showdown in the movie. What terrible plans did she have for him? He suddenly thought: she enjoys this. She enjoys the danger. It was the right mix for this kind of woman: revolution, love, danger.

She looked deeply into his eyes. "It is the way it always comes to me," she said. Vague, ominous words. "Suddenly, without plan." Her hand went to his face now, and traced lines gently upon it.

Sawchuk saw no easy solution to the complexities of this. "Kathë, shouldn't we shift down to low for a little while?" Better: put it in reverse and back up a few miles.

She spoke sharply. "Look me in the eyes, for God's sake. Don't let this fall away from us, don't let the lies take over, or the guilt. We have joined more than our bodies, Jacques. We have . . . don't you understand?"

She looked at him with an expression of disbelief or pity, Sawchuk wasn't certain which. It began to dawn on him that this woman had a neurotic obsession of the most terrible kind—the need to feel in love. It was an explosive mix with nymphomania.

"Let's cool it," he said, drawing her hand away. "I'm going to Berlin with Karl. We can meet afterwards." A soft lie. Afterwards Wurger and his band would be under arrest. Sawchuk would put a good word in for this confused lady.

"Solomon?" she said softly. "Oh, God, not that horrible business. Why, Jacques? Why are you joining in all this blood smearing? Don't go with Karl. Oh, God, take me away."

"I'm exhausted, Kathë. I've got to be allowed to think."

"You don't know what's happening between us. You don't want to face it because you're afraid you can't deal with it. You're afraid like Karl, but in a different way." She said this softly, and moved beside him so the length of her was touching him. "Look me in the eyes, Jacques."

He looked into her sad, deep eyes, and they reached out to him, held him like tight fists. He was awed by the grand edifice of her self-delusion. He had the sense of her aura billowing out in front of her, reaching, grasping, pulling him in.

"Kathë, no."

She kissed him deeply, and he found not the power to resist and responded. She stood up then, and untied a thin cord that held her blouse to her waist, and she shrugged from it, letting it flutter to the grass, baring her breasts. She stepped out of her pants.

"Take me here, by the river," she said, coming toward him, "Take me quickly and I will wait for you in Amman next week."

A bargeman stared goggle-eyed as his craft chugged slowly upstream, and then its pilot house disappeared behind the tall grasses of the riverbank. Sawchuk, looking at her, felt all defences collapse. "What if someone comes?" But he was unbuckling his belt.

"Lovers are invisible."

"Lovers are blind. That is the expression."

That evening, Cuyfer visited Sawchuk in his room. The Dutchman was clutching a bottle of wine and was drunk.

"I have a friend now," he slurred. "I hate these other creeps. You are my fucking brother, Jacques." There was affection in his ugly rat face. "You will be my right gun at Mecca. Our job will be taking out the fucking bunkhouse of the palace guard. We'll bomb them. Bomb, bomb, bomb."

He thudded the heel of the bottle on a chair arm and wine
splashed to the floor. He passed it to Sawchuk, who sipped,
and imagined he could taste Cuyfer's spittle and germs.

Cuyfer wanted to talk about Operation Mecca, and Sawchuk
was happy to let him.

The operation would be an enormous one—upon the palace of a Saudi prince, Aziz, a commission agent whom
Sawchuk knew was reputed 'to be the richest man in the
world—and it was to take place a week from Sunday before
dawn. A force of a hundred and fifty Libyan-trained Rotkommando guerrillas would arrive in Jeddah from Ankara, dis-
guised as Turkish pilgrims on a chartered flight. Already arms
and explosives—enough to blow up the entire palace—had
been stockpiled in a warehouse in Jeddah. The hostages
would include the King of Saudi Arabia and his entourage,
the defence minister and his, and several Americans from the
Typhon Corporation, the Pentagon, and the State Department. They were all gathering at the palace for a ceremony to
sign the deal between the United States and Saudi Arabia for
the provision of a ground-launched Cruise missile system.

Sawchuk had read about the controversial deal in the
newspapers which had made their way to Gran Paradiso. But
he was stunned. How had the Rotkommando gained enough
information about the palace—which seemed detailed—and
how were they to get inside?

"We got somebody inside," Cuyfer said. "Arab chick by the
name of Latifa. Aziz's secretary."

After another half an hour of suffering Cuyfer's friendship—
and playing to it—Sawchuk expressed a tiredness that he did
not have to feign. There was some coarse questioning from
Cuyfer, who wanted to know "what it was like" with Kathë
Zahre, but Sawchuk declined to provide the sought-after
titillation, and finally the Dutchman retreated.

Sawchuk rejoiced inwardly. Operation Mecca, on a grander
scale than anyone from the Group had speculated, had now
been bared to Sawchuk. And there was no need to reduce it
all to code: Sawchuk had recorded all of Cuyfer's words in the
microcircuitry of his watch recorder. All he had to do now
was pass the tiny spool of tape to a Group pick-up man, along
with the Solomon plan, all reduced to code now.

Sawchuk undressed and went to bed. The room still reeked
of Cuyfer's bad smells and bad karma, but finally he powered

himself to sleep, into a darkness of unpleasant-smelling dreams, of nightmares of himself being pursued across a limitless desert, of his body racked with pain, of a billowing ball of flame, and a palace crumbling to the earth.

21

Thursday, May 31, Gran Paradiso

Hesselmann was in his cabin, shrouded with gloom. The agents who had been assigned to follow Sawchuk had slipped up badly last night. They had been drawn off his tail by a false radio call, an order they believed had come from Group radio control in Paris. How could this have happened? And Sawchuk had been identified as the killer of two PLO gunmen in a Rive Gauche bar. God, had Sawchuk gone over to the Rotkommando? Had he himself engineered the false radio call? But Sawchuk had not been told he was under surveillance.

Hesselmann was sipping antacid from a spoon, pondering these imponderables, as Hervé Arnup, one of the bright minds of the combined radio-cryptography group, came bursting into the cabin.

"We have his voice," he said.

"Whose?"

"Wurger."

Hesselmann followed Arnup to the intelligence building.

One of the tasks of radio-cryptography was to scan the amateur radio frequencies. Hesselmann had thought it unlikely that the Rotkommando would be so open as to use the public airwaves, but the use of telephones was also dangerous: internal traces were easily accomplished. And it was clear, with a network as far-flung as the Rotkommando's, quick communications often had to be made between linked cells. So the radio team had been instructed to scan the airwaves for anything that sounded like code, particularly if the pattern repeated itself.

The Gran Paradiso computer had been programmed to scan and record all short, repeated phrases that fit within cryptogram parameters. But there were thousands of these— jargon codes were used by many operators, legitimate and illegitimate.

In the radio-cryptography room, Hervé Arnup played a tape.

"*Gefährlich ist's den Lau zu wecken,*" came a voice.

"That's not Wurger," said Hesselmann. They had tapes, recordings of Wurger's old university lectures.

"No, not yet. It is someone trying to make contact. Every Monday and Thursday at twenty-two hours, twelve minutes, the same phrase. Usually there is no response."

"*Gefährlich ist's den Lau zu wecken,*" Hesselmann repeated. Iambic pentameter. He said it over in English: "It is dangerous to wake the lion."

"The call just came in?" said Hesselmann.

"Yes." Arnup was holding the pause button with his finger. "And at twenty-two hours, seventeen minutes, on a slightly different frequency—just a lucky hit on our scan—we picked this up."

"*Yah, Griffin.*" A high voice.

Then another voice, in German, a sentence that translated as: "*The grapes are fruiting in Lorraine. Over.*"

Arnup again pushed the pause button. "The voice scanner says it is the same person who spoke the phrase about waking the lion."

"Yes," said Hesselmann. "And the other voice?"

The tape played again. "*Unfortunately they do not do so well here.*" Again, a high voice, in German.

"That is Wurger?" said Hesselmann.

"Yes, we have compared voice prints."

"Can you be sure?"

Arnup seemed to take offence. "Voice printing is an exact science with our equipment."

"The phrase about the sleeping lion, that is always on the same frequency?."

"Yes. Then Wurger, I gather, is expected to call back three minutes later for the message. On a second frequency. We have him only the once, but we are monitoring both frequencies continuously now, of course."

"And what do you think they are saying, Hervé?"

"'It is dangerous to wake the lion.' God knows why they picked that phrase. There is not enough in it for us to break it down. It probably means nothing, just a phrase asking Wurger to make radio contact."

"Yes."

"'Yes, Griffin.' Griffin will be Wurger's code name for these broadcasts."

"Griffin. I see."

"'The grapes are fruiting in Lorraine.' I would hazard the theory that refers to the place, date, and time of a proposed meet." Arnup shrugged. "The place might be Katmandu, for all we know. We do not have much material." Arnup sounded apologetic. "The next phrase, 'Unfortunately they do not do so well here': it is formulated as a negative response, but could have an affirmative sense. Wurger is saying, 'I will be there,' or 'I cannot be there.' I could be wrong about all of this."

But Hesselmann knew that Hervé Arnup had an instinctive sense for cryptological meanings.

"Play the voice again," he said.

"*Unfortunately, they do not do so well here,*" came Wurger's voice. Calm, but with an impatient inflection.

"No," said Hesselmann, "the other voice."

Arnup rewound the tape.

"*It is dangerous to wake the lion.*"

"Stop. Replay it."

"*It is dangerous to wake the lion.*"

"Every Monday and Thursday nights?"

"Yes."

"The second phrase, please."

"*The grapes are fruiting in Lorraine.*" An old and tired voice with a barely perceptible wheeze.

"Play for me the other tapes on which you have this voice."

"It is the same phrase: 'dangerous to wake the lion.'"

"I want to hear the voice on the other tapes."

"Do you know who it is, sir?"

"Hervé, in my cabin there are several slim volumes of poetry by Schiller. Find one that is entitled *Das Lied von der Glocke*, The Song of the Bell."

22

Friday, June 1, East Berlin

"It is dangerous to wake the lion, Destructive is the tiger's fang . . . ."

Hesselmann walked east along Unter den Linden and rejoiced at the wonders of the restoration. Methodical and perfect. Communism knows how to do this, to preserve, to return the old things to us. Maybe that is why von Hertz had made his option for the East. The man is essentially a devotee of changeless things, a conservative. And so, essentially, is communism.

"Gefährlich ist's den Lau zu wecken." The voice on the tape had been slower, gruffer than Hesselmann remembered it. But that was thirty-seven years ago.

Hesselmann had not been in East Berlin since the restoration of the Mitte had begun. The buildings and churches of Bismarck's reign had risen from their rubble as if by magic, more perfect as replicas than the buildings they replaced. The great Dom Cathedral on Karl Liebknechstrasse, St. Hedwig's, the German and French cathedrals, and the other churches that the communists had so painstakingly rebuilt—if God is not worshipped here, are not the temples of his religion?

The Dom reflected with dark perfection upon the bronzed-glass wall of the Palashotel by the River Spree. He walked over the bridge and entered what seemed another city, a modern showcase with boulevards and skyscrapers, the great radio tower throwing an immense, spike-like shadow. All so impressive, he thought. So ordered, so correct. He thought of West Berlin with its crass tinsel and vulgarity, but he also thought of its gaiety, its manic life, and he felt sorry for the people walking by on this street, with their forlorn eyes.

He had tried to still his concern about Sawchuk, the man the Group had recklessly bet so many chips upon. If witnesses at the bar in Paris were correct, Sawchuk had fled from there the night before last in the company of Cuyfer and Zahre. Why had he not called in?

It was time to end this strolling about. Hesselmann turned back to the Wall, to the river where the Wall abutted the riverbank above the Reichstag. Here, where a narrow street bumped against the Wall and ended, was a building whose faded sign proclaimed it was the Institut fur International Politik. But Hesselmann knew it was the headquarters for the Intelligence Group of the state security police of the DDR, the Nachrichtendienst. He walked in.

A man in a suit, but with the stiff mannerisms of someone accustomed to a uniform, rose from a desk in the anteroom. "Yes?" he said.

"I wish to speak to the director."

"Who are you? Your identification?"

"Tell him it is Die Schlange. He will see me."

There was something in Hesselmann's manner and speech that caused the officer to know he was used to giving orders. Hesselmann could hear him from a small office, speaking into an intercom. Then the officer called him in, passed a metal detector over him, and pointed to the elevator door. "Go to the fourth floor, sir. Someone will show you in."

On the fourth floor, Hesselmann was taken into a large office encumbered with filing cabinets, with books stacked on library shelves, with Delacroix and Courbet prints upon the walls. Helmut von Hertz, a large, jowly man with a sagging paunch and breasts, was standing with his back to him, staring out a window which framed the deserted and terrible splendour of the Reichstag and the Brandenburg Tor. He wore no jacket and the sleeves of his sweat-stained shirt were rolled to the elbows.

"A scene of ancient glory, Helmut. So still now. Without the drummers and the banners."

Von Hertz turned and looked at Hesselmann, but did not speak for a while.

"You are an old man, Heini," he said at last.

"The knee has finally surrendered. I think most of my stomach is useless. But you are an old man, too, Helmut."

"Nonsense. I am younger than you. By three months, to be exact. I have preserved myself well, don't you agree? I do not look like a wizened, starving goat. Don't they feed you at Paradiso?"

"Nothing feeds the ulcers. Perhaps it is a cancer. I am afraid to find out. I am afraid of doctors. But you have obviously lived better, Helmut. Perhaps the conscience doesn't bother you."

Von Hertz gave Hesselmann a pained look, which made Hesselmann understand that their conversation was being recorded.

"Turn off the tape, please. We will be more comfortable."

Von Hertz sighed, then reached under his telephone and flicked a switch.

"We were so young," Hesselmann said. "It didn't seem so then. Although we were babies, we felt like men when we were in our twenties, full of the Führer's promises of conquest and manhood. We were strong and prideful. Hegelian heroes, fated by a mysterious providence to carry out the will of the world spirit."

"How mindless all that seems to me now."

"You have stopped believing, Helmut. Now you are for the common man, the downtrodden proletariat."

Von Hertz said nothing. He pulled at his shirt where it stuck wetly to his skin.

"How many times have you asked yourself, Helmut, what the Party would do if they found out that during the war you were selling underground fighters to the Gestapo?"

Now von Hertz looked at Hesselmann with the sad eyes of an old beagle. "So. The time has come. You are seeking payment."

"Yes, Helmut, payment." The general found a wooden chair and sat on it, stretching out his game leg, wincing as he adjusted it with his hands. "For double agents, the past is always with us, waiting for the payment of dues."

"What would the Party do? Put me against the wall, I suppose. But no one knows our secrets but ourselves, and you were Himmler's man, too, Heini. What do you think *your* government would do if they found you had been planted by Himmler into von Stauffenberg's camp? The revolt of the generals—what a mockery! Two hundred German officers strangled by piano wire while you pretended to escape across the Swiss border." Von Hertz sighed. "But they would not execute you, would they? It would be too embarrassing. Die Schlange, who penetrated Allied intelligence, gave false briefings, then gave evidence at Nuremberg to implicate former friends, and rose to be head of NATO intelligence. They would not execute you, they would bury you in anonymous retirement and you would be allowed to keep your medals and honours."

Von Hertz turned to the window again, and gazed outside, across the Wall at the winged angel which glowed gold from atop the Victory Column in the centre of the Tiergarten.

"I walked down Unter den Linden, Helmut. It was as if time had stood still."

"Beautiful, beautiful. But my agents come back from the West with their arms full of Western gadgetry, their stomachs full of Western pleasures, and I think they scorn the spartan style of socialism. And I sometimes wonder, too, if I should not have turned to the West. But then I hear about the riots on the other side of the Wall—children hurling cobblestones at police—and I realize that in the end we must win."

"They don't throw rocks at the police here, do they?" Hesselmann said.

"Of course not. This is a peace-loving country. Dull as a medieval hermitage, but no one is unemployed, including me. The Red Army made a good offer. I had the experience and they believed I had the loyalty. It is a job." He groaned and eased into a wooden swivel chair behind the desk, moving a leg up onto a padded stool. "Gout. And to tell the truth, the heart works sluggishly. I should retire."

"I mean it, Helmut. I have come to seek payment."

Von Hertz shook his head sadly. "This is stalemate, is it not? Perhaps I even have the stronger pieces. I did not go to Auschwitz. I did not know. I guessed, but I did not know."

That got Hesselmann like a dagger in the heart. So evil, he thought, so evil. I saw and I knew and I stood by. Would the Rotkommando, the Jew-killers of today, be the final payment? Would destruction of the Rotkommando seal my wounds and give me peace? That is why he feared doctors: he had seen the worst of them. He knew von Hertz had noticed him wince.

"That conscience that you speak of, Heini? Perhaps they *would* arrest you. Bonn is always seeking sacrifices to assuage the anger of the Jews."

Hesselmann had told himself to be ready for this, to take it if it came. "You know I was there only a month, that I had no part in what later happened. You know that Auschwitz sickened me. You, of all people, know. We confided our darkest thoughts."

"But I also know you did nothing about it. At the trials, I recall no evidence from you about Auschwitz. But your war records had been destroyed. By me, your closest friend. Yes, you confided your darkest thoughts. To ensure the survival of our *Weltanschauung* it was necessary to perform those experiments. We must be *hard,* you said. We must be *strong*." Von Hertz thundered the phrases at him cruelly.

Hesselmann spoke slowly. "We were mindless and we were cruel as only mindless men can be. I am now ready to pay the price for youthful venality, the price for Auschwitz, the July plot, everything."

Now there was a long silence, and von Hertz looked deeply into his old friend's eyes, and he knew that Hesselmann meant this.

"So. We are not in stalemate after all. A player can win who makes a bold sacrifice. What do you want, Heini?"

"Wurger."

Von Hertz narrowed his eyes until they were hidden by the folds around them. "Wurger? Who is Wurger to us?"

"I know you are his case agent, Helmut. 'It is dangerous to wake the lion, Destructive is the tiger's fang. But the most terrible of all terrors ...'"

Von Hertz completed the passage for him: "'Is fanatical man.'"

"You live in the eighteenth century, Helmut. Schiller still owns your soul. 'The most terrible of terrors is fanatical man.' You couldn't resist your little joke at Wurger's expense, but he has probably never read Schiller."

Now a soft smile came to von Hertz, and he started to laugh, a hoarse, big laugh, full of admiration, full of relief. "You have monitored the frequency! Excellent work! And so, a tawdry contract is proposed. Former Oberlieutenant Hesselmann wishes to buy from his once-devoted adjutant a worthless piece of merchandise. You may *have* Karl Wurger.

He is yours, a last gift from an old friend." He began to chuckle again.

"Worthless merchandise, Helmut? How long have you been running him? From the beginning?"

Von Hertz dragged himself to his feet and went to a filing cabinet and unlocked it. He shuffled about in a drawer for a while and drew out a photograph. "These were my boys. They were the cream."

Hesselmann studied the picture of young officers grouped in front of a camera. In the middle, with his cold eyes, in a grey uniform trimmed with green, was Karl Wurger.

"He was the best of them. Moody, evil, disobedient, but the best. Born out of the chaos and death of the last days, as the Russians poured across our borders. His mother was a prostitute, a blonde Berlin beauty. She died in the artillery barrage, but we saved the baby. His father was close to the Führer, but his father died, too, in the last days. I once thought I could be the father to replace his own, but he wanted no father; perhaps he could not love. I believe he has a sickness, verging on psychosis, something that is carried in his blood. Anyway, we sent him to Lumumba University in Moscow, then to Finsterwald Camp for the guerrilla training. So much effort spent, and so much training, and so much wasted. But there you go—you send a man into the world to foment a little trouble, and he becomes ambitious, leaves his company, and starts his own. We've lost him, Heini. He is a weed which has gone wild."

"I don't believe you."

"No? Listen to this." Von Hertz reached once again inside the cabinet and drew out a sealed envelope from which he took a reel of tape. He pulled open a drawer of his desk, into which was built a tape recorder, and clicked the reel into it. "As you listen to my voice, you hear a petulant old man whose eyes can barely read the newsprint in front of him."

Von Hertz's voice, reading in English: "'Temperate bachelor, sixties, enjoys bridge, wishes to meet prospective partner of opposite sex, view to enhancing mutual relations.'" The voice switched to German. "That was in the Guardian a month ago, Major. A month ago."

Von Hertz spoke over the tape: "You know the drill, Heini. The advertisement sets the meeting date."

His taped voice again. "Major, are you listening to me?

Three of these, each one week apart, and you ignored all but the final one. I am damned impatient!"

"*I have been very busy, sir."* Wurger's voice, high-pitched, with a distinctly irreverent tone.

"*Very busy with random assassinations. They must end. I see them as quite purposeless. Stop grinning out the window as I am addressing you!"*

"*I was looking at the Reichstag, sir. It must still have a terrible beauty for you."*

"How I would have loved to slap the supercilious smile from his face," von Hertz said to Hesselmann.

"*I thought I had a free hand with this program,"* Wurger's voice continued. "*We don't fight wars with armies any more. That was what you taught. 'Guerrilla Insurgency as an Aspect of Policy'—your paper that we studied. You meant terrorism of course. Divide and confuse. Divide and conquer. Boil up the Middle East stew. I have been fighting the unofficial war while everyone else in the Comintern armies has been playacting."*

"*You have been involved in some damned nonsense. The world doesn't shift a millimetre forward when you take a gun into some Jewish artist's hotel room and slaughter him in front of his wife. What cause is advanced? What conceivable cause?"*

"*I was told to make my alliances where I could. Ghaddafy has given us a list. Am I not to maintain my friendly relations with him?"*

"*How much is that posturing idiot paying you?"*

"*Two hundred thousand Deutschmarks for each name. Not much. It pays for upkeep. May I sit?"*

"*What a liar you are, Wurger. Ghaddafy is paying God's fortune. Just stand where you are."*

"*Is there a reason for that, sir?"*

"*A reason?"*

"*Is there a reason why you want me to stand here? Is it because of this, sir?"* Wurger's voice increased in volume. There was a loud scraping sound.

"The recording device is in the telephone mouthpiece," von Hertz said. "As bold as brass, the man unscrews it and sets it before me. But its batteries continued to work."

"*I thought all our meetings were to be entirely confidential,"* Wurger's voice resumed.

*"I'll be frank, Major. We are pulling back on your reins—
all right, sit down for God's sake. We do not like the way you
ride roughshod over orders, interpret strategies for yourself,
and tactics within those strategies. And, yes, I am keeping
records of our meetings from now on. And we shall be going
on radio control. Twice a week, Major. Monday and Thursday nights."*

"Yes, sir."

"Memorize and destroy."

"I have just given him a note with the frequencies," von
Hertz said to Hesselmann. "The smirk on the man's face
never entirely retreats. It sits there in bud, ready to bloom
again."

"You will remember the first rule," his voice continued.
"Always obey orders."

*"Oh, yes, of course.. Treitschke, one of your Führer's
favourite philosophers. 'It does not matter what you think, as
long as you obey.'"*

"You will remember you are in our service, not Ghaddafy's."
No response.

"And who is next on his assassination list?"

*"Gebayesh, the former Libyan ambassador to Italy. Ghaddafy
has fired him, but he won't return home. We have been asked
to send his corpse back."*

*"To shut his mouth. He has been saying honest things
about that swine. You will not kill Gebayesh. And you will kill
no more Jewish artists and entertainers. We are all disgusted
by your excesses."*

"Even you, Herr General?"

Von Hertz looked at Hesselmann with an expression that
said: what a swine this man is. "As you see, a disobedient
soldier. He killed Gebayesh in Geneva Wednesday night."

"These targets," Wurger's voice went on, *"they are just
pawns in the larger, overall strategy, are they not? It will be
difficult to persuade the Committee to withdraw from our
contract with Ghaddafy. I don't control the Committee. It
enjoys notions of democracy. It is comprised of a confusion of
idealistic morons whose idea of struggle is about as primitive
as a pack of farm dogs. I use them, but I don't quite control
them, General."*

*"Gebayesh will not be killed. And no more Jews. All
assassination issues will be vetted by me. That is understood?"*

"I will do what I can."

"*You will do what you're told!*" Von Hertz's voice roared from the speaker. "*You savage butcher. I see it in your eyes: you love to kill. The bigger the name, the bigger you feel.*" The voice calmed. "*Mondays and Thursdays at twenty-two hours, twelve minutes, the callback three minutes later on the other channel. The radio key will be as follows: 'It is dangerous to wake the lion.'*"

"*Is that Schiller? The seminars were always larded with your literary opinions. I find Schiller rather vapid myself Sir.*"

Von Hertz clicked off the machine. He looked gloomily at Hesselmann. "As you see, Dr. Frankenstein has produced the perfect monster. A monster who finds Schiller vapid. A monster with his own growing army. You can have him, Heini. We would help you eliminate him if we could—he is a liability. But we are not sure if we can find him. I hear now that the Canadian, Sawchuk, has joined up with them. I think Wurger will want to watch that fellow. He may be dangerously ambitious."

Hesselmann found himself sinking into the black gulf of despair. He had been willing to expose von Hertz's anticommunist past—and risk disclosure of his own misdeeds—for Karl Wurger. He would return to Paradiso with nothing. The thought came to him: had Sawchuk become to Hesselmann what Wurger was to von Hertz?

"How many others like Wurger do you have, Helmut?"

The East German general put his hands about his sagging paunch and smiled. "Come, come, Heini."

"You run agents of terror. And the men in Dzherzhinsky Square run you: they smile innocently and show their clean Kremlin hands to the world. As do you. It is the dirtiest form of warfare."

"Show me your clean hands, Heini. Have you washed the blood of Auschwitz from them?" Von Hertz looked scornfully at him. "Anyway, do not tell me that the West does not play these games. Your Group has agents with similar licence. Yes? Perhaps even in the Rotkommando? One of Wurger's 'idealistic morons'? Is that what led you to monitor our frequency? But never mind. To answer, you would have to lie to me, and that would make us both uncomfortable. Well, we have completed our bargain. Now we are both at a standoff again, my ancient friend. Do you want to stay for tea? Schnapps?

We might reminisce. We might remember the days when we were not so old. Poor Heinrich Hesselmann. Poor Helmut von Hertz. We were such innocent, wide-eyed Nazis."

23

Saturday, June 2, Near Paris

"I am not experienced," said Oskar Grubbler. "I will be nervous." He was behind the wheel of a Simca 1308, one of the anonymous-looking cars from the garage of the chateau. They were driving to Orly Sud, along the A-5, through the gloomy forests.

"This your first one, kid?" said Sawchuk from the back seat. His mind was on the problem of getting to a telephone.

"Yes," Grubbler said.

"You're always nervous the first time," said Sawchuk. This Grubbler was a serious one, like his mentor, Wurger, beside him. "Let me tell you a little secret, Oskar. I'm *always* afraid." The grizzled sergeant with the pimply-faced buck private. Sawchuk was feeling better this morning, rested by a long sleep alone in his bed. The sleep would have been more nourishing had he not willed himself to stay near the edge of consciousness. He had wanted to be immediately alert if his bedroom door opened and a visitor came, a visitor such as The Shrike, undergoing an agony of sexual self-doubt that could only be conquered by the discharge of a bullet.

Sawchuk leaned toward the front seat, his head between the right ear of Grubbler and the left ear of Wurger, and he spoke in reassuring tones.

"When I walk into a public building, I'm afraid. I'm afraid when a stranger looks at me. I'm afraid of capture, of torture, of death. I am going to be afraid to walk into Orly

Sud terminal." Sawchuk was denigrating himself in his effort to maintain good terms with Wurger. "I'll tell you something else, kid, I'm scared to pull the trigger. The moment when a man's life eclipses . . . the thought of it torments me."

"It is wrong to feel sorrow," Wurger said in a tired, strained voice. "The face of a man who knows the people have taken vengeance upon him is a revolutionary lesson that renews and renews."

"That's the difference between Karl and me, Oskar. Karl has got steel, the kind of stuff Lenin was made of." He believed that praise fulsomely given reaches the inner heart of all.

"When the guerrilla slays his enemy," said Wurger, "there is a double act of liberation in a single act of pure violence. The victim has been freed from his false role, and the victor has freed his own spirit for authentic manhood. Death is life."

Sawchuk, with elaborate display, pulled his notepad from his pocket and began writing. He was encoding a message now that when deciphered would read: "Request meet, urgent."

The car moved onto the freeway. The sky was low and spitting summer drizzle.

As he wrote, Sawchuk could sense Wurger had turned around and was watching him. He looked up. "I had to get it down. It was one of those pictures that evaporate into the sky if not captured quickly. I am a poet first, a communist second, Karl. I have always believed that the only true poetry is that which joins spontaneous overflow of feeling with rhythmic language in order to embody the correct dialectical visions of the future. Don't you agree, Karl?"

Wurger cleared his throat. "Of course."

Sawchuk turned to Grubbler. "Karl says he has also shared with you the fact that he is a poet."

Wurger seemed uncomfortable. "I am not published, of course."

"Have you read any, Oskar?"

"It is true revolutionary poetry," said Grubbler.

"I'll bet you write some excellent stuff, Karl," Sawchuk said, continuing his seemingly guileless teasing. "More in a classical style would be my guess."

"One day my works may be published," Wurger said. "After I die."

"It's a good way to be remembered," said Sawchuk with false heartiness.

They took a minibus from the parking lot to the terminal.

The airport strategy involved reserving tourist-class seats as far forward on the plane as possible, then separating to arrive at the departure lounge at the last minute, to avoid sitting in one place for half an hour.

Sawchuk separated from the others. He headed for a newspaper kiosk and bought a *Herald Tribune*. Bakerfield's Book said that transfers were to be made inside a folded newspaper, placed on an empty seat in a public area. But the rule also said: don't make a drop unless you are sure a pick-up man is around. And Sawchuk had no reason to believe one was. From the back of the Simca, he had been watching for a tail, had seen no one.

Sawchuk knew he could miss the plane, phone in, ask to be let out of Operation Sawchuk. They would have Wurger and Grubbler at the other end. But not Cuyfer, he thought sadly. Not the rest of the Central Committee. Cuyfer and Zahre were headed to Jordan by plane already, on a safe route across North Africa.

He spotted some coin phones near a brasserie. Wurger was talking into one of them. To whom? Why? Sawchuk decided he would wait in the bar, wait for the last moment, until they were headed for the plane, then phone in fast. The Group could make the pick-up at Tegel. But time was getting short. In eight hours, at twenty-one hours forty-six minutes exactly, Sawchuk and Wurger were supposed to kill Sir Isaac Solomon.

He found an empty table in the bar's darkest corner, ordered a vodka martini, straight up with a twist, and hid behind his newspaper. He looked for the baseball scores. Would this be the year for the Expos?

Only ten of the forty seats in here were occupied. A few stewardesses having coffee. The rest looked like salesmen killing time between planes.

Now a fat little gentleman came stumbling through the smoked glass door. He blinked in the darkness, then took a table next to Sawchuk's. He was dressed in a shiny dark dacron suit that strained to enclose him. He had straight black hair that seemed to grow not just from his scalp, but from his forehead, giving him a simian look. The name tag on his lapel said, "Hi! I'm Frank!" Sawchuk squinted and took in the small print: "Alternate delegate, 34th annual convention, American Society of Mortuary Directors." A little Stars and Stripes pin decorated his lapel.

Frank addressed himself to the bartender. "Hey, fella, you speak English?" The bartender nodded, sizing the man up for tips. "Double bourbon on the rocks."

Frank glanced across at Sawchuk. "You're American, huh? I'm tryna get out of this country. I been here two days, that's enough for me. I can tell you're American because of your face. You got an American face. I know faces. I see faces of the fresh dead. That's my business, making them look good. Also I can tell you're an American because you're holding an American newspaper there, and you're looking at the baseball."

Sawchuk wondered how he could politely ignore him. The waiter brought Frank's drink, and he dropped half of it back in one frantic gulp.

"Here's what happened. I told the guys back home, the Pittsburgh chapter, anyone comes to the convention in Paris with me, I buy them all a meal. The restaurant is the Sink Columns. Watch for it." Sawchuk figured out he meant the Cinq Coulombs, a famous four-star.

"Ended up seven of the guys came over from Pittsburgh, plus four of their wives, plus one of them brought a hooker to the restaurant—she didn't speak English, anyway—and it is like they haven't been eating for a month. Tony Prapp was drunk and started ordering champagne. 'Since, it's on you, Frankie, baby.' Christ, did I get shafted. The bill came in just under sixty-two thousand francs. I asked the waiter to translate this into dollars. I was turning white by this time. I was hoping this was one of the currencies that is worth a thousand to the dollar. It ain't. The bill came to eight thousand, u.s."

Sawchuk checked his watch. Forty minutes before takeoff. He felt like buying this guy a drink, felt like getting loaded with him, flying back to Pittsburgh. He sighed. He had to make that phone call.

"When they phoned the American Express number, they

found my maximum wouldn't cover it. They took every traveller's cheque I had, twenty-five hundred bucks, and they've given me two weeks to pay the balance or they'll start an action. I need a lawyer."

Frank downed the rest of his drink and the bartender was there like a dart with another.

"Fix you up?" Frank asked. "What's the poison?"

"Vodka martini. Thanks."

"So how did the Pirates handle the Expos Wednesday night?" Frank said.

"Seven-four."

"Pittsburgh up? That's great. Gullickson didn't have his good stuff. That puts the Pirates ahead by three. You're an Expos fan, I can see it in your face. Like I say, I read faces. My name is Frank Fager. Fager the Undertager. Food wasn't that great in the Sink Columns neither. What a rip joint. I could of ate better at the McDonald's on Monongahala Boulevard. They had garlic on everything. I came out of there smelling like a skunk's asshole. That's why Pittsburgh smells. It ain't the steel plants, it's the garlic. Them Hunkies eat garlic like hippies smoke dope. It rots out their brains, that's why they're so dumb. Give me a rundown on Berlin quickly. Why are you going there?"

Sawchuk blinked a couple of times, realized he was not at the Mad Hatter's tea party after all. "This isn't by the Book," he said. "No one's supposed to talk to me."

"Fuck the Book. We've got eyes on Grubbler and Wurger, they're nowhere near us. The tickets say Tegel Airport. What's happening? If you've got anything for me just leave it in the newspaper. By the way, we've had a tail on you all along. Bumper beeper under the vw 1300 that Cuyfer was driving when you left Barney's American Bar."

"I've never met you before," said Sawchuk, carefully doing the Book. But he was familiar all right—there had been so many agents flitting in and out of Gran Paradiso. "What's the recognition code?" Only top-level Group had been given his code number.

"H-V seven, double K, three."

Right on.

"I'm still Fager to you. Washington office. I been brought in because I'm known to be good at this."

"You've been following me all along?"

"What do you think we are, Sunday school teachers? Spit it out."

Sawchuk let go a whoosh of release. "All right. You've heard of Isaac Solomon. He's it. The Berlin Philharmonie at twenty-one forty-six hours tonight. In his dressing room during intermission. They've done a hell of a book on Solomon, and they know he insists on being alone during intermission. We go in through the south staff door and wait for him in the guest dressing room. Rotkommando seems to have keys for the whole building. Grubbler is wheel man, Wurger and I do the kill. We pin a note." Sawchuk pulled out the envelope with the micro-negatives and tape and slipped them inside the *Herald Tribune*.

"The general won't want to cancel the concert," Fager said. He looked with hard eyes at Sawchuk and spoke in a low, emphatic voice. "Go in without Wurger. Find some way to volunteer to do this on your own, to keep him out of the building. You don't know Hesselmann—he may be prepared to sacrifice Solomon just to preserve your cover. I've got to split now."

"Don't bullshit me, Fager the Undertaker. No one is going to be sacrificed. *No one*. That includes me. Tell kindly old General Hesselmann that. I've got to have a meet, Fager, right away."

"In the guest dressing room of the Berlin Philharmonie," said Fager. "Tonight at twenty-one forty-six hours. Be there. Don't bring a friend."

Fager stood, picked up the newspaper from Sawchuk's table, and walked past him. "Call me if you ever come to Pittsburgh to die," he said.

24

Saturday, June 2, West Berlin

They met in the parking lot at Tegel, where their sedan was waiting. "I call it my Baader-Meinhof Wagen," Wurger said as he unlocked the trunk. "You see? BMW?"

Sawchuk got it. A real rascal, this Wurger, with a real great sense of humour. He watched as Wurger removed cloth wrappings from two Heckler-Koch nine-millimetre parabellum pistols, and an HK-54 submachine-gun. He handed Sawchuk one of the pistols, took the other, and closed the trunk.

They sat as before, Sawchuk alone in back, Wurger up front beside an unhappy-looking Grubbler, who took the car past the cargo terminal, across the Hohenzollernkanal and along its south side, along Saatwinkler Damm. Sawchuk wished he had a good map. He had been here only once, for a week, many years ago.

"Still nervous, kid?"

Grubbler nodded his head. His face was the colour of yellowed newspaper.

"You look like you're going to throw up," Sawchuk said. "You want to stop the car some place?"

"Just get to the pension," Wurger said.

"Karl, if he's going to get sick on us—"

Wurger spoke sharply to the shaking Grubbler. "All you do is shoot out the terminal box. That is all. You will have the submachine-gun, you know where the terminal box is. Yes? Yes?"

"I can do it."

"At exactly twenty-one hours, forty-six minutes."

"I know. I can do it."

154

"After that, all you have to do is *drive*. You are driving now. It is *not* difficult, yes?"

"I will do my part."

They were heading into the heart of West Berlin. Sawchuk could see the golden angel atop the Victory Column in the Tiergarten. Now they crossed the River Spree, cruised past the Technical University, and moved into the busy streets above Kurfeurstendamm, near the Bahnhof and the zoo.

Grubbler parked about fifty metres from the front door of a five-storey building which bore the sign, "Pension Schickle." They walked to it, past spray-bombed graffiti on concrete walls and hoardings: "*Kampft Mit Den Gefangenen im Hunger Streik*." "Fuck Militarism." The anarchist symbol, the encircled A, was everywhere.

The sign on the heavy, worked doors of the Pension Schickle announced that no rooms were available. Wurger rang four dots and a dash on the buzzer, and the door buzzed back at him, unlocking. They went up a stairway where they were met by a group of Rotkommando recruits. As in Paris they were faceless, witless, staring with wonder at Sawchuk and rushing to press his hand. Wurger seemed annoyed, hissed at him: "We must work. We have final rehearsal."

A tall, sinewy woman, about thirty, gave Sawchuk a firm handshake. "I am Dharla Sayeed. I am the operator of the house. So you are the famous French-Canadian cowboy who never misses." She was smoking a black Sobranie cigarette in a holder. "We must find some time to talk."

"Please," said Wurger, "not now. We must go to the conference room."

Sayeed gave Wurger an unfriendly look. "How is Kathë, poor darling? Do you still beat her?"

Sayeed turned to Sawchuk. "I gather you are to be presented to the Committee in Amman on Sunday. Have you been there, to Jordan?"

"No."

"From Mount Nebo you can see my home, my country."

"Palestine? You were born there?" She shook her head. "I am a second-generation refugee. I have never seen my home except from a distance." She spoke bitterly. "But it *is* my home. Not Jordan, where Hussein massacred our people. Not Beirut, where the Israelis killed my parents. Not Israel. Palestine. One day, comrade, one day."

*   *   *

"We will do this again." Wurger was exasperated. Sawchuk watched as Grubbler drew a shaking hand across his chin, wiping the saliva off.

"Do *you* have it down, Jacques?" Wurger asked.

"At twenty hours, thirty minutes and thirty seconds, we walk from the car in the parking lot," said Sawchuk. "Twenty seconds later, you and I enter the Philharmonie through the south-side staff door, location Number Three. In fifteen seconds we will be in the storage room, which is precisely eleven and one half metres down the hall from the guest dressing room. We wait there until Solomon has completed the concerto. At twenty-one forty-six hours, during intermission, Grubbler shoots the electrical system out from location Number Six, outside. In the darkness we walk eleven steps down the hall, enter Solomon's room, we each fire at him, we pin a note to his chest announcing that we have taken revenge for the Palestinians killed last week by Zionist bombs. Grubbler picks us up just outside location Number Three. We return here."

"So simple," said Wurger. "Even a child can do this work. Do you agree, Oskar?"

Grubbler smiled with white lips.

"We will rehearse it now in fifteen-second phases," Wurger said. "From the beginning."

Sawchuk was standing, pouring coffee into a cup. "Refill, Oskar? You're not going to soil your pants out there, Oskar? Are you?"

"I will be in control of myself." Grubbler's complexion had turned to mottled grey.

"From the beginning," said Wurger. *"Please."*

Sawchuk came over to Grubbler, put a gentle hand on his shoulder, handed him the coffee. "We're counting on you, Oskar. If you screw up we can all be killed. If they capture us, we'll be tortured, you know that." He squeezed Grubbler's shoulder, in a not-reassuring way. "I knew a comrade once, they put him in a cage with thirty starving rats. Ate his face off."

While Wurger in his whining teacher's voice took them through the quarter-minute drill, Sawchuk watched Grubbler as he began to break apart. Grubbler was the ticket. Sawchuk gave him long, cold, and menacing stares.

In twenty minutes, as they were about to leave for the Philharmonie, Grubbler, trying to rise from his chair, almost knocked it over as he turned quickly and headed for the conference room door.

"Grubbler!" Sawchuk barked. Grubbler stopped. "Turn around!"

Grubbler turned around. Sawchuk and Wurger stared at the wide, wet stains on his blue jeans, between the thighs.

Wurger spoke sharply to him in German, a shrill expletive followed by a rain of vituperation that had Sawchuk in awe.

A few moments of fearful silence, then Grubbler began to weep.

"I won't go with him," said Sawchuk. "It's too late to get anyone else."

"I will drive," said Wurger after a few minutes. "It is not necessary to have Oskar. We will not cancel."

"What about the blackout? Who shoots out the lights?"

"You will. You will remain outside. I alone must do the execution."

This was about to backfire, Sawchuk realized. He could not allow Wurger to go into the Philharmonie alone. "This is my initiation, Karl, remember?"

"I am the leader. I will face the danger. It is how I lead."

"Karl, I should be the inside man. Let's apply some cold, hard logic to the situation. The one who should bear the lesser risk is the one more important to the revolution."

Wurger suffered no dilemma, Sawchuk knew, about who that person was.

"There are arguments on both sides," Wurger said after a while.

Sawchuk pulled an American fifty-cent piece from his pocket. "Winner gets to do the people's work," he said. "Call it in the air."

"I will make the decision, comrade."

"Easy one to make, comrade—heads or tails. Call it in the air."

Sawchuk's thumbnail snapped and the coin rang a quivering, low note as it tumbled up toward the ceiling, then started down.

Wurger suddenly screeched: "Heads!"

Sawchuk let the coin fall nearly to belt level, then caught it flat on the back of his left hand, where it hit but bounced as he gave a slight flex of his wrist. The coin wobbled, settled, tails up.

"You will have to kill anyone else who comes into the dressing room, you understand this?"

"Yeah." Sure, Karl, anybody who looks at me, I'll kill. Free the victims from their false roles. Death is life.

"After I have taken out the power, I will wait for you at Location Three. Thirty-five seconds. After that you are on your own."

From the open doorways of the foyer of the philharmonic hall came the dinging of bells. A few late arrivals scurried by, hurrying to the main entrance doors on Matthäikirkplatz. Sawchuk and Wurger crouched low in their car.

"Please, we will synchronize watches again."

That done, Sawchuk left the vehicle, strolled to the building, and quickly let himself inside, unobserved as far as he could tell. He didn't pause at the storage room, but went straight to the guest dressing room, entered it with his key, stepped into the darkened room, closed the door.

"Don't shoot him," came Frank Fager's voice. "He's one of ours."

A dim table lamp clicked on in the corner. Two men dressed in the uniform of the Berlin police were standing in the far corners, pistols aimed at him. Fager was standing just beside the door, his own gun out.

The allegro sounded from a speaker overhead, the themes being introduced, Solomon's fingers rippling over the keyboard.

Fager was dressed in tails, black tie. Sawchuk guessed there was a pillow down the front of his pants. His hair was grey, curly.

"You figure I've got the right weight for him?" Fager said. "Solomon's kind of a paunchy guy. Doesn't have to be perfect—the photographers are only going to get a view of my back, with a bullet hole in it. We have men in the lot outside. We know Wurger's there. Good job, Sawchuk."

Sawchuk sat down on a wooden chair. "You can't fake Solomon's death for very long. Does this mean I'm being pulled out?"

"We'd like you to stay in the ring for the whole card, comrade. Only a few more rounds to go." Fager sat at the dressing table, began to affix a grey goatee to his chin. "We want you to go with Wurger to Jordan, to the Central Committee meeting in Amman."

"I should have known." He had dared hope this would all be over here.

"We figure the Amman office will have everything, addresses of the other houses, details of the Mecca plans."

"You've got everything. Wurger's notes. Forty-seven pages that I photographed.

"You don't read German, do you, Sawchuk? I'll tell you what you photographed. Forty-seven pages of an epic poem. Wurger's own vision of Götterdämmerung. Watch your ass, man, this guy can really write poetry." He grinned at Sawchuk. "And it's not in code, that's what the cryptanalysts say. Can you tell me anything more about Mecca aside from what was on your tape? How did you get Cuyfer drunk? That was good."

Sawchuk shrugged. "Did the tape read all right?"

"Perfect."

"That's all I know about Mecca. What does it matter if you're taking them in Amman?"

"Maybe we want more than the Committee. Maybe we want to grab the army, too, all hundred and fifty of them."

"I'm not going to Misurate. Or Mecca."

"Don't be such a chickenshit."

"Listen, things have got kind of sticky for me. Kathë Zahre has been coming on pants afire. I'm into a *domestic* scene, a triangle. With a psychopathic killer at one of the points."

"Good. Keep using that midnight magic."

The sound of scattered, delicate coughing from the speakers. The adagio began.

"We can keep Solomon under wraps only for a week or so," Fager said. "Mecca is planned for next weekend, and that's when we'll make our move: at Mecca's gate. Wurger, Cuyfer, the Committee, the army—we'll net the whole school of fish at one time. That's when we'll pull you, Sawchuk."

"One more week," Sawchuk said.

"A week—that's not too much when you figure what we've got invested in you. Then you can retire and go to seed."

Sawchuk heard flutes, then Solomon's fingers moving over the keys, dancing.

"One more week," Sawchuk repeated. "Somehow I'd like to see that in writing from Hesselmann."

"I got Hesselmann's proxy," said Fager. He smiled and reached into a small bag, pulled out a bottle of stage blood. Then he took off his tails, cut a ragged hole in the back with scissors and splotched some of the stage blood on it. "The photographers won't be allowed past the door."

"I don't like this job," Sawchuk said. "I've got Fatah gunmen all over the place looking for me."

Fager's voice went soft. "Listen to that music. The Shrike would have destroyed that sound. You saved Isaac Solomon's life and you saved his art. Save some more art. Maybe the next famous Jew will be a poet."

"Maybe the next famous poet will be me."

"We're taking Solomon to a private room at intermission," Fager said. "He'll stay there until everyone leaves, then we'll sneak him off to a safe house. You got the note?"

Sawchuk handed him Wurger's revenge note. Fager glanced at it, pinned it to his sleeve, checked his watch.

"We'll try to make contact again in Amman," he said. "I'm going to give you a phone number and some safe addresses there. Incidentally, the European Group Seven number is scrubbed as of now. We'll give you a new one and a new agent recognition code. Okay, we've got twenty minutes for a full debrief. When the lights go out, you fire a couple of shots into the wall, then get the hell out, jump into Wurger's car. Nobody's gonna shoot you by mistake, and we'll have a tail on you."

The room was still echoing with gunfire as Sawchuk slipped out the door in the darkness.

"I guess we'd better tell the local *polizei* what's going on," said one of the men in uniform. Hysterical crowd sounds came through the speaker. A voice on the p.a. system was trying to give calm directions to evacuate the building. "Your friend Hesselmann is going to be unhappy."

"He ain't a friend of mine," said Fager. "Sawchuk is ours now. Belonged to us all along, anyway. Get out and guard the door."

The two uniformed men hurried from the room. Fager smiled a pleased smile to himself, then went down on his stomach and played dead.

Wurger was sure they were being followed. He could not figure that out. A car had picked them up just outside the

Philharmonie parking lot, had stuck with them despite his
evasive tactics along the streets south of the Tiergarten. He
turned north, toward the Hallesches Tor U-bahn station.

"Where are we going?" said Sawchuk, slouched low in the
seat beside him.

"We must shake them. I have an alternate route, where
they cannot follow."

They parked near the subway station, and Wurger led
Sawchuk quickly down the steps to the northbound Number
Six platform of the Alt-Mariendorf-Tegel line. It was an old
subway route, built many years before the war, and it passed
beneath the Wall, beneath the centre of the old city, the
Mitte, where the East sector bulged like a distended gut into
the West.

The trains which ran this route, carrying West Berliners
across the Mitte, were required to slow at the darkened,
empty underground stations of the East Sector, but they were
not allowed to stop—except at Friedrichstrasse which, like
Checkpoint Charlie, provided a border crossing for visitors
from the West. Then the train, after trundling by more
ghostly stations, would pass under the Wall again, into the
District of Wedding, in the West city.

They worked their way into a boisterous, late-night crowd
at the subway platform. A group of young men and women
sang beery football songs. A long-haired youth, his upturned
cap in front of him, played a saxophone. An aging drunk
tottered down the stairs.

Not so drunk, Wurger thought. Maybe not so old.

He and Sawchuk nestled into the thick group at the edge of
the platform as the north-bound train swept into the station.
They found seats near the back of the coach, and the drunk
sat across the aisle, closed his eyes. As the train moved
ahead, the man seemed to rock himself to sleep.

Why were they being followed? Wurger wondered again.
If the pigs were onto them, why did they not try to make
an arrest? They would have two of the world's most-wanted
men: the guerrilla king and the man whom Wurger believed was a secret pretender to his throne, the killer of
Isaac Solomon. One more shiny badge for that bastard
tonight. His last. Wurger thought of Kathë Zahre. He
remembered the welts that he had seen on Sawchuk's

back, remembered the smile on his face, the smug, sneering, deceitful smile.

A headache suddenly claimed him. He tried not to think of her, for when he did, such headaches always came. And lately he had been suffering something worse than headaches; temporary slips from reality. Von Hertz had told him his mother had been schizophrenic. He had begun to fear it was hereditary.

The train accelerated then braked as the deserted platform of Stadmitte station came into view. Wurger saw the lone guard pacing outside, grey uniform trimmed with green, his head bowed, not interested in the train. As it slowed further, Wurger suddenly stood up, pulling Sawchuk by the arm. He wrenched the doors open and the two men skipped onto the platform, running lightly to keep balance. The guard did not see them, but from the train the drunk did. Wurger turned around, smiling a little, and caught a glimpse of him in the coach, his eyes wide open now and conceding failure.

Wurger led Sawchuk to a darkened stairwell, and they moved up toward Mohrenstrasse, dark at night as most streets were in East Berlin, even on weekends.

"I hope you know what you're doing," Sawchuk whispered.

"I know what I am doing. They do not expect people to sneak into this country. Only out."

"How do *we* get out?"

"I have friends, comrade." Von Hertz would have heard the news about Solomon by now. He would not be pleased. But fuck him. Fuck them all. Wurger was his own man.

They walked for three-quarters of an hour, staying away from the activity to the north, the Mitte, Marx-Engels Platz. They came to a wooded park. Wurger pointed to a bench. "Wait here. I will make arrangements."

Sawchuk did not like this at all. He had been on this bench an hour. A nightingale had sung to him for a while, but its notes had grown sadder and sadder, and finally faded.

Seven more days. He could make it. Hell, he was doing okay. In the space of two days he had already worked his way into the heart of the world's most feared terrorist group. Jacques Sawchuk, Master Spy.

He had a time limit now. He could begin to think about the future—happy years playing his flute and tossing basketballs into hoops. Happy years contemplating the foolishness of man, a source of much poetic inspiration.

Happy years. Like those years in Cuba. But he felt altered. Could he go back to that former life? Did he want to?

Questions such as these played in his brain as it was smashed nearly to oblivion by a foot-long length of stainless steel water piping that bent twenty degrees upon his head.

25

Saturday, June 2, Palo Alto, California

"Yes, Hank?" George Boschuff, a sixty-five-year-old with a whispery voice, leaned back against his brother's personal office computer, a Typhon 2090. George and Fred Boschuff each held one common share in the corporation that built the machine, the only two voting shares ever issued.

Naiboldt always felt a chill when near these men. The chill one gets when near power. And the Boschuff brothers *were* power. They had parlayed guns and silicon into an empire that stretched from California around the world, with a major intermediate stop in Washington, D.C. The President took advice from them, Naiboldt knew, and they were "Ronny" and "George" and "Fred" to each other.

"Yes, Hank, is there a problem?" said Fred Boschuff. He was eight years younger than his brother, was more relaxed, had more West Coast America in him. Fred *related*, the California way. But menace lurked behind his bland smile. Fred Boschuff was standing by his brother at the console of the computer playing an Atari program.

"It's about a reporter, a man named Charles Rubinstein," Naiboldt said. The three were alone in the air-conditioned jungle of indoor plants that was Fred Boschuff's office. Naiboldt had asked for the meeting. Senator Stoffard Johnson had been on the phone this morning.

"Rubinstein is the man who wrote that newspaper article about you two years ago," George Boschuff said.

"The article that got you pink-slipped by the Pentagon," said Fred. "The article about kickbacks." *Bip, bip, bip,* went the computer.

"I've got fifteen messages from him in the last three weeks." Naiboldt cleared his throat. "He wants to interview me."

"No," said George. A softly spoken syllable that made the hairs tickle on Naiboldt's neck.

"This morning he left a message saying he wanted to talk to me about the Glickums sale."

"Hank," said Fred, "you promised no problems. If there are problems, we cut the line and you swim to shore yourself. If you can make it." *Bip, bip, bip.* Zang. "Got him."

"What newspaper does he work for?" George said.

"He sneaked into a Stoffard Johnson press conference with *New York Times* credentials. I've found out they're false. Johnson is shitting bricks."

"Find out more," said George.

"I have a tail on him."

"No problems, Hank," said Fred. "No problems, remember?" *Bip, bip, bip.*

Charles Rubinstein was in his Upper West Side apartment, drowning in a cesspool of despair. The Senate vote was a little over three weeks away, and the story was as much a non-item as when he had started on it. Nailing it down had become a neurotic obsession, something threatening to break him.

He had made phone calls, attempted to arrange interviews with the three suspected senators, but had been unable to get past the third or fourth secretaries. Several days ago he had gone to Washington, used his false *Times* identification to sneak into a press conference given by Stoffard Johnson, who was announcing a new nuclear submarine facility in his State. Charles's questions about the Cruise bill were cut off. So was his question about dealings Johnson had with Typhon lobbyists.

Charles was living on credit cards, was three thousand dollars in the hole. Not knowing where his next dollar was coming from, he pulled out his wallet, examined those seven bleak one-dollar bills in it, and decided to spend them on a six-pack of brown ale.

He trudged from his apartment to the nearby deli-cum-grocery, picked up the ale, and was wending his way back home when a large man stepped out from the shadows and began to walk beside him.

This is how it will end, then, thought Charles. A switchblade between his back ribs. Mugged by a New York psychopath. *Well-known journalist Charles Rubinstein today was stabbed to death fifty yards from his apartment building. He was thirty-two.*

"Just relax. Don't look behind. Act natural."

"I'm going up to my apartment. The next building."

"I know where it is. I'm going there with you."

"You like Newcastle Ale?"

"I could use one. I'm going public, Charles."

Charles unlocked the door, held it open for Rufus McKay, and they walked together to the stairs and went up to the fourth floor without talking. Nor did they talk until they were sitting around Charles's rickety kitchen table, glasses of foaming warm ale in their hands.

"I drove all the way out from Washington," McKay said. "I've been waiting outside ever since it got dark. I felt I owed it to you to let you know first."

"You're giving me the story? First shot?" The world had suddenly proved to be a grander and more beautiful place.

McKay pulled a portable tape recorder from his pocket. "Hank Naiboldt phoned yesterday morning to make an appointment to see me. I set up a bug under the desk." He pressed fast forward and watched the numbers spin by, found his place.

"Look, Ruf, there are a few, er, dollars floating around over this thing. It's tied up with your joining the board of Typhon when you get into civvies."

"What are you talking about, Hank, a payoff?"

"Naw, an up-and-up deal. I know you're a straight soldier, Ruf. I just want to see if I can change your mind about something here, just a little matter of philosophy. I'm not trying to buy any votes. We'll be asking you to join Typhon whether or not you go along with us on this thing."

"Would that matter of philosophy have anything to do with our policy towards Israel, Hank?"

"You know you're wrong, Ruf, you know it in your heart. Israel is no longer the key piece on the chessboard out there. We've bought their line for thirty-three years, and we've lost everything in the Middle East now except Egypt and Jordan and Saudi Arabia, and Jordan has started to turn to Russia, and I'll give you eight to five that Egypt goes back to them soon, too. Then it will be the Saudis. We picked the wrong side. Russia picked the right one. They're better chess players."

"Remember when we were both at the Point, before the war? You said then, too, we picked the wrong side. We should be with Hitler, you said. Destroy the Russians."

"The history of this century hasn't all been written. We could have destroyed communism if we'd gone with Germany. In twenty years communism will destroy us. Not with nukes. The Reds nibble at the world like an artichoke, leaf by leaf, until they reach the heart."

"I know who our enemies are, Hank, and I know who are friends."

"Our friends are the people with the oil. Oil still fuels the world."

"You're wrong, Hank, but what difference do my opinions make? I'm a soldier. I have no right to express them."

"Don't play those innocent games with me, Rufus. I worked under you for too many years up here. You're part of the strategy team. You've been trying to swing other generals behind you on the anti-Cruise thing you've been organizing in the Pentagon."

"What difference does it make now? The President lost in the House, but he's got the votes in the Senate. The votes you told me you bought and blackmailed from three guys."

"Hey, Ruf, that was drunk talk. I hope you haven't gone around repeating stuff like that. There's been a reporter nosing around. You wouldn't have talked to anyone, would you?"

"Oh, come on, for Christ's sake, Hank."

"You must have been making some waves," McKay said to Charles. "He was scared."

"Look, pal, the vote's just hanging in the balance. When the bill comes up on June 26, who knows if someone's gonna change his mind because he hears of the rumblings you're making in the strategy team. Let the State Department run foreign policy, Ruf."

"Maybe we should let Typhon run it."

"*Better than letting the Jews run it. And they're doing that, aren't they? That gorgeous Jewish artist you keep in New York—are you letting her help run our foreign policy?*"

There was a pause. No voices out of the recorder for a few moments. Charles was embarrassed.

"*You know about her.*"

"*Well, you know, Typhon's got this investigative team.*"

"*An investigative team. Are those the guys that go around getting the goods on people? Like Senator Budd, that lover of little boys?*"

"This is based on some of the stuff you came up with, Charles," the general said, smiling, taking a gulp of beer.

"*. . . Budd—how did you guess? I don't remember I said his name. Rufus, I told you that stuff in secrecy.*"

"*While you were drunk. Anyway, what's your offer, Hank? How much is my vote on the strategy team worth?*" The voice was like ice. "*Maybe not eight million, maybe I can't demand a senator's price.*"

"*Ruf, I know you haven't told anybody. I'd have my ass in a federal jug by now if you had. As far as the file on the lady in New York is concerned, look, I had nothing to do with it. The Boschuff brothers ordered reports on everybody who might have some influence over this. You wouldn't believe how many senators keep mistresses. I ordered your file destroyed.*"

"I'm sure he was lying all the way," McKay broke in.

"*. . . Ruf, we've been buddies since we shared up-and-down bunks at the Point. We've duck-hunted in the prairies every year since the forties. You and Joan and Janey and me, we used to be like one family before Janey and I moved to Palo Alto. I know you sometimes think I get into shady things. Sergeant Bilko, right? Made it all the way to four-star general. But I've always felt you were the one guy I could talk to, the one guy I could get it off my chest with. That's why when we were out hunting last fall, maybe I opened my mouth a little too much.*"

"*Who were the other two senators, Hank? Let's see how honest you're prepared to be with me.*"

"*Ruf, this room isn't bugged?*"

"*Of course not*"

"*You aren't going to fuck your best friend around. You'll never say anything.*"

"Hank, you're still my friend, despite everything." He pushed the stop button.

"I felt shitty. But he wanted to talk about it, wanted to boast. That's what they say about crooks, isn't it? They get hanged by the tongue. They feel compelled to talk to someone."

The tape resumed. "Nobody knows but the Boschuff brothers in California. And Aziz, who's got the tapes and the film in Mecca. I did a fuck of a job, Ruf. Had cameras secretly installed in their homes, transmitters. These weren't Watergate plumbers we put together for this one, they were Grade A ex-Agency. Only bad thing about it is I'm in the movies, too. Couldn't avoid that. These guys weren't going to talk to underlings."

"Satisfy my curiosity, Hank. Who did you buy?"

"Well, you got Senator Budd, all right. He's the baby-snatcher. Set him up in his Boston bedroom. A kid prostitute, fuzzy cheeks, thirteen. Stoffard Johnson, he's the eight-million-dollar man. He ran into a little land investment hassle down in New Orleans, but he's bailed out now. Jack Grodsky came in a little cheaper, at seven, but he was the easiest of them all."

"He was looking at me as if I should be applauding," McKay cut in.

Charles Rubinstein was blinking.

". . .the offer?" McKay's voice.

"Okay, we can be square with each other now? My cards are all face up. Ruf, it's a good offer. We'll wait until you're out of uniform. Typhon will take you onto the board, full director's salary of three hundred grand a year. Plus a bonus the first year. It's not like being a civil servant, old buddy."

"How much is the bonus?"

"Seven hundred and fifty big ones."

"That's the starting offer? Am I supposed to negotiate—work up from there?"

"Typhon gets good tax advice. You'll get to keep most of it."

"Is the money from Saudi Arabia?"

"That's who we're doing the contract with. And we'll get it if the Senate goes our way twenty-five days from now. But we don't want any waverers in there who think the Pentagon is just lukewarm. Give us some more support in there, Rufus."

"Hank, as Typhon builds the Glickums installations, they

*are at the same time training Saudi technicians to program
the missiles."*

"I started to blow it here. Couldn't hold the anger back."

*"We haven't been making any public statements about
that,"* said Naiboldt's voice.

"They'll use them to first-strike Israel, Hank."

"Aw, for Christ's sake."

*"You're not trying to buy my vote on the strategy team, are
you? You know my opinion means very little outside the
Pentagon. You're trying to buy my continued friendship.
Because with that comes silence. For nearly a million dollars
the first year, three hundred thousand every year after that,
you buy my loyalty."*

*"Get on board, for Christ's sake, Rufus. The contract is
worth thirteen billion to the u.s. government. These are hard
times in America. The White House wants this one bad."*

*"They won't want it so bad if they find out about the
gratuities to the senators. Get out of here, Hank. You can tell
the Boschuff brothers to piss up a rope."*

McKay stopped the tape. "I'm prepared to blow this whole
thing sky high. You can run the story in the *Times* the day
after tomorrow. I need a little while to get myself prepared. I
am going to write an open letter to the President."

Charles felt as if he had drawn the million-dollar ticket in
the State lottery. Why not the *Times* indeed? He would get
the political editor on the phone tonight. Thoughts of Pulitzer
prizes danced in his head.

"Do you have a dupe of the tape?"

"I made one. It's in the glove compartment of my car. But I
should keep both."

"Let me put this on my machine. I've got five thousand
dollars' worth of stereo equipment here. It'll take fifteen
minutes."

McKay looked at his watch. "I'm expected at Barbara's for
dinner. I'm late. And I should stop off for some wine."

"My mother gave me a bottle of '53 Thérie Côtes du
Rhone. It's for when I get married. I'm a confirmed bachelor,
General. Fifteen minutes. She loves you, she'll wait for you."

McKay smiled. He had grown fond of this idealistic young
reporter. "Charles, you've stuck with me for four and a half
months on this thing. Sure, take the tape. There's a liquor
store on Seventy-Ninth Street. Do they have a reasonable

selection there? Never mind, a good California will do. Bring my recorder and the tape when you've finished, meet me there."

The general left. Charles was almost freaking out at the riches that had been bestowed upon him. He babbled to himself as his fingers fumbled about the reel-to-reel recorder, pushing buttons, flicking switches. "Get the quality right, check out these record levels, left channel, right channel. There is a God. There is a God after all." There was a moment of paranoia. "No, not the reel-to-reel. That's the first place anyone would look. Put it on a cassette. They'll never look there."

He fumbled through his enormous library of stereo cassette tapes, several hundred of them filed alphabetically on shelves. "What do I hate most? What do I hate? Punk rock. Here. *Mad Morgan and the Assassins of Moog*, one of the all-time worst albums. I'll tape over that. Volume level. Amplifier on tape one to tape two. Check these wires. Jeez, have I got that right?" He scrambled through the jungle of cords leading to receiver, amplifier, pre-amp, recorders, speakers, making connections from one cassette machine to another.

Okay, come in General Naiboldt. Speak to me. Whisper sweet words of corruption."

"Look, Ruf, there are a few, er, dollars floating around...."

Charles filed the tape back under M for Mad Morgan, and raced out of the apartment with the original and the general's portable machine.

McKay was standing in the shadows near the liquor store. "Thank you," he said. "Good luck on the story."

"Thank *you*, General. And God bless you."

McKay flicked a wave at him, then walked down the street. Charles saw him go to the driver's side of his parked Buick. He saw him unlock the door and bend to get in.

Suddenly there was a flash of fire and a *whump*! as if a land mine had exploded. Another explosion tore the roof of the car off. Nearby apartment windows swelled inward and burst. Bits of upholstery and glass and General McKay showered the street.

Charles, half a block away, felt the rush of hot wind, felt it like a wind from hell, and staggered back a step. He became nauseated.

He was aware of people yelling, people pouring into the street, people pushing past him as he stood there dazed, mouth open, doing nothing, waves of horror passing through his head. He watched as a human ring formed tentatively around the wreckage of the Buick and of the cars nearby. The Buick was a charred shell and flames were licking at it. A distant wail of sirens.

A car-seat bomb, Charles thought.

Get out of here, he said to himself. Phone the *Times*. Jesus, phone the *police*.

He shouldered through the crowd to his apartment building. Five people were standing at the entrance, agitated.

"What happened? Was someone killed?

"You could hear it from my bedroom."

The sirens got louder.

Charles ran. up the stairs to the fourth floor. He unlocked his door and stepped inside.

"Hello, Mr. Rubinstein. We're your new roommates. We're going to be living with you for some time. And we are going to have long talks."

V

The Land of Fear

Still eyes look coldly upon me,
Cold voices whisper and say—
He is crazed with the spell of far Arabia,
They have stolen his wits away.

Walter de la Mare

26

Tuesday, June 5,
the Casr al-Akbhar Saudi Arabia

Sawchuk had broken contact with the continuum. Time had separated into unrelated particles. One distant memory: of surging forward from a park bench, and the grass rising up toward him, and then death coming, blackness within pain, the way he had suspected it would be, blackness within pain, regret, lost chances, oblivion.

In death, still other memories. Memories of his corpse surrendering its captive mind-spirit, memories becoming fragmented, misshapen memories of the body being carried, of speeding darkly, of a broken-toothed smile.

Rolling, rolling. A sensation of climbing fast into the air, the roar of jet engines... fragmented, unrelated pictures of wrists and ankles all bound together by loops or rope. The cabin of a plane, coldness... his body rolling on the floor, the broken-toothed man smiling... the plane climbing into yawning space.

A fragment of stillness. Then the sound and feel of a great roaring wind, hands grappling, knees bumping over gravel, the *wang-wang-wang* of helicopter blades at idle speed, their great roar now, another force carrying him away from the earth.

Awakening to another silence. And heat. A fragmented memory of being a trussed animal in a baking oven as large as infinity, and a great sun sitting cruelly and high above a barren plain.

Sawchuk's doubting, agnostic soul had been delivered into hell. For two days and two nights his mind continued to emerge briefly from blackout, continued taking snapshots, pictures of the hot, dark pit of Hades where the tormented writhed and screamed, naked men like him, and where fires scorched the walls to whose stones the damned were chained.

During the third night the concussion abated and he was granted the cruel gift of consciousness. He became aware of the mad drummer in his head. He was hungry and dehydrated. He did not know where he was or how much time had passed.

He found he could not stand fully upright, for the chain which bound his wrists was welded to a ring in the wall only two feet from the floor. He could sit down, he could lie down, or he could stand in a crouch. When he lay down, lizards and rats ran over him.

Hell is where you cannot stand up and stretch. Hell is the sound of the moans of the men chained to the wall on either side of you. Hell is a place where there is no water.

Oil-soaked torches licked flames upon the walls. Battery-powered lamps shone spotlights upon each of the six naked prisoners. A generator chugged from somewhere behind the walls.

Collating the disconnected bits of information that his brain had recorded, Sawchuk knew he had been kidnapped, flown to an Arab country, was in a terrible prison, a long hall, two hundred feet long, only twenty feet across. Sawchuk was near one end of the hall, between two other men. The other three prisoners were at the far end, near some stone steps which led up to a thick trap door. All six men were chained to rings cemented into the rocks. The man to Sawchuk's right, about six feet away, was young, had a trim moustache and terrified eyes. He tried to say some words to Sawchuk, but could speak only Arabic. The man six feet to Sawchuk's left was elderly, with long, wild hair. He spent most of his time in prayer.

But when the morning light entered through the high, slit windows, the old man turned to Sawchuk and said in English: "Do not count the days of the months which may never belong to thee."

"What place am I in?" said Sawchuk in a hoarse voice.

"A place called Death."

Upon receipt of his damaged goods, Colonel Bisharat had been angry, because Mohammed ibn Mohammed had clearly

not measured his strength, had delivered a blow that might
have cleaved a normal man's skull apart. But this Sawchuk
was a giant of a man, a Samson in the pay of the Marxist
infidels.

Bisharat controlled his anger, submitted it to the discipline
of Islamic ethic. What is written is written. If he dies, he
dies. As God wills. *Insha Allah.* And if the terrorist lives to
talk about the Rotkommando and its plans for Mecca, then
praise be to God.

Of those plans, the head of the Saudi Special Security
Force knew nothing. Only the one word: Mecca. A word that
General Hesselmann of Group Seven International had passed
on to him almost nine months ago. Bisharat understood,
although it was not said in so many words, that the Group
had unsealed the lips of a Rotkommando detainee before he
was killed.

Mecca. Colonel Bisharat had been embarrassed in 1979,
when several hundred fundamentalist zealots had seized the
Grand Mosque, which was rewon only after a week, and only
with the help of French advisers. The eighty captured men
had been beheaded in public ceremonies in the major cities
of Saudi Arabia. Bisharat was determined not to be caught by
surprise again. Especially where Islam's holiest city was
concerned.

So Bisharat had made the PLO an offer of major funding—a
third of a million dollars in gold—should that organization
deliver to him a high-ranking member of the Rotkommando.

Four days ago an anonymous caller—perhaps responding to
the PLO's own hundred-thousand-dollar reward for such
information—telephoned the PLO mission in East Berlin to
advise that a high-ranking Rotkommando guerrilla would
soon be visiting that city. He had called again that night,
giving precise information. Mohammed ibn Mohammed, at-
taché to the PLO mission representing Fatah, the military
wing, had delivered the goods, one Jacques Sawchuk,
transporting his coffined cargo from East Germany under
diplomatic cover in a PLO executive jet. The plane had flown
directly to the huge Saudi military base at Tobuk, not far from
Israel. From there, Mohammed and Sawchuk had been removed by helicopter to the Casr al-Akbhar near the western
sands of the Nafud Desert in north Arabia.

The Casr al-Akbhar had been built by the Christians at the

time of the Fourth Crusade, one of a string of such fortresses
from Antioch south to the Red Sea. It sat beside a wadi, a
six-foot-deep gulch, whose winter floodwaters had over many
centuries chewed stone and gravel from a high bank,
undermining one of the fortress's great square walls. Now
that wall was held up by reinforced concrete buttresses, but
some of the massive stones of the wall had loosened, were
cracking and separating.

The walls were three feet thick. Huge chambers surrounded
an inner courtyard which was open to the sky. Some of the
chambers were open, too, because their roofs had fallen in.
The basement dungeons had not held prisoners since the
Dark Ages, but held them now.

A thousand years ago there had been an oasis here, where
the Nafud's enormous western dunes—mountains, really, thousands of feet high—surrounded the little wadi, a tributary of
the great Wadi Fajr which carried winter waters north, to the
depression of the Sirhan in Jordan. There was no oasis now.
The tamarisk and date palm and *ghaf* trees had withered and
the waters had dried up within a hundred years after Saladin
stormed the fort and quartered all the people within it. A
superstition of the bedouin tribes of the Nafud held that the
blood of slaughtered Nasrani had dried the waters. Now only
a well existed, surrounded by scrub trees, and the water was
flavoured with camel urine.

The signs posted on the desert tracks nearby, used by
herders of sheep and goats, advised that restoration work was
being done here by the Division of Antiquities of the Minis-
try of the Interior. A few prefabricated structures had been
trucked here, set up near the crumbling south wall of the
fort. The workmen who had built the concrete buttresses had
been housed in those buildings, but the workers were gone
now, and the buildings were used as bunkhouses and kitchen
for the officers of Saudi Special Security who were stationed
here.

The castle had been saved from ruin not for the sake of
history—the history of the brief Christian occupation was a
shameful one—nor for tourists, for the gates of the Kingdom
of the Sauds were closed to all foreigners except businessmen
and contract workers. The castle had been restored solely to
serve as cover for operations that the sss Force wished to

carry on in privacy. Those operations mostly involved the questioning of political prisoners.

It was a good location, far from the vestiges of Saudi civilization. Occasionally a Western journalist found his way into the kingdom, and because such persons pried into matters best shared between only the masters of the kingdom and their God, the existence of this facility was known to very few.

Bisharat did much of the interrogation work at this place by himself. He was good at it, enjoyed it.

Colonel Kamal Bisharat was a man of medium height with a grey goatee and the sharp eyes and nose of a desert hawk. His uniform was the long Arab shirt, the *thaub*, which dropped almost to his feet, and a red-checkered *kaffiyeh*, the headdress, which was held to his head by a double cordless *agal*, used in former days on the desert to hobble camels. Bisharat's only signs of station were a curved dagger which hung from a loop at the centre of his belt and a large sapphire ring which he wore on the middle finger of his left hand. He had a string of worry beads around his neck which he often fingered.

Bisharat was a second cousin to the King. Under him, the SSS Force enacted its own laws for its conduct. It was unquestionably the Arab world's most efficient secret service—trained by the American firm, Interset—and its main role was to seek out and arrest anyone who expressed sympathy to communism. It did not try to re-educate these people.

Bisharat himself had attended the CIA school in Langley, Virginia, spending two years in America. He had hated that country, an evil place where infidels mocked the true and only God, attempted to replace Him with a panoply of pagan gods—publishers of obscene magazines, female communists from Hollywood, the New York leaders of the Moscow-allied Zionist conspiracy. In America, women were even allowed to drive automobiles, and wives could disgrace their husbands with adulterous acts and never be tried or sentenced.

Bisharat was the son of an Ikwhan, the fanatic tribe of religious warriors whose guns and swords had welded the kingdom together for King Abdul Aziz ibn Saud in the early decades of this century. He was as fanatical as his father, who had put whole communities to the sword for refusing to bow to the domination of the ibn Saud. In his heart, Bisharat

deeply questioned the Western ways of many of the royal
family, yet he was almost as loyal to his king as he was to his
God.

Bisharat arrived at the Casr al-Akbhar every morning by
helicopter when he had work to do there, and departed late
each afternoon, returning to his three wives and his estate
near Tobuk, the base from which his AWACS aircraft patrolled
the kingdom's northern skies. He kept a fifteen-man staff of
SSS agents at the castle, and when they travelled to Tobuk for
leave, they used a military truck, heavily armoured, equipped
with wide sand-dune tires.

The only other vehicles here were camels, providers of
fresh milk and recreation. Most of the men stationed here
had never lost their love of the desert camel, for they had
been drawn from the White Guard, bedouin soldiers blindly
devoted to their king, men from the tribes of the Otayba, the
Harb and the Mutair, men of the camel. Often in the
evenings these men would ride their camels up into the hills
and with expressionless eyes watch the sun die in splendour.
Then they would dismount and bow low to the south, to
Mecca, and offer their sunset prayers.

Now it was Tuesday morning, and Kamal Bisharat's heli-
copter had arrived. He was informed that the fearsome
Western giant in the dungeon had returned to consciousness.
Bisharat was pleased. The questioning might begin.

Two SSS agents led Bisharat to the dungeon. Mohammed
ibn Mohammed, who would be staying at the fort until the
PLO reward arrived, followed behind.

The terrorist struggled to his feet. Bisharat could see he
was still dazed from his head wound. God in his infinite
wisdom had demonstrated that this Marxist criminal was
made of human flesh, weak as all are weak in His eyes.

"Can I have water?" the terrorist said, his voice scratchy
with the lack of it.

Bisharat had forbidden that the man be allowed food or
drink. He said nothing, contemplating this naked hireling of
the devil, his white, well-muscled body gleaming whiter
under the spotlight above his head.

"Water, please."

This Jacques Sawchuk, however strong he might be, obviously lacked the leatheriness of desert people, and already
water was much on his mind. Perhaps, thought Bisharat,

therein would lie the route to the hidden bounty of this
Westerner's mind, his knowledge about Rotkommando's plans
for Mecca.

"Who are you?" said Sawchuk. "Damn it, where am I?"
His voice offered too much challenge, too little respect. The
questioning would probably take some time, Bisharat decided. Haste comes from the devil.

"I am Kamal Bisharat ibn Shehadah. As I am God's servant, I am the servant of His nation. You are a guest in His
nation. Do not think we have scruples, infidel. When it
comes to Mecca, we have no scruples."

"Am I in Saudi Arabia?" Sawchuk rasped. "Look, Kamal
Bisharat, servant of God, this is a mistake. I am not a
terrorist!"

"What words did he speak?" said Mohammed, who knew
little English. He was a short, squat man with a mouthful of
broken and decay-stained teeth, and he wore the khaki
uniform of the Fatah. "What words, Sheik Bisharat?"

"He said he is not a terrorist." Bisharat now understood
that the way to the truth would be an arduous one, but he
had travelled it many times before. Speaking English again,
to Sawchuk: "Of course you are not a terrorist. You are
Jerome Miles, an American citizen, a student of the University of Paris. Your false papers are excellent. The Rotkommando
has borrowed many of the best skills from Satan."

"Listen, I'm not a *terrorist*—" Sawchuk began, but Bisharat
swung a hard backhand at his face, and the sapphire stone of
his ring split the skin of Sawchuk's cheek.

"For lies, there is only pain. Only pain. That is the rule by
which you will live. And while you live, God will find honest
words to fill your mouth."

The prisoner tried to say something, but Bisharat struck
him across the face again, this time with the flat of his hand.
"We start with this truth: that you are Jacques Sawchuk, a
communist, and a member of the Rotkommando. And we also
start with this truth, that the Rotkommando is run by Zionist
infidels from behind the wall of the Kremlin. From these
truths we will build." It was understood by Bisharat, as by all
leaders of Saudi Arabia who had not allowed themselves to be
seduced by the lies of international conspirators, that the
Western Jews and their Zionist entity called Israel were
financed from Moscow as a part of a plan for world domina-

tion. Marx had been Jewish after all. And did not most of Israel's immigrants come from Russia? Never mind that the Rotkommando killed Jews—these were just internecine wars for control of the Zionist mob.

"Listen, damn it, I am a police agent, undercover—"

Bisharat talked over him, in Arabic. "He has insulted God, Mohammed. Teach him courtesy."

Mohammed, his eyes blazing, spat on the floor twice, then stepped forward and drove a fist with his full weight into Sawchuk's solar plexus, and continued his attack with both fists, his broad slabs of shoulder muscle moving his short arms like pistons. Sawchuk gagged for air, slumping. Mohammed, aiming for his testicles, swung his boot but missed slightly, connecting at the upper groin.

"Do you think you can play with us?" Bisharat screamed at the prisoner. "Do you think we are simple bedouin fools? Do you dare show such conceit to the leader of Saudi Special Security?"

"I like kill you," said Mohammed, speaking a few of the only words he knew in English. He kicked at Sawchuk's lowered head before Bisharat's men could restrain him, and Sawchuk's head snapped back, and the prisoner collapsed.

Sawchuk's face was turned to the side, lying in some sticky bile which he had vomited. He struggled to his knees, tried to beat his way through the fog of pain, then stilled himself and tried karma yoga. Focus on the pain, focus everything on the pain, and that isolates the pain and reduces it by the force of massed energy.

But the pain came from so many places, his head, his groin, his empty stomach, his scalding throat. He heard a prisoner scream from the far end of the hall. He could not understand the words that followed, but they were clearly pleas. Mohammed was squatting not far from Sawchuk, but looking down the hall at Bisharat, who was asking questions calmly of a prisoner, a thin boy on his knees, his head bowed.

Sawchuk tugged at the steel ring which was embedded into the stone behind him. He tugged as if he felt some remote hope that it would come free. The ring held fast, but he felt a trickle of sand and cement dust his buttocks.

The man screamed again. Sawchuk saw that Bisharat had

his ceremonial dagger out and was touching the point of it to the young man's chin, forcing him to raise his head.

Karma yoga failed Sawchuk. He felt all his pain and his thirst, and he felt frustration and anger and fear. Somehow he had to convince this Kamal Bisharat that Jacques Sawchuk was, to give the word its roughest meaning, a friend of his country. He had to get the man to call Hesselmann, just convince him to phone or radio to Group Seven. Someone would pay in blood for this. He would see that the Saudis would arrest this man, jail him for his unbelievable blunder.

I have got to come up with something very good very fast, thought Sawchuk. But the facts seemed to be these: Hesselmann and Group Seven had created in Sawchuk a spy whose cover was so deep, so credible, that these men might kill him for speaking the truth.

The next two hours was a trial by ordeal for the four prisoners charged with robbery. Sawchuk was unable to watch much of it, but unable to avoid listening. At one point, one of Bisharat's aides went up the staircase and returned, bringing a rectangular black metal apparatus about the size of a stereo receiver and with as many dials. As the man came downstairs he unrolled loops from a long electrical cord which dragged behind him and which, Sawchuk assumed, was plugged into the generator.

Such equipment, he knew, was standard among the security forces of certain Latin American republics and some of the closed societies of the Middle East. The procedure was standard, too. A man would be tortured brutally in front of his comrades, and one by one the others would break. The kidneys, the ears, even the eyes would be the targets of the electric pulse.

When it was over, the young man chosen by Bisharat for his demonstration was hanging forward, his arms straining at his chains. Sawchuk assumed he was dead or dying. The other two men, weeping, praying, were freed by an SSS officer who took a key from a ring at his belt and unfastened their locks. The prisoners were marched up the stone stairs.

Bisharat called to Sawchuk from the bottom of the stairs. "We will talk tomorrow, Jacques Sawchuk, and in God's good time you will tell us the truth. I am taking these thieves by helicopter to Tobuk. In the square, in front of all the town, their right hands will be cut off. They raided a government store, but I have judged them not guilty of being communists, and thus they have been saved from far worse punishment."

"Your Excellency, please!" Sawchuk shouted in a ragged voice. "Please listen to me." But Bisharat had disappeared up the stairs where Sawchuk's voice could not reach him.

Tomorrow, if Bisharat would only listen, Sawchuk would offer a deal: he would promise to tell everything to him in return for the favour of Bisharat making a simple call to the Group Seven number that Agent Frank Fager had given him.

But a feeling of hopelessness settled over him.

His fingers scraped at the mortar around the steel ring behind him. The rock had been hollowed out there and filled roughly with cement. Not an expert job of masonry. Particles of dust fell softly on his back as he worked.

He heard the sound of the helicopter leaving.

27

The Fourth Night, the Casr al-Akbhar

"What is the news?" The old man to Sawchuk's left was looking at him with sad eyes.

"What is the *news*?" said Sawchuk.

"It is how two men greet in this country. One asks, 'What is the news?' The other responds, 'The news is good, thanks be to God.'"

"But the news is bad."

"That is never said."

"Who are you?" Sawchuk's voice was a croak.

"I am Abu Ali Rag. I learned English serving the British at Aden. And I led Theringer on his explorations of the Empty Quarter. I have known the closeness of death. I am not afraid because I have done no man injury who has not done injury

to me. I am God's property and He will use me as He
desires."

Sawchuk saw that there were many scars on his skinny
body. His hair was to his shoulders, grey, matted.

"Why are you here?"

"I am a nomad, sir, a wanderer, a receiver of hospitality
from the desert tribes. I repay that with my gift for song and
words. I have not written ballads in honour of the family of
the Saud, and in truth I do not honour them above all other
families. That is my crime. That is my treason."

"You are a poet?"

"Yes. And you?"

"A poet, too."

"Ah, how wonderful. And American, by your voice?"

"Canadian."

"I have never known a Canadian." Abu Ali Rag's voice held
respect. "Is it true that snow makes no noise when it falls? Is
it true that your deserts are of snow, and that men go blind in
the whiteness of the storms?"

"Yes, this is true."

"And that you have houses made of ice, yet they are warm
inside? And there are great oases also made of ice, that one
can walk upon?"

"Yes, Abu Ali Rag. And in spring, they melt. Is there room
service here? Who is in charge of the water?"

"Ah, a man of jest. How wonderful."

Sawchuk continued working as they talked. When he could
stand the pain at his fingertips no longer, he began scraping
with his knuckles. The wall at this corner of the fortress
seemed to be collapsing outwardly, and the stones at the base
had separated in some cases, and cracks went through them.
Sawchuk had felt the seam of a crack running through the
cement near the ring.

"And are you a poet respected in your country?" Abu Ali
Rag said. "That monster Bisharat said your name was Sawchuk.
I regret I have not heard of you."

"Mine is a country which does not much respect poetry or
its poets. And yours?"

"How sad for you. In this country it is said that a book of
poetry is like a garden carried in the pocket. Poetry is loved
here. But not all poets are, such as I, who speak not praise
for the family of the Al Saud, the usurpers of our tribal lands.

And in your country, I have heard, it is not forbidden to speak ill of your President?"

"Prime Minister. No, it's not forbidden. In fact there are men and women who are paid to speak ill of our leaders. They are called the Opposition."

"The Opposition. How excellent. Such a wonderful custom. Here, there is no Opposition. But why should there be? All is perfection in the Kingdom of the Sauds. In a country of such perfection it is not understood how hungry men could steal from the government without being under the influence of communist agitators."

Sawchuk wondered what time it was. It was still night. He had been unconscious, but for how long he did not know.

The prisoner to Sawchuk's right was curled up, sleeping.

"That is Kamal Bisharat's view of the world," Abu Ali Rag went on. "Raiding has always been an honoured occupation of the desert, but in these modern times, Bisharat seeks to find conspiracies in the assault by bedouin raiders upon a government store. As for me, I compose songs about freedom, and Kamal Bisharat has informed the King, in answer to my petitioners, that my orders come from Moscow. The King believes him. In this country it is said: 'If the King at noon-day says it is night, behold the stars.'"

Rag looked away from Sawchuk, and closed his eyes, seeming to envelop himself in his thoughts. Then he looked at Sawchuk again. "Are you one who is truly a communist? I have never met a communist."

"I was a communist."

"And are you godless?"

"Well, yes, I guess I am."

"How extraordinary. But surely, since you are a poet, God will send for you, and you will enter His gate. How astounding it will be for you when you encounter paradise. I pray I can meet you there and together we can praise the beauty of the heavens."

"I will set you free yet, my friend. I have the means if I can find the words. Who is this man?" He gestured with his head to the man at his right.

"His is a crime which has brought shame to Prince Sultan and great loss of honour. This man was one of the prince's palace guard and it is believed he seduced the old prince's youngest wife. That woman will be stoned to death in the central square of Riyadh. He will be tortured here to make confession, and will be beheaded at her side. Death is a glass, and all will drink from it."

Sawchuk asked questions about where they were and learned he was in the Casr al-Akbhar, a few hundred miles east of the Red Sea, on the western edge of the Nafud. The old man told some stories of the desert, simple and enchanting, and spoke about its haunting beauty, its colours and its moods, and of the days when Arabia was primitive and free, the days before oil and the Saudis.

Sawchuk recited poems about freedom.

The old man began to pray. Sleep came mercifully to Sawchuk.

Sawchuk was awakened by an ear-splitting scream. So deeply had he been asleep, the cortex of his brain still bruised, still demanding the healing of sleep, that he cursed aloud as he wrenched into wakefulness, not aware of where he was, only of his pain and the horrible scream of the man chained to his right.

He saw that copper wires were wound around the scrotum and penis of the man alleged to have seduced Prince Sultan's wife. The wires collected into a black cord that ran to the rectangular box with its many switches. The box sat on the floor. Bisharat was holding a small device in his hands which, Sawchuk realized, sent remote control directions to the black box. When Bisharat touched a button, the man jolted wildly forward and uttered screams that echoed clangorously from wall to wall.

Abu Ali Rag was bent in prayer. Sawchuk felt mad with revulsion and fear.

"Colonel Bisharat, let me say something to you," he mumbled. "I will tell you everything if you will call a number—"

Mohammed, at a nod from Bisharat, swung his fist, catching Sawchuk fat in the throat, causing him to gag and retch.

"Do not insult me with your tricks," said Bisharat. "Watch in silence. Observe how resistance is broken. The shocks have already rendered this sensualist impotent, have rendered his sex permanently useless to him. But of greater concern is the pain."

As Bisharat began asking questions of the prisoner in a voice that seemed bizarrely respectful, Sawchuk, struggling

to breathe through a swelling throat, felt himself descending
into an abyss of despair and helplessness. A presentiment
visited him: Bisharat was never going to believe the truth. So
committed was he to his belief that Sawchuk was in the
Rotkommando, so far had he gone in allowing Sawchuk to
know of the terrible things that were done in the Casr
al-Akbhar, that he would subdue his every doubt in an
obsession to believe that Sawchuk was a terrorist. And for
what Sawchuk had already seen, and was seeing now, he
knew he would not be allowed to remain alive to give
testimony to the world.

Another little trickle of dust.

The seducer of the princess mumbled words and shook his
head, and tears rolled down his cheeks. Bisharat now shouted
again, and flung a loose end of his *kaffiyeh* over his shoulder
with an angry gesture. The man seemed to be gasping pitiful
denials. Bisharat pressed the button again, and again the man
pitched forward to the length of his chain, and the ligaments
and veins of his neck protruded, his face became contorted,
and his mouth came open in a noiseless scream.

"That one is no stronger than a woman," said Bisharat.
Then he announced something in Arabic. He and his three
assistants and Mohammed walked quickly away to the stairwell.

"Prayer," said Abu Ali Rag. "It is time for the midday
prayer, but they will not try to speak to God from within this
prison, as I must do." The old man bowed in the direction of
Sawchuk—and Mecca.

After a while, he said, "I have prayed that you will be
transported with me to God's garden of streams and flowers.
What will come is God's will."

Sleep had claimed Sawchuk again. When he was brought
awake, he found that two men were trying to stand him up
against the wall, and the copper wires, with their cord
leading to the black box, were strung tightly around his
testicles, around his penis.

He heard Bisharat ask a question about the Rotkommando.
He didn't hear it clearly over the whine and buzzing in his
head. But it didn't matter. When he tried to speak, no words
came out. His larynx had been damaged by Mohammed's
uppercut.

"You are a member of the Rotkommando, yes?"

Sawchuk opened his mouth, emitting no sound, only a pink drool that Bisharat watched drip slowly to the ground. He looked at Sawchuk with disgust and pressed the remote-control button.

An unbearable, searing pain exploded through Sawchuk's penis and groin, sending needles into every organ. His body was hurled forward as if shot from a cannon, and the surge ended with Sawchuk limp, on his knees, little chunks of cement debris scuttling onto the backs of his legs and feet. Two men lifted him again, pushed him against the wall.

"As God is great, you will answer."

No words came out. Another high voltage current went through Sawchuk, rivers of fire in his groin and every limb, and again he came jolting from the wall, surging away from the men holding him up. And this time he came forward with such force that the ring pulled from the wall, a heavy clump of cement adhering to it. His mouth open in a noiseless bellow, Sawchuk continued to move forward, and he swung his body around, and twenty pounds of steel and cement whirled around behind him, smashing against the hands of Bisharat's men, smashing against Bisharat's arm, sending the remote control device spinning through the air.

Sawchuk kept whirling about in a blind madness, the rock of cement and steel behind him sweeping backwards and forwards like a giant shot-put ball that would not release. Mohammed got around to Sawchuk's unprotected front, and charged low at his stomach. Sawchuk snapped his right knee upwards and the bony point of it thudded into Mohammed's chin, crushing crooked teeth into lip and gums.

But the other men were on him now, powering him against the wall, bringing him down, and the wall, undermined here by the encroaching wadi and poorly buttressed from outside, shook as the men pummelled him into unconsciousness.

28

Thursday, June 7,
the Casr al-Akbhar

Bisharat's helicopter returned in the morning bearing Bisharat, his elbow massively bruised and in a sling; Mohammed, with stitches in his lips; and a doctor from the Tobuk military hospital.

The doctor examined Sawchuk and reported back to Bisharat: "His larynx is damaged. He cannot talk."

"For how long?"

"Two days, three. I suggest water, or he may die."

"We will let the thirst possess him. Its madness loosens the tongue."

"I think there are fractures of the cheekbone, but they are hairline," the doctor said. "If his spleen has been ruptured, it will have to mend by itself."

"He is like an ox," said Bisharat, "and he will take time to die. Until then he will cling to the threads of hope that we will spin for him. But in the end, terrorists must die. It is wise policy."

The sun had risen over the wall. The ceiling had collapsed here many centuries ago and the curving stone ribs that had once held it now reached up starkly into the sky fifty feet above Sawchuk's bed, and the sun, fierce over the desert, drowned the blueness of the sky around and dried the sweat upon the racked flesh of Jacques Sawchuk.

This was the isolation room. He was on a bed with bars on all sides. A steel crib. The mattress was of ticking, whose lumps bred desert fleas. A single wooden table and chair. A

windowless door of heavy handsawn timbers reinforced by
bolted strips of steel. A ledge with two high, narrow openings, once used by bowmen who had sped their arrows
through them at the hordes of Saladin.

The noises. The throbbing of a gas-powered generator
outside. From the speakers above his head, the monotonous
intonations of Arab music, singers in blended choruses, their
songs alternating with the plaintive recital of Koranic prayer.

Bugs ate everywhere at his flesh, and left his body a quilt
of red welts.

And the shadows of the wall were now fleeing the sun, its
rays were searing him, as they would for three hours before
the sun moved behind the western wall.

Sawchuk's lips moved. Water, they spoke—two silent syllables. He tried to swallow the phlegm that had collected in his
throat, and the effort made him wince in agony.

His wrists and ankles were tied by leather thongs to the
cast-iron bedposts. A wide strap was across his chest, fastened
so tightly he could not take normal breaths. His breathing
came in pants, like a tired dog's.

The pain came from everywhere. Not generalized: specific
to every place in his body.

He heard the door being unlocked, and saw the apparition
with the broken teeth and swollen lips walk in. Mohammed
stood by the bed and spoke to him sharply in Arabic, the
sounds of curses.

"Ah-er," Sawchuk croaked.

Mohammed took a knife from his belt and ran his thumb
along the cutting edge.

"I kill you," he said softly in Sawchuk's ear. Then he left.

The flies and mosquitoes. The flies fed themselves on the
nutrient from his rank sweat. The mosquitoes, on his blood.

He had dreams of water. Clean and bright and flowing.
Cold water. Gurgling between clumps of ice. Break-up on
Lac du St. Joseph. Ice floes rolling down the St. Laurent.
The drip of spring icicles, and the sweet crunch of them
between the teeth.

Mohammed visited, smiled, cursed, and left.

During times of consciousness, minutes crawled by sluglike.
His mind was taken by fearful hallucinations. Lizard devils
spitting flame. Confusions with the sun. Anger returning

sanity. The maddening chant of Arab choruses. Distant screams. A helicopter rising above him, then chattering away into the distance.

Every effort that he made to wrench one of his arms free from the bindings caused pain.

Time no longer had meaning, and all sense of it was lost.

I don't want to die. But I am dying.

He felt his flesh wither and his bones reduce to dust.

A terrible hallucination. Colonel Bisharat holding a crystal pitcher, and the glass sweating with large drops of wetness, the pitcher heavy with water, and ice cubes gleaming atop the water like enormous diamonds, and the light shining through the water, and Sawchuk's throat muscles constricting, swallowing dryness, working convulsively.

"You are a member of the Rotkommando." Bisharat leaning over him. "Please confirm."

"Ah-er."

"You will have water when you have agreed to help us."

"Ah-er!" A burning scream.

"An improvement. Perhaps tomorrow you can speak." Bisharat dipped his hand into the pitcher and flicked water on Sawchuk's face. "Feel the water. Know that it is there for you."

Sawchuk whispered hoarsely, "In the name of God, listen to the truth. Call this number . . . ." But his words disappeared like dry puffs of smoke and died amid the chanting of the Koran from the speaker above his head.

Bisharat went to the door and was about to leave. But he paused, returned, and set the pitcher of water on the table, smiled at Sawchuk, then went out the door. Sawchuk could hear the bolt click.

All of Sawchuk's senses came meshing together as he stared at the pitcher. Twenty feet away. Beads of perspiration sliding down its sides. The ice cubes still gently rolling. The silver-blue liquid within.

Water is life.

Soon after, he heard the helicopter depart.

He meditated, achieving some peace, collecting his deepest reserves of strength, reserves which were compacted into a small, hard nut, a tough living fist of will to live that was really all there was left of Jacques Sawchuk. A will.

He ordered himself to move. He ordered himself to move toward the pitcher of water.

He did this by thrusting his body sideways, powering it with every muscle in his body, thrusting sideways in the bed. It moved about a fifth of an inch.

29

Just Before Dawn, Friday, June 8

In eight hours, Sawchuk and his bed had travelled twenty feet to the edge of the table, had inched there like a relentless snail.

Sawchuk's hand was a foot away from the pitcher now. But that hand was bound by the wrist to the bedpost, and the fingers clawed the air through the bars of the bed in futility.

He rested again. He stilled his body.

Water is life. Life.

The pitcher contained two quarts of water. Life.

Arab song whining from the speaker. Fat green flies circling the bed. A memory of the man with the broken teeth. A memory of Abu Ali Rag, the poet: *Death is a glass, and all will drink from it*.

Now with his fingers he grasped the edge of the table, and those fingers had the strength of steel, strength born of his will to live, and the table began to tilt slowly toward the bed, and the pitcher seemed stuck on the incline for a moment, and then as the tendons and muscles of Sawchuk's arm tightened and seemed almost to reach snapping point, the crystal container slowly began to slide toward the bars of the bed.

Then it came fast. And splintered against the metal bars. Long wedges of sharp glass flew onto the bed. A splash of water hit his chest; the rest dribbled from the table to the floor.

He passed into a state of delirium. When he revived, the sky was still empty of all light save that of stars.

And one hand was free.

He was unsure how that could be. But he observed that his free right hand held one of the shards of glass, and he observed blood running from the cuts on the hand and wrist. And he saw that he had sawn through the leather thongs that bound that wrist. Some element of his mind had worked while he was in his brief state of mania.

Now, with that hand free, he was able to pick the knots that held his left wrist bound to the bed. But he was still unable to raise himself up—the leather strap across his chest had been buckled beneath the bed, and that buckle was out of arm's reach.

With two hands working, Sawchuk splintered some more glass from the pitcher and he began to cut into the five inches of strap, and as his cutting edges dulled he broke the pieces of glass into smaller shards, working feverishly against the moment that one of the sss men would come into the room to check on him.

Time passed. Was there a slight paling of the sky? Did the stars seem dimmer? When would Mohammed come, who visited at strange hours to watch him die?

The strap finally frayed and pulled apart, and Sawchuk felt a great rush of release as his body was freed. He undid the knots at his ankles, then climbed creakily from the bed, his wounds shooting knives into him. He leaned over the table and lapped at a small pool of water that had collected there, enough to soften the dryness of his tongue and throat.

Now he moved the bed back to its place. He tied two strips of leather thong until he had a cord three feet long, its ends wrapped around his fists.

He prayed that the first person into the room would be stupid and incautious. A person like Mohammed of the broken teeth. Yes, he would do. Mohammed: *I kill you.*

He stood beside the door. He waited, seeing spots in front of his eyes; feeling vertigo. If you are still there, God, don't fail me, don't let me pass out.

Finally, the sound of the outer bolt being released. The massive, steel-reinforced door swung open.

Mohammed ibn Mohammed stared stupidly at the empty bed.

Sawchuk's foot flew at his ankle, and Mohammed began to fall forward, but his fall was stopped abruptly as the thong looped over his head. Sawchuk crushed his fists into the back of the man's neck, revolving them, tightening the choke, and Mohammed's tongue thrust out and his face went scarlet. His hand grasped the knife at his belt, but Sawchuk drove his head forward until the neck cracked, and the lifeless sack that Mohammed had become slumped sadly to the floor.

Sawchuk was, for all practical purposes, fearless at this point. He had lived in death's shadow for what had seemed an endless time, and now he was prepared to take any risk that seemed necessary to save his life. And he knew that what he had to do, he had to do fast.

He peered into the corridor. It was windowless, dark. A stairwell led up to the towers, an open trap door led down to the dungeon. A door at the far end had a wire-reinforced window at eye level. That door led to freedom.

Mohammed, you served me poorly in life. Serve me better now.

Sawchuk crawled down the corridor to the door, holding Mohammed's knife in his teeth, dragging the Arab's body behind him. When he got to the door he raised himself enough to look through the window.

It was a large anteroom. A sturdy metal door was to the left. There was a window in the door with bars in it, and above it a battery-powered lamp that provided light for two guards who were playing dominoes on a table nearby. Only two men in here. How many others elsewhere in the fortress? How many outside?

Sawchuk's eyes fastened hard on three submachine-guns leaning against one of several lockers. His eyes switched to the urn of tea and the flat loaves of pitta bread that were on the table.

He pulled lightly at the door handle. It was locked from the other side.

He looked down with distaste at the white death mask, Mohammed's face. He slid the eyelids open, tried to arrange the features into some kind of smile. The eyes stared emptily into the void and the smile spoke only of death. Who might think this was something living? But it was dark enough.

He hoisted Mohammed's head to the window and rapped on it loudly.

"Ya, Mohammed," he heard one of the men call.

A brief silence, then the scuffling of feet, the sound of a key turning. The door swung open.

Sawchuk stepped from behind it and plunged the knife into the centre of the guard's chest, and with a quick, fluid motion as he stepped inside the anteroom, hurled the body aside, and went for the other man, who had knocked the table over in his haste to get to one of the submachine guns. Sawchuk was like a panther; in five great bounds, he reached the man and smashed him against the lockers. He was about to deliver a death chop to the man's ear, but he pulled, hitting him only hard enough to render him unconscious.

Sawchuk closed his eyes briefly and steadied himself and tried to quell the demons that burned his throat. He feared to look at the wreckage on the floor, the spilled dominoes, the shattered tea urn. But then he did look, and he saw that the urn had only cracked, was otherwise undamaged. It was on its side and tea was dripping from its mouth. He lifted it and put its narrow opening to his lips, and although causing pain to his still swollen throat, each swallow was an exquisite delight. Nothing more sublime, more perfect could ever have been distilled by the gods than this sweet, spiced Arab tea. He felt the liquid caress his throat, felt it soak into the tissues of his stomach, felt life flow back into every limb and organ.

And he felt his mind now begin to retreat from the edge of insanity's abyss. Damaged as he was, the side of his face broken and ripped and swollen, his stomach and groin black with bruising, his naked body scorched red by the sun, his sex riven from the terrible bursts of electric fire, Jacques Sawchuk yet felt a joy, the joy of life returning, life preserved— for however brief a time. And he felt a hope. That was the best. There was a hope.

Because now he was armed.

The submachine guns were American M-5s, poorly maintained, in need of oiling but apparently in functioning order, with magazines loaded. Against the wall was a radio communications set. He wondered what else was here. He unclipped the ring of keys from the unconscious man's belt and found one that opened the lockers. Clothes in two of them—his own shirt and pants and boots, some Arabian *thaubs* and headdresses.

He felt he would be more comfortable in a loose-flowing

thaub, and he found a large one and pulled it over his head.
It dropped almost to his ankles.

Two of the lockers contained arms: spare clips for the
submachine guns, sniper's rifles, pistols, M-26 grenades, tear-
gas canisters, even a few lightweight missile launchers: hand-
held U.S. Vipers with disposable plastic tubes. A box full of
Viper warheads. Saudi Special Security was ready for a minor
war. But so, now, was Sawchuk.

How many men stationed here? He guessed that Mohammed
and the two-man guard that he had surprised were the only
ones who had been awake. But the first glimmerings of
twilight showed through the window of the door; soon this
encampment would be rising with the sun.

A flat steel bar held the door fastened from inside, but the
door itself was unlocked, and it would be easy now to escape
outside. He could see the faint outlines of the gravel riverbed
out front, and in the depression, a few scrubby trees. And
some movement. Large figures. A snuffling sound. A snort.

Camels.

Abu Ali Rag, show me your deserts.

The man whom Sawchuk had clubbed into unconsciousness
was coming to, and Sawchuk slapped him fully awake, and
held the tip of Mohammed's bloodied knife to his voice box.
The man seemed quickly to understand that if he tried to call
out, he would produce little sound. Sawchuk grabbed one of
the submachine-guns, then prodded his prisoner into the
corridor, down the stairs to the dungeon.

Abu Ali Rag was the only one left here. He lay sleeping on
the floor. Sawchuk gave the trembling sss man the ring of
keys, and pointed to the lock on the old man's chains. The
guard hesitated but felt the knife prick his throat, and he
freed Rag, whose eyes opened weakly.

"Come to the desert with me," Sawchuk said.

Rag seemed momentarily confused. "What is the news?"
he murmured.

"The news is good, thanks be to God." Sawchuk spoke
hoarsely, his voice beginning to function again.

Rag smiled. "I expected heaven when I awoke. I am not
there yet."

Sawchuk wound the chain around the guard's wrists and
clicked the lock shut. "Find out from him quickly how many

men inside this building, how many outside, when do they go on shift, what vehicles do they have."

Rag received his answers: Twelve men in the barracks behind the fortress. No one else in the fortress. A day shift of five armed men were to relieve him and his fellow night guard soon after the sun broke over the eastern sands—less than half an hour from now, Sawchuk guessed. The only vehicle was a military truck, between barracks buildings.

The good news was that Colonel Bisharat would not be arriving today. It was Friday, the Holy Day.

"Ask him how many kilometres it is to the northeast, to Iraq."

Two hundred kilometres.

Sawchuk ripped a strip of linen from the guard's tunic and gagged him with it. Rag was slow in mounting the stairs, so Sawchuk carried him, bounding three steps at a time. He found a *thaub* for him to wear and passed him the tea urn and a loaf of the unleavened bread.

The old man drank cautiously, and split some bread with Sawchuk, who chewed it despite the pain in his jaws.

In the faint light, Sawchuk could see more clearly now through the window. The camels were unguarded, five of them, kneeling. He made out the outlines of objects around the well: several empty pails, ropes, a trough, saddles and other riding paraphernalia sitting under the trees.

"Can you saddle the camels?"

Rag took a swallow of tea. "Am I Arab?"

"Can you use a gun, Abu Ali Rag?"

"I repeat: Am I Arab?"

Rag, looking much stronger now, chose a Fasil F-1 sniper's rifle and slung it over his shoulder, found a belt with .233 cartridges and tied it around his *thaub* at the waist. He showed Sawchuk how to position a *kaffiyeh* on his head, and put one on his own.

Sawchuk found a khaki duffle bag, put two submachine-guns into it, extra clips, and a Viper launcher and four warheads. He put on his boots. Rag found a small leather bag and tucked the remaining loaves of pitta bread into it. Sawchuk smashed the radio set with the butt of a rifle. Then the two men released the bolt from the door and slipped out into the fading night, stirred by the breezes that twilight brings to the desert.

Rag worked quickly, efficiently, saddling two camels who spat at him in ill temper. He filled goatskin water bags and tied them to the tall, three-pronged saddlehorns. Sawchuk looked anxiously at the great beast which had been allotted to him, a female animal that delivered a terrible odour and grunted with displeasure as Rag rapped her sharply with a stick, causing her to rise from her knees. He pulled the cinches tight around the body.

"Can we make it?" Sawchuk said.

"We call the desert the Land of Fear," said Rag. "Between here and Iraq there is only desert."

"We are not going to Iraq."

"And which way shall we go?"

"How many days are we to the Gulf of Aqaba?"

"Ah. Seven days, perhaps. It is a longer journey, and there is not only desert but the southern hills of the Tubayq and the mountains of the Hijaz. After they have searched for us to the north, they will search for us to the west, my friend. They have an armoured truck, and we have a hundred miles of desert dunes before we reach the shelter of the hills, and today we will be moving beneath the sun." He shook his head with a sad smile. "In a few minutes they will know we have gone. Look at the eastern sky." A pink blush showed there.

Sawchuk stared at it and thought. "Stay behind the gorge, Abu Ali Rag, and cover me if you have to. Have the camels ready when I return, because when I return, I will be running." He removed the missile launcher from the duffle bag and inserted a warhead. He also removed a submachinegun, took an extra warhead, then tied the bag to the saddle.

"May God protect you," said Rag as Sawchuk crept away, along the wadi beside the castle wall, where the ancient river gorge had chewed away at the foundations. From around the tower corner he could see a few prefabricated buildings near the north side of the castle. A few early risers were stirring pots upon small gas stoves near a military truck which was protected with steel armour.

He climbed a narrow trail up the riverbank, got onto his stomach, crept forward under the shadow of the castle walls. He stopped, took careful aim with the Viper, and he fired.

The engine of the truck exploded in a hot, red ball, and flames licked up the sides of it, and in a few seconds the gasoline tank went with another roar. Sawchuk didn't wait to see the second explosion. He ran, inserting the second warhead into the launcher, slinging the submachine-gun over his shoulder.

He scrambled down the gravel of the wadi gulch, his *thaub* whipping behind him. Wild, random shots came from the area of the barracks, but he was out of sight, behind the castle wall, running for the trees he saw outlined against the western sky near the well.

Two shots rang out from the area of the well, and when Sawchuk arrived there, he found that two of the camels were lying dead, a third was on its feet, weighed down with extra waterskins and tethered to Rag's camel which, like Sawchuk's, was on its haunches, roaring in fright.

"Be careful as the animal rises," Rag shouted as Sawchuk leaped upon the saddle atop the camel's hump.

Sawchuk had no idea what to expect. The sensation was of a roller coaster. The rear legs went up first as the animal rose onto its hind knees, pitching Sawchuk forward onto its neck. The camel raised up on its forelegs and Sawchuk was thrown back, almost falling, and he turned around, grabbing the hump. Now his mount threw him forward again as the hind legs went straight. As the forelegs came to full extension Sawchuk found himself sitting backwards on the animal's neck and shoulders, his legs wrapped around the camel's neck as it began to surge forward, his arms pressed to the hump, the submachine-gun in one hand, the Viper launcher in the other.

Rag's camel, towing the pack animal, was already racing toward the western incline of the wadi. But Sawchuk's camel began running in the wrong direction, toward the fort, up the wadi bank, with great lunges of its powerful legs, and Sawchuk, facing backwards and trying to crane his neck around to see where the camel was going, bounced crazily from side to side, the camel's legs moving rapidly·in disjointed rhythm.

Suddenly a flare rose in front of them, a great yellow phosphorescent light which enveloped the dark shadow that had been Sawchuk and his camel. The animal, in ·a renewed state of terror, seemed to skid sideways to a stop like an automobile braking on an icy road, then took off in the opposite direction, back toward the wadi and the buttressed corner of the fortress.

Sawchuk, still riding backwards but facing the bunkhouses

now, fired wild bursts with the submachine-gun in his left hand at the men he saw outlined in the mauve sunrise, men scrambling, ducking to the ground, then running again, firing pistols. They disappeared from view as the camel sped surefootedly down the wadi trail and around the crumbling northwest corner of the fortress.

As the camel began to mount the opposite bank, Sawchuk could see seven or eight men racing along the riverbed, around the castle corner. They all stopped as they saw their target clambering up the gravelled slope a hundred metres from them, and they took up firing positions with handguns and rifles.

His legs still clinging to the animal like a vice, Sawchuk took what aim he could and fired a Viper missile at the weakened corner of the castle.

An enormous crash of flame and sparks. The tower rocked and tottered, and the buttresses wobbled, and some stones thudded to the ground near the sss men, and then, all at once, the entire corner of the fortress gave way, an avalanche of ancient stone whose thunder drowned the shouts of the men being crushed and buried in the wadi.

30
Friday, June 8, the Palace Near Mecca

"Women are your fields," says the Koran. "Go then into your fields when and how you will."

Prince Aziz ibn Saud had four wives, the full complement allowed by Koranic law, and kept an average of twenty concubines. Most of them enjoyed separate lodgings within the walls surrounding Aziz's summer palace. But he had of late been spending little time with his concubines and none at all with his wives. Sweet Latifa, his secretary: it was she who occupied him most.

On their first occasion of intercourse, she had seemed stiff and frightened. Aziz had taken her from behind in the traditional way. She had expressed pain, but there had been no blood.

That had been over four months ago, in January, when the Americans had first been here. Now they were back at the palace again: the Typhon people, the men from the Pentagon and State Department. They included Aziz's pliable but good friend Henry Naiboldt, with his assurances that things were well in hand in Washington. Tomorrow, King Fahd, Defence Minister Sultan and their entourages, would arrive for the signing ceremonies.

Tonight, after the rigours of entertaining his American guests, he would entertain Latifa in his great circular bed in his fourteenth-storey penthouse suite. With Latifa he enjoyed a kind of pleasure that his other women seemed unable to give him. They were always too compliant. But Latifa would fight his charms, back away from him like a frightened fawn, apologizing. This tantalized him, for her reactions went beyond the normal modesty. He felt strong when he took her. Always, his feeling of conquest was complete.

One of the reasons he preferred her, he had to reluctantly admit, was that Latifa had lived in the West, had studied there, knew a wider world of ideas. She was almost as intelligent as a man. There was something of the rebel in Latifa, and this made the conquests richer.

The service here is something else. Raise a little finger and somebody comes running up to you and puts another Southern Comfort in your hand. With a spray of juleps, no less.

Henry Naiboldt had arrived that morning with the Typhon-U.S. government team, eight in all. In their rooms, upon the bed pillows, they had found gifts: eighteen-carat white gold, diamond-set Piaget watches. When you've got that kind of money, flaunt it, he thought.

Naiboldt was a millionaire himself, on his way—as soon as the Senate passed the Glickums bill in eighteen days—to his first billion. But he envied Prince Aziz for being tens of thousands of times richer than himself.

His own home was a seventeen-million-dollar hobby ranch chewed out of the redwood forests of Santa Clara County, an hour's drive from the Typhon complex near Palo Alto. But he had heard that this palace, together with the other buildings in the compound, and the lavish grounds inside and outside the walls, had cost Aziz a few hundred million. Petrodollars. The country's oilfields held twenty-seven per cent of the world's oil reserves, enough oil to last fifty years. That is where America's future lay. Saudi Arabia and its soil and its rapacious thirst for American guns and luxury items: the free world's benefactor and its true frontier.

Water, so scarce in Arabia, was flaunted at Aziz's palace, came cascading down in torrents from different levels of the tower into pools surrounded by potted palms and bougainvillaea vines and their paper-petalled flowers of red and violet, hanging cages with rare songbirds, sculptured fountains and statuettes, flowered islands in the pools and walkways over them.

Naiboldt was relaxing now beside the ground-floor garden pool, in a bathing suit, on a gilded lawn chair, enjoying the sun which beat upon his belly.

His only worry now was the reporter Rubinstein. How had that guy got involved with Rufus McKay? How many times had they met? Had McKay, after his promises of silence, told him about the business with the three senators? The men who had been following McKay and Rubinstein must have picked up the reporter by now, as well. By now they must have found out if Charles Rubinstein knew anything. And then eliminated him.

Naiboldt wasn't going to feel badly about Rubinstein, who had been his nemesis once before. But he felt badly about Rufus McKay. The man had been his best friend.

"This is Charles Rubinstein. I am currently in California studying opportunities for further enhancement of my journalistic career. I will be back in New York by June the fifteenth. At the sound of the tone, your message will be recorded." Charles had said this into the telephone recorder while looking into the muzzle of a snubnosed .32, the kind that police officers carry.

The men who packed these particular pieces did not, however, appear to be policemen. Not New York policemen, with their informal, sloppy ways. These guys were too professional to be cops. And the accents were not New York.

On every one of the seven evenings since Charles had been taken captive, the leader of the men, a sallow, wiry fellow in his forties with a Fu Manchu moustache, would turn the speaker on, and they would listen to the day's collected telephone messages. Macy's demanding payment. Aunt Yosephine begging, for the twentieth time this month, that Charles call her to discuss the state of her health. American Express demanding payment. His freaky sister Paula, always spending her tuition money and always harassing him for loans. His mother' phoning to vent her fury about Paula. ("A hippie, my God, at twenty-one—what have I done to deserve?")

His brother Rocky even phoned once, across a line that crackled and popped. "Have I got a story for you. I told you I'd get the inside dope. It's even better than we thought. I'll call you when you get back from California. What's the matter, schmuck, you lose your job again?" Fu Manchu had snickered at that.

None of the phone calls involved a job offer. However, the prospect of returning to work was not immediate in Charles's mind. The prospect of continued life was the important thing. If these men were from the Typhon Corporation's "investigative team," to use the words of ex-General Naiboldt, and if they were the same men who had wasted Rufus McKay with a car bomb, they would have no scruples about doing away with an unemployed reporter. Especially if they believed that Charles was the possessor of the dark secrets that Naiboldt had passed on to McKay.

And those secrets were on a punk rock tape buried deep within the enormous bowels of his cassette library. One of the kidnappers, a young, dark-skinned man, fluid like a cat, played certain of the tapes during his breaks. But *Mad Morgan and the Assassins of Moog* did not entice him. He was a jazzhead.

The three men took equal shifts. One would always be sitting there like a sphinx with a Smith and Wesson in his hand. One would be taking a break. One would question him. Always in a casual way, never with hostility. They were leisurely, as if they had all the time in the world. Charles thought this odd, and he constantly held himself tight, like' a man in a dentist's chair, waiting for the rough stuff to begin. They questioned him about General Rufus McKay. How Charles had met him. The nature of their conversations. Charles played dumb—not so much because he was nobly honouring the journalist's precept about protecting sources, but basically because he figured if he kept his mouth shut his chances of living were better. But how strong would he be when they started sticking splints inside his fingernails?

The men were silent when he countered—in a nice-mannered way—with questions of his own. They did not identify themselves, said nothing about their mission.

As for the death of McKay, the police, according to the newspapers, were stumped. Mindless terrorism directed at a prominent military figure, that was the best bet. Charles thought of McKay's pretty girlfriend, Barbara, and of his wife and children. He thought of the general's revelations of intrigue among Prince Aziz and Typhon and the three senators, whose names he now had. The whole scandal was there on the Mad Morgan tape. Charles Rubinstein was sitting on the story of the decade, and was unable to file it anywhere. And the Senate vote was two and a half weeks away.

The newspapers were brought up every day, along with hot deli food, by the third man of the kidnap team, also young, who wore a jogging suit when he left and who quietly conferred with Fu Manchu upon every return.

Once in a while one of the men would go to the front window and peer down into the street from a slit in the curtains. On one such occasion, Charles caught the dark-skinned man giving Fu Manchu a nod of his head, a signal. The leader then went to the window himself, looked out and mumbled something. Charles was never allowed to come close to the window.

He lived tensely but well, was allowed to watch television, play his tapes and records, sleep (if you could call it that) in his own bed—though always with one of the men nearby, holding a gun.

31

Friday, June 8, the Desert

Sawchuk named his camel Sopwith. The two of them had eased into a relationship in which disrespect was mutual. Sopwith swore at her burden, with roar and spit, and punished

Sawchuk with fearsome farts. Sawchuk cursed back in a frog-like voice.

He was now high in the wooden saddle, facing forward, having managed to get up there when Sopwith had slowed and then stopped altogether in a patch of sedge grass, where she began to feed. A couple of thwacks on the neck with the bamboo stick had got her going again. Sawchuk had learned that he could control Sopwith's direction with taps on one side of the head or another. They were heading west, under a sun which rose steadily behind him like God's spotlight.

But nothing seemed to be searching for him under that spotlight. Twice he had heard the distant drone of planes, but had not seen them. He was waiting for a helicopter—that is how they would search. But nothing.

Not even Abu Ali Rag. The old man had doubtless found his private way into the desert, and the desert might protect him, one of its own children. Whether it would be so kind to Sawchuk, a trespasser, fortune would ultimately determine. But he had two goatskins full of water and a loaf of bread that Rag had placed in one of the saddlebags. The water tasted of camel piss, so Sawchuk was forced to sip at it only sparingly.

There were a few scattered clumps of dried grass in the lee of the hills, but otherwise the desert was all sand here, dunes which rose three and four hundred feet. Sawchuk was urging his camel around the twisting valleys, staying low. Sopwith's huge feet were like snowshoes in the sand, which was rippled and shone white and yellow and hot. Moving among the dunes, Sawchuk felt as if he were in a suffocating sand-pit, hemmed in by burning walls on every side.

He was still in much pain. His face was swollen where Mohammed's boot had cracked the cheekbone. His throat and body were still badly bruised. But the worst was the fear of not being a man, of having been unsexed by the fire that had torn through his lower organs.

He was driven as much by anxiety for safety as by lust for revenge. He saw Bisharat's face in his mind's eye. And Wurger's. For surely it was Wurger who had betrayed him to the PLO in East Berlin: that had been no accident.

And where was Wurger and his Rotkommando army now? Sawchuk knew that this was Friday, the Islamic Holy Day. The attack on the palace at Mecca was to take place before dawn on Sunday. He wondered if Group Seven had taken them all in Amman....

Sawchuk was immensely tired, and he felt himself shrivelling under the unforgiving sun of the Arabian summer.

The desert had begun to flatten. On the western horizon there was nothing, just the shimmering of blue mirages, ever-retreating, a vast sea of fire. Sawchuk fought his body's demands for a deep and penetrating sleep. He would give in, then jerk awake, and turn and look behind him, to each side, searching for his searchers, seeing nothing but the terrible stainless beauty of the yellow sands.

"You've got to find us some shade, Sopwith," he muttered. "Then we'll sleep."

Sopwith snorted, tried to alter course to the south, but Sawchuk prodded the camel west with the sun. The Gulf of Aqaba. And Israel.

They were moving from the dunes toward salt-caked plain, dried and cracked and empty of anything living, a flatland that extended to the far distances and promised no pity.

Sawchuk sipped at the brackish, awful water from one of the goatskins, then wrapped his *kaffiyeh* around his mouth, and stared with unhappy eyes at the barrens beyond.

There was a distant growl of an airplane engine, but far in the east, behind him. Sawchuk and Sopwith, lone moving figures on a trackless landscape, would surely be seen if the plane came near. But its sound faded. He presumed the Saudis were concentrating their search northeast of Casr al-Akbhar, along the routes to Iraq. But soon, tomorrow at the latest, they would be looking for him here, to the west, the only other escape route from this part of Arabia.

The sun crept with sullen slowness over a sky of blinding blue. Sopwith's long eyelashes acted like sunshades, but Sawchuk had no protection from the glare, and he often had to shut his eyes. He thought again of Kamal Bisharat, felt a surge of anger at what that man had done to him. He feared that the desert would deny him his accounting. He felt himself falling into a black gulf of desolation.

He awoke to a soft voice behind him.

"It is said that a camel driver has his plans, and the camel has his."

Sawchuk opened his eyes, turned to his right. Beside him, Abu Ali Rag, his *kaffiyeh* drawn away from his face, was smiling. He was atop his camel, the other animal still following behind.

"You are travelling to the south," Rag said.

Sawchuk glanced up at the sun. It was to his right, falling slowly to the horizon. How long had he been asleep, moving south into the heart of this woeful country?

"You are travelling to the south because the camel knows there is water there, the oasis of Qumat. The camel does not care that there are soldiers at Qumat."

"Abu Ali Rag, how did you find me?"

"The bedouin say there are three things cannot hide themselves: love, a mountain, and a man on a camel. Two men and three camels are even more obvious to the eye, and it is only through God's generosity that we have not been seen. But the desert is a vastness, and men's eyes are small. Come, follow me."

They turned to the northwest, still tramping over the salt-cake.

Rag gave Sawchuk's camel a thump on the behind, and it trotted forward.

"Sleep. I will be behind you. We will be travelling through the night."

Sopwith slowed to a rocking gait, and Sawchuk felt sleep mercifully shrouding him again.

He awoke as the sun began to release its grip, turning the desert ochre. The sun turned red itself, glided toward the horizon, flattened, and was sucked away.

Rag smiled, reached over and patted Sawchuk's hands. "They will never find us, Jacques Sawchuk. They have lost the day, and we will have the night. Tomorrow, the hills."

They rode through the night, the stars guiding them, the camels exhausted and making complaint. Abu Ali Rag sang ballads to them, his soft voice caressing Sawchuk's ears.

"In the desert," said Rag, "one forgets everything, one remembers nothing."

"I do not forget," said Sawchuk.

They were on sand again, with a few scattered rocks. The land had become more rolling, and when the crescent moon rose Sawchuk could make out pimples thrusting from the flatness of the horizon: distant hills. The sand seemed to glow red in the darkness.

As twilight came, Sawchuk could see a few lone escarpments standing boldly against the sky. They began to toil upwards, Rag working the camels with his stick.

At one point Rag stopped, just as the sun was colouring the cliffs ahead with tips of orange. He tapped his camel on the snout, and it went down on its knees. Rag got off. He stirred the sand with his hands and fingered what looked to Sawchuk like animal droppings. He moved to another spot, sifted through more such droppings. He walked around, staring at the ground.

"Men of the Awamir tribe. Four of them, with twelve camels, have passed by two days ago. If they have a camp, we will trade guns for food, of which we have little. Hunger is an infidel, we say. It has no moral scruples."

He remounted and they continued forward.

"Will that be safe?" Sawchuk said.

"They are bedouin."

The sunrise was glorious in a cloudless orange sky. The sand was russet here, flecked with red light. The escarpments ahead were of multicoloured sandstone, painted fluorescent by the sun.

"There we will find cover from the sky," Rag said, pointing to a huge rockface that soared five hundred feet from a hill of sand about half a mile away. Rag and Sawchuk urged their exhausted, complaining mounts upwards.

As they drew closer, Sawchuk could see they were heading for a gap between two spurs of the sandstone cliff, between which there would be permanent shadow from an overhang. They trudged up the incline, around the spur, and into the safety of a pocket protected from sight by land or air. They dismounted.

"Now we will stay until it is night again. Thus we will travel: only by the night. It is a miracle that we have not been observed." Rag went down on his knees. "I have to ask God's forgiveness. Yesterday I was forced to make all my prayers from the back of a camel. It is ungracious to pray from a camel."

He bent forward, to the south, murmuring soft words.

Sawchuk, too, faced Mecca. Was the Rotkommando army gathering there? Had Hesselmann decided not to have the

Committee arrested in Amman, determined instead to lay a trap for them at the gates to the Holy City? But Bisharat had seemed unaware of the plans to take Aziz's summer palace. Sawchuk thought it incredible that Hesselmann had not informed the Saudi ss chief of the plans of the Rotkommando.

The Rotkommando—it had been a week since he had been in their midst, yet it seemed a lifetime ago. He thought fleetingly of Kathë Zahre. That last encounter by the bank of the Seine, so twisted and hard with her neurotic obsession to feel herself in love. And he thought of Bisharat's black machine.

Rag hobbled the camels. He began to milk the pack animal.

Sawchuk's eyes widened.

"It is why we have taken this female, although usually only the bull is used as beast of burden. Drink. It is excellent."

He passed a goatskin with frothy milk in it. To Sawchuk, it tasted of the richness of life itself.

"We call the camel *ata allah*, God's gift. We take His generosity as He gives it, and He has given this cow in milk. Her calf has doubtless made a feast for Bisharat's men, may they roast in eternal fires." Rag pulled some more milk for himself from the camel's teats. "God's gift. The hair is used for rope, the hide for leather pouches, the dung for fuel, the urine to kill the lice in the hair, of which I fear I have many."

The old man slipped off his *kaffiyeh* and drew his hand through his tousled grey hair, which fell long and dirty over his shoulders. Sawchuk realized he was no less filthy and thought of how a bath might feel.

Rag sat cross-legged on the sand, his rifle nestled in his arms, and he stared out onto the desert. Sawchuk found a knife in one of the leather packs, and began to carve flute holes in his bamboo stick. Abu Ali Rag sang softly.

All day, it seemed, there came the sound of searching planes and helicopters. Rag had explained they were near one of the main routes for winter-grazing herds of sheep and goats that came down from the hills in December. He had travelled here many times in the course of endless wanderings. He knew the deserts of north Arabia, of Jordan, and he knew of the Negev. But of the Negev, he said: "I will not return there. The British seized it from us, and gave it to the Jews." Rag was a political man, resentful at what he called the

British treachery over partition. But he asked no questions of Sawchuk, asked not why he wished to go to Israel's southern gate.

"I will take you there," he said. "I will show you the way. But this—" he spread his arms apart as if to encompass the northern deserts of Arabia—"this is my home."

Sawchuk felt secure in this man's protection.

32

Sunday, June 10, the Palace

It was three a.m. Henry Naiboldt was out of bed again, burping, hiccupping. He had always been a poor drinker. Last night he had drunk too well, and his body was now rebelling.

Too much champagne on top of the stupefying banquet that Prince Aziz had spread. Yesterday his host had announced to Naiboldt and the other Americans that they would enjoy a traditional Arab feast in honor of the presence of His Majesty and the royal entourage. Naiboldt had counted nearly fifty roast lambs, all with their teeth grinning macabrely on the platters. Craters of white rice, wet with juice and melted butter and grease, with limbs and ribs and haunches of baby goat floating on top, together with clumps of liver, kidney, and salted knots of intestine.

Naiboldt had followed custom, had sat in discomfort, cross-legged on the floor, and thrust his right hand into the piles of rice and meat. Never the left hand, he had been warned. It never touches food.

But he had declined with barely suppressed horror the sheep's eye that had been offered to him by Aziz, who had laughed at his guest's unease.

"Tradition holds that he upon whom the eye is bestowed has honour bestowed as well," Aziz had said.

Twice earlier Naiboldt had got up, feeling vaguely nauseated at the memory of a single, awful eye staring at him from a dish, his stomach a noisy cauldron, his throat parched with the dehydration caused by too much Mumm's Cordon Rouge. Now he was up a third time, and had uncontrollable hiccups. Nothing seemed to stem them, and it was as if something were in his chest, kicking him up the throat every twelve seconds.

He slid open the doors to the patio and walked outside in his pyjamas. The night was starlit but the moon was only a narrow slit and he could see nothing but the glow of Mecca in the distance. Muted sounds came to him: the scrape of a night guard's boot on the tiles below, the clucking of a caged bird, and the furred sound of the wind. The rumbling of his stomach.

He was a billionaire. If the price of celebration was a hangover and hiccups, he could stand it. The documents had been signed and all that waited was the Senate vote.

His attention was caught by the flicker of a light outside the wall, but it disappeared almost instantly. He thought nothing of it, hiccupped, turned around. As he glanced up nine floors above him, he saw a light click on in Prince Aziz's penthouse.

Latifa whispered in Aziz's ear. "We have friends at the gate."

The prince woke from his deep and happy sleep and when his eyes cleared they saw the barrel of an old Colt .45 single-action revolver, one of the prizes of Aziz's gun collection, a weapon said to have been used by Doc Halliday. Its hammer was cocked, the cylinder quite definitely had bullets in it. It was being held in Latifa's hand. It was pointing at his nose.

"We have friends at the gate," she repeated. "We are going to the office now, and we are going to release the gate's lock. You will order the guards there to put down their arms."

Aziz was sure this was a joke. He smiled uneasily, went up on one elbow and reached the other arm out for the gun. "Don't play with that, my dear."

She brought the prince's bejewelled scimitar from behind her back and slashed at the hand, taking off three fingers.

He screamed.

"They merely want to rob you, Your Excellency. They will

leave afterwards without harming you. But if you do not order the men at the gate to put their guns aside, I will kill you. Then I will kill myself, and I will be pleased to go wherever God sends me."

A loud explosion cured Naiboldt of his hiccups. He could not see the palace gate from where he stood, but he saw a rush of flames and rising sparks from behind the wall of one of the compound buildings, the one in which the rangers of the palace guard were quartered.

Then there was another explosion, a much more violent one, as if from a missile launcher, then several more, and the guards' quarters became engulfed in billowing red clouds. Men ran screaming from the door, and submachine-guns bellowed and the men were cut down. Others crawled from the windows, their night clothes ablaze, and the walls of the guards' quarters collapsed upon them.

Naiboldt was too stunned at first to move. Lights went on all over the palace and compound, and he could see black-faced forms with submachine-guns racing alongside the wall, into the passages between buildings.

This isn't happening, he thought. However, it was not a dream.

He dashed back inside his suite, put his suit jacket on over his pyjamas, and ran into the corridor of the fifth floor. The other Americans who were guests on this floor—men from Pentagon and State and Typhon—were stumbling from their rooms, their eyes wide with astonishment and fear, and they were yelling. The guardsman on duty in the hallway had his pistol in his hand, but was standing against a wall, seemingly rigid with fright. Naiboldt ran up to him.

"Give me the gun!" he ordered.

The guard, dressed in the khaki tunic and white *kaffiyeh* that was the palace uniform, stared at Naiboldt with panic and incomprehension.

"Give me the gun!"

The man did not move, so Naiboldt simply grabbed the pistol, a Browning .38, peeled the guard's fingers off it, and ran with it down the hallway to the stairs.

He went up, not down, towards Aziz's offices eight floors above. On his way, Naiboldt met frightened guests, members of the royal family, their staff and guards, standing wide-eyed and open-mouthed at the landings. Naiboldt shouldered past, shouting, "Get to your rooms. Lie down. Get to your rooms."

Prince Sultan, the defence minister, was standing at the landing to the tenth floor, a pistol in either hand, three of his elder sons behind him.

"For God's sake, put those away, or you'll get killed!" Naiboldt said. "They probably want hostages. Don't throw away your life."

"Where are you going?" the Prince Sultan stammered.

"To the radio, to call for help." But he would be happy to do that from the radio of Prince Aziz's helicopter, which should still be sitting on the pad atop the building.

Another frightened guardsman was at the locked door that led to Aziz's offices, the command centre for all the palace. Naiboldt heard two shots from inside. He shoved the guard away, tried the door, then fired at the lock and wrenched the door open.

He stepped inside, his .38 held forward from the waist.

He saw Prince Aziz, a bloodied cloth wrapped around his right hand, his face white as death. He was sitting behind his great circular rosewood desk in his great circular office. The secretary, whom Naiboldt knew as Latifa, was standing behind Aziz and slightly to his left, a gun in her hand. Smoke rose from the emergency radio equipment where she had shot out the command console.

Latifa saw Naiboldt step inside, did not recognize him for an instant. "Have we won?" she shouted. Then she realized who he was, and she became confused, swivelled her gun toward him, then toward Aziz's back, then at Naiboldt again. "Put the gun down or I will kill you."

Naiboldt heard her voice crack, saw that she was terrified. It seemed bizarre: she was wearing a filmy nightgown. He remembered that Aziz had given her affectionate looks during the business sessions of yesterday, when she had been quietly subservient.

Naiboldt made no sudden moves, tried to face her down, but began to move the .38 around in an imperceptible arc.

"I said put the gun down." Her voice was high and tight.

She took a step to try to put Aziz's body between her and Naiboldt. That one step brought her chest just in Naiboldt's line, and he squeezed the trigger.

She jerked back, and a splotch of blood was at her left

breast, on her nightgown. There was a look of astonishment in her eyes, then her face resolved into an expression of agony, and she crumpled to the floor.

"I can fly a helicopter, Aziz."

"She cut my fingers off," Aziz whimpered. "Oh, merciful God, she cut my fingers—"

Naiboldt checked his complaint harshly. "The helicopter—is it on the roof?"

"She said they are here to rob."

The sound of gunfire could still be heard outside. And it reverberated through the building, and Naiboldt knew the guerrillas had probably made entry into the ground floor.

"My ass they're here to rob. They're terrorists."

"The helicopter, yes, it is fuelled, ready." Aziz began to go to the stairs.

Naiboldt paused to think. "Open the vault."

Aziz stood, ashen-faced, uncomprehending.

"Open the vault, for God's sake!"

Aziz went unsteadily to the wall behind the desk, touched the button that sent the false wall sliding open, twirled the combination for what seemed to Naiboldt to be an eternal time. When he finally got the vault open, Naiboldt towed the prince inside. "The film, the tapes. Where do you keep them?"

Aziz blinked, then went to a filing drawer and drew a large envelope from it. Naiboldt dug inside, located the strips of movie film and the tapes of the senators' voices, then stuffed the envelope into his jacket pocket. They quickly mounted the stairs to Aziz's revolving penthouse suite, then to the rooftop terrace and the helicopter landing pad. Naiboldt climbed inside, helping Aziz in after him.

They could see human carnage on the grounds of the palace. Men with guns were lining people up with their hands behind their heads, marching them into open spaces. A few random shots. But most of the fighting seemed over.

"I will pay you God's fortune for this," Aziz said.

Naiboldt would not be shy about reminding him of that. The twelve-passenger executive helicopter roared to life. Naiboldt brought it surging into the air.

Half an hour later, as they sped across the hills to the nearby city of Taif, Naiboldt burned the film and tapes in an ashtray, then scattered the ashes across the desert.

33

Saturday, June 9,
New York City

It was eleven o'clock at night.

Fu Manchu had put his .32 in his shoulder holster and was in the kitchen making hot chocolate, but keeping his eye on Charles Rubinstein, who was working his way through the *Times* crossword. The jogger man was napping on a sofa. The swarthy-skinned music fan was snapping his fingers, headphones on his ears.

Charles by now had been reduced to a network of quivering ganglions. These men were starting to ask questions in a tougher way, with threats. This was stage two they were into. Stage one had been a period of gentlemanliness. Stage three will be actual torture. By stage four, he thought, I'll be remembering how nice it was at stage one. I'll tell everything to get back there.

Another matter was of deep concern. The music man had slaked his thirst for jazz, had moved into rock, and was just sampling. Charles's tape library was arranged alphabetically, from Abba to Neil Young. And stereo man, randomly picking his way through the alphabet, was up to L now. A Led Zep tape. Just a half-dozen tapes down the row was *Mad Morgan and the Assassins of Moog*.

The master tape had been destroyed along with Rufus McKay. This tape was the only accessible testimonial to the treason that was taking place in America, a treason that was to culminate in a Senate vote seventeen days from now.

It has to be protected at all costs. Even if I don't get to write the story. Even if they kill me.

He thought of Israel, which had no defence against an invading barrage of Cruise missiles. No country on earth yet had a defence against those things.

And why wouldn't they kill him after the tape had been found? He thought of making a mad dash for the front window, crashing through it to the pavement four storeys below. Then these men would have to leave here and the tape could await detection ultimately by a Mad Morgan fan.

"What's a nine-letter word meaning 'convert into cash'?" Charles asked, trying to appear natural.

"Liquidate," said Fu Manchu.

The music man put the Led Zeppelin tape back in its place and began to finger his way down the row.

"What's an eight-letter word," said Fu Manchu, "meaning a kind of canary?" He offered Charles a cup of hot chocolate.

"A kind of canary?" Charles put the cup to his lips, scalded them, sputtered. A portent of torture.

"As in, sing like a canary. An eight-letter word beginning with N that also means a former general from the Pentagon."

"I never heard of him."

"Who?"

"Whoever." Charles eyed the music man, now poking through the cassettes under the Ms.

Fu Manchu checked his watch. "Turn the radio on," he ordered. "Mr. Rubinstein, I think the time has come for us to be frank and open. You will tell us what you know. I promise you that." There was a measured certainty in those words.

Classical music from an FM station.

With the music man's search through the tapes momentarily arrested, Charles was emboldened. "How much I know, I'll give you a five-letter word starting with Z and ending with ilch." His voice cracked.

"We will know before this night is over." Fu Manchu impaled him with his eyes. Charles bobbled his cup and hot chocolate slopped over the sides. He made up his mind to go for the window. NEW YORK(AP)—*Reporter Charles Rubinstein, 32, died Saturday following a four-storey fall from his apart-*

ment building here. Mr. Rubinstein was reported to have been in a depressed mental state. There were no witnesses.

Charles looked at Fu Manchu through the corner of his eye, then pencilled in small block letters along the newspaper margin the words "Mad Morgan." He tore the little note off, rolled it into a ball in his hand. *Police say a note was found crumpled in his pocket. It said, "Mad Morgan." They are investigating further.*

On the radio, the violin sonata was cut off in mid-adagio and an announcer came on.

"We have just received a bulletin from Associated Press that an attack has occurred on the royal palace in Saudi Arabia where a high-level American delegation are staying. It is understood his Royal Highness, King Fahd, was also staying there. First reports indicate a large band of terrorists stormed the palace with apparent success and have taken prisoners."

More was promised later. The music came back. Charles was reeling.

"Now we will talk," said Fu Manchu. "Make yourself as comfortable as you can, Mr. Rubinstein. On the chair there."

Charles's head was in majestic turmoil.

"Was that it?" said the jogger man, rising on his elbows from the couch. "Mecca?"

"Mecca," said Fu Manchu. "Now we will talk."

To Charles's numbed ears came the sound of voices now, from the hallway outside the apartment. Two laughing voices, male and female.

A key turned in the lock.

"Get rid of them or we will kill them," said the leader. The other two men unbuttoned their jackets.

Before the door even opened, Charles knew who it was. His sister Paula had the only spare set of keys.

She gaped at him, then glanced at the others. "Charles, you're supposed to be in California." Her college football player friend was standing behind her with a sheepish smile.

The three men all had their right hands raised, ready to dip into shoulder holsters.

Charles started talking quickly. "Uh, listen, honey, these boys and me are having an acid trip right now. We're exploring the dimensions of life. Make it tomorrow night, okay? You can have the whole place, bed and all, to yourselves. Hey, guys, it's my kid sister Paula. Jake, Frank, Bill, this is Paula.

Another time, baby. We're heading to the centre of the macrocosm."

That was weird enough. Get the hint, Paula, and get out, call the cops.

But Paula stood there dumbly. "It doesn't look like you're on any acid trip," she said, assessing the scene. Her friend stood behind her grinning foolishly, appearing a little drunk.

"We're into something heavy, Paula. I mean it." His voice was too full of warning.

"Something strange is going on, Charles. Who are these men? Who are the guys who followed us into the building?"

The music man uttered a curse and dashed to the window and glanced quickly out. "They have a car waiting," he told the others.

Fu Manchu pulled his gun and said sharply to Paula, "Get in here and get down." He went to the open doorway and grabbed her arm, pulling her roughly in, throwing her to the floor. Paula's date followed and, his judgment impaired by alcohol, lunged for the gun. The knife edge of Fu Manchu's free hand chopped his wrist, snapping it.

As the young man turned and began to run out the door, there came the sound of a soft *thunk* from the corridor, and Paula's date staggered to his knees, clutching his shoulder.

Fu Manchu dropped to one knee, and began to fire through the doorway, his gun hand braced on the other forearm. Charles heard a strangled scream from outside.

"How many men?" the jogger hissed at Paula, his gun to her head.

"Two," Paula said, wide-eyed with terror on the floor.

The music man hurled himself through the doorway, firing first to the right, the wrong way, then to the left, too late. The sounds of two more bullets passing through a silencer. *Thunk, thunk.* The music man, though hit twice in the stomach, emptied his revolver, then collapsed against the wall outside, clutching his stomach. "Damn, damn," he muttered.

"Don't call the police for ten minutes or we will kill your brother," Fu Manchu said to Paula, and he grabbed Charles by his elbow and thrust him toward the door. The other man picked his injured comrade up in his arms and the four of them went to the stairs, stepping over two dead bodies and

Paula's date, who was trying to crawl away, leaving Paula still on the floor, somewhere between total numbness and hysteria.

34

Sunday, June 10, the Desert

A grizzle-faced bedouin inspected the proffered M-16 submachine gun, played with it, admired it.

"He will give us rice and vegetables, maybe tinned meat," said Abu Ali Rag. "Tinned meat was not known when I was a young man. Lo, the wonders of progress."

Sawchuk was sitting in a circle of Arabs under a black goat-hair tent, smoking a nargilhe with them, sharing dates and cheese.

The man with the submachine-gun spoke in Arabic to Rag. "Where are you going, Abu Ali Rag?"

"Myself—towards God's gate. My friend—and this is truly a friend, whose life is worth more to me than mine—he seeks another country."

"A better one, I suspect." The herdsman hefted the gun. "I know where this will fetch a price." He smiled. "But not a good price."

Rag spoke to Sawchuk. "We will sleep here today, under their tents. But look to your animal. There is a saying: 'Trust in God, but tie your camel.'"

He returned to his bargaining. "You will see that my friend is of abnormal size. He is one who has the appetite of an elephant. Come—it is worth double. There are many rounds of ammunition, as you can see."

"My respect for you is great, Abu Ali Rag, and I will therefore say three additional tins of this excellent cured mutton. Although I suspect the infidels who prepare this food add pork. But it is given on condition that you will sing to us. Sing about the days when the desert was free."

* * *

During that night they travelled through the hills of the southern Tubayq, where the rocks were sharp, making the camels jerk and wince with pain. The animals became more churlish, made roaring complaints about their thirst. Rag explained that in the winter, when grazing was good, a camel can last thirty days without water, but in summer, without grazing, only five.

The several goatskins of water that had been tied like saddlebags to the third camel were not, Sawchuk realized, intended for Rag and himself alone. In the shadows of a rock formation where they stopped at dawn, Sawchuk watched as Rag poured water down the throats of the kneeling animals.

As the sun rose, and as Rag bowed south, Sawchuk lay on his back, watching a griffon vulture wheel slowly around. Friendlier birds, sand larks, visited their little encampment, pecked about, then disappeared.

Rag lifted his head from the sand. "Prayer is better than sleep, Sawchuk."

Sawchuk had created a wooden flute from his bamboo camel-stick, and he played simple, wistful folk tunes for Rag.

He felt his body slowly get well in the dry, healing air of the Arabian desert.

At night, when they rode, he played flute accompaniment to Rag's soft Arabic chanting, and this quieted the camels, made them less surly. They would ride well into the dawn, then start again before the sun set ahead of them. Always it went down red and angry, as if protesting, and always the night was warm and caressing. Sawchuk surrendered to Sopwith's rolling gait, but never felt as comfortable as Rag looked, who seemed one with his animal. Sawchuk no longer noticed Sopwith's stink; it had blended with his own.

Towards dawn on the fourth day, they came to a plain and it became a sand desert, interrupted later by an enormous wadi, tumbled-down boulders in cuts and valleys that slashed across the surface of the plain. Rag, working easily with the stars and a new moon, calmly picked invisible trails and brought them to the other side, as a rosy hue began to take over the sky. Sawchuk saw ahead that the desert was bleak and infinite. A wind, the northwest khamsin of the Saudi desert, had begun to hurl the fine sand into the air.

Rag stopped at the far side of the wadi, and for a long time he studied the sky, its high cirrus, whipped by the wind into the shapes of filmy sails. Behind them, the sun was dark as blood.

"The khamsin blows hard here," he said. "It is fourteen hours across the desert to the mountains. We will not stop. The desert will protect us." He wrapped one of the ends of his *kaffiyeh* around his mouth and nose. "Be ready for what the desert gives."

The desert gave birth to a sandstorm that obscured them from the sky and the sky from them. All was a blind greyness. Gusts scraped at Sawchuk's face, dust choking him. But the wind was from behind them, and drove them like sailing craft, and although the camels moaned pitifully, they plodded on.

Rag stayed beside him, directing the animals with his stick as if somehow able in this fog of driven sand to know north from south and east from west. Sawchuk could see Rag's dark eyes smiling at him, surrounded by caked yellow dust.

The heat became scorching, but Sawchuk followed Rag's example, and sipped little water during the journey. The wind dried him up, and he began to think again of the terrors of thirst. And to remember Bisharat.

Nothing seemed to have meaning out here. There was just the thunder of the wind, the drunken, rolling walk of the camel, the struggle to breathe, the thirst, the loneliness of a savage land.

Then, like an apparition, a huge diesel trailer-truck, its headlights glaring white and yellow, swooped past in front of them, left to right, and disappeared with a powerful rumble of engine. Sopwith bucked and started to bolt, but Rag grabbed her by the ear and controlled her.

"It is the desert highway to Amman and Damascus," Rag shouted in his ear. "Beyond it is the Hejaz railway."

"And beyond that?" Sawchuk shouted.

"The desert."

At the end of that laboured day, as the wind slackened, they came to the first scattered rock that led to the foothills of the Hejaz range, the long spine of intruded and volcanic rock that divided Arabia's narrow coastal plain from the vastness of its deserts. They began to toil upwards. Sawchuk knew his camel was exhausted, barely able to put one foot ahead of another.

But Rag seemed to know where he was going, as if he had passed this way every day of his life and, eventually, as the sky darkened, he took them down into a little valley sheltered from the wind by cliffs. Some yellowed grass and tribulus dotted the valley bottom.

Rag hobbled the camels and they hopped about, grazing.

"We will stay the night, and the day." Rag was a ghost, coated in dust. "For the mountains, we need rest."

Sawchuk and Rag were walking. The camels were limping, their thick feet cut by shale. The hours seemed unending as they worked their way through canyons, granite massives towering above them, and climbed up the rock-strewn passes. At the top of each pass, Sawchuk always saw mountains rising to the west, the ranges taller, seemingly impossible to breach.

But Abu Ali Rag assured him this was a route that nomads had followed for as long as there had been Arabia.

Rag turned to him once and said, "The mountain that one climbs with a friend should be for him a road that goes downhill." He smiled.

When the sun rose on the sixth day, Sawchuk could see, in the aqueous light near the horizon, a dun-coloured plain below them to the east. The flat blueness beyond was sea, the Gulf of Aqaba.

That night they crossed the coastal highway. The coastal plain was dry, but supported some plant life, and the camels slowed to graze from time to time. They travelled past bedouin encampments and their sleeping flocks of sheep and goats and camels.

After the sun rose, Rag visited one of the camps: several long, low, black tents supported by sticks, with naked children running and playing nearby. Rag fetched Sawchuk, and they shared some tea and drank water, and ate bread. The children peeked at the awesome white giant with the sad eyes and ripening red beard. They hung to their mothers' dresses, giggling. The mothers had hurried into their tents to don their veils when the guests came. They looked, said nothing. There were four families here.

The men did not talk much either. "They will not ask

questions," said Rag. "Only on the fourth day does one ask questions of a guest. They have invited us to stay, of course: 'Honour thy guest, though he be an infidel.' We will travel with them tomorrow."

Sawchuk felt like living with them, melding into them, walking the plains with them in search of pasture, being a child with their children. Those children were bug-eyed as he played his flute for them after breakfast. Then the bedouin struck their tents. Sawchuk tried to help, got in the way, and was tolerated. They moved west to pastures near the sea where winds brought moisture and grass.

Rag and Sawchuk had ridden all night and now walked all day, sleepless, exhausted. But Sawchuk felt good leading his camel with these other men, felt comfort as a hidden member of this extended family.

Once a pair of military helicopters flew above them, but did not slow and continued to the north.

They came to the low hills that fringed the coast, and Sawchuk, enervated, plodded to the crest of a grassy knoll overlooking the sea. He and Rag said goodbye to the others here.

"*Fi amanillah*," said the headman. "Go in the safety of God." The herders began to raise their tents in the shelter of the knoll.

Rag and Sawchuk carried on north, continuing to walk because the camels' feet had not healed. They rested a few hours before sunset under a grove of tamarisk trees. Sawchuk tried to sleep—he had been awake twenty hours now—but his mind would not rest. As the days had passed since the escape from Casr al-Akbhar, as his mind had become less preoccupied with the fundamental struggle of surviving, its vacated spaces began to fill with hate. Sheer, unadulterated, voluptuous.

Formerly, he had hated only himself. But those days seemed long, long ago. When had that been, when he had been a wasting, failed poet, screaming obscenities at his Remington and his macaw, Chamberlain? How many centuries had passed since then?

And he remembered his political emptiness, those final days of frantic search for his lost Marxist ethic, his desertion, at the end, even of Marcuse. The purposelessness of it all.

But no longer. He was filled with purpose. It had very little

to do with the creation of a brave new world and very much
to do with one of the cruellest of human emotions: revenge.
How sweet was the lust for vengeance. Bisharat may have
stolen from him the power of his sex, but Sawchuk's glands
were filled with richer juices now.

Sawchuk stared down over the waters of the Gulf, aquama-
rine where coral reefs webbed out hundreds of feet from the
shore. In the distance, tankers crawled across the waters. The
faint outline of hills was pencilled along the horizon across
the Gulf.

They travelled all night, and those hills had moved closer
when, on the morning of the eighth day in the desert, the
sun's rays touched the sky. Rag took them back inland a way,
and when they came around a rise, Sawchuk saw the flags of
Saudi Arabia and Jordan—the border. He saw one small
plaster hut, but the other buildings were cut off from view by
the hillside. Up the coast, on the Jordan side, was an
enormous dock facility with freighters, transport trucks.

"From here we can see four countries," said Rag. "Jordan
to the north, Egypt on the other side of the water. Beyond, at
the head of the Gulf, is the land of Palestine, which you call
Israel."

Sawchuk could see the city of Aqaba, white among lush,
irrigated fields. Beyond that was Elath, a tiny jewel at the
southern tip of Israel. Sawchuk felt giddy with lack of sleep.

"My home is back in the Najd," said Rag. "There are ways
across the border into Jordan. I will show you one. Will you
not be secure in the country of King Faisal?"

Although friendly to the West, Jordan might mean compli-
cations. In Israel, the Mossad knew that Sawchuk worked for
Group Seven, was not a terrorist.

"Come with me to Israel," he said. "They are not devils,
although they often seem to be. They will be pleased to
harbour a political refugee from Saudi Arabia. You are hunted,
Abu Ali Rag. I will find you safety."

"I will find my safety among friends. I have many. Some of
those friends once lived in the Negev, and cannot now. More
than that, we should not discuss. Come, we can go behind
the hills, where there is no fence." Rag tapped his camel on
the knee with his stick, and it snorted and went down, and
Rag mounted.

Sawchuk did not move. He stared toward the head of the

Gulf of Aqaba, to Israel, twenty miles away. The Gulf was as calm as the waters of the lake where he had spent his summers with his father.

He turned to Rag. "You may have the camels."

Rag smiled. "If I have three camels I am a rich man."

"Thank you, Abu Ali Rag."

"Who gives not thanks to men, gives not thanks to God."

"*Salam alaikum*," said Sawchuk. "Peace be on you."

"*Alaikum as salam*," said Rag. "On you be peace."

Sawchuk, his robes gently flapping behind him, walked down the hill toward a pebbled beach.

Rag watched, expressionless, as the tall *nasrani* removed his headdress and laid it on the pebbles, then removed his *thaub*, and stood naked, a white giant in the morning sun. He watched as Sawchuk walked slowly into the water, and watched as it rose to his thighs, his hips.

Sawchuk then began to swim. Long, sure, clean strokes through the water.

VI

Götterdämmerung

*Time consists of two days—
one for thee, the other
against thee.*

Arab proverb

35

Friday, June 15, Elath

Judy McKenzie and Henriette Flosser, attractive women of about sixty, one recently divorced, the other widowed, took their solace every evening at the poolside bar by sipping complicated drinks of rum or vodka that Yev the bartender teased them with.

The Orange Lizard, vodka and grenadine and fresh orange juice poured into a glass filled with crushed ice: that was the favourite of Judy McKenzie. Henriette Flosser, succumbing to the sugary descriptions of smiling, mustachioed Yev, was on her third Burglar's Surprise.

They were booked for one more week in Israel, then on to the dark mysteries of Cairo.

The bar was empty of other customers because dinner was being taken inside the hotel. Judy McKenzie and Henriette Flosser refused to join them just yet. They saw themselves as intrepid and independent travellers, not like the rest of the Americans on the tour, who gathered together like sheep to eat or play cards according to the advice of the benevolent dictator who was their tour director.

The sun had fallen behind the hills, but the evening was still hot, and their cotton dresses were sticky. They talked about their husbands, one with anger, one with happy memories.

Henriette Flosser, who had been bored on this trip, who had been looking for excitement if not romance, held the Burglar's Surprise in her two hands, her upper lip curled over a pair of straws, and she was straining her eyes, looking out to sea.

"That is something," she said. "What is it?"

229

It was a little furrowing of the waters far out in the bay.

"A shark."

"No."

"Yev, what is that?"

The bartender came up to their table and he, too, peered into the distance. "I think it's a man."

"Goodness."

They watched in silence as the man stroked toward the beach. They saw him duck under the rope that warned of deep waters, and he cleaved the water slowly, a long, unhurried Australian crawl, toward the sand.

He stood, and was in water to his waist. He tried to walk forward, wobbled, lost his balance, then moved forward again. Now they could see he was naked.

"Goodness *gracious*."

Jacques Sawchuk walked very slowly up the beach, to the steps which led to the terrace. Judy McKenzie and Henriette Flosser were flustered but unable to keep their eyes off him as he advanced toward the bar. He didn't seem to see them, or to be looking at anything in particular.

He leaned against the bar and turned to Yev. "Double vodka martini, straight up with a twist," he said.

Yev made the drink.

Sawchuk sipped it, continued to stand, staring vacantly at the bottles arrayed at the back of the bar. He turned around and for about thirty seconds stared at the sea whence he had come. The women were wide-eyed and speechless, straining not to look at him.

He stepped away from the bar, finished his martini, then took two steps to the side of the bar.

He collapsed in a heap of naked limbs.

36

Saturday, June 16, East Berlin

"Wie geht's?" said General Helmut von Hertz, easing his aging bulk onto the stone bench beside the Permagon Museum, near the river. It was a fine morning. Too beautiful a day for more of this business with his old but demanding friend Heinrich Hesselmann. This was their second meeting in two weeks, and it was seeming like the start of a bad habit. A habit with worrisome implications. "We must stop meeting like this, Heini. People will talk."

"We have not completed the contract, Helmut."

"The contract? It was for Karl Wurger. I told you that you could have him." Von Hertz smiled benignly. "All you have to do is walk into the summer palace of Prince Aziz and take him. We will not complain."

Hesselmann was feeding bread crumbs to a flock of bobbing pigeons. Von Hertz did not like these dirty birds, wanted to shoo them away. "Yes, it is Wurger I have come for," said Hesselmann.

"Perhaps you have not read the newspapers, Heini. On the front pages are to be found stories about the taking of Aziz's palace by Karl Wurger and a hundred and fifty of his commandos. They have the Saudi royal family, the defence minister, their entourages, plus a little group of friendly arms dealers from America. That is where the object of your interest is to be found: in a palace near Mecca. I doubt that Major Wurger will come out of there and surrender to you even if I ask him very nicely. As I have told you, he escaped from us."

"The Saudi government has asked us to take charge of the negotiations. I think you know that."

"Yes, your man Bakerfield. Is he not supposed to be an expert in these hostage things? Three prisoners shot in cold blood while he's been on the job there." Von Hertz made a *tsk-tsk* sound. He kicked feebly at the pigeons with his gouty leg.

"You can give us Wurger yet," Hesselmann said. "You have evidence we could use. And we would be pleased to have your co-operation in getting a man inside the palace."

Von Hertz had no idea what his old friend was driving at.

"Helmut, we have decided to give in completely on Wurger's demand for a prisoner exchange—the palace servants for thirty-seven jailed terrorists—because if we go along with it, we may be able to get a Group Seven agent into the palace. All we need is a little help from your government."

"I see we are not keeping secrets. Who is this agent?"

"Jacques Sawchuk."

"That fellow who calls himself a poet? But he killed Isaac...." Von Hertz listened to his own words die. He tried to ignore the pigeons fluttering near his feet and looked up at the urn-like bulb of the East Berlin television tower. The city's penis erectus. Could that be? he thought. My, they have done quite a job. "All that business about him on a robbing and killing spree in France a few months ago—you organized that? And they say the Eastern press is managed." He patted Hesselmann on the shoulder. "Still the master, Heini. Still the master. I am glad you did not elect for the East. You would have had my job."

Von Hertz looked down and peered sadly at the white gob on his shiny weekend walking shoes.

"I remember wondering about that fellow," he said. "I had read some of his complaints about the influence in Cuba of our beloved comrades from the Soviet Union. The worst sort of heresy: made up of truths. It seemed to me he had lost his zeal for the Cause, then suddenly regained it in Canada when he went on trial for a political murder. I remember sniffing at the bad aroma. But there are so many strange smells about these days. Did you set up the trial, too. Heini? A masterwork. But one thing disturbs me. If your man infiltrated the Rotkommando, how is it you did not know in advance of the attack on Mecca?"

Hesselmann said nothing for a while. He tossed the last of the bread crumbs. "We knew. And we didn't know."

Von Hertz let it go. "How would we be able to help?"

"Sawchuk disappeared in this city. Why he was in East Berlin, I don't know, but he was kidnapped by a PLO squad, and smuggled to Saudi Arabia by plane."

Von Hertz was embarrassed. He had had no wind of this: someone smuggled out of the city under his nose.

"He resurfaced last night in Elath and is in an Israeli hospital mumbling 'Arabia' in his sleep. It occurred to us that since we and the Saudis are working side by side in the Mecca hostage negotiations, we might ask Saudi Special Security what they knew about our Sawchuk, if anything. It appears he escaped eight days ago from a Saudi prison. After having been tortured for claiming he was a Western agent."

Von Hertz slapped his knee and his jowls bounced with merriment. He enjoyed it when the opposition walked Chaplin-like into closed doors.

"Colonel Bisharat has been working with Mr. Bakerfield at Mecca for the last four days. Only last night and only upon blunt questions being asked did he admit that Sawchuk's kidnapping in your country had been engineered by his security agency, with the help of the PLO."

It galled von Hertz that all this had happened without a whisper of gossip to any of his security police. He realized Hesselmann knew this, too, and was appealing—quite correctly—to von Hertz's sense of damaged honour.

"Bisharat is a man of dubious ability, but he managed that one rather well," said Hesselmann, his expression bland. "The Saudi royal family, however, I fear is quite put out that Bisharat had so mishandled the questioning of Agent Sawchuk. Had the colonel listened to our man's account of being an anti-terrorist agent, the taking of Aziz's palace would never have occurred, and the Rotkommando would have been smashed."

Von Hertz chuckled again. "History writes itself with irony."

"The Council of Elders is prepared to pay billions to free the King and his brother and the others. They will, unless you help us. Do you want Karl Wurger and a division of armed fanatics roaming about the world trying to trigger a great power war? Because that is what we will have if Wurger succeeds when it comes time to ask for money. Helmut, we

don't think Wurger knows Sawchuk was kidnapped in East
Berlin. He believes the PLO killed him. If you will announce
he is in jail here, arrested two weeks ago in a city park,
Wurger will believe Sawchuk was picked up before the PLO
assassins got to him. He will have no reason to suspect
otherwise."

Von Hertz was wearying of this sales pitch. "And what
then?"

"You will agree to release Sawchuk as part of the prisoner
exchange that Wurger is demanding."

Von Hertz sighed. "Surely you will appreciate that the East
German government has no wish to interfere with the foreign
affairs of other countries. We are like the Israelis over this
business in Mecca. Politics makes strange bedfellows. We
share their delight and share it for similar reasons. The
Israelis hope the U.S. government will conclude that the
Saudis are clumsy and unreliable allies, and will not complete
the sale of Cruise missiles to that curious country. My good
friends in Moscow believe these missiles will be aimed at
Baku and Ashkabad and Aden. The Israelis believe they will
be directed at them. Probably we are both right. The world is
a complicated place, is it not?"

"Helmut, it is painful for me to do this."

"Do what?" Von Hertz felt his old friend's unease, felt
more shadows drifting between them.

"I have in a safety deposit box my confession as to my role
as a counter-agent inside the Allied command. In that document I also speak of the work you did in turning over to the
Gestapo the communist leaders of the French Resistance. If I
fail to give a countermand order within the day, someone will
open that box."

The pigeons had begun to withdraw from the feast, and
von Hertz saw a white, wet mark on the toe of his other shoe.
He groaned. "I am to be held hostage by a seventy-year-old
terrorist. Blackmail becomes an addiction, Heini. If I let you
keep this up, you will be running me, you will be my case
agent. A very unsatisfactory situation."

The ignominy of his friend stooping to this. But he thought
he knew what drove Hesselmann to these extremes: the guilt
over what had happened to the Jews, and Hesselmann's role
at Auschwitz, however minor. One month there, as an observer-
delegate for Admiral Canaris of the Abwehr. Before the mass

killings to be sure—but during the experiments. Hesselmann had been spending the rest of his life paying off dues.

But von Hertz, too, possessed *mens rea*—the guilt of knowledge—and he had been utterly sickened later by the Holocaust. "It is not your crude extortion which sways me to help you, Heini. It is Isaac Solomon's death. I told that *Schweinehund:* No more Jewish artists. Solomon! The greatest interpreter of Beethoven of this generation, greater than Schnabel in his." He pulled out a handkerchief, bent forward with a grunt, daubed at his shoes. "So it was not Sawchuk who did that assassination—it was Wurger after all. I should have thought so. It was his style. Destroy the great and thou shalt be great. A paranoid schizophrenic with a megalomania complex, that is what the doctors wrote of his father. Like father, like son."

"And who is this father?" Hesselmann asked.

"My government will want compensation," von Hertz said. "More than the Saudis are prepared to give to the other countries. About five million in Western currency: that will sell this scheme to the ministers." He looked sharply at Hesselmann. "Then all debts are paid."

"Yes. Helmut, who was Wurger's father?"

"He used to prefer his whores blonde and plump, and he ordered most of them killed afterwards in case he had passed them secrets in his sleep. But Wurger's mother managed to survive both the Gestapo and the war, although the baby killed her in birth. The Shrike's first victim." Von Hertz put his old arm around Hesselmann and patted him on the shoulder. "The boss, Heini. Not Canaris. The man we *really* worked for."

Hesselmann's usually passive face seemed to rupture. "Himmler?" he whispered.

"He was madder than the Führer. Perhaps that was why each was the only man the other trusted. They say that before he died, before the Russians moved in, Himmler descended into a raving mania."

"I have heard that. My God, Himmler."

"Who despised socialism with such fanatic passion. So we played a joke upon his memory and made his son a fanatic socialist, and we hoped young Karl would give us his father's sharp policeman's mind. But Wurger inherited a disease of that mind. And the genes of hatred."

There was a long silence.

"We should go to your office now, Helmut."

37

Saturday, June 16, the Negev

He opened his eyes to the touch of soft fingers on his wrist. A nurse, slim, dark-haired, was holding it.

"How am I?" he said.

"I don't know. I've never tried you. Your pulse is good, but you have bruises on your bruises. We found a small fracture on your left cheekbone, but no displacement. You were screaming terrible words, so we had to pump some tranquillizer into you." She spoke with an American drawl.

"How long have I been asleep?" Sawchuk felt secure, almost at peace, in this darkened, antiseptic room.

"Seventeen hours and thirty-five minutes. That's since they 'coptered you out here. We are in the Negev. This is the Mossad 101 field clinic. God, we thought you'd never wake up. We want to put you through a full physical, but you don't seem to be missing any toes or anything."

But Sawchuk felt he was missing something. He remembered Bisharat's electric gelding and tasted bile.

But God—he was out. His emotions were a complex mix of exultation and sorrow and implacable hate.

A voice from the doorway. "You got yourself into a real mess, Agent Sawchuk. Have we got to wet-nurse you or something?" It was Frank Fager. He was wearing a white T-shirt, khaki shorts that showed knobby knees, ugly wraparound sunglasses that bespoke a fear of the desert's harsh sunlight.

"Fager the Undertager," Sawchuk groaned. "You are like an ill omen. The last time I saw you, I got my head smashed in an hour later."

"Told you to come to Pittsburgh to die, not Saudi Arabia."

"Please, Agent Fager," said the nurse, "not until the doctor sees him."

Fager ducked under her outstretched arm, came up to the bed. "So go get the doctor."

The nurse fled and Fager took Sawchuk's hand. To Sawchuk he seemed thinner, uglier, with his wonky nose, his mop of straight black hair.

"We know what happened in East Berlin. Bisharat finally filled us in. Even if he told us only part of the truth, what he told us convinced me it was the worst horror show since 3-D movies." Fager put his hand gently on Sawchuk's shoulder. "I'm sorry. But you look okay. You survived in one piece."

"Bisharat. That fucker."

"Yeah, he's a real mean machine."

The nurse came to the door, the doctor in tow. He moved Fager out of the way, urged Sawchuk to a sitting position, began probing him with a stethoscope.

"Tell me, Fager," Sawchuk said, "did Bisharat explain how the PLO kidnap team knew where to find me in East Berlin?"

"Tip-off to the PLO mission there. Caller a German-speaking male."

"With a high, authoritarian voice? Sort of like a bird? Say, a shrike?" He lay back down.

"Shrike?"

"Only Wurger knew where I was."

"Wurger—that's kind of unbelievable."

"Why?"

"Because he wants you back in the fold."

"What do you mean? You *have* picked him up, haven't you?"

Fager stuck a stick of Juicy Fruit in his mouth, chewed strenuously.

"Did you take them in Amman or wait for Mecca?" Sawchuk asked.

Fager just chewed.

"Hey, Undertaker, I gave you everything at Orly Airport. And in Berlin."

"It kinda got fucked up."

The doctor plunged a thermometer into Sawchuk's mouth. Sawchuk pulled it out. "What do you mean it got fucked up? What happened?"

"Bisharat wouldn't let our guys into the country. And he

wouldn't believe Aziz's summer palace was the target. Impossible to break into it, he said. They didn't know there was a terrorist inside."

"But *you* knew. I told you. It was on the tape, the Cuyfer tape."

"Well, there was some garble on it. Anyway, Bisharat flat didn't believe the tip."

"I flat don't believe *you*." The doctor replaced the thermometer in Sawchuk's mouth, and Sawchuk wobbled it like a toothpick as he talked. "Bisharat was torturing me to find out what I knew of Operation Mecca. Nobody had told him *anything*. What kind of shit is this, Fager?"

"Please, Mr. Sawchuk," said the doctor.

"Yeah, just keep your mouth shut for a few minutes. I've given you the truth." He shrugged. "As we know it. Okay, this is the scene: They have the palace. They have the King and fourteen members of his family. They have the minister of defence and his eleven. A royal entourage of twenty-seven. A hundred and twenty-three palace servants and their families. A Saudi government staff of twelve. The assistant undersecretary of State for the U.S., three of his juniors, six men from the Pentagon, three from the Typhon Corporation. They were all there to sign the Cruise missile deal, right? They are also holding forty-seven soldiers of the palace guard, supposedly an elite ranger corps, but not very brave. Less some who were killed, maybe thirty or so. Minus three they shot in cold blood yesterday. Two escaped: Prince Aziz himself and the executive veep of Typhon. By helicopter."

Sawchuk stared at him, incredulous. Fager made a few snapping sounds as he chewed his gum, then carried on.

"We figure there are a hundred and fifty terrorists in there. Some must've got killed in the assault, but they still got an enhanced company of pretty-well-trained soldiers. Wurger heads the bargaining group. Cuyfer, Zahre, almost all the Committee are inside. They're threatening to bump three of the palace guard every day until their first demand is met."

Sawchuk's eyes were squinting and disbelieving. "And what is their first demand?" he said in a muffled voice.

"Big prisoner exchange. It's gonna happen this evening. Five Western countries have agreed—they'll get paid plenty by the Saudi government—to release thirty-seven jailed terrorists in return for the hundred and twenty-three palace staff and families. They're innocent proletariat, see? And we guess Wurger wants to cut down on the numbers he has to guard and feed. Okay. They've promised no further hostages will be shot if we free the jailed terrorists by eight tonight. It's three o'clock now. Most of the terrorists will be flown to Libya."

"And their second demand?"

"They haven't got to that yet. From the briefing in Berlin, I'd guess they want lots of money, to equip and train Wurger's army. The negotiations have been going on for the last week. Hamilton Bakerfield is in charge, stalling them like mad, trying to negotiate numbers of bodies. We're in there because the Saudis requested our help. Bisharat extends his apologies. He says sorry. God curses him for his stupidity."

Sawchuk glared at Fager, still incredulous. The doctor wrapped a rubber cuff around his arm and pumped it up.

"We got terrorists being released from Italy, France, West Germany, Turkey. Those governments agreed once they found out we could get you inside."

Sawchuk almost bit the thermometer in half.

"Eighteen of the released terrorists have elected to join the Rotkommando in Mecca. Wurger insisted that option be left open for them." Fager worked at his gum. "General Hesselmann has just been across to East Berlin. It seems he has some leverage there. This is what he's set up: the East German government has just announced you were arrested a couple of weeks ago on a terrorist mission in East Berlin. And so your name has now been included in the list of terrorists that the Rotkommando wants exchanged. What we figure we'll do is fly you to a staging area in Cyprus, where you'll join the other eighteen. Then to the palace at Mecca. By eight o'clock tonight."

"Are you kidding?" No one was laughing. The doctor was studying x-rays and the nurse was heating chicken soup. Now the doctor grabbed the thermometer from Sawchuk's mouth, looked at it, nodded, snapped the mercury down, handed it to the nurse.

Fager went on. "I better tell you that Rotkommando claims to have wired the bottom five levels of the palace with high-explosive plastic bombs. Most of the captives—all the big names, for sure—are held on the seventh to twelfth floors. If the Rotkommando had pros do it, the building should collapse when the bombs go off. Bakerfield figures that's the main thing, disconnecting the fuse. Once that's done, we can feel free to rush them. We've got commandos at Taif, fifty miles away. You would be equipped with a transmitter to tell us when to go in."

The doctor had Sawchuk sitting up again now, his arms raised, his various glands being examined.

"I see you are not laughing, Fager," said Sawchuk. "But you have a keen, subtle sense of humour, and you are having one off at the expense of Agent Sawchuk, the garlic-munching Ukrainian oaf who has provided so much entertainment to the boys of the Group."

"One other thing. As an additional safeguard, Dr. Laurent Pétras, the crazed chemotherapist, will be laying on you a chemical known as DNT-17. If you can get it into those assholes' drinking water, they'll become as harmless as slugs. The crawling kind."

"You should go to Hollywood. Write slapstick like this. Make a fortune."

"He calls it the 'love drug.' He's coming here by helicopter in a few minutes. He's been at Aziz's palace, advising Bakerfield."

"Cough," said the doctor.

Sawchuk coughed.

"One more week, you said. That was in Berlin, Fager, in the guest dressing room of the Philharmonie. You remember. 'I got Hesselmann's proxy,' you said. That was two weeks ago. I'm now a retired civil servant." Sawchuk laughed a soft, bitter laugh. "Bisharat bungled this and in the process almost killed me. And that motherfucker wants me to go in there to try to save his ass. Well, the Group can collectively kiss mine."

"Look, man, after what you went through we know you don't owe any debt to Saudi Arabia. But the palace is full of innocent people. You can help save about two hundred lives."

"Innocent people: Pentagon generals selling Cruise missiles to a feudal autocracy." He yelled "ouch" as the doctor poked him in a tender spot. "Wurger wants me back in the fold—who do you think you're kidding? He wants me *dead*, you jerk. He wants to finish me off, that's why he wants me back in the palace." But God how he would love to get back at Wurger. And a little idea began to burst from a seed in his revenge-filled mind.

Fager put a second stick of Juicy Fruit into his mouth, chewed hard. "The Saudis are prepared to pay you a lot of bread, Sawchuk. They're talking about a Zurich account with a couple of million bucks."

"They can't afford me. They haven't got my price." But Sawchuk said this abstractedly, softly, not really thinking about the money. The idea was sending out rootlets.

Fager chewed gloomily, not looking Sawchuk in the eye. There was a long pause. Then he pulled some photographs from his pocket, a group of Polaroid prints. "We just got these," he said in a low voice.

When he looked at the first one, Sawchuk felt revulsion. It showed Abu Ali Rag, blood coming from his mouth, standing in front of three camels. Kamal Bisharat was beside him.

"Taken this morning," Fager said. "Came by special air despatch."

The other photographs offered similar proof of Rag's capture. In the last one he was on his hands and knees and an sss agent was holding a rifle to his head. There was no subtlety in that last message from Bisharat.

"He said the man confessed his crimes against the royal kingdom," Fager said, his voice strained. "As he puts it, God's will is to be exacted on his head tonight."

Sawchuk watched the doctor pack his instruments away. Fager nervously pulled a third stick of gum from his pocket, folded it a few times, tucked it into his mouth.

"Tell him," Sawchuk said finally, "that Abu Ali Rag must be produced at the gates of the palace before I enter it tonight. In good health. With a full pardon. A visa to get out of Saudi Arabia. He will be in Bakerfield's safe conduct. Will you tell the slimebag that?" His voice was level, controlled.

"Yeah, okay. Sorry. His idea, not ours."

"Of course, Fager. I quite understand." A faraway look was in Sawchuk's eyes. Yes, he thought. The Group has used me. Now it is time to use the Group. He owed them nothing now. Not after this last sickening attempt at extortion. *His idea, not ours*. What users these people are. How venal.

"We've only got two hours to debrief you," Fager said, "and then to run you through the layout of the palace and the state of the siege. Then we take you by Saudi plane—it'll look like they brought you in from East Germany—to the staging area in Cyprus. When you get to Cyprus, Hesselmann will have a small packet waiting for you. A little material you can use against Wurger. I'll fill you in after you fill your stomach. *Sholom aleichem.*" He wandered out.

"You look good," said the doctor. "We want a urine sample, and we have some tests, but you can put some clothes on now." He handed Sawchuk clean clothing from a locker, grey cotton slacks and shirt, boots. Sawchuk looked at the labels: East German issue.

He sighed, sat down at a table and had chicken soup with matzoh balls.

Sawchuk was debriefed quickly, then intensively lectured by Fager and two others about the palace, and shown photographs and layouts.

What was known about the situation was: all military prisoners, the surviving members of the palace guard, were locked in Aziz's enormous wine cellars. The Americans, the Saudi royalty and government people, the royal entourages, were confined in their rooms on the upper floors of the palace, all escape routes from the building being guarded by Rotkommando soldiers. The 123 staff and family who were to be released were under guard in a compound building. The palace kitchens served food to hostages and terrorists alike, and enough food was available to last them several weeks after they reduced their numbers by trading away the servants. Water had been cut off, but the swimming pools were full. Power had also been cut off from outside the palace walls—the cables had been cut, and any battery radios were subject to jamming. The compound gate had been unhinged by a missile during the attack, and was partly open.

Wurger had been doing most of the negotiating. Pétras, posing as Bakerfield's second-in-command, had been at the table, set up just inside the gate, and he had drawn the conclusion that Wurger seemed to be on the verge of a nervous breakdown. The negotiations had been lively, with Wurger bursting into wild rhetoric about the military-industrial conspiracy, and making ugly threats about the hostages. "You will know that we are not weak," he had repeated many times.

The specific negotiations as to Sawchuk had been odd, in that Cuyfer and another man had done most of the talking, with Wurger nodding, apparently in sullen agreement.

Bakerfield believed there had been bitter fights among the Central Committee between sessions, and Pétras hypothesized that Wurger was offering clues to a paranoia in which he saw conspiracies within conspiracies, and not all of them outside the palace walls.

Wurger's deteriorating mental state, his jealousy over Zahre—these factors were going to make life's path a slippery one in there. He remembered Kathë Zahre's descriptions of Wurger's moods and delusions. Zahre—she brought added problems.

During part of the briefing, Sawchuk sat rigidly in a tilted dentist's chair while a large hole was drilled into a lower-left molar, a transmitter packed in with the filling. Contact with a strip of copper sewn into his belt would set it off.

Now he was alone at a desk, poring over charts and diagrams, memorizing. A squat man with a brown walrus moustache came up to him. "I am Major Arvad, Unit 101, camp commander. I know you are busy, Mr. Sawchuk, but I would like a word with you before you leave."

"Let's have the word now."

"I'll be quick. I ask a little favour, if it is at all possible. We have classified information that, ah, even Group Seven has not been informed about." A delicate smile under the big moustache.

"Don't trust them, huh? I'll tell *you* some classified information. I don't either."

"You are aware that the contract for purchase of land-based Cruise missile systems was signed in the palace the day before the terrorists struck."

"Thirteen billion dollars' worth of the world's most sophisticated weaponry. It is like giving three-year-olds live grenades to play with."

"We were of the view that you might see it that way. You know that the U.S. Senate is to approve or veto the President's bill in ten days. It looks like ayes may have it by two votes. I am now going to tell you something rather interesting. We have information—reliable, but please don't ask me how we came upon it—that two of those votes have been bought by fifteen million dollars in bribes. Saudi money, but a Typhon operation. A third senator has been blackmailed: also a Typhon operation. We believe there is evidence of these matters, in the form of taped conversations and two strips of film, in Aziz's private vault on the thirteenth floor of the palace. Since the Saudis supplied the bribe money, we assume they wanted proof in their hands that their investment was sound."

Sawchuk tried to digest this new information: more complex mental food to work through his system.

"I have become cynical with the passing years," he said, "so I'm not surprised. I've got nothing else on my plate except dismantling some bombs, saving a few hundred lives, and overpowering an enhanced company of trained killers. I'll look around for you. It'll give me something to do on my off hours." Sawchuk almost laughed aloud. The whole transnational capitalist conspiracy: it had all been happening in Aziz's palace. He remembered the sixties—creating dark scenarios about how the multinationals controlled the world and corrupted its politicians.

But those were the days when Sawchuk thought of himself as an honest revolutionary. Before he joined the enemy. Whoever that was.

Dr. Pétras's helicopter landed just fifteen minutes before Sawchuk was scheduled to depart for Cyprus.

He minced into the briefing room as Fager was hammering home some final points. "Night is the best time, Jacques. Best time to dismantle the detonator, best time to rush them. There'll be tear gas, but just come running out with the others. No one will shoot. But if *you* have to use a gun, well, you know what you gotta do. Good luck." He left.

Pétras had no time for small talk. The hand he offered Sawchuk was damp and soft. "DNT-17. Developed by a team from the Bayer labs. Properties similar to LSD-25. Promotes feelings of, ah, brotherhood. But no physical symptoms that will warn them they have been drugged. No increased heart rate, no tightening of the bowels, no temperature change, no furring of the mental processes. One simply becomes unable to perform harmful acts."

Sawchuk was suspicious of this psychiatrist and his strange drugs.

"They will become malleable for a short but significant time frame," Pétras continued. "Within fifteen minutes of ingestion, they will find they are unable to squash a cockroach."

"Who has this been tested on?"

"A few dangerous psychopaths, volunteers in prisons. They

have all become quite lovable, and are being kept on it orally now. Model prisoners, Jacques, model prisoners."

"And how will my comrades ingest this stuff? Am I going to walk around putting tablets on their tongues?"

Pétras pulled a paperback book from his pocket, passed it to him. The title read: *101 Ways to Improve Your Health.* "Pages forty through eighty have been dipped. They are made of special fibres that will dissolve in liquid. Cut them up into tiny squares."

"And what—drop them into the stewpot?"

"You are trained to think for yourself."

"I almost forgot."

38

Saturday Evening, June 16, the Palace

She stood like an Indian sentry, shading her eyes from the falling sun, leather sandals, tassled shirt, a rifle slung on her shoulder. She waited. She and the palace were enveloped in a taut stillness, disturbed only by the mutterings of those who prayed below her.

Kathë Zahre had had presentiments of death. Black, shining birds, like ravens, had flown silently in her dreams, their claws red. She had awakened as they spiralled downwards, and had listened with horror to the sound of Wurger's teeth working together, a mill of agony and illness. She always slept poorly, fearing him, his black aura covering her like a shroud.

Jacques was alive. Had she known that all along? Despite Wurger's story that Jacques had likely been assassinated in East Berlin, she had felt in her heart that he lived; in her heart, where the true information was kept, where she knew that Wurger had played some treacherous sport with her new lover.

She had travelled to Amman, to Tripoli, to the Misurate camp, to Ankara, to Jeddah, and to the palace of Prince Aziz. She had done so only because her heart had told her Sawchuk was alive and they would come together in perilous, provocative connection. God, the excitement.

It was half-past seven. She looked below, to the great marble stairway that cascaded down the hill from the palace tower to the tiled terrace below, near the gate. There she saw the intended sacrifices: three soldiers of the palace guard trussed against the wall, gagged, their eyes crying for mercy. The fourth, fifth, and sixth sacrifices. The first three bodies had been removed from in front of the open gate yesterday afternoon, taken away by Saudi officials for burial in the desert.

Murder, murder unceasing, she thought.

She looked at the figure pacing beside the terrified guardsmen, pacing the tiles of the courtyard, back and forth, back and forth, like a caged tiger. Karl Wurger, holding his automatic pistol, studying it intently as if it were a graven image of his god.

Over the last few weeks his mind had seemed to separate, rejoin, separate again. He had trespassed to the edge of a final madness, she felt, was hovering at the abyss. Everyone on the Central Committee had begun to realize that, even those once blinded by devotion. Yet they had followed him here, unable to deny him. Perhaps because of his madness, the Rotkommando had succeeded in conquering the palace. And they held the King of Arabia and his court, the American arms merchants—and the attention of all the world.

Zahre was one of a dozen guards standing sentry on the lower balconies of the tower or atop the compound buildings. Like her, the other sentries stared into the west, shading their gaze from the great orange eye of the sun.

Zahre could see the tents spread upon the golf course outside the walls, seven of them, headquarters for the men from Riyadh and the team of so-called terrorist experts from Group Seven International. She saw Bakerfield, the American, and he was looking westward too.

The stillness enveloped everybody, even the crowd of servants and their families who stood near the gate, guarded by guerrillas with submachine guns: the kitchen and the room slaves, the innocent poor who had been caught up in revolution. They were praying softly. They would leave in groups as the exchanged political prisoners entered through the gate: the comrades from Action Directe, the Italians jailed during the Moro trials, the men and women of Baader-Meinhof, the Armenians from Turkey. And Jacques Sawchuk.

In Amman, at the Central Committee meeting two weeks ago, Wurger's praise for Sawchuk had been elaborate. "If he gave his life, he gave it for the revolution. We are inspired by him." The new martyr had been elected in absentia to the Committee after Wurger's paean of praise: a death tribute, delivered in past tense. Wurger had told everyone earlier that the two of them had crossed into East Berlin after the Solomon execution, that they had become separated, that Sawchuk had disappeared. Wurger had been vague, and his eyes had met no one else's.

Kathë Zahre had felt a wrench.

But that wrench was nothing compared to Wurger's when he learned earlier today that Sawchuk was alive. What a shock had shown itself on her cruel lover's face as Bakerfield, during negotiations just inside the palace wall, informed them that East German state security had taken Sawchuk prisoner two weeks earlier in East Berlin. Wurger had seemed to gag, as if he had swallowed something foul, then, looking at the jubilant faces of the other Rotkommando negotiators, he had composed himself. "Add him to the list to be traded," Cuyfer had ordered triumphantly, a great smile opening over rotting teeth.

Wurger had muttered brave words about Sawchuk joining them, but this afternoon he had lapsed into a dark silence when Bakerfield, to everyone's surprise, told them that the East Germans were proving malleable—and that Sawchuk had elected to join those coming to the palace. He would be coming tonight, by Saudi army helicopter from the staging area in Cyprus. It was due in fifteen minutes.

If it did not arrive, Wurger would kill three times.

The look on his face after the executions of earlier had been a horrid mix of pain and pleasure. But even more terrible was that Wurger had killed the badly injured—seven of the palace rangers who had had limbs blown off or who had suffered severe internal damage during the assault upon the palace.

Wurger had not asked approval of the Committee. It had been done according to the plan, which said no hostages would be released in whatever condition—unless there was payment for their lives.

God, the utter stink of death percolating through the marble floors. The bodies had been removed to an underground cold storage room, but there was no refrigeration now, and the smell rose secretly from the basement of the palace, a nauseating air that everyone pretended not to notice.

Standing there, death's aroma wafting up through the windless evening air, looking for a helicopter from Jeddah, she felt another warning of death, a silent scream, the shrill song of The Shrike.

And then she saw the helicopter, caught it in a sparkle of light below the sun.

The big Chinook-47 seemed to balloon towards them, and there were sounds of excitement in the palace grounds; the prayers of the crowd below grew louder, a chorus of chanting and thanksgiving to God.

The helicopter grunted noisily onto the putting green beside the gate, and its engines stopped, its blades swished, slowed, died. The passenger door opened.

An armed officer of the Saudi National Guard stepped off the aircraft first. Then came the prisoners, all handcuffed. The twelfth one was Jacques Sawchuk.

She saw him hop to the ground and look about. His eyes seemed to settle on the figure of an old Arab in a wheelchair near the American, Bakerfield.

She raised her rifle in the air and fired four times. Sawchuk looked up. Yes, he had seen her.

Another sentry fired into the air. And another. Guns began to shoot in triumph all about the compound.

39

The Palace

Sawchuk felt powerful amid these grimy faces, the fourteen members of Rotkommando's Central Committee: quarrelsome technocrats who played at democracy with motions and points of order. He was reminded of tamer radical groups he had belonged to in past years—the unbalanced dialectic of the angry Left, antithesis seeking synthesis, rarely finding it.

The Committee members sat on cushions spread about the poolside, with cigarettes and wine, with a portable cassette deck which played a Simon and Garfunkel tape—unlikely background music, music of peace. All the faces were red masks, painted by a sun that boiled into the sea.

Sawchuk felt powerful. He could bend these humourless seekers.

Their leader was mad. He would be taken out first.

He felt powerful because he had known the worst of fear, had conquered that, and was driven now only by anger. He felt powerful because he had given freedom to Abu Ali Rag.

A wheelchair. How had they harmed him? So solemn had Rag's face been.

The idea that had sprouted that afternoon in Israel had, during the flights to Cyprus and to Mecca, sent strong roots into his mind, and flowers had blossomed. The fertilizer had been in a packet that had been slipped to him in Cyprus by an agent from Hesselmann. He had the means now to destroy Wurger. He felt he had the power to sway these deluded mindless men and women. And the power to take revenge on Bisharat and his foul kingdom.

Chairperson Wurger, brittle, domineering, giving way to tirades which caused nervous exchanges of looks, was driving like a bull through an agenda that seemed interminable: food spoilage, the electricity outage, the jammed radios, the election of three new arrivals to the Committee.

Not once had he looked Sawchuk in the eye. Not even as he had greeted him at the palace gate, where he had pulled Sawchuk away and said in a stiff voice: "There are matters to discuss, of course. After the Committee meeting—you are a member now."

Matters to discuss. Yes.

Beside Wurger, cowering, was Oskar Grubbler, the secretary.

Cuyfer was several feet from Wurger, to his right, just a little behind him. Sawchuk saw him pop a few caps of speed into his mouth.

Kneeling, staring into the garden pool, where big orange carp swirled in long, hungry circles, was Kathë Zahre. Her face seemed drawn inward, pinched, her features like a surface of many planes, ready to shatter. Sawchuk had encountered her on the stairs leading to the palace entrance. She had given him a look that was molten.

Cuyfer had then drawn Sawchuk away, to guide him on a quick tour of the palace grounds before the Committee met.

"Fat man on the tenth floor, he's the King," Cuyfer had said with pride. Sawchuk had looked up, seen the lone figure of King Fahd on his balcony, staring balefully down at them. Other hostages, including some of the Americans, were here and there on other balconies.

Cuyfer had taken Sawchuk to the fifth floor, introduced him to the platoon of Rotkommando sentries there. They were on orders to kill anyone who tried to come down without permission.

Sawchuk had seen that the threat to the hostages' lives was convincing. The detonating device, operating from a pair of twelve-volt batteries, could be activated by flicking a simple on-off switch after turning a timer button to fifteen seconds. Whoever turned the power switch on would have that much time—no more—to run from the main floor of the building, down a marble stairway built into the slope of the hill, to reach the safety of open ground. At the end of the fifteen seconds, a current would pass through wires that had been strung up the elevator shaft to the first five floors. At each storey, a twenty-kilogram lump of Flex-U high-powered plas-

tic explosive would detonate, blowing the bottom floors out-
wards, rendering the palace into a hill of rubble and bodies.

The detonator was guarded by three commandos. One was
relieved every eight hours, Cuyfer had explained, and three
were on duty round the clock. The device sat just outside the
elevator entrance on the main floor, not far from and in view
of the Committee members now meeting beside the garden
pool.

To Sawchuk's trained eye it appeared that the terrorists'
explosives team had done everything right. He had peered
up the elevator shaft, had seen the plastique stuck between
ladder rungs imbedded into concrete. The explosive was
yellow, like children's plasticene.

The palace tower had been built upon the highest point
within the compound, which was situated upon a gentle
incline of the mountain. From its main floor, the stairway
widened like a fan toward the tiled terrace and the other
buildings within the walls. The garden pool was set into tiles
with Koranic designs glazed upon them, and the area was
surrounded by a balustrade, below which was the open
ground, the other buildings, the wall.

There were sentries everywhere: on the tops of the buildings, in the grounds, behind turrets.

It was an outstanding military operation: Sawchuk had to
give them that.

The tension around the poolside was like a thin coating of
ice. Piersanti, newly elected to the Committee from the
Milan Nine, was shrewd and cold and distrustful. Beside him
was Dharla Sayeed, the leader of the West Berlin house—a
sinewy masculine woman who seemed to hate Wurger—and
Erik Vosburgh, ex-Baader-Meinhof cell leader, just released
from a long prison sentence in Frankfurt—old-looking and
bitter. The other faces were lined despite their youth.

Sawchuk felt old, too, as if in the last two weeks since his
brutal plunge into the world of terror and anti-terror he had
advanced through phases of age, instant, bitter years. An old
but vengeful mind.

Wurger's words made their way into his inner ear.

"Three billion dollars." The phrase worked like magic on
everyone, stilled side conversations. He had come to the final
item under new business. "Gold bullion and safe currencies
only, to be deposited in the Libyan National Bank. And our

safe conduct to Tripoli. It is a great deal of money, but they will pay for their king."

But Sawchuk thought three billion was a piker's sum. They had the leaders of a country that was prepared to spend thirteen billion for Cruise missile installations. He remembered the film and tapes that Major Arvad had mentioned. He would have time to look for them. After Wurger was dethroned.

"Yes? We have no problems with this?" Wurger looked from face to face. Sawchuk understood the plan had been agreed to many days ago, at the meeting in Amman. "Three prisoners will be shot every day until the demands are met. The method has been agreed to, has been tried, and works."

"After we have killed the palace guard, who is chosen next?" said Piersanti, a burly man with watery eyes.

"Then we begin to draw names by lot. As it has beer agreed."

"We should give the government more time." Anothei Italian, kneeling beside Piersanti. There seemed a number here who were displeased with all the killing.

Wurger looked at each of the Committee members. "Are there problems about the executions? I think I have heard some whispers about dissent. But the talk is never open, is it? Behind my back. Yes, it is so. Behind my back."

"We should explore it with them first before we talk about more killing," said Piersanti. Sawchuk knew he had been jailed for a terrorist bombing in Milan—but he did not seem ready for murder on Wurger's scale.

"That is weak," said Wurger. "Yes, that is what they want: one cowardly hint of irresolution. Then they will know they can be at our throats." There was silence. "If there is no discussion, we will tell the pigs we will meet with them in the morning."

Now Sawchuk spoke. "I have another idea."

Wurger looked past Sawchuk's head. "This is your first meeting, comrade. You do not understand that we have discussed these plans. We have agreed."

"We can unagree." Sawchuk smiled a soft, malicious smile. "I think we're lying to ourselves."

"We have an agenda," said Wurger. "Later on there will be additional new business."

Sawchuk snapped at him: "We have old business, Karl."

"You are new among us, Comrade Sawchuk. You would be wise to listen, not talk."

"Don't be boring, Karl," Dharla Sayeed hissed. "Let us hear him."

"Isn't it about time we let the world know what we really stand for?" Sawchuk said. "What the hell is this all about, if it's not about justice?"

Sawchuk felt he could persuade them of this. They could not deny an appeal to social conscience without admitting they were not that which they claimed. They had come into the Rotkommando with an ideal, although it had become warped in the means used to pursue it. "*Are* we lying to ourselves?" he said. "Are we just like those we condemn, grubbing through the filth for our profit? Worse than the enemy because we add hypocrisy to the crimes that we share with him."

Wurger said nothing. He shut his eyes, and his forehead became furrowed, as if a headache had overtaken him.

The other faces all turned to Sawchuk.

"Jacques," Sayeed said, "we are talking about three billion dollars. What are *you* talking about?"

"I'm talking about thirteen billion. And I'm talking about giving it away."

Wurger's eyes opened at this. He blinked, focussed. "Giving it away," he said slowly. He looked from face to face to see if they were sharing some joke that he was not a part of. But no one was smiling. "We will give the money, perhaps, to Reverend Moon?"

Sawchuk, in a relaxed lotus position, centred on the person of Karl Wurger, glaring at him as if he were a bug. "You're an asshole, Karl."

That bald statement stopped all conversation. Wurger's smile sat on a frozen face.

"In Eastern Africa, the babies have balloons for bellies," Sawchuk said. "In Somalia there are a million refugees in desert camps, where the women dig with their bare hands to gather moisture from mud ten feet below the surface. Overnight the holes dry up, and they start again in the morning. Just so their families can survive. We're sitting here talking about bank accounts in Libya, about grabbing off three billion bucks like a bunch of Mafia. There have been twelve years of drought in northeast Africa. Tens of millions are starving.

Children are growing old and wrinkled and aged. When they starve so young the brain and the body never recover. Sixty percent of the refugees in the Somali camps are under fifteen, so a whole generation is being destroyed. And we sit around here like the Roman court, Caligula on his throne, and we talk of making profit. We have the means to do a deed for humanity."

"We are building an *army*." Wurger's voice was a squawk. Sawchuk was reminded of Chamberlain the parrot. "Do you think that giving away what we have earned will bring the revolution? Three billion dollars will train and arm divisions of guerrillas. Let us have our army—and then we can end starvation. You know what we have planned. We have *talked*."

"We haven't talked about some things, Karl."

Their eyes locked darkly in late evening light. "We will talk about what is on the agenda," said Wurger tightly.

"I wish to address a point of personal privilege to the chair," said Sawchuk.

"If you and I have some issues of a private nature, comrade, I will be pleased to discuss them with you later. This is not the correct time."

"It is a *good* time," said Dharla Sayeed.

"But it is not the *correct* time."

"The correct time," said Sawchuk, glancing at his watch, "is nine-fifteen, and it is getting late."

"I do not like the way you presume to interrupt this meeting, as if it is run for your benefit." Wurger hissed his words. "I don't think anyone else does."

"Why don't we hear what he has to say?"

Wurger studied this new source of treason: Piersanti, the leader of the Italians.

"My point of personal privilege has to do with betrayal."

Eyes moved from Wurger to Sawchuk and back again.

"I also have a message for you, Karl," said Sawchuk. "It is from General Helmut von Hertz. He says you are fired."

Wurger's eyes snapped wide, bright and frantic in the gloom.

"You are not working for East German intelligence any more," Sawchuk said.

"What are these lies?" Wurger shifted uneasily.

"Comrade Wurger has been working for the false socialists of the East," Sawchuk said. "And thus he has been working for the PLO. The East Bloc supports them, of course. Our glorious leader works for the enemy. He is a police spy."

"That is a lie. A *lie!*"

Sawchuk addressed Wurger. "So it was easy to set me up in East Berlin. That's your home town. Thats where you were trained by General von Hertz's special subversive unit. You told them where I could be found. You expected they would kill me."

Sawchuk could hear breaths being sucked in, eased slowly out.

Wurger said nothing for a while. His face was lined. He seemed to be in pain. Then he looked around dully and addressed Sawchuk. "There are those who wish to sabotage the leadership. You are in league with the others. They have entrusted the knife to you."

"You are psychotic, Wurger. Von Hertz understands that. It is in your genes. The East Germans think you are dangerous, a disturbed megalomaniac, and becoming worse. General von Hertz wants people he can trust, people who obey orders. Always obey orders, Wurger, it is the first rule of the police spy."

Wurger glanced to his left and saw Cuyfer, a cold grin on his face. He turned back to Sawchuk. "You are being used to *subvert* me." His voice rang about the palace enclosure. The Rotkommando soldiers patrolling the terraces below and the men guarding the detonator looked in the direction of the pool.

Zahre seemed unable to raise her eyes from the swarming fish in the pool. Grubbler had dropped his pen and had both hands at his mouth.

Wurger got slowly to his feet. "You think I will give in to you. You think I am weak! I have *will*. I have *will!*" He whirled around, staring wildly at the men and women who surrounded him.

The lines of pain seemed abruptly to disappear from Wurger's face, and it took on a look of craftiness. "There are those who do not understand my strength. It comes not from my organs. It comes from my *will!*"

Sawchuk drew an envelope from his shirt pocket. "He holds the rank of major. This is a photograph of his unit, when they were in training." He passed among them the photograph that von Hertz had given to Hesselmann in East

Berlin. It had been given to Sawchuk in Cyprus along with a tape which Sawchuk had listened to. "The older man, standing to the right: that is von Hertz, chief of state security for the DDR. They say he used to be a Nazi. But the East Germans don't care—he brings special skills."

Erik Vosburgh looked hard at the photograph. "It is von Hertz," he said softly. "He once tried to recruit me."

"He gave me the picture," Sawchuk lied. "And this." A laminated plastic identification card showing Wurger in a major's uniform. "And this." Sawchuk removed the Simon and Garfunkel tape from the cassette player and inserted the tape which he had withdrawn from his pocket. From it came von Hertz's voice: *"What a liar you are, Wurger. Ghaddafy is paying God's fortune—"*

Sawchuk moved the tape forward, saying, "This was taped in von Hertz's office a few weeks ago, during one of Wurger's visits there. This is the interesting part: *"...our contract with Ghaddafy. I don't control the Committee. It enjoys notions of democracy. It is comprised of a confusion of idealistic morons whose idea of struggle is about as primitive as a pack of farm dogs. I use them, but I don't quite control them, General."*

Sawchuk stopped the tape. "You can hear the rest at your leisure. General von Hertz told me Wurger had telephoned him, had suggested I be assassinated. But von Hertz had me arrested instead. When the Saudis offered five million dollars for my release, the East Germans were happy to have the foreign exchange. And this chance to rid themselves of an embarrassment." It was weak, but it would do.

"I used *them*," Wurger cried. "Don't you see? I used *them*." Pain had returned to his face with the awareness of what was unfolding around him. "All of you know what I have done. Without me there was no movement, no Rotkommando. I see doubt in your eyes! And cowardice! Without me, you are nothing! All *this* is nothing!" He waved his arm, a sweeping motion that seemed to take in the entire palace compound.

Now Oskar Grubbler got unsteadily to his feet. He said some soft words to Wurger in German, and tears came into his eyes. Suddenly he ran for the pool, and the carp rushed hungrily for his retchings.

Then Dharla Sayeed had a pistol on Wurger, who had

subsided to his knees. He was holding his head between his hands. "Now we will have a leadership election," she said. "We must do it pursuant to the constitution, according to the bylaws to that effect."

Wurger placed his hands firmly over his ears as if to shut off an inner scream. Sawchuk knew he had thrown him over the edge.

It was two o'clock in the morning. Sawchuk had escaped to a hammock under the stars. A young man with a pistol guarded him. The Committee—minus Wurger—had met until midnight, and Sawchuk had felt his strength grow, as though he had finally mastered his myth, had become in truth the revolutionary hero that Group propaganda had projected to the world.

And certainly he was that person: no longer Hesselmann's super agent, who had moled so far in he was at bedrock. He was about to become the world's most successful terrorist. Like Karl Wurger, Jacques Sawchuk had become nobody's property.

What a role could be filled here. These people demanded living legends, and they would follow someone who gave off the brave scent of a candidate for martyrdom. He rocked himself in the hammock, his leg gently pushing at one of the pillars that held it, and stared at a sky of a trillion stars and the curl of a moon.

The police spy and the terrorist. Could one play both parts and succeed? Maybe he could pull it off.

Sawchuk had skilfully spun consensus from the meeting after Wurger's demise as chairperson. He had been composed and forceful, had dominated the meeting in subtle and graceful ways. He had given an aura of leadership, and they had all sucked in that powerful perfume. At the end he had proposed, generously, a triumvirate to take command alongside him. Dharla Sayeed was elected, as was Piersanti.

Wurger had lapsed into something like a catatonic state, snapping alert only when he saw Kathë Zahre vote with the others to remove him from office. He had been placed under a form of house arrest, was being guarded now, appropriately, in the royal playground. A people's trial would be held when they were freed in Tripoli.

Sawchuk remembered the look on Wurger's face, like

shattered glass, as he was being led away, as he saw Zahre take Sawchuk's arm, silently announcing to all by this choice that she felt free of Wurger.

Zahre had wanted to be with Sawchuk tonight, but he had made excuses, explaining to her that he needed to be alone to think. The fact was he did not want to be alone with her. He felt in no condition to stand up to her.

Sawchuk had held the Committee rapt. His appeal had been to ideals that had first put them on the road to revolution. He had spoken of their opportunity to strip the blinders from the world, and demonstrate that revolutionary acts can bring change, can benefit the masses.

There were the dissenters, those from Wurger's school who had seen Operation Mecca only as the means of equipping a great army. But Wurger was discredited now, and so were his dreams.

"The army of the Left needs fighters before it needs guns," Sawchuk had said. "How better to attract to our cause those prepared to fight for ideals than by demonstrating our power to commit acts for humanity. If we have a few hundred soldiers now, in a month we will have ten thousand."

He went on to describe his proposal: Oxfam, the Oxford-based international relief organization, would be requested by the Saudi government to set up safe accounts in Switzerland to which thirteen billion dollars would be transferred. When the Rotkommando was satisfied that serious measures were under way to disburse these funds with outlays of food and medical aid to Somali refugees, the guerrillas and selected royal hostages would be ferried to Tripoli by Libyan troop helicopter. The Saudi government would have forty-eight hours from noon on the coming day to make the bank transfers. Otherwise hostages would begin to die again.

Sawchuk had had time earlier only to compose a rough working draft of his plan, so they had discussed details, made amendments. Those who were mercenary, like Cuyfer, had wanted profit for the Rotkommando. Sawchuk had compromised, agreed to an amendment demanding payment of three million dollars to the guerrillas. A commission, as it were.

Sawchuk pushed again at the marble column, and the hammock swept up and dipped back, a lulling, pleasant sensation.

He felt good. He thought of Bisharat and his cruel country.
He thought: Poetic justice.

40

Sunday, June 17, the Palace

Psychologists have proven statistically that terrorists, primed
at the beginning for death, for sacrifice, have the edge of
their excitement ground away as minutes, hours, days pass
by. So Hamilton Bakerfield's Book for hostage situations
advocated a policy of co-ordinated delay. The main thing was
to deflate any hopes that demands could be satisfied early.
Outsiders had to be blamed, people who weren't able to
mobilize fast enough.

The Book required a quid pro quo for every concession,
involved counter-offers that seemed attractive but so complex
that the terrorists would be forced to take time to study
them. The quick and easy way out was to be suggested with
increasing frequency: safe passage in return for hostages'
lives.

But it seemed to Bakerfield that Wurger had read his
Book, had rewritten it, had thrown the old version in the
American agent's face. Wurger had refused to listen to counter-
offers. The edge of his excitement had not seemed to wilt but
to become finer and more dangerous as the days passed.

But the whole game had now taken on a lopsided structure,
with Sawchuk in there. Bakerfield decided to continue the
policy of co-ordinated delay this morning with Wurger. Delay
would give Sawchuk time to get things together inside the
palace.

The time now was a few minutes after ten a.m., and
Bakerfield rose ponderously from a collapsible chair behind a
collapsible table. "Hold your piss, I'm coming," he said to an
anxious Laurent Pétras, who was standing by the entrance of

the command tent—a nervous grouse scratching at the gravel with his toe. They were a few minutes late for the meeting scheduled with Wurger inside the palace walls. That was deliberate.

Bakerfield joined Pétras, who was posing as his assistant; Kamal Bisharat, whose job was on the line over the Sawchuk debacle; and an aide to Bisharat. These men comprised the combined Group-Saudi negotiating team, and were the only outsiders allowed inside the walls.

They walked past the palace gate, which was twisted back and held on a single hinge. They walked past the area where, two days ago, three men had died. Bakerfield swore to himself that there would be no more hostages killed. He could smell death in here, in the compound.

He was ready. He had steeled himself. He was determined to get back to his Book, to delay, delay, give Sawchuk time enough to dismantle the detonator.

He looked at the terrorists sitting along one side of the table, and saw that the centre chair was occupied not by Wurger but by Jacques Sawchuk. His agent. Smiling like the cat that ate the bird.

As Sawchuk recited the Oxfam proposal, Bakerfield made detailed notes, trying to deal with his astonishment, to control it. He looked with concealed wonder at Sawchuk, glanced at Pétras, whose mouth was slightly open, and at Bisharat, whose face was frozen into an expression of suspicion and confusion.

Sawchuk retained his smile throughout. It was the smile of a car salesman dealing with rubes from the country.

Bakerfield's best guess was that Wurger, on the edge of a nervous breakdown, had finally snapped. Now Sawchuk, of all people, seemed more than vaguely in charge. Sawchuk, an agent whom Bakerfield was supposed to be running. Who was running whom?

"Thirteen billion dollars is impossible," Bisharat mumbled.

"You have a hundred times that sitting in banks in New York and London and Switzerland." Sawchuk spoke with a relaxed voice. "Saudi oil revenues, what are they—a third of a billion dollars a day? Don't tempt us to raise the ante."

Bakerfield had recognized Piersanti, to Sawchuk's left, a former Red Brigades captain. Dharla Sayeed, to his right, had been a P.F.L.P. leader before she joined the Rotkommando. They seemed prepared to let Sawchuk do all the talking.

"You are giving us two days," Bakerfield said. "It's a very short time."

"At noon on the day after tomorrow, three members of the palace rangers will be executed," Sawchuk said. "Unless by then the funds have been secured unconditionally in Oxfam accounts." He leaned toward Bisharat at this, and eyeballed him, but Bisharat did not look up.

"Where is Comrade Wurger?" Bakerfield said. "I miss him."

"He is not quite up to par, Bakerfield. I think it's the meat. It's spoiling in the lockers because you have cut off the electricity. His Majesty has been forced to eat rice and dates. I think he prefers kid."

"We will send in food for His Highness," Bisharat said.

"And we'll have to send some people in to locate the cable breaks and do the splicing," Bakerfield said. "A team of technicians. It may take them a few hours."

He handed this to Sawchuk like a big hamburger. Bite on it, Jacques.

"No one else comes inside the walls. Anyone who tries will be shot."

"Mention the radios, Jacques," Piersanti said.

"Yes, we have transistor radios but no sound comes out of them, just a loud hum. We know the BBC World Service is available here on the AM band. Stop the jamming. We want to hear the news."

What was this? Bakerfield thought. Why was Sawchuk making an issue of this? Isolating terrorists, monopolizing information flow into them: these were standard strategies. And Sawchuk knew them all, had been trained in them.

Now Sawchuk handed him a sheet of gold-embossed stationery. "It is an order from the King that the Oxfam plan be carried out. He was all in favour of it when we explained the idea to him early this morning."

As Bakerfield took the letter, he felt Sawchuk tuck something into his hand. It was a square of paper, folded many times.

Sawchuk gave nothing away, continued to smile. "I beseech you, Bakerfield, not to screw us around. This evening we want to listen to the BBC news. We want to make sure the world is being told what a good bunch of fellows we are. And we want to hear about the progress in making the thirteen-billion-dollar transfer."

Bakerfield slipped the piece of paper into his pocket. He was relieved. The note seemed like a contact with reality.

The deadline was just a little over forty-eight hours, and that meant Sawchuk had decided he would be able to dismantle the detonator within that time. When he gave the signal, it would take fifteen minutes for the Group commando unit, enhanced by members of Division B2 of the French D.S.T. and by British Special Air Services, to find their way into the compound.

"Bank transfers of such sums can't be made like a fine being paid over the counter—"

Sawchuk cut Bakerfield off. "They punch out a Telex," he snapped. "You'll find out how fast banks can move when their gears are lubricated by oil money."

"Oxfam might refuse to administer extorted moneys."

Again Sawchuk spoke sharply. "Work out those problems for yourselves. Understand that we will kill everybody in here if we have to. And then we'll fight to the last man and woman. Get out. The meeting's through."

"This is crazy," Bakerfield said. Sawchuk and his team were standing. "We have to take instructions—"

"That will take two seconds. If by Tuesday at noon the thirteen billion has been transferred, we will be prepared to discuss stage two of our proposal." That had to do with their being taken to sanctuary in Libya with selected Saudi hostages, the latter to be released on arrival. Sawchuk beamed. "Trust us, Bakerfield."

Sawchuk and his seconds walked away. Rotkommando soldiers menaced Bakerfield's team with their rifles, and the four of them got up and walked toward the gate.

Sawchuk shouted from the palace steps: "Colonel Bisharat, would you be interested in offering yourself in exchange for one of the prisoners? One of Prince Muhammed's whores, maybe." He laughed, turned, and continued up the steps.

Outside the command tent, Bisharat said with a strained smile: "The man is a perfect actor. May God forgive me for what I have done to him in error. He is the best agent I have ever encountered. See how he has them all fooled in there. See how he has taken control."

"Yes, he is very good," said Pétras. "I am amazed. I remember from the tests we did, I had concluded he would be a risk, that we could not trust him."

Bakerfield unfolded the note that Sawchuk had passed to him.

It said: *"I'm not kidding."*

41

Monday, June 18, the Palace

It was now close to thirty-six hours after the meeting with Bakerfield, and Sawchuk and a group of Committee members were listening to a portable radio in the servants' cafeteria.

"This is the news from London. Here are the latest developments in the Saudi hostage crisis. Following the emergency resolution of the board of Oxfam this morning, an international consortium of banks has begun to channel thirteen billion dollars into a series of Swiss accounts. However, bank officials have expressed doubt that all transfers of funds can be completed in time to prevent the murder of three more hostages, which is threatened for tomorrow at noon . . ."

Sawchuk was wondering what his father would have thought about this gamble. He remembered that his father had always liked the long odds. Those who played it safe, went for the margin, laid off the big money—they were just small-time businessmen. But he remembered too that his father had busted out at the end of his runs. Almost always.

". . . despite urgent attempts to enter into further talks with the terrorists, there has been no response from inside the walls. . . ."

Bakerfield, don't call my hand, I've got wild cards, Sawchuk said to himself.

Sawchuk had ignored his loud-hailer shouts during the day. He had spent his time in the last two days getting to know people better, making friends on the Committee, talking to the soldiers, keeping their spirits up, being a good general. In the palace music room, he had found a flute, had entertained his soldiers with happy music.

He had been enjoying the expression that he had caught on Bisharat's face in the meeting of yesterday morning. There was the sss chief's former torture victim, at the helm of Rotkommando's ship, negotiating over the lives of Saudi royalty. You know I mean it, don't you, Bisharat? I'm not kidding. Can you take the chance that I am?

Three men to be killed tomorrow at noon. Sawchuk had told the Rotkommando that he would carry out the executions. He felt clammy.

Please don't call my hand, Bakerfield.

The Committee had just eaten dinner. The day was fast drawing to a close.

Kathë Zahre was at his side now, had been there every waking hour. Last night he had again escaped from her, democratically choosing to sleep in the men's dormitory with the other soldiers. She had looked at him reproachfully this morning. And she had been like fly paper all day. He wanted to be alone, to think, to plan. But he had won her; he was expected to take advantage.

"I'm going for a walk," he said to her.

"Where?"

Where. I would like to go down to the corner tavern and order *une draffe*. "I'm going to the tower, to Aziz's office."

"I'll come with you."

"The building is mined. I'd feel better if you didn't come." He knew the eyes of the other Committee members were on them.

"I will feel safe with you," Zahre said.

She doggedly followed him out the door.

At the top of the stairs, while Zahre waited for him, he walked to the front of the elevator door, wedged open by a marble bust of King Khalid. As he had many times before during the last two days, he inspected the detonator there, pretending a casualness. So simple. Turn the rotating knob.

Flick the power switch on. The knob and dial go *tic-tic-tic* from fifteen seconds to zero. The current travels up the elevator shaft to the Flex-U plastic bombs. The walls of the lower five floors of the tower blow out, burst away in a tangle of steel and concrete and glass, and the upper nine floors topple onto the compound grounds. All die who are in the building.

Sawchuk inspected the faces of the three detonator guards to satisfy himself that they looked reasonably sane. Fortunately, the Rotkommando's chief madman had been removed from the danger area.

From where he stood, Zahre close beside him now, Sawchuk could see down into the royal playground, which contained elaborate dragon tunnels, a slide down a clown's sheet-metal tongue, a wading pool with a large playship, and swings and seesaws. The play area was surrounded by an eight-foot wall interrupted by a fancy storybook gate. Sawchuk could see Wurger on the swing, head bowed, shoulders slumped, staring into clasped hands. A Rotkommando guard was near, holding a pistol. Another was outside the playground gate with a submachine-gun.

Maybe you'll be able to plead insanity, Karl. A future in a padded room.

As for his own future, he had until noon tomorrow to ride his long shot.

Sawchuk, with Zahre behind him, went up the stairway which spiralled around the elevator shaft.

On the thirteenth floor—where light from the falling sun cast Aziz's office in bronze—Sawchuk talked to his search crew, a group of six persons he had assigned to comb through the files and the vault for the tapes and the film. They had found numerous documents evidencing the sale of Cruise missiles to Saudi Arabia, but nothing the world did not know about, no evidence of pay-offs to U.S. senators, no evidence of the blackmail that Major Arvad had spoken of.

But the vault had been open when the palace was stormed, and it was likely that evidence had been taken and destroyed. Mossad and the Israelis were going to be disappointed.

"What is the film you are looking for?" said Zahre.

"Nothing. I had a theory." Whatever Latifa had known about any plot to bribe or blackmail senators, she had not passed the news on to the Rotkommando with her smuggled messages.

"Maybe we can find something upstairs," Zahre said.

"Upstairs? What's upstairs?" He remembered, uncomfortable.

"Let us see how the richest man in the world spends his nights." She tugged at his sleeve. He felt himself being drawn toward that final flight of stairs that led to the penthouse floor and Aziz's bedroom. He was conscious of the eyes of the others in the office.

The dying sun made richer the gold and silver touches that were everywhere in the bedroom. On the walls facing the curved-glass windows were Persian tapestries. The floors were of marble of many hues. At the centre of the room was a huge, circular bed. The mirrored ceiling reflected rumpled, blood-stained sheets.

Zahre seemed not to notice the blood, and walked to the balcony door, slid it open, walked out and looked below to the terraces and the pools, to the royal playground where Wurger sat hunched.

"He has lost even the dream," Zahre said softly. "How easily you have broken him, like a plaster figurine." She was a black silhouette against the sun. Her hair was gathered behind with an elastic, and hung in a long ponytail. Sawchuk thought of an unbraided whip.

"We had better get down for the Committee meeting," he said, leaning against the balcony door, talking to her back.

"The Committee. It is always meeting. And we are never alone. You seem fearless with everyone else. Why are you afraid of me?"

But he felt not fear—only a yawning gap between this woman and himself. He admired her beauty as one might a sculpture, aesthetically. He wondered if he would ever know physical arousal again.

"Jacques," she said softly, "where are you?"

"Thinking. About where it will all end."

"Will it end? What will happen to us, Jacques? If we succeed here, then Libya awaits, and it will be terrible there. After Libya, what? The police will hunt us all over the world. They will follow our trails of blood. Can't we make it stop?"

Sawchuk remained silent.

"Don't kill tomorrow. If I see you kill those helpless men tomorrow, I will begin to fear you, and that will corrupt what we have between us."

What we have between us. A structure made of her self-delusion, his acquiesence. "I won't have to kill."

A hard laugh. "Do you think they will not test you? You will kill to prove your resolution. Instead of Karl presiding at the butcher's block, it will be you, Jacques. Don't become like him."

"Become like Karl? It would be impossible."

"Perhaps we should be certain of that." Her hands went to her shirt buttons, undoing them as she stared past a falling sun that painted her an iodine colour. The shirt hung loosely now.

She shrugged. It fell.

She turned around and looked at him intensely.

He edged back into the room.

"We're on enough explosives to take down the Aswan dam. It doesn't turn me on." He tried to smile.

"It adds an edge." Her voice teased. "Touch me. I want to feel your hands." He didn't move, and she came up to him, took his hands in hers and pressed them to her breasts. He felt a trembling within her. Now she crushed her body into his, thrust her hands into his tousled hair and pulled his head down toward her mouth. She kissed him brutally, with the click and slide of teeth.

He answered her with very little.

She drew her head back, her eyes showing hurt. "For God's sake," she whispered.

"I'm sorry." He glanced at the splotch of blood on the sheets, felt revulsion.

She looked only at him. "What are you afraid of, scandal? We have stolen some time—please, let us use it."

"I have things on my mind."

"Stop the revolution for a few minutes; I want to get off. God, Jacques, the struggle doesn't fall apart because its new leader escapes from it for half an hour and becomes human."

"We don't have half an hour." He had felt so much power upon entering the palace compound. But he felt none now with Zahre. His hands dropped from her chest and they closed into fists of frustration.

She pressed her face into him. "Love is more important

than the rest of it. Please make love to me. I am ashamed that I have to beg."

"I can't."

She stepped back, her face hot with the spurning. "You *are* the same as Karl. As one form of power grows, another dies. Will you, too, be saving your orgasms for your pistol? Is it the killings tomorrow, is that what you are saving it for?"

"Kathë, let me be frank with you." He took a deep breath. "Whatever you believe you feel for me, I do not share. I have no desire for you." A blunt, quick truth.

She blinked. "God, I have had my fill of cruel men." She stopped, picked up her shirt, began to put it on. She fought tears as she did up the buttons. "I feel ashamed." She whirled around, went to the door, slammed it shut behind her.

Sawchuk walked out onto the balcony and stood looking at cruel Arabia.

Karl Wurger scrutinized the pumpkin-like face of his Rotkommando guard. Jurgen, you were nothing when I found you; you are less now. Is this a German?

Another headache had begun to take him. They visited whenever they wished. If he fought them, he remained lucid. When he was lucid he understood that he was having a breakdown. Had von Hertz told him the truth? Had his mother suffered from schizophrenia before she was killed by American bombs? He feared he carried her curse in his cells. He knew not how to conquer it.

If he gave in to his headaches they went away. But then he passed into insanity, and when in that state he saw that Sawchuk had mysterious, malevolent powers. He had weaved a hypnotic web about Kathë, clouded her mind as he had the minds of all the others. He held them with a satanic force. If his grip could be released, they would return to Wurger. Kathë would return.

Wurger fought his headache, stayed sane. He swung back and forth, his heels scraping the dirt. His hands hung loosely between his knees, but sometimes he would raise them and press them tightly to his head.

A while ago, Wurger had glanced up, over the playground wall, and had seen Sawchuk and Zahre at the top of the palace stairway, near the elevator. She had been close to

Sawchuk, touching. And they had been watching him. He
had bowed his head, unable to let her eyes meet his in a
terrible shared understanding of the things that had happened.
Wurger knew that they were seeking a place to be alone,
where the Canadian—a man of mixed blood—could take his
pleasure from her. He thought of them naked, writhing on
the sheets. Vile. Vile.

He fought the pain, the jarring, cutting pain in his head.
He fought its release too, because with it would come the
hallucinations. Again he studied the young guard, his nervous
hands clutching his gun. The pumpkin face of a stupid child.
A chinless coward. It was a face of weakness. Not German.

"Jurgen," he hissed. "I brought you into the revolution. I
taught you. Do you not feel like a traitor?"

"I am sorry, Comrade Wurger."

Wurger closed his eyes. His mind went back, as it had
many times in the two days since Sawchuk's arrival here, to
the events of Berlin. How had von Hertz found Sawchuk
before the PLO assassination team had got to him? Von Hertz,
who had been like a father. Has he bought Sawchuk, sent him
here to replace me? It was a puzzle that refused to fall into
place. It caused his brain to spin. Conspiracies behind conspiracies, wheels whirling through the void. He squeezed his
eyes shut against the pain.

"You have been deceived, Jurgen. You have all been
deceived."

"I believe we are doing the right thing now," Jurgen said,
his voice small and worried. "I was not sure before Comrade
Sawchuk spoke to us." He stood eight feet from Wurger. He
saw pain crease his former leader's face. "Are you not well?"

Wurger looked up at him with reddened eyes, stark. He
pushed his fingers against his temples, digging there as if
trying to reach into the cortex, the pain centre.

Where had he taken her? In what room above was he
overpowering her, pouring his foulness into her? He looked
up, over the playground wall, and saw Committee members
assembling near the garden pool for their nightly meeting.
What were they without him? He had been their heart, their
mind. He had been the revolution.

His eyes travelled up the glassed front wall of the palace
tower. His eyes saw the frightened, staring faces at the
windows, the American arms dealers, the feudal royalty of

the Saudi kingdom. But they did not seem important now. Nothing was important but preserving his mind and proving his will and strength.

Now his eyes went to the penthouse balcony of the bedroom of Aziz. And there he saw her. His Kathë, illuminated by the low sun.

He remembered the first time they had met, at an exclusive party of West Berlin's radical chic, before the university lecturer had submerged and joined the Röte Armee Faktion. His eyes had followed hers as she drifted from group to group. There had been a crackle of energy, like lightning. Later, when she had taken him to her bed, she had said: "I knew we would come together. I knew it when I looked into your eyes. It was as if a current had connected us."

Now he made out the tall form of a man up there. And he saw her hands undoing the buttons of her shirt. And he saw the shirt fall from her shoulders, baring her breasts. He saw her turn toward the man.

Wurger snapped.

He saw a horned beast on top of her, saw the beast expelling vapours of potency, conquering her, thrusting at her, thrusting at her, filling her with poison seed, mixed, impure.

He began to swing, pulling forward, back, in increasing arcs. His headache was gone. In his insanity, he was free of it.

He looked at Jurgen, looked at that slack-jawed, chinless distortion of a human being, too misshapen in mind and spirit for the race of great leaders that Wurger had been destined to create.

"You are nothing," Wurger shrilled at him.

Jurgen looked at the crazy eyes, ran a tongue over his dry lips.

"You are refuse. The refuse of history." Wurger swung higher, catching his heels on the dirt, pumping the swing. "You will not be remembered, because you are nothing, a piece of shit. You do not know, do you? He is up there, spinning his webs for General von Hertz. But I have *will*."

"Who is up there?" Jurgen felt a chill. The sun had disappeared from them, but reflected off the mountains and off the tower. He looked up.

Wurger flew off the swing as if launched. Coming down, he caught Jurgen in the neck with the heel of his boot in a hard

karate snap from the knee. Wurger rolled as he fell. His mind
was full of chaos. Jurgen was woozily scrambling for the gun
which he had dropped, but before he could get to it, Wurger
pounced like a leopard, bringing the cutting edge of his
hands down on the back of Jurgen's neck, snapping it. Jurgen
screamed and grunted and died.

Hearing the noise, the guard outside the gate rushed in
and met Wurger racing toward him. He did not have the
chance to level his submachine gun before Wurger was upon
him, fearless in his insanity. He smashed the guard back with
hammer blows, throwing him against the playground wall,
beating him until his face was a pulp and Wurger's fists were
scored and raw.

Yes, Wurger exulted to himself, it is good. It gives strength.
Death is the true orgasm.

He picked up the submachine gun.

When I kill him, it will all stop. All this turning and
whirling will stop.

He crouched and ran from the gate, up the terraced incline
toward the palace, toward the great stairway that led to the
elevator—and the detonator.

42

The Palace

Sawchuk had remained for a few minutes at the balcony door,
letting settle the silt of his roiling emotions.

Then he saw Wurger attack the playground guards.

Now he saw him racing toward the stairs, toward the
detonator, firing wild bursts with his submachine-gun.

His mind for a few seconds seemed sluggish as if he were
trying to work himself out of a harsh dream.

Sawchuk ran to the door, grabbing the gun from his belt.

*   *   *

The twelve members of the Central Committee were gathered at the poolside around a transistor radio, listening as the world was to the story—distorted by the capitalist media—of the heroes of Mecca. They felt righteous and they felt important. They waited for the news that would tell them they had succeeded in turning history in new directions.

The great financial institutions of the world were racing to meet the deadline of noon tomorrow. The banks of the world and their richest customers were dancing to the Rotkommando's blood music. And, best of all, they were saviours now, not scum, heroic men and women for whom many leaders of the Third World were offering careful praise. And they had their own hero—Sawchuk.

None of them was near the railing, so none saw Wurger running toward the palace stairs. And when the gunfire began, they were stunned into immobility.

It was only when Wurger had neared the top of the stairs that anyone moved, and then the twelve men and women were suddenly like a hive of hornets, pulling guns, racing toward the elevator. And they saw the three young comrades stationed by the detonator being raked with a line of fire from Wurger's submachine-gun. Then Wurger emerged in front of them, firing with gritted teeth and crazed eyes, and they were diving to the tile as bullets spit past them.

Cuyfer, from the ground, got off a shot with his automatic pistol as Wurger dove, somersaulted, fired wildly. Cuyfer's bullet slashed into Wurger's stomach, but didn't stop his headlong rush to the detonator, and suddenly he was there, on top of it, and everyone held fire for fear of setting it off.

They looked at Wurger and he at them, with a cocked smile, blazing eyes.

He had turned the power switch on and they could see that he had moved the timer button to the three-second mark on the dial, and was holding it.

Three seconds to eternity.

Kathë Zahre, gun in hand, had raced down the spiral staircase of the tower. She stepped out on the ground-floor landing and stopped. She saw him there, his submachine-gun on the floor beside him, one hand clutching his stomach from which an ooze of blood came, one hand on the timer button.

He was smiling, hurt but possessed of power.

Her gun was pointing at him but she dared not fire.

"If I let the timer go," Wurger said, "we all pass into hell."
She saw in his face insanity's cruel mask. She felt nauseated,
fought to control the tremors running through her body.

Rotkommando soldiers were hurrying toward the stairway.

"Get back!" Wurger shouted.

And they saw him at the detonator, and slowly they began
to inch away. Some of the Committee members also began to
sidle toward the stairway, their eyes fixed on Wurger and his
deadly machine.

"Stop!" he screamed. "No one leaves!"

They stopped. All but Grubbler, who seemed stunned, in
shock, uncomprehending, and taking uncertain steps toward
the stairs.

"You will stay!"

Another step.

"He has clouded your mind, do you not see? Because you
are weak! He has seized control of your mind!" A pause. Still
addressing Grubbler, menacing, low: "There is coward's blood
in your veins."

Now, slowly, Wurger removed his left hand from the wound
in his stomach, and he picked up the submachine-gun, and
cradled it under his arm, his finger on the trigger. His right
hand was still on the timer button.

"Those who run—they are weak. The weak fall. The strong
conquer."

Now Grubbler panicked, turned, bolted for the stairs.

Wurger's gun thundered.

Grubbler's thin body lurched forward and sailed like an
ungainly bird toward the stairway, bounced down several
steps, and lay there limp and lifeless.

And then there was a deep and penetrating silence.

Below, in the courtyard, the soldiers began to drift away to
the inner edges of the walls, as far from the tower as they
could get.

Zahre spoke softly in German. "Karl, it is I, Kathë."

He turned to her. She was six feet from him, at the bottom
step of the spiral staircase. She was still pointing her gun at
him.

"I know you." He barked a laugh. "Do you think I don't
know you?" He shouted the words.

Zahre began now to move slowly toward him, tried to hold
him with her gaze. Her smile was a stony, glacial smile, false,

learned in modelling school. "We will go away together, Karl, just you and I. Yes?"

"No." The word was uncertain, almost a question.

"It will be as it used to be. Do you remember?"

He said nothing for a moment. He looked away from her, then quickly back. "He has sent you," he said in a cautious voice. "He has spewed his poison into you, then sent you to me."

She kept her eyes on him: dark and potent and eloquent. "Could you not see that I was only pretending with him?" A soft laugh. "I am yours, Karl. Look into my eyes, and you will know. You are hurt—let me care for you. See? I don't want this thing." She stooped slowly, keeping her eyes on him, and laid her pistol on the tiles. Then she straightened and took three slow steps toward him.

"No," he said. But again the tone was unsure, questioning.

"I love you, Karl," she said.

Something human and real came into his face as she leaned closer to him. "Did you tell him everything?" he whispered. "Did you tell him how I could not satisfy you? Did you tell him how I cried in front of you?" His face was white and bloodless.

"I told him only that I loved you."

Now her hand went toward him as if to stroke an unruly blond lock from his forehead.

Then her fingers darted down to the on-off switch, but with a lightning snap—with the hand that had been holding the timer button—he grasped her wrist.

"Karl!" she screamed. He jammed a finger onto the needle of the dial and it stopped at the one-second mark. "*Treachery!*" he screeched.

One shove, one push, one stumble, one second: if Wurger released his finger the palace would blow up. Zahre's hand was crushed by his against the steel surface of the detonator box, and her fingers were flattened there, inches from the power switch.

"Treachery!" He dropped the submachine-gun and with his free hand grabbed her by the hair, snapping her head back hard. "Whore of the revolution! Cunt! Filthy sewer of a cunt!"

The Committee members were bathed in a fearful silence,

motionless like the impassive busts of the Saudi kings that guarded the hallways.

Zahre saw Cuyfer inching his gun in Wurger's direction. "Don't shoot, for God's sake," she cried.

Wurger looked down sadly at his abdomen. The wound was not sealing and the wash of blood across his shirt front was spreading. He looked as if he was weakening but he seemed strong as a demon—her hand was numb with the force he exerted upon it.

"I am not afraid," he said, still staring at his own blood. "Not of death. Not of my death, not of the death of brothers and sisters whose minds he has clouded. Not of the death of one *who betrays with her stinking body!*" He screamed those words, snapped her head back again.

Now Dharla Sayeed spoke from near the pool. "What do you want, Karl?"

"I want Sawchuk." Wurger spoke English now. "His body. I will give you a prisoner exchange! Sawchuk for the whore!"

Sayeed saw a mangled smile work its way across Wurger's face. "No," he said, "I will offer an even better trade." He began to laugh. The laughter was disjointed, hysterical. "Your lives! Bring his body to me and I will turn off the detonator!" His breath was rasping, ragged.

"I will die anyway," he said, calmer now. "But you will live to carry on my work. When you have killed him you will realize that in obeying me you have freed yourselves from the webs he has spun." His voice went high and sharp. "But if you do not present him to me dead in fifteen minutes, I will explode the bombs!"

"Karl, let us take him prisoner," said Dharla Sayeed. "We will try him . . . for his crimes. And you can give evidence—"

"I want his *death!*" Wurger looked at his watch. "Now there is fourteen minutes." He jerked Zahre's head back by the hair again, harder than before. "He is upstairs, yes? In the bed of Aziz!"

Zahre could not get words out, was prepared for death.

"We will capture him." Sayeed's voice was strained and raw. "We will tie him with rope. You will see—he will be our prisoner."

She heard Cuyfer whisper behind her: "It won't work. We're running out of time."

Sayeed tried again. "We are your friends, Karl, your broth-

ers, your sisters. We must talk about this. Tell us about
Sawchuk—how is he evil? You must help us understand."

"Oh, I know what you are trying to do. You seek delay. I do
not bargain with the enemy, and I do not bargain with false
friends. Thirteen and one half minutes! He will die anyway!
And if you do not kill him, all of you will die! And the King of
Arabia will die! And the warmongers in the tower will die!"
His voice became hoarse.

"Let's go," said Cuyfer. In a louder voice: "Yeah, we'll kill
him for you, Karl. He's evil, right? I know now he has
clouded our minds. Yes? We'll go upstairs now, and get him."
He took a hesitant step toward the spiral stairs near the
elevator.

"Yes," said Wurger. "Everyone to the hunt. Except my
darling Kathë, who promised she would love me."

Now, starting slowly, but moving faster as they neared the
steps, the eleven members of Rotkommando's Central Committee moved past Wurger and Zahre. Then they began
scrambling wildly up the stairs.

43

The Palace

Sawchuk, after hurtling down thirteen storeys, stopped at the
second-floor landing, where from the open, doorless stairwell
he heard Wurger's shrill diatribes and his commands for
Sawchuk's death. He realized that Wurger was in control of
the detonator, that he had retained the leaders of the
Rotkommando to destroy him, their services extorted by a
bargain for their lives. The hostage-takers were hostages now.

He heard their footsteps coming and abruptly he swung his
parabellum pistol at the second-floor sentry, a frightened
teenage boy. "Give me your gun."

The guard tried to back away but Sawchuk grabbed his arm with his free hand and pulled the gun from him.

"Run down and meet them," he ordered. "Tell them I want to talk." He checked his watch. Twelve minutes. He had to think of something.

Now he turned, ran up to the third floor, stationed himself behind a pillar where he could have a view of those coming up, and shelter from any bullets. There was no sentry on this floor but he knew a platoon was stationed two storeys above. It was getting dark. An amber evening light entered through a small window.

In a few seconds he heard Cuyfer's voice, tentative. "Jacques? Are you there?" Then he saw the Dutchman come partly into view around the stairs, Sayeed behind him.

"Is that you, Jacques?" she said.

"Yes. Don't come any higher."

"He has the detonator," she said. "He has the dial at one second. He wants us to kill you."

"I heard him."

Sawchuk held the submachine-gun in one arm, braced against his shoulder, his pistol in the other hand. His mind had been racing but had arrived nowhere.

"He's off his nut, Jacques," Cuyfer called. "Give us a better answer, man. Give us a better answer quick, because I only got one I can think of now."

Sawchuk heard other footsteps, knew they were all crowding behind Cuyfer and Sayeed.

"Let me take him," he said. "Everybody clear off and let me take him."

Cuyfer's voice was frantic. "You can't take him, Jacques. Maybe you don't understand. If you shoot him, he lets the dial go. That's it—you, me, all of us, the whole building. Jesus, Jacques, I'm sorry, man."

Sawchuk could dimly see his eyes in the darkness. The cold rat eyes, flecked with sparks of panic now.

Sayeed spoke calmly. "No fighter can be said to be expendable to the revolution. Sometimes a person must make an example to others, must sacrifice. You understand that, Jacques, don't you?" She paused. "There is no choice. You would die anyway. It doesn't matter about the others, the American and Saudi pigs. But it matters whether the vanguard of the revolution survives."

Sawchuk understood what she was saying: Perform a noble act. "Give me ten minutes—we have that much time. Give me room and stay out of my way." His brain was still working at it, trying to solve it.

But he could see that Cuyfer, his sworn brother, was coming apart. His lips were drawn back in a tight grimace. He wiped sweat from his eyes with his free hand.

"We'll stage a shooting," Sayeed said, "carry you downstairs as if you're dead."

"No," said Sawchuk. "Tell him I'm shooting back. Buy some more time."

"You're not going to take us with you, Jacques," said Cuyfer.

And Sawchuk saw a sudden hardness in his eyes, as if a decision had been made.

Cuyfer stepped into the open, his gun pointed at Sawchuk's face.

He ducked back as Cuyfer fired with his .22-calibre Baretta and the bullet hit his scalp, grazed it. The shock caused a momentary blackness, and he fell back, fighting the great onrushing cloud. Almost instinctively he fired with his nine-millimetre pistol as Cuyfer began to scramble up the steps, and he was dimly aware that the Dutchman had jolted back, astonished, blood spurting from a hole in his chest.

Some of the others now started firing in panic, but Sawchuk was for the moment out of view of them, lying on the floor. He struggled to his knees, a fat target for them once they reached the third-floor landing. He put his pistol in his belt and grasped his submachine-gun with both hands and fired bursts down the stairway, heard screams. Still woozy, he got to his feet, made for the stairs to the fourth floor as bullets whipped into the plaster of the stairway wall beside him. The guerrillas, crazed with fear now, came pouring up the stairs, paused only when Sawchuk fired behind him.

He reached the fifth-floor landing, where confused sentries—the twelve stationed there plus a few who had come down from upper floors—were milling about. They recognized Sawchuk, and began shouting questions.

"It's the pigs," he yelled. "They're storming the building. Hold them with your lives!"

And he fired another burst down the spiral stairway as two of the Committee members emerged dimly into view, and he saw their bodies crumple and fall. The soldiers at his side began firing streams of 7.65-calibre bullets down the stairs, red-streaking tracers flashing like darts of lightning, the crash of gunfire echoing up the stairwell and down the corridors.

Sawchuk, his head clearing now, raced up to the sixth floor, the seventh floor, both empty of guards.

By the glow from his watch he could see the time left: seven minutes.

The seventh-floor corridor was empty, the hostages still in their rooms. Sawchuk wheeled, found the elevator door. Firing was still coming from below. Yells, curses, screams.

There were no windows here, and the darkness was complete. Sawchuk felt the elevator doors—heavy, bronzed doors closed tight upon strips of rubber. He laid the gun down and dug his fingers between the strips, but the doors wouldn't give, wouldn't divide open. He bunched his chest and shoulder muscles, took a great breath, pulled, pulled, and slowly the doors gave, a few inches, and then, as he was able to get his hands between them to take a stronger grip, they separated a foot, then came open wide.

The gunfire stopped, he heard more curses, footsteps running up, and as he stooped and felt about for his parabellum pistol, he saw the murky outlines of his pursuers racing up the stairs to the floors above. But one stopped at the seventh floor, and Sawchuk guessed he had been assigned to look for him here.

Sawchuk remained crouched, waiting, sensing the terrorist stepping softly toward him. He dared not shoot, dared not alert those who had gone to the upper floors to continue the search.

He heard the man curse softly in Italian, realized it was Piersanti, his own co-leader of the Rotkommando, a burly, powerful man.

Now, as Piersanti stepped in front of him, Sawchuk suddenly raised up, and as he was able to bring the knife edge of his hand across the man's neck, Piersanti lunged back, bringing his gun around, and Sawchuk kicked wildly, catching the man's wrist, sending his pistol twisting into the air. As Piersanti recovered, charged, tried to grapple with Sawchuk, his warning yell to the others was cut off by a fist in his throat. But the man's rush was not wholly expended and with his arms now wrapped around Sawchuk's chest, he pushed the Canadian to the edge of the elevator shaft.

Sawchuk cracked the butt of his pistol across Piersanti's forehead with a bone-splitting thud and felt the other man release him, felt himself teetering, and he dropped his gun grasping wildly at one of the elevator doors to stop his fall. But he failed to get a grip and went backwards into the shaft, his arms flailing, reaching for something to stop his fall, but there was nothing but a seven-storey space to the bottom. He wrenched himself about as he fell, and managed to grab one of the steel elevator cables, and felt a searing pain and smelled the flesh of his hands as the cable cut into his palms, but he tightened his grip, wrapped his legs around the cable, and he came slowly, cruelly, to a stop, and he felt the cable shivering in his hands. For a few deadly moments he wondered if Wurger, six and a half storeys below, in front of the open elevator door, had heard the soft twanging of that cable.

He clung there, trying to clear his head.

By now the Committee members—those who had survived— had either killed the guards whom Sawchuk had turned against them, or had convinced them to join in hunting him down.

He was unarmed.

He was being sought by some of the world's best-trained guerrilla fighters.

He was—he looked at his glowing watch dial—one and a half minutes from oblivion.

He knew there was a metal ladder against one of the walls of the elevator shaft, but the walls were too far away to reach. He had one option.

He tightened his legs and thighs against the cable, was able to ease the tight grip of his burning hands, and now he began to descend, hand over hand. He heard distant calling, the thud of racing feet.

Sixth floor.

Fifth floor.

As he descended, he was able to see a little better—dim evening light was entering the shaft from the main-floor door, jammed open by a marble bust. He could see the metal ladder rungs imbedded into the concrete wall now.

He then saw the wires. And he saw the twenty-kilogram lump of plastic explosive through which the wires were drawn, a lump of high-powered Flex-U sitting between the rungs.

Sayeed came racing out of the building. "Please, Karl, give us another fifteen minutes. There are hundreds of rooms, and he could be anywhere. You have heard the guns—he has been fighting back." Her voice cracked with despair.

"No time, no time," Wurger's voice hissed. He was like a ghost now, and he still held his finger on the one-second mark of the dial, that hand still crushing Kathë Zahre's on the detonator panel. The power switch was still in the on position. He held the submachine-gun jammed into her ribs with his free hand. His eyes were dim and awful, as if much of him had departed into a distant dimension. "Thirty seconds," he droned, staring at his watch. "Thirty seconds." A broken cackle. "Do you hide him? Where is the body, please? In death I will be remembered. I am a martyr, yes? Death is life. Death is the reward. Death."

Sayeed was pleading, her eyes inflamed, but her words went unheard, drowned in Wurger's babble.

"Don't you see? It was necessary that you fail, because it is I who am called upon to destroy him, not you, not the others. It is I!" He was excited, speaking as if he had discovered an important truth. His eyes rolled back into their sockets, and the whites were like dying light bulbs. He stopped talking, seemed to be listening with a great intensity, and when Sayeed continued to plead, he screamed at her. "Shut up! Now, *now*, Götterdämmerung!"

"Time to pack it in, Karl. You blew it."

Wurger's eyes snapped alive. He slowly turned around to see where the voice was coming from. Sawchuk was just inside the elevator, leaning against the door, slumped there wearily.

Wurger uttered an animal scream, a howl that might have come from the jungle. "We die!" His crazed, high-pitched laugh. "We explode!"

He lifted his finger from the dial.

Sawchuk watched it.

The dial clicked the one second to zero.

Nothing happened.

But the silence was shattering. Wurger's face seemed

peaceful, as if he had gone to his afterlife. Dharla Sayeed was bloodless, staring, a ghost with a gun. Kathë Zahre unlocked her gaze from the detonator dial, from Wurger's quivering hand raised now a few inches above it, and she turned to look at Sawchuk, feeling the hardness of the gun barrel in her rib cage, but feeling numbed by events, outside emotion.

In Sawchuk's hand was the broken end of the wire that he had torn from the lump of plastique at the bottom of the elevator shaft, severing the circuit. With his foot, he pushed away the marble bust that held the elevator door open, and advanced one careful step.

"Put the gun down, Karl," Sawchuk said.

Wurger looked at Sayeed, at the several Rotkommandos who were straggling down the stairs. "Destroy him," he said, "or he will destroy all of you!" No one moved. Their guns were not pointed at Sawchuk but at Wurger. But his body was shielded by Zahre.

A sadness came into Wurger's face, and a look of pain. His expression became sentient as he passed from his hallucinatory phase. There was a long silence. Darkness began to envelop them all.

"Put the gun down," Sawchuk repeated. He was only a few feet from Wurger. But Wurger's finger was on the trigger.

Now Wurger squeezed his eyes shut, then blinked, then studied Sawchuk, and spoke in a soft voice. "I know I am ill. When I fight the illness, my head seems to split apart. As it is doing now. What a tragedy a jealous lover creates for himself, Comrade Sawchuk. And what a tragedy he creates for others." He sighed. "I have lost everything now, even the final reward of martyrdom. I can already read the words that will be written of me: 'A man driven to insanity by a jealousy as devouring and twisted as his fanaticism.'" He laughed softly. "The insane monster of the revolution."

"Karl, it is over," Zahre said in a level voice. "Please put the gun down."

He continued to hold the submachine-gun to her. "But tragedy demands tears and I fear that none are to be shed for me. Perhaps in the end it is not tragedy after all, but comedy. At the end, I am a joke. One of history's fools. Who terrorizes the terrorists? The sick jester of the revolution. We say terrorism is aimed not at the victims but at the people watching. Terrorism is theatre, and is this not excellent theatre? Will you applaud after I am gone?"

The guerrillas began to form a ring about Wurger and Zahre.

"What do you think of all this, Kathë?" Wurger said. His speech was rational, his voice wistful. "Do you not laugh? Can you not applaud? But you do not see the humour. Do you steal the strength of all your men, Kathë? Do you take everything from them before you cast them off like old skins? What about this poet Sawchuk, is he better than I at resisting your lies of love? Sawchuk, you may have all of this: the Rotkommando—for you are its new emperor—this palace and my place in history as well. But I will not let you have everything. Tell me that you love her, for then she becomes a thing I can destroy that is yours."

"She is nothing to me, Karl, nothing that you can take from me. Release her, and you will not die."

"Ah, but I die nonetheless." Wurger flinched with pain, and blood now seeped from his lips. "Love happens quickly, Comrade Sawchuk, like the discharge of a bullet."

An angry, screaming roar from the submachine-gun. Zahre's chest exploded out and her face twisted with pain, and as the firing stopped, as her body sagged forward to the terrace floor, her face composed itself into an expression not of hurt but of sorrow, of fate acknowledged.

Wurger put down the submachine-gun and slid it toward Sawchuk. "Now you may execute me. Experience that climax. I know the lust of death is within you, or else you could not kill so well. Feel the rush, feel the power."

Sawchuk was frozen, unable to move. He looked at Wurger as if at a slug that had spread a trail of slime.

Wurger got to his knees, and clutched at his stomach with both hands. He stumbled as he tried to rise, then steadied himself with a hand to the floor, and slowly raised himself onto his legs.

"Kill me," he said. Blood bubbled at his lips.

Sawchuk stared at him. Wurger turned to Sayeed. "Kill me." She looked at him with repugnance. He turned to the circle of Rotkommando soldiers. "Kill me."

He took a few steps toward them, and they moved away. He staggered toward the stairs. At the top of the stairway, he studied the bodies sprawled below him. Tears were in his eyes. "Kill me," he said. He took one step down, then lost his footing, stumbled, fell onto the steps, and rolled and bounced to the bottom.

Sawchuk stepped forward and clicked off the detonator. He looked at Sayeed. She lowered her gun, then lowered her gaze. It seemed to all a gesture of submission.

Bakerfield's tent reeked of sweat. There had been that one last burst of gunfire, and then silence.

No one dared guess at what had been happening behind the walls. They knew only that the bombs had not exploded, that the worst had not happened. And they knew that Sawchuk had not transmitted any messages from the transmitter imbedded in his tooth.

Now Bakerfield heard Sawchuk's voice calling to him from the palace gate. He strode outside the command tent.

"Yes, this is me."

It was dark now, only a purple glow to the west. Bakerfield could see him by the gate, tall in the shadows.

"There has been a palace coup," Sawchuk shouted. "It seems that I am in charge of things in here. Is the money in the Oxfam accounts yet? The scythe of time hangs heavy on us all."

"It is happening," Bakerfield called. "When do we ask the Libyans to come?"

"Tomorrow we will go. After the money has been paid."

Then he disappeared. Bakerfield called to him, but he did not return.

After a while, he heard from within the walls the sound of a flute trilling Bach arpeggios.

44

Tuesday, June 19, the Palace

Sawchuk had not allowed the Rotkommando explosives team
to rewire the bombs. There had been mild protest at this, but
Sawchuk was now, as Wurger had proclaimed him, the new
emperor here. Seven of the Rotkommando Committee—
including Piersanti—were dead, and Sayeed, the third member of the triumvirate, was content that all power be rendered
to him. There was no discussion, no formal decision. The
Rotkommando leaders had tried to kill the man who later
saved them. They assuaged their guilt by tendering the
throne.

Sawchuk was regarded as more Christ than emperor by the
hundred and twenty young soldiers under his command.
They were hero worshippers, as most soldiers are, and Sawchuk
had been sent by the gods of revolution to redeem their
sense of morality, to direct them upon the correct Left path.
His strategy of squeezing the rich to help the African poor
had won them. His heroics in saving the palace and conquering
the mad Wurger satisfied them with instant, living folk
legend.

Sawchuk allowed himself to sample the flavour of power
and acclaim, a flavour bittersweet, spiced with guilt. He
played his flute to the swirling fish in the garden pool while
men and women shuffled by like ghosts in a graveyard,
removing bodies. Wurger's body was the last but one to go.
Everybody had avoided the form lying at the bottom of the
stairs, as if all feared that his disordered spirit would claim
the person of anyone who touched him. His body was
finally removed, carried into the vaults with the other
dead.

Sawchuk fluted a sad song for Wurger, a song for a weak man, a song for a madman.

The last of the bodies to be taken was that of Kathë Zahre. He played the blues for her: love and loneliness and revolution.

Finally, he just played for himself, recalled the songs of Quebec, improvised, worked their melodies and reworked them.

He did not sleep. All night his people visited him with reports from the radio. The bankers of Zurich were awake tonight, too, it appeared, working round the clock to complete the transfer to Oxfam. His potshot bet, his fifty-to-one-shot bluff, was about to pay off. His body was too worn, his mind too ragged, to feel the thrill of this. And little darts of pessimism kept sticking at him, hinting at some last-minute betrayal, a sabotage of the multi-billion-dollar almsgiving that he was demanding from this rich and ungenerous country. He feared Bakerfield would, in the end, force his hand—to test him, find out whether he could kill hostages. The killing was over—of that he was certain—but if Bakerfield had guessed that the death threats were a sham, if he called Sawchuk and demanded to see his cards, then the game would come to an ignominious end. And the men outside the walls would laugh a hearty, cynical laugh.

And what would they do to him then? Well—what did it matter?

Later in the morning, the BBC news was cause for rejoicing. *"...has confirmed that all funds have finally been secured in Swiss accounts under control of Oxfam, which has announced that purchases are already being made in international grain markets for cereals to be airlifted to the Somali camps ...."*

Soldiers fired into the air as the word spread about the palace grounds.

Several soldiers and Committee members gathered around the transistor radio with Sawchuk and all were in a delighted mood. Behind Sawchuk, at the top of the fan of stairs leading to the palace door, was a table with fifty-three bottles of champagne—for a celebration that Sawchuk had promised. The champagne had been part of the wine collection that had been removed from the vaults when the palace rangers were locked inside.

Now an interviewer was drawing from the weary chairman of the Oxfam Board its plans for buying medical supplies and hiring health workers. All about Sawchuk were staring at him with wonder. A great master was among them. A Buddha for all guerrillas.

"And will there be a possibility, Sir Charles, that any of these monies will be returned to the Saudi government?"

"None whatsoever," said Sir Charles gruffly. "Unless, as we have warned, there are further killings, or the hostages are not immediately released."

Sir Charles Whitcomb. Sawchuk had heard him interviewed once before, not many months ago. Something puzzled him.

The news announcer's voice returned. He said four Libyan troop-carrying helicopters were to arrive at the palace at noon today to take the terrorists and selected Saudi hostages to the sanctuary offered by Moammer Ghaddafy.

"You have made it seem easy." Dharla Sayeed sat next to him on the steps and smiled.

Too easy, he thought. Too perfect. It was disquieting.

"Tonight we will be in Tripoli," she said. "They have estates in the suburbs where comrades may rest before it is time to return to the field. It is like a holiday camp. You will meet the new recruits being trained at Misurate. Your army, general."

"Our army." Sawchuk was distracted, thinking.

"Your army. Maybe one day you will lead us into Palestine. Lead me to my home."

"We will let the Committee decide what is next."

"There is no Committee. You are the Committee."

Suddenly Sawchuk broke out into laughter. He reached over and spun the radio dial. Every other station jammed. Only the BBC World Service. It *had* been too easy. So absurdly easy that he had been an egotistical fool to have swallowed it.

And there was no way to change his course now. But he would not take hostages' lives. He had been playing against weighted dice, and all he could do was try to come out of this smiling. In Bakerfield's face. He would do what he had to do now to save his own skin. And to save face.

Upon his command, all the guerrillas of his army were

brought together in assembly below the palace stairway. They were jubilant, firing their rifles into the air. Sawchuk motioned them to stay put and walked up alone to the top of the stairs and went to the table set up there. He selected a bottle of champagne and popped the cork. An ecstatic roar. Sawchuk held the foaming bottle aloft.

"We have proved to the world that small bands of dedicated men and women can defeat the fascists with their great armies." His rich baritone rolled over them like thunder. "Drink with me in honour of what we have done."

He raised the bottle to his lips, took a great swallow, and wiped his mouth with the back of his hand. He beckoned to Sayeed and passed the bottle to her and she took it down the stairs, into the crowd. He popped open another. Again shouts of rejoicing.

He had promised a celebration. He would give them a celebration.

"The world knows that what we do, we do for love of fellow man," he roared. "It is the pigs who act out of hate, the militarists, the oil monopolizers. We are revolutionaries. We act out of love!" He heard these brave and vacuous words echoing back to him from the walls. He was sick with disappointment at what he had failed to do.

At each pop of cork they cheered.

Sayeed offered to help open the bottles but he waved her away. "It is my gesture to the cadres," he said.

He continued to play a Mussolini to them, reciting the kind of revolutionary cant that he had grown to despise. These acne-faced soldiers, lured to revolution by Wurger's seductive siren call, bent to his words like swamp reeds in a breeze.

A mob totalizes itself into obedience. The intelligence of the masses is restricted. *Mein Kampf.* Had it felt like this for Hitler, for the other demagogues who had tried—and too often succeeded—to alter history?

After the last cork had been popped, the last cheer had been cheered, and the last of his rhetoric declaimed, he watched as his soldiers continued to drink.

We are revolutionaries. We act out of love. What love had these embittered young people known? He suddenly felt sorry for them. They wanted so badly to believe.

Several minutes later, as Sawchuk was cleaning the flute

with a dry cloth, Sayeed came and stood beside him. "You shouldn't let all this carry you away, Jacques. It is not good to forget who you are."

"I have not known who I am since I could think about such things."

"As long as you know where you stand, I suppose that's all that matters." She lit a black Sobranie.

From below came a chorus of somewhat intoxicated voices, singing disjointedly.

"But you understand the language of the struggle," she said. "You understand the theory, and that is important in a leader."

"The language of the struggle," he repeated, and smiled. "'Struggle is the father of all things.' Do you know who said that, Dharla?"

"Marx?"

"Adolph Hitler. He also wrote that force is the first law, that only blood rules. Anyone can use words, the tools of the trade of demagogues."

She looked woozily at him, blinked.

"Who said this? 'The street is where policy is made. Conquest of the street means the gain of the masses. He who has the masses conquers the state.'"

She drew deeply on the cigarette, blew out again. "Lenin?"

"Goebbels. Dharla, do you sometimes think we are that which we despise?"

"What are you talking about?" she said softly. "A while ago you were talking about love. What we do we do for love." She giggled. "I feel strange. Maybe it is the champagne. I feel giddy."

Sawchuk put his mouth over the embouchure. He ran off some rapidly-tongued notes, traced lightly the melody of a Cuban folk song, returned to it, tried to give it a happier sound.

A young woman below him who had been swaying with the music took a few steps, spun, laughed.

"Libya!" someone shouted. "Libya by tonight!"

Another cheer.

45

The Palace

Bakerfield turned to Pétras and Bisharat with raised eyebrows as they heard the cheering and the singing. "It is simple," said the psychiatrist. "They are celebrating unprecedented victory. They had never quite believed that they could win."

They had heard Sawchuk's loud oratory, although the words were distant and unclear. Agent Sawchuk playing Reverend Moon.

Bakerfield prayed that Hesselmann had been right. By radio from Gran Paradiso, the general had said to gamble on Sawchuk. And Hesselmann was the shrewdest judge of man Bakerfield had ever known.

I'm not kidding, the note had said. But there had been an insistent voice inside Bakerfield that said his agent had not turned. And would not take innocent lives. Everyone knew that Agent Sawchuk had a droll sense of humour.

Sawchuk was still playing his flute amid the clamour of revelling voices.

Now, distantly, came a harsher sound, the noisy churning of helicopters. Bakerfield went outside the tent with his field glasses and scanned the horizon toward Jeddah. He spotted them rising above the black hills, and soon they were whirling above him, circling the palace and the grounds outside, four huge CH-47 airships with camouflage colouring and Libyan Air Force markings.

Some of Bakerfield's men raced out to the first fairway of the golf course and began to signal the helicopters to land. The machines fluttered toward the grass and plumped down. Their engines stopped and their blades swished and braked.

All that could be heard then were the flute inside the walls and the soft gabble of voices inside the radio tent.

After a few minutes, Bakerfield called over his loud-hailer. "It is Bakerfield. The helicopters are here."

The flute played on.

"Wait here," he told Bisharat. "I'm going in."

"They will shoot you. You will expose yourself where even God cannot aid you. It is not wise."

"The sentries are all down. I am going in."

Bakerfield slapped a white tropical hat on his head—bald and badly burned already—and as he stepped toward the gate he found himself walking to the rhythm of Sawchuk's music, a bouncy march. No one was on guard inside the gate, so he carried on in, along the inside perimeter of the wall, past the negotiating table, into the open terrace below the palace stairs.

All over the terrace, the Rotkommando guerrillas were dancing—alone, with one another, in groups.

Many had laid down their guns in a circle, and they danced within that circle. Some still carried pistols in holsters.

Bakerfield saw that they were looking into each others' faces, smiling. They looked up at Sawchuk from time to time with open, trustful faces.

He wondered at first how Sawchuk had got the DNT-17 into their mouths, but then he saw the empty champagne bottles littering the tiles. Pétras, the mad drugger, had finally come up with something that worked as advertised.

He looked up and made out faces in the upper floors of the tower: hostages staring with astonished expressions at the scene below.

He caught Sawchuk's eye. There was nothing, not a wink, just the pinched smile of the flautist, and the smile was denied by the sadness in his eyes.

He stopped playing and announced to the people below him: "We will go to Libya now."

"We must take hostages," someone said in a slurred, uncertain voice.

"There is no need. The Libyan soldiers are here, and they are our security."

There was dissent, but it died and the voices stilled as Sawchuk again put the flute to his lips. He walked slowly down the stairs, and as he did, he drew the pistol from his belt and laid it on a step. Then he beckoned to them to follow him.

There were uneasy looks at the weapons arrayed on the ground, and a few went toward them, but most did not, seeing their leader begin to walk toward the gate unarmed. Many of them were stepping to Sawchuk's march.

Bakerfield watched Sawchuk walk slowly past, fluting his troops outside the walls. One young man stopped and spoke to him.

"We are revolutionaries," he said. "We act out of love."

"Love, huh."

"Now the world will understand. We even love those who are pigs."

Bakerfield followed them outside the gate to the golf course. There he saw Pétras and Bisharat gaping at the scene: Sawchuk pied pipering the rats past a water hazard toward the four big Chinook helicopters sitting on the yellowed grass. He saw Sawchuk stand aside while Saudi soldiers in Libyan Air Force uniform guided their guests aboard the airships, which had Libyan insignia painted over the original Saudi markings. The terrorists were laughing, smiling, waving. Those who still had guns gave them up to the soldiers as they climbed inside.

The helicopter doors shut. The engines started. The aircraft lifted into the air one by one, and began flying to the northeast, toward Riyadh.

Bakerfield walked slowly down the short fairway to where Sawchuk was standing alone, looking wistful.

"Hullo, Ham," he said.

"Jesus," Bakerfield sighed.

"As you see—music calms the savage beasts. A little DNT-17 in the champagne helps."

"What happened to your hands? They're badly cut. What happened in there?"

"Debrief me some time, and I'll tell you about it. Or send Fager the Undertager. He's good. First time he debriefed me was in Berlin, and I told him the Rotkommando was going to try to seize this palace. What fuck-ups you guys are."

"Actually he doesn't work for us, for the Group."

"Who?"

"The man you call Fager."

"Who does he work for?" Sawchuk could see Bisharat

standing by the command tent, smiling, waving to them. Sawchuk tasted something foul.

"Mossad."

"Come again?"

"They stole you from us in Paris. They've been running you since then. They didn't tell anyone about the taking of the palace. They wanted the palace to fall."

"My God."

There was a moment of mental blankness and then a lightbulb clicked on. Sawchuk saw a rat but could not make out its features.

"Debrief me some time," said Bakerfield, "and I'll tell you about it."

"I think we have an informer in our midst, Ham. Who is it?"

"It could be anyone at Gran Paradiso."

There was still no activity near the gate. A group of sss men were standing around Bisharat, waiting for orders. A Group tactical unit was also there. Bisharat was still beckoning at Sawchuk, who was in no hurry to deal with him. Nor was Bakerfield, it seemed.

"The note you passed me—was that your idea of a good joke? You didn't really think you were going to do that, did you? That big number for charity?"

"Come on, Ham, you think I'm some kind of fellow traveller or something?"

"'I'm not kidding.' The note had that silly fucker Bisharat going up and down the walls of his tent. Almost wore out his worry beads."

"Sure, that was the idea. Just getting back at him a little. Not enough." A lie that would probably satisfy Bakerfield. He steered the subject elsewhere. "Wurger's dead. Cuyfer. Half the Committee."

"Okay, Sawchuk, that was a hell of a job." Finally Bakerfield stuck out his hand and shook Sawchuk's. "A *hell* of a job. Congratulations."

Sawchuk kept to himself the truth—a knowledge of failure.

"Any booby traps in there?" Bakerfield gestured toward the palace. "I think that's what Bisharat wants to talk to you about."

"No. The bombs in the elevator shaft have been defused. You can bring the hostages out. How is Abu Ali Rag?"

"The wheelchair is temporary. Some broken bones. In a guy as old as he is, they will take time to mend."

"Not with that man. He is made of iron and leather."

As they arrived at the command tent, Bisharat came rushing forward and tried to plant an Arab kiss on Sawchuk's mouth.

He brushed him aside savagely. "Keep out of my sight. Bisharat. When I look at you, I want to kill you."

Bisharat bent, touched his head to the ground, muttered words in Arabic.

Sawchuk spat on the sand beside him, an Arab gesture of contempt that he had learned from Mohammed ibn Mohammed. "Pray for your own soul, not mine." He turned to Bakerfield. "The palace guard are all locked in the wine cellars. They should be released first. Some may be in bad condition. The hostages in the tower are well, I think. Make sure nobody tinkers with any switches."

Bakerfield started giving orders to his tactical unit to go in and secure everyone's release, but Bisharat, standing now, looking sour, cut him off. "That will be the task of the Saudi Special Security Force. I will personally attend to His Majesty."

"You better let our people go in, Colonel," Bakerfield said. "They know what they're doing."

"No foreign person will go into the palace grounds," said Bisharat.

"We have anti-demolition experts," Bakerfield complained.

"We have our own. Your work has been completed, Mr. Bakerfield. We are pleased to thank you for the expert assistance you have rendered us."

"Assistance? You did piss all." Bakerfield was furious. He had wanted to put a team of investigators inside. His anti-terrorist police agency had much to learn from this palace attack to help in future operations. Bakerfield could see that Bisharat—in a delicate position because of the bungling over Sawchuk—would attempt to redeem himself by taking major credit for quelling the terrorists.

"I am sending soldiers in to seal the entrance to the grounds," Bisharat said. "After the hostages have been removed, no one will be allowed inside except by my order." He barked commands in Arabic to his men and they raced inside. He returned to Bakerfield and said icily: "I would be pleased if you would ask Agent Sawchuk to meet with our bomb-disposal unit and explain about the placement of the explosives in the building."

But Sawchuk had wandered away from them, to Abu Ali Rag, in his wheelchair near a tent, an umbrella shielding him from the afternoon sun.

"What is the news?" said Sawchuk.

"The news is good, thanks be to God."

Sawchuk bent down and the two men kissed.

"Once again you have saved my life, Jacques Sawchuk. Broad is the shadow of generosity. I have written a song for you."

"You will sing it for me on the desert. I will go riding there with you again. Peace be on you."

Sawchuk squeezed the old man's shoulder, then walked past him, toward the tent from which high aerials protruded. He stood outside listening to a voice from within, enunciating with a cultivated English accent.

"...and now we go live to the capital of the Somali Democratic Republic."

Another voice, speaking over a tape that might have been recorded in a busy African bazaar: "This is Lawrence Nugent, reporting to the BBC from Mogadishu, capital of the drought-stricken war-ravaged land of Somalia, the country of a million refugees. Today the President of Somalia said his country would be open to all members of the Rotkommando, whom he claimed had demonstrated the use of terrorist force for the good of mankind ..."

Sawchuk whipped open the tent flap. Two men were crouching on either side of a microphone, and four others were standing around a large transmitter. An engineer was working at another table, with headphones on. A young woman was sitting, pencilling changes from wire-service copy coming over a teletype.

The man from Mogadishu droned on about honour being bestowed on the terrorists.

"That's painting it pretty thick," Sawchuk said. "It's over, for God's sake. Didn't you hear the helicopters taking off?"

"Er, we're supposed to continue until Agent Bakerfield tells us to stop," one of the announcers said. But he clicked off the transmitter. "Well, you're Sawchuk, then. Did we fool anyone in there? I'm Palmer. Ex-BBC, actually."

"You had them all fooled, gentlemen. Very good job. I liked

the interview with Sir Charles. More of a thin, piping voice, like this, don't you know, old chap." Sawchuk gave his own poor rendition.

"I say, you're rather good," said Palmer. "We thought we might have laid it on a little rich, but the intelligence people said none of these youngsters are too bright—they'll gulp down anything we serve. Didn't fool Agent Sawchuk, though, did we?"

Sawchuk smiled a seraphic smile.

46

Tuesday, June 19, the Palace

Prince Aziz ibn Saud sat beside his helicopter chauffeur, his right hand, minus three fingers, swathed in bandages. He had taken off several minutes ago from the grounds of Prince Muhammed's palace in Taif, the resort city high in the mountains east of Mecca, where he had been attended by his staff of Swiss and American physicians. He had received word that his own palace had been retaken, and he was in the air in time to see the Libyan-marked troop helicopters chugging over the mountains toward Riyadh, to the northeast.

The relief he felt that his half-billion-dollar showcase palace had been saved from ruin was so strong he felt intoxicated.

Everything had been rescued from disaster. The King and Prince Sultan—his uncles—had been saved, as well as the lives of their families, and the Americans. Perhaps more important, one was dead who could have brought the Typhon-Cruise deal to an embarrassing and doubtless complete collapse: Latifa.

As for the evidence—the film and tapes which compromised the senators—this had been burned. But such records were no longer necessary. Senators Budd, Grodsky, and Johnson were publicly committed and would be voting to ratify the arms sale exactly one week from today.

Naiboldt would be visiting Aziz soon to make arrangements for his share of Aziz's commission of over a billion and a half dollars. A third of that to Naiboldt: a great deal of baksheesh. But Naiboldt had rescued from annihilation that one luxury item even more valuable than Aziz's palace—his life.

Colonel Kamal Bisharat had taken confident control over the tail end of Operation Mecca, had gone bravely inside the tower with his troops and had personally escorted out, with much panache, King Fahd and the other hostages. The soldiers from Aziz's palace guard were removed from the wine cellars, and they were in miserable shape, although they had all survived.

Bisharat was solicitous in tending to the royal family. Bakerfield watched him warble and chirp and bow and scrape about the ample person of the King, with some generous attentions being paid, too, to Prince Abdul. Two of the larger tents had been furnished with mats and cushions, and the guests of importance were ushered there.

All but King Fahd himself who, Bakerfield observed, seemed to have been invited by Bisharat to observe the chief of the Saudi Special Security Force in action, mopping up, having vanquished the enemy. The King accompanied Bisharat to a briefing by Sawchuk to the 355 bomb squad. Sawchuk explained through an interpreter that the explosives in the elevator shaft would be dangerous to handle, that the heat of heavy friction could set them off. And it was too dark in there to work safely.

Throughout the briefing, Bisharat was in a blind rage, not listening to a word. He had introduced Sawchuk to the King, and Sawchuk had expressed himself as being honoured, then had added these superfluous and shocking words: "I feel it is my duty to Your Majesty to advise you that your chief of the Special Security Forces is incompetent and a dangerous sadist."

Bakerfield, standing nearby, had been stunned. But King Fahd had never lost his smile as Sawchuk went on, in a normal voice, to brief the bomb people. The King gave no reaction that he had even heard Sawchuk's defamation of his Special Security chief.

"What you want to do is go in there with flashlights," Sawchuk was saying. "Rig up something so you can lower the explosives in a sling. There is a ladder that goes all the way up but you don't want someone slipping and falling with twenty Ks of Flex-U in his arms."

One of the team directed some words to Bisharat in Arabic. The SSS chief, his face still hot, looked puzzled, said something to an aide, who scurried away, came back. There was another conversation.

Bakerfield watched all this with impatience. He would have the bombs out of there by now if his men had been allowed inside.

"It seems we have left the flashlights behind in Riyadh," Bisharat said finally, in English. "We will have to requisition some from you."

"You will, huh? Requisition them, huh?" Bakerfield looked scornfully down at the man.

Bisharat started as if a thought had just come to him. "But it is not necessary, is it? There are electric lights inside the palace."

Bakerfield smiled as if Bisharat had made a joke.

Now Bisharat yelled in Arabic to a man who was standing at a switch box just outside the palace gate.

Bakerfield was distracted momentarily by a helicopter flying toward them, from the direction of Taif. He had not understood Bisharat's shouted command, and although he had a momentary qualm, he said to himself, no, the man couldn't be that stupid. And then he saw the SSS agent by the switch box reach down toward it. "No!" he screamed.

"Mr. Bakerfield," Bisharat barked, "you are not in charge."

Lights went on all over the palace: the spotlights on the walls, the lamps on the terraces, in the interiors of the many suites. Water began to gush in the fountains as the electric pumps started to function. And Bakerfield was running toward the switch box, a hundred metres away, screaming, "No! No!"

"What is he *doing*?" Bisharat said.

Sawchuk explained in a resigned voice: "It's about the elevator, Bisharat. You see, if only one person in the last two weeks pushed a single elevator button on any floor, the carriage will start rising from the basement—"

Bisharat cut him off with a shriek in Arabic to the man at the switch box.

"And when the elevator cage hits one of those lumps of plastique ...."

The man in charge of the power switch was staring stupidly at Bisharat, mesmerized by the huge form of Bakerfield barrelling toward him. He reached down for the switch.

"The friction heat will result in ignition, and the palace will thereby be razed to the ground."

King Fahd was looking at Bisharat with a combination of pity and horror.

Aziz's helicopter came over a rise, a rocky outcropping of Mount Arafat, and there, to the north, glowed his jewel, glass and marble and concrete, in a setting that had been green before the terrorists attacked but was now brown. The golf course had not been watered, and looked like a large dried doughnut around the palace walls. But he could see that the water system was working again now, and sprinklers were on.

Aziz directed the pilot to hover over the palace, over the tower, not to attempt to land on the big painted H on the roof but to hover above it—Aziz's demonstration of the fact he had regained sovereignty over his little walled kingdom.

Suddenly the prince felt an oppressive sensation, a sickening thud in the centre of his stomach.

His helicopter jumped and tossed like a small boat on the sea.

Aziz looked down, saw the lower five floors of the tower distending, as if suddenly pregnant. An enormous cloud of dust and smoke billowed fiercely out in all directions.

Then he felt and heard the roar as the lower floors ballooned farther, disgorging slabs of concrete, twisted steel framework, panes of glass spinning through the air.

The top nine floors seemed motionless for an instant, as if suspended from the sky, and then the tower began to descend. And it went down with a whoosh, setting up a vacuum that the helicopter could not defy.

Aziz was sucked to the bosom of his summer palace.

VII

The Rocky Horror Show

Laugh then at any but at fools or foes;
These you but anger, and you mend not those.
Laugh at your friends, and if your friends are sore,
So much the better, you may laugh the more.

Alexander Pope

47

Tuesday, June 19, Athens-New York

From Athens, where he was debriefed by Group Seven interrogators, Sawchuk phoned Rocky Rubinstein in Montreal to ensure that the solicitor general's pardon was waiting for him.

"I just got back from northern Quebec; big win up there," Rocky exulted. "Torch job on a bankruptcy-bound night club in Chicoutimi. The twelve gentlemen of the jury, business-minded townspeople, felt more sorry for my guy than for the insurance company, and they acquitted. I read from the papers you outfoxed them in Mecca. Good win for you, too, Jacques. But I got some bad news from New York. Can you meet me there tomorrow? Charles has disappeared. Kidnapped. About a hot story he had picked up. Payoffs to senators over the Cruise bill."

It was at that point that Jacques Sawchuk hit on the key to the heart of the interlocking puzzle, and began to fit the pieces around it.

What Bakerfield had told him in Mecca provided much of the glue for this puzzle. While fire raged in the palace, they had found time to talk; then, after trading a few desolate laughs, they had parted, Sawchuk taking a helicopter ferry to Jeddah and flying from there to Athens.

Sawchuk flew sleepless with the sun from Athens to New York, pondering, going back over events. The Group had lost contact with him in Paris. Then, in Berlin, Mossad intercepted him, to allow the palace takeover to happen. Rocky's brother had discovered the story about the bribed and blackmailed senators. Charles had been kidnapped. Charles was at the centre of it all, the information link.

When Sawchuk arrived at Kennedy Airport, he had time to make a phone call before meeting Rocky, who greeted Sawchuk with his usual flurry of pulled punches, then hugged him around the waist. His delight in seeing Sawchuk was seemingly softened, however, by his concern over Charles.

In the cab to Charles's apartment, Rocky told Sawchuk: that he had phoned his sister a week ago; that Paula had filled him in about Charles's kidnapping, about the shooting that had taken place. Paula's former football friend had been wounded at the doorway and two men killed—mobsters, whose fingerprints had also been found in General McKay's bombed vehicle. Charles had been hustled away by three men who had shot and killed the hit men, had not been heard of since. Because of his month-long trial, he had not been able to get down to New York sooner.

"They killed him," Rocky moaned. "They killed him because he got ahold of the story that would stop the Cruise bill. There's got to be notes in his apartment."

The vote was set in the U.S. Senate for a week from today. The White House had wielded muscle in the Senate chamber, and as the expected lineup now stood, the result would be fifty senators in favour of the sale, forty-eight opposed, two senators ill but their votes paired.

Sawchuk was willing to help jam up the Saudi Cruise deal, but it appeared the only hope would be to find some evidence that Charles had collected, something that would hold up in libel court. Sawchuk knew that Charles's record wasn't good in libel cases.

"You didn't tell me you knew about this Cruise scandal," Sawchuk said. "Charles must have told you months ago."

"What a journalist tells you is privileged."

"But you told Mossad." Sawchuk remembered Major Arvad's words: *We have information—reliable, but please don't ask me how we came upon it.*

"What do you think I am—an informer?"

"Rocky, you told Mossad."

Rocky said nothing. Sawchuk took his expression as one of poorly concealed guilt.

*   *   *

"This is my dizzy sister Paula." Rocky, from the entrance to Charles's apartment, stared sadly at the wreckage. Paula stood aside and let them in. "Look what the bastards did," Rocky said.

"I did most of it," Paula said. "You told me, tear it apart. I couldn't find anything. No notes about the Cruise missiles, nothing." She was thin, intense, sexual. She looked at Sawchuk appraisingly. "The bulls were here, too, homicide, but they didn't take anything but bullet slugs and fingerprints. A couple of hired killers, Mafia types: that's what the police told the reporters. The other guys, the kidnappers, who knows?"

"Shit." Rocky slumped onto a chair that had stuffing ripped out of it.

"So you're Jacques Sawchuk?" Paula said. Her hands were on her hips. She scrutinized him with what she thought was her erupting volcano look. "You're cute."

"Lay offa him," Rocky said. "He's been to hell and back. Although he is of steel." He turned to Sawchuk. "She's dangerous, could be going through that phase where the girls make the advances."

Paula closed the door behind Sawchuk, who stepped over some magazines and leaned wearily against the kitchen counter.

"All he ever wanted was the big story," Rubinstein groaned. "All his life had been a search for that one big scoop, that screaming headline with his name below it. *Saudi Millions Buy Senate Votes.* Up there in eighty-point type. And below that, still in big letters with maybe a little picture of him, *By Charles Rubinstein. Exclusive. Copyright.* He had it and they stole it from him. They bumped my brother to make a thirteen-billion contract go."

Rocky looked up at Sawchuk and Paula with reddened eyes. "He could've stopped the Cruise deal. They'll be getting nukes for them soon, from Pakistan."

"Hey, come on, man," said Paula, "who says he's dead? We don't know, Rock. Come *on.*"

Sawchuk looked from the corner of his eye at Rocky, said nothing, searched for a place to sit down. Papers and magazines were strewn over chairs and sofa, books were tossed about on the floor. There were old newspaper clippings, record sleeves, tapes, and everywhere was pillow and mattress stuffing. Sawchuk brushed some papers off a wooden chair and sat backwards on it, his arms folded over the straight back. And he studied Rocky.

"Who were the guys who kidnapped him, Rocky? Maybe they didn't plan to kill him. Some *other* guys were trying to do that. Those three who were in here when Paula came to visit with her friend—"

"We weren't close," she interrupted, then realized she sounded cruel. "He was a linebacker for Duke," she mumbled irrelevantly.

"Yeah, well, those three guys, who knows who they were," Rocky said.

"Don't *you*?" said Sawchuk.

Rocky looked sideways at him. "What do you mean? He leave any beer in the fridge, Paula?"

"No."

"Check and see."

"I already have."

"You're a good actor, Rocky, but I think you know who kidnapped him," Sawchuk said.

"Paula, go out and get some beer."

"Who was your butler last year?"

"Here's ten bucks. Jacques and me are thirsty."

Paula took the money, leaned over Sawchuk's shoulder. "I want you should know I think you're okay," she said.

"Don't act like a whore, Paula. I asked you to lay offa him."

Paula gave Sawchuk a Goldie Hawn eye flutter as she left the apartment.

"Nice sister," said Sawchuk gloomily.

"You see how innocent and soft she is? She's only twenty-one. Keep your hands off her."

"You don't have to worry."

There was a short silence.

"I think you know who kidnapped him," Sawchuk repeated. "Maybe you arranged it."

"Maybe you could use some r. and r., Sawchuk. You're kind of babbling there."

"There is nothing worse than the feeling one has been a *poisson*, as we say in Quebec. *Un dupe*."

"What is this all about already?"

"You've got to stop playing these games, Rocky."

"Hey, here's a pinochle deck. That's the only game I play with you, Jacques. Let's have a couple of hands. As I remem-

ber, you got the luck, but I got the good card memory." He
pulled a coffee table between them and laid the deck on it.
"Cut."

"It was the biggest scam of all, wasn't it, Rocky?" He cut
for deal, won it, and began shuffling the pack. "I thought it
was really, ha-ha, ludicrous at first. I sat there on the plane,
thinking about it, and started laughing at how stupid it was.
Then I stopped laughing, started choking."

"What have you been snorting—angel dust? Diamonds is
trump." Rocky began to sort out his hand.

"Those two years—'73 and '74 when I was in the States on
the run—you said you'd been on a kibbutz. It was a different
kind of kibbutz. Royal marriage, forty points. Keep score,
Rock." He put down a king and queen of diamonds, drew a
card from the stock.

Rocky frowned at his cards, glancing quickly up at Sawchuk
and down again.

"Unit 101—I've heard they have a special training camp for
their sleepers. Some of the candidates they choose are kind of
unbelievable on the surface. Sort of like you."

"A sleeper? Sixty for queens."

"Aw, come on, Rocky. He's put back at his old job—say he
runs a two-bit law practice—and he waits around until he's
called. Waits until Mossad sends the word. Spies around a bit
in the meantime. It wasn't just Sammy Rubinstein playing at
his funny little spy games. You were living the role." He took
a trick and laid down his aces. "Hundred for aces."

"Shit." Rocky studied those four big bullies on the table,
decided he'd trump them all if Sawchuk tried to lead them.

"Mossad knew Group Seven wanted a man who could get
inside the Rotkommando. So you sold me to them, made a
deal with Hesselmann. What a deal. Your words in the office
at Mirabel, what where they? 'What do you think of the deal
your diabolically clever lawyer put together for you?' You
drew up the contract with Hesselmann. I was the chattel
being transferred. You worked it out with the Canadian
Intelligence Security Service, the Group, put together a little
frame over the murder of the labour minister. To all the guys
at Gran Paradiso you were just my loud, annoying sidekick
who had somehow finagled his way into the Group Seven
camp, but to Hesselmann—and I suppose Bakerfield was in

on it, too, although he wouldn't admit it—to them, I was *your* jolly, lovable, gullible sidekick. A patsy."

"That *all* you got—aces?" Rubinstein grumbled as Sawchuk melded a second set of them. Rocky had nearly run out of trump.

"Did Hesselmann know that you were handing everything to Mossad that you picked up at Gran Paradiso? Or was that part of the deal, part of the package that you traded? But I guess he wasn't expecting you to steal me back. Yeah, it seemed pretty weird to me that you were at Gran Paradiso at all, but you were learning my routines, the note drops, the poetry code, the places I would be hanging out in in Paris. That's how Mossad were able to pick me up in Paris, to tail me."

"I've got every fucking nine and Jack in the deck. You stack this? I can't remember cutting after you shuffled."

"Some of this I got from Bakerfield. What he didn't know—or wouldn't tell me—I figured out for myself. Ham thinks Mossad sucked the Group agents away from me in Paris with a false alarm call on the Group radio frequency. Some guys from Mossad followed me from Barney's American Bar, they slipped a bumper beeper under Cuyfer's car—to Wurger's chateau on the Seine. Later they tailed me to Orly Sud. That's where Frank Fager the Undertager, that great lover of the Pittsburgh Pirates and four-star restaurants, did the pickup, took my notes and tape and film. That guy Fager—he was a real pushy fellow, not the Group's style at all—his job was to get my notes before Hesselmann's men did. But Hesselmann had no idea by then where I was."

Sawchuk studied a queen of clubs that Rocky had led.

"Bakerfield said the Group lost all track of me until I turned up in Berlin. Isaac Solomon had agreed to let Mossad feign his death, but since Mossad agents had to pose as West Berlin police, and couldn't maintain that lie without some official sanction, Fager had to call in Hesselmann, explain to him that Mossad had borrowed me for a while. The Group missed contact with me in Berlin. Mossad phoned Hesselmann, told him, 'Jeez, we're sorry, we sent him back into the Rotkommando before you could talk to him.' They had given me a new contact number, a new phone number, so I wouldn't connect with the Group. Fager, whoever he is, never did pass on to the Group my tapes about the plans for

Aziz's palace, never mentioned to them at all that the palace was the target of Operation Mecca. Sure, Mossad wanted to destroy the Rotkommando, but by now they had learned that there was evidence in Aziz's vault which could sabotage the Cruise sale to Saudi Arabia. What better way for the evidence against the senators to come to light than for the terrorists to find it, and broadcast it to the world? Wurger would have loved to have done that. Israel *wanted* the palace attack to succeed. Anything to embarrass and destabilize the enemy."

He hadn't played a card, was still staring at Rocky's queen.

"Are you going to take the trick or not?" Rocky said. "Shit or get off the pot. What's the matter, running out of aces?"

"I don't think you guys counted on me being picked up by a PLO kidnap team. Wurger took me into East Berlin, in the process of shaking the Mossad tail, and I ended up getting a free ride to Arabia."

Sawchuk trumped the queen.

"After you left Gran Paradiso, my bet is you went right into the Mossad network. Oh, I guess you went back to Montreal for a few days, maybe flew up to northern Quebec for that so-called trial."

"So-called trial? Twenty for a marriage. I got to salvage something."

"I phoned the daily newspaper in Chicoutimi when I got off the plane. The arson charges against your client were dropped almost three weeks ago, Rocky. Where have you been since then?"

Rocky didn't answer, peered close-eyed at his hand.

"By the way, do you guys run Hesselmann or something? It was that easy. Have you got something over him from his Nazi days? Is that why he gave you the run of Gran Paradiso? I've got the king and his whole family, Rocky." Sawchuk laid down a sequence. "A hundred and fifty points."

Rocky leaned wearily back in his chair, laid his cards down. He pulled a cigar from a waistcoat pocket, bit the end. With his thumb he snapped a wooden match alight, and began to puff. He removed the cigar from his mouth. "These Ritmcester Milds are too dry for me. I shoulda got the Cubans at the duty-frec. They're juicier."

"You really put me through it, Rocky."

Rocky puffed quietly for a while. "You got it figured out

pretty good," he drawled. "Now I'll have to kill you. You know too much."

"Somehow that sounds just like Edward G. Robinson."

"Lee Marvin. Get with it."

"You were always crazy about theatre, Rocky. Always the frustrated player, and you always wanted the big spy role. We used to hang around the campus after the library closed, get a little wrecked, and talk about it. That was your big pipe dream: international double agent. You want to play this game out?"

"Naw."

"Let's have another. Your deal."

"You deal."

"It's your deal, Rocky. Pick the cards up from the table and deal them. Deal cards, Rock."

Rubinstein sighed. "It seemed like a kind of trip at first, you know? I was kicking around Tel Aviv. I applied for laughs. Fuck, they accepted me. I was going to be James Bondchik. Cut the deck. I'm gonna watch your hands this time. That last game you card-sharked me. I was two years in the camp. They called it a special intensive unit, like in a hospital. They drove me crazy with all the technical bullshit. I was too headstrong or something for them, so they wouldn't graduate me up to the field school. That's what I became—a sleeper. Plus a small-time information collector. No money in it—I still had to support myself with the law practice. Wasn't like I thought it was going to be. Kind of boring. Like this hand. Jeez."

"What information collecting? Stuff you got from Charles when he was on the Pentagon beat? That sort of thing?" Sawchuk led a ten which Rubinstein couldn't beat, then exchanged his deuce for the trump ace of clubs.

"Naw, mainly what they want is people checking out the New Left scene. Got to ferret out them pro-Arab sympos, radical Jewish kids who think it's groovy to support the Palestinians. Most of Israel's bread comes from North America. Israel don't want no long-haired nephews going around to Uncle Moishe's house—he's been a mensch, he supports Israel—saying don't buy no more bonds because Israel's just an imperialist tool. I mean there's a lot of that sentiment around the Jewish community, especially after Beirut."

"Eight kings, Rocky. You used to come down and spend a

few weeks with me in Cuba every year. Just checking out the goods, I guess."

"Aw, come on. Okay. When I talked to you down there the last time, read your letters about Cuba, about the Russians, I figured we've got a change of heart. You knew Cuyfer. You had great cover. I figured Group Seven could use you. Not Mossad. Never thought you'd work for Mossad."

"But I might conceivably work for Hesselmann—with a little shove. So Mossad lent me to him, borrowed me back. He didn't complain very much."

"Yeah, well, he couldn't. You're right—we had a little something on him. He used to give us pretty well what we asked. He had helped run Auschwitz for a month. Nothing he was proud about."

"You're as slippery as snot on a doorknob, Rocky."

"Give me a break, Jacques. You remember how it was when we were first pals, teenagers in the sixties? You were always the guy who'd go charging off in the underbrush and I'd be the runty kid following fifty yards behind, picking my way among the snakes, wiping the drips from my nose. Maybe I had to think of something to get back. I never figured things would go as far as they actually went. Shit, you got *aces* again? What do you, breed them or something?"

"I ought to beat the crap out of you."

"Yeah, well, look at it this way—I got you a real interesting job."

"It was a *shitty* job."

Rocky sighed. "Jacques, I hope you don't think I've been fucking you around for fun. You're my best friend. You're not Jewish, but I'm not prejudiced. I like you. It's hard for me to say that. Fuck it, I *love* you, okay?"

Such expressions of solicitude did not come easily at all to Rocky Rubinstein, and his voice cracked.

Sawchuk couldn't help but smile. "You love me, Rocky, but you've got a higher loyalty."

"Yeah." Rocky looked sadly at the score, another wipe-out in the making. He got up and wandered into the kitchen.

Sawchuk heard the refrigerator door open then close.

"She's right. There's a negative beer situation in this apartment. Where the hell is she?"

Sawchuk studied the riches in his hand. Queens to be melded and a good chance to fill in on another sequence.

He felt very lonely. Not only had he learned a great deal about himself in the last few months, he had learned a great deal about the vagaries of friendship. But with all of Rocky's faults—and they were exceptional—Sawchuk could not hate the man. Rocky was a joyful person, a fraudulent oddball who enjoyed the send-up as no man Sawchuk had ever known. And he had sent Sawchuk up like a Roman candle.

In spite of himself, Sawchuk admired that. For years he and Rocky had plotted funny scams against each other. *Le Grand Slaque* had won most of them, but he had just been bested in the biggest.

There had been major kindnesses, however. Rocky had helped Sawchuk run the border when the RCMP were looking for him. He had brought him here, in fact, to the safety of this same apartment, where Charles had hidden him for a month. And, thanks to Rocky, Sawchuk could now enjoy a lifetime pension, a new home in the country of his choice.

Sawchuk decided to forgive him at the level of strained friendship. What was over was over.

There was relief at that decision. But he still felt numbed, his tension of recent weeks unabated, unslackened. And although he knew that most of his body would continue to heal, he had yet to feel a return to manhood, a recovery from the fires that he feared had gutted his sex.

"You're right about the stage," Rocky called from the kitchen. "I could've been great. A little nose putty, a little padding here and there, and you got Falstaff. Remove the padding, show off my natural, heroic proportions, add a little more to the nose, we got Cyrano." He swished back into the room, parrying and thrusting with his cigar.

"Play cards or play Jose Ferrer, take your pick," Sawchuk said. The only way he would be sure to beat Rocky was to destroy him on the pinochle table. He studied his trump, enjoying them.

"Or we got this guy, say, a geek from Pittsburgh, shiny black wig, kind of a fucked-up guy." Rocky assumed a voice. "The Sink Columns, what a rip joint. The food ain't fit for anybody but Hunkies, there's so much garlic."

Sawchuk looked up from his cards. Rubinstein was holding a mop over his head to effect a wig and had shoved mattress stuffing down his pants. "Yeah, the thirty-fourth annual convention of the American Society of Mortuary Directors, the year that Fager the Undertager got stiffed in a French restaurant."

Sawchuk gaped at him. He was unable to react with words. It was mental overload. Rocky beamed at him quietly for about half a minute, and Sawchuk began slowly clapping his hands, feeling anesthetized, benumbed.

Rocky bowed low. "In the eternal war for supremacy between the gigantic but slow-thinking French-Ukrainian poet and the brilliant superspy lawyer with his steel-trap mind and his many faces, there is only defeat for the poet, while the guy who is only five foot five enjoys continuing and glorious victories. I can't believe it, man. I figure you'll recognize me right away at the Orly Airport, when I come waddling into that bar with the Fager routine. You are going to recognize me and I am going to do the pick-up. Major Arvad said that when you recognize me, you'll think I'm doing the job for Group Seven, and give me the tapes and photos. That would be the surest way to glom onto your stuff before Hesselmann's boys finally fumble-footed their way back onto your trail. But you didn't recognize me."

The airport brasserie had been dark, as Solomon's dressing room had been, Sawchuk remembered. He closed his eyes, tried to bring back pictures. The Mossad camp in Israel: Rocky had been wearing those ugly wraparound sunglasses. The knobby knees—should he have known the knobby knees?

"And when I realize I am taking you hook and sinker, shit, I just recite the agent code number and carry on as Fager the Undertager."

"Undertager, substitute undertaker," Sawchuk said in a dim voice. "Fager, substitute Faker."

"I was pretty proud. This was my first big field job and Arvad the Great was running me."

Sawchuk remembered that Major Arvad had been in charge of the show at the Mossad base. He had been running Rocky alias Frank Fager, who in turn was running Sawchuk. Pétras had visited the camp, too, but doubtless had not known the real identity of Fager. Hesselmann had, of course. And Bakerfield? Yes, probably. He had hinted at Mecca that his boss seemed to have been unduly influenced by the Israelis. He had been bitter, obviously felt used.

"So I go back to Arvad not only with the goods but with the news I've got you completely blarneyed. I knock Arvad dead with this. He gives me the go to stay in, to keep playing Fager of the Group, and to switch the recognition code and the toll-free number on you. It was Arvad's masterstroke, I got to admit, but I had some input. The Mossad makeup crew have another go at me, and I meet you again inside Sir Isaac Solomon's dressing room, debrief you, snatch you away from Group Seven. We had two Mossad guys in there dressed as Berlin police. They were going to ice Wurger if he came in with you. But with or without him, you were going to be sent back into the Rotkommando. We had the whole story on your tape by then, and we knew the main thing was to keep the Rotkommando's Operation Mecca on line. We figured if we pulled you away from Group Seven for a week or so they wouldn't find out about Mecca in time to stop it. And you're right—we wanted the palace to be taken."

Rocky's rapidly-tongued syllables trickled through Sawchuk's eardrums, sounds only vaguely heard. He remembered Fager in the Philharmonie dressed to the hilt in tails. Playing Isaac Solomon. Playing Sawchuk like a fish.

"We clued in the West Berlin police fast to what was going on, and phoned Hesselmann at his hotel—he had just been across in the East city talking to von Hertz—and he got formal police co-operation to let us play it out, keep Solomon under wraps for a while. Nobody planned on you being kidnapped or taken to Arabia or nothing like that."

Sawchuk just wanted to escape from it all, escape from Rocky, escape from the world of spies. He would choose a slow-moving little country, Samoa or Costa Rica, where he could be alone, live off his Group Seven pension, and write.

"By the time you turned up in Israel, the palace had been ransacked by the Rotkommando. It was obvious they hadn't found the film or tapes or Wurger would have made something of it, so Major Arvad wanted to get you inside to search. So we gave you back to Group Seven."

Rocky leaned the mop against the wall and returned to his chair and picked up his cards. He grimaced. "I remember this hand. It's awful." He folded it. "Listen, Jacques, I don't want you to tell Charles when he comes about my secret life."

"So a Unit 101 team is holding him."

"Originally, the main thing was to protect him from the icemen that Naiboldt had hired. Our team had been following

both Charles and General McKay ever since Charles told me
about his tip-off from the general: the bribes and the blackmail. When McKay got greased, the team grabbed Charles,
held him here while the hit men were hanging around
outside, then moved him off after the shootout. Also, we
wanted to keep him from blowing the palace takeover with
his story, hold him until Wurger took over the palace and
discovered the stuff that was supposed to be hidden in the
vault. Later, Arvad told our boys not to release Charles until
I got to New York to talk to him. He hasn't talked to his
kidnappers—he probably still thinks they're Typhon's men—
but he'll talk to his brother."

"But he hasn't got anything," Sawchuk said. "All that effort
for the tapes and film. They've probably been burned. Now
there's no evidence, no story for Charles. And the Senate
votes in a week. You guys muffed it."

There was a knock at the door. Rocky got up, opened it,
and Paula bounced in, beaming.

"Guess who I've got?" she said, dropping two six packs of
Bock on the floor. She swung the door wide open. Charles
was there, his eyes glinting suspiciously around the room.
Behind him was an innocuous-looking man with bifocals.

"Bloody God!" said Charles. "My *apartment!*"

"Easy, easy," Rocky cautioned. Charles opened his mouth,
shut it, repeated the process like a fish. "I asked Paula to go
through your stuff to try to find your notes about the Typhon
payments."

"Notes? *Notes?* I kept no notes here. My music collection!
It is like taking a knife in the heart!"

"Stick the shtik. Who's the gentleman with you?"

"You wouldn't know a famous newspaperman if he fell on
top of you," Charles said. "When those geeks let me go this
morning, I went straight to the Times Building. This is
Grunalt J. Swain, their political editor. Mr. Swain, this is my
brother Rocky, who I am surprised to find here, and this is
the famous Jacques Sawchuk, who I am also surprised to find
here. . . ."

He stopped. What was going on here? Charles had been
held in a smelly tenement in Queens, where he had been
kept in near darkness for the last ten days. His captors had
asked no questions, made no threats. At six a.m. this morning
they had driven him to Rockaway and had dropped him.

When Charles had presented himself at the city desk with the story of his abduction, the city editor whisked him into the office of the man who was now standing nervously inside the door, looking for terrorists in dark corners.

Charles had not been able to find out who his captors had been. And he had no idea what his brother was doing here with Jacques Sawchuk. But answers to questions would come later. Only one thing was critical now—find the tape. Charles went down on hands and knees on the living-room floor and grubbed through hundreds of cassette tapes spread about.

"What a bitch," he moaned. "They vote in seven days. This story will be the Watergate of the U.S. Senate, Mr. Swain. I am taking copyright. The *Times* has taken a hard stand against the Cruise deal, so I'm giving you first crack, although Rupert Murdoch would probably give me half a million."

Swain smiled nervously. "We'll talk," he said.

There was a scream of jubilation from Charles. He held a tape in the air. "*Mad Morgan and the Assassins of Moog.* You folks like rock and roll? I'll give you rock and roll."

He set up his cassette deck, plugged in the tape. "*Ain't no God, ain't no heaven,*" came the ragged screech of the lead singer.

Charles's face went dark with horror. "Come in, General McKay, come in," he called. "Do you read me?"

Now there was a click on the tape, then silence, just a furry background sound. Then the voice of ex-General Henry Naiboldt: "*Look, Ruf, there are a few, er, dollars floating around over this thing—*"

Charles moved the tape forward. "Want to make sure I got all of it."

"*Nobody knows but the Boschuff brothers in California. And Aziz, who's got the tapes and film in Mecca. I did a fuck of a job, Ruf. Had cameras secretly installed in their homes, transmitters. These weren't Watergate plumbers we put together for this one, they were Grade A ex-Agency. Only bad thing about it is I'm in the movies, too. Couldn't avoid that. These guys weren't going to talk to underlings.*"

Grunalt J. Swain's eyes were bugging.

"*Satisfy my curiosity, Hank. Who did you buy?*"

"That's McKay," said Charles. "Half of Washington can identify his voice."

"*Well, you got Senator Budd, all right. He's the baby-*

*snatcher. Set him up right in his Boston bedroom. A kid
prostitute, fuzzy cheeks, thirteen. Stoffard Johnson, he's the
eight-million-dollar man. He ran into a little land investment
hassle down in New Orleans, but he's bailed out now. Jack
Grodsky came in a little cheaper, at seven, but he was the
easiest of them all."*

Charles, satisfied, stopped the tape, rewound it.

The eyes of Grunalt J. Swain began to glow. His mouth
formed a soft smile.

"They sealed his lips that very night, Mr. Swain," Charles
said. "Now you know why. You like the story?"

"Mr. Rubinstein, why don't we wander back to the Times
Building? We'll see if we can't set you up with an office, a VDT
and a research staff."

"Rocky, you're my lawyer," Charles said. "Do a deal for
me."

"Do one of your famous deals, Rocky," Sawchuk said. "I'm
going to check into a hotel room where the beds are soft."

"I'll help you find one," Paula said brightly.

He looked at her wistfully. She returned her Bo Derek
smile.

"Lay offa him," Rocky warned. "He uses women."

"I want to be used," said Paula.

There is nothing like being used, Sawchuk thought.

48

July, New York City

Under an assumed name, Sawchuk stayed in a small hotel on
West Forty-Fifth, not doing much, reading Burton's and
Theringer's accounts of their journeys in Arabia, reliving in
his dreams his own desperate travels. His brief Arabian saga
had scarred him like a branding iron—his body, his psyche.
And he was suffering from adrenalin withdrawal: he was

lethargic, made no friends, was unable to summon the strength to escape New York City, was content to dissolve into its anonymity. New York was like the desert: one could hide within its lonely reaches.

In the Public Library one day he read some back issues of *Monthly Review*, drew out and studied some other examples of new Marxist thought. He sought an awakening of dormant ideal. He failed to find it. The new Marxist thought was the same stale dialectic: no answers to be found there.

You never sold *what* out, dad? I can't find it any more.

A self-flagellating mind kept returning to the palace of Prince Aziz. What could he have accomplished there with all that power he had possessed? Why had he given up so softly in the end? He had owned undreamed-of power to aid helpless multitudes, and he had given it all away to play the policeman again.

He couldn't write. He had bought an old upright Remington, like the one he had in Cuba, but it was as dry and milkless as the other had been. He was not in a tropical beachside cabana, but in a hotel in the pounding heart of midtown Manhattan, but the creative results were the same.

And he found out he could not make love either.

A week after settling into the hotel he had gone to a rally in Central Park for International Ecology Day, and had met Paula Rubinstein there, and she unabashedly picked him up. In her apartment that night, she offered herself, but he felt no passion. He kept staring at the great Save the Whales poster on her wall. And he remembered the young student in Paris, the girl from the Polytechnique with her Save the Whales button on her shirt. The first death. And then there had been so many.

"I think I was injured," he had said to Paula. He didn't explain further.

But those few words unlocked the wide gates of Paula's compassion and she secretly determined to give salve to this man and heal him. She moved him and his typewriter into her apartment, off Prospect Park in Brooklyn, went every day to her summer job in a second-hand bookstore, came home to smoke reefers and stare curiously at Sawchuk, feeling his tension-packed vibrations. She tried her fourth-year university psychology on him with indifferent results. She drew him out about his deceased parents, and understood the terrible curse that his father had left him with. *I never sold out.* She understood that although Sawchuk's deeds had been heroic, he was immersed in the gloom of sensed failure.

She tried to get his mind off it all, talked about the newer causes, tried to convince him that the real political struggle had to do with things like renewable energy and preserving the earth's life forms.

At night they slept together. He offered nothing physically. She never pushed it.

As the New York summer moved to a sweltering apex, his lassitude grew, softening and spreading with the heat. He often thought of the desert and Abu Ali Rag, who was in Iraq now, free to roam the hills and the salt flats and to sing of a lost homeland. *What is the news, Abu Ali Rag?*

There was enormous tension behind his ennui that Paula tried to and couldn't massage away. Sawchuk feared that some of the DNT-17 might have gotten in through his pores. But at least he was not suffering the blissful damnation of the terrorists who had been in the palace. Most had been flown from Saudi Arabia to countries where warrants were held, but none of them, it appeared, could come to trial. Dr. Pétras had once again miscalculated. All Rotkommandos who had shared in the doctored champagne were now permanently damaged, in an enduring condition of nirvana. That was the conclusion of doctors at the hospitals for the criminally insane where they were being held. Pétras was said to be off Group staff, back at the drawing board of his clinic in Brussels.

Charles Rubinstein came by a couple of times to tape some material for follow-up stories he was doing for the *Times*. He had taken a twelve-year no-cut contract there instead of the money they had offered him, and soon would be in the *Times* bureau in his favourite city, Washington. Ultimately there would be a book, one with a happy ending: the President had withdrawn the Cruise bill and the deal now seemed permanently scuttled. The President had issued brave pronouncements about the reliability of Saudi Arabia as an ally, but the furore over that government's role in providing bribery funds for U.S. senators had killed the possibility of any new arms deals with the kingdom.

As for the conspirators, Henry Naiboldt had agreed to turn state's evidence for a maximum five-year term, had formally implicated Senators Budd, Johnson, and Grodsky, and even named the Boschuff brothers as co-conspirators. A grand jury was sitting. Impeachments were expected in the Senate. Cynical America rejoiced to find that its distrust of politicians was proven justified.

Rocky Rubinstein phoned one evening from his office in Montreal. He was back at his old slot, working part-time as a Mossad spy. "I've got a criminal trial in the morning, so I'm working late. A flasher. Made the mistake of showing it—in the bloom of full erection—to the eleven-year-old daughter of a Montreal police lieutenant. Which leads me to the issue of you and my little kid sister. I want you should stop making it with her unless your intentions are serious."

"I'm not making it with her."

"It's on your mind."

"It's not on my mind."

"Touch her, you have to marry her. Listen, Bakerfield—you know he's acting head of the Group now—has been trying to get hold of you. That's actually what I called about tonight. It seems a little snag has shown up in that contract we drew up for your lifetime pension. Don't know how it happened, because I remember scrutinizing those pages with a fine-tooth comb. It turns out there's this option clause that allows the Group to continue to employ you for a few years before the pension takes hold."

"Rocky—"

"It's at their sole election, and Bakerfield has this idea he'd like to keep you on staff—"

"Rocky, you told me that was just a throwaway clause. For form. They didn't intend to exercise it."

There was a pause from Montreal. "Gee, I can't recall saying that to you. That would have been bad legal advice. I might have said it's highly unlikely—"

"Rocky, you haven't told Bakerfield where I'm hiding, goddamnit, have you?"

"Nobody knows but Charles and me and Paula. I told Bakerfield I'd get ahold of you."

Paula came to Sawchuk's chair, perched on his knee, held a slice of hot anchovy-and-pineapple pizza to his mouth, and took the telephone. "Guess what? Charles has got an advance for his book."

"I'm writing one, too," Rocky said. "I'll get it started one of these days, got to find the time. Is Jacques doing one, too?"

"He doesn't do anything."

"I bet. This guy is dangerous, Paula. He loves them and leaves them in the lurch. In for a fast screw. He's using you."

Sawchuk took the phone. "How's General Hesselmann?"

"It's malignant. Three-quarters of his stomach gone. Apparently he refused to see doctors until it was too late. They say he wants to die, isn't fighting it."

Sawchuk felt the gobs of pizza heavy in his stomach, doughy indigestible stuff. He thought sadly of General Hesselmann, who had lived with so many secrets, even that of his own death. Sawchuk had hoped the deaths were over.

The last one had been Bisharat's. He had been crucified in the central square of Riyadh in front of television cameras and before the King and most of the Council of Elders of the Saud family. The Koran had been recited by the *muttawiun*, the religious police: "The angel who bends over a dying man asks what good deed he has sent before him."

"Hamilton says he's in no hurry," Rocky said. "Take a rest, he says, maybe a few more days."

"There is not God's chance," said Sawchuk. "Good luck with the flasher."

"I'm going to argue irresistible impulse. He can't help himself."

On the twenty-second morning of July, a sweltering Sunday, three and a half weeks after Sawchuk moved in with Paula, they lay in bed naked, sheets cast aside.

"What the hell is going through your head?" She laid her newspaper aside, turned to him.

"I didn't have the guts to go all the way. At the end I was what my father had always detested most."

"What we have here," she said, nuzzling up to him, "is psychological trauma causing neurotic blockage of the libidinal impulses. Maybe you'll get rid of it if you'll stop carrying your dead father on your back. Bury him for God's sake. He's dead, man. You are alive. And I think you're as healthy as a horse."

"Hardly."

"Stop fighting yourself. It's so damned masochistic. Your father represents something that is past, honey. It's the old politics, second wave. Climb onto the third wave. The march today to save the national parks—you're going?"

"I guess."

He went on the march that day. At night, at ten o'clock, all the fury and anger and triumph and passion of his encounter with Group Seven and the terrorists imploded, and he felt his body go limp.

"God, I'm crying," he said.

It was over.

And that night Sawchuk made love to Paula. And the next day he began to write.

ABOUT THE AUTHOR

Born in Regina in 1937, William Deverell began his writing career as a journalist, working for several newspapers across Canada and for the Canadian Press in Montreal, while studying for his law degree.

He has had a law practice in Vancouver since 1964, and has acted in over one thousand criminal cases. A former president of the British Columbia Civil Liberties Association, he describes himself as a political, cause-oriented lawyer.

Deverell's previous two best-selling novels, *Needles*—winner of the $50,000 Seal Award and voted Book of the Year by the Periodical Distributors of Canada—and *High Crimes*, have been published in Canada, the U.S., and U.K., in hardcover and paperback. They have also been translated and published in numerous foreign language editions.

William Deverell balances his time between Vancouver, where he practices law, and a west-coast island retreat, where he writes.

SEAL BOOKS

Offers you a list of outstanding fiction, non-fiction and classics of Canadian literature in paperback by Canadian authors, available at all good bookstores throughout Canada.

THE CANADIAN ESTABLISHMENT	Peter C. Newman
THE IVORY SWING	Janette Turner Hospital
A JEST OF GOD	Margaret Laurence
LADY ORACLE	Margaret Atwood
THE SNOW WALKER	Farley Mowat
ST. URBAIN'S HORSEMAN	Mordecai Richler
MALICE IN BLUNDERLAND	Allan Fotheringham
THE STONE ANGEL	Margaret Laurence
THE BACK DOCTOR	Hamilton Hall
JAKE AND THE KID	W. O. Mitchell
ZEMINDAR	Valerie Fitzgerald
DADDY'S GIRL	Charlotte Vale Allen
BODILY HARM	Margaret Atwood
PREPARING FOR SABBATH	Nessa Rapoport
SUNDAY'S CHILD	Edward Phillips
THE DIVINERS	Margaret Laurence
HIGH CRIMES	William Deverell
THE ESTABLISHMENT MAN	Peter C. Newman
THE HAUNTED LAND	Val Cleary
ROSEGARDEN	Kurt Palka
THE CANADIANS (six volumes)	Robert E. Wall
COMEBACK	Dan Hill
MURDER ON LOCATION	Howard Engel
NEVER CRY WOLF	Farley Mowat
LIFE BEFORE MAN	Margaret Atwood
WHO HAS SEEN THE WIND	W. O. Mitchell
GOING THROUGH THE MOTIONS	Katherine Govier
THE ACQUISITORS	Peter C. Newman
MEET ME IN TIME	Charlotte Vale Allen
THE SERPENT'S COIL	Farley Mowat
BODILY HARM	Margaret Atwood
PERPETUAL MOTION	Graeme Gibson
JOSHUA THEN AND NOW	Mordecai Richler

The Mark of Canadian Bestsellers